CW01460848

YOUNG MAN
FROM LEEDS

First published in 2025
by The Black Spring Press Group
Maida Vale, London W9,
United Kingdom

Graphic design by Edwin Smet

ISBN 978-1-917788-21-2

BLACKSPRINGPRESSGROUP.COM

YOUNG MAN FROM LEEDS

Neil Hunter

THE **BLACK SPRING**
PRESS GROUP

"O! sure I am the wits of former days, to subjects worse have given admiring praise." — **SONNET LIX**

CONTENTS

HUNTER.

SPRING

I.I

PEACE, HO! CAESAR SPEAKS.

'Good morning, ladies,' he said, with a doff of his wide-brimmed black top hat.

'*Good afternoon*,' said Mildred.

That one brought the general to an abrupt halt. He found himself standing sentinel, staring into the eyes of a colossal carved Buddha.

A moment of reflection, then he turned on his heel and strode stiffly back, down the Mongolian goatskin rug.

'What tidings dost thou bring, Miss Scragg?' he enquired, locking eyes with the fierce tribescreature. 'Speak once again.'

'I said, *good afternoon*,' Mildred reiterated.

'*Good afternoon*?' Caesar questioned, a quizzical brow raised.

'Yeah. *Good afternoon.*'

Pause.

'What cryptic language is this?'

'Oh my God, how thick is he,' interjected Gertrude, standing next to Mildred.

'I mean you're *late*, Glenn,' said Mildred, scowling. 'And you missed the delivery.'

'*Again*,' added Gertrude.

And just as the epics of old would begin with the bugle's grim blare, so too did his tale unfold.

The significance was not lost upon him.

The general wished to respond to the provocations of these wild islanders by at once inflicting heavy slaughter on them (his *dignitas* being dearer than life itself). However, his number being inadequate for such an action, he instead employed an *exitus diversus*:

7

He smiled amiably.

'Princesses! What grief hath set the jaundice on your cheeks?' he said, chuckling. 'Why dost thou garter up thy arms o' this fashion? Thinkst that you have ta'en a tardy sluggard here? Alas, thou hast misconstru'd everything, for I was at the dentist.'

'The dentist,' scoffed Gertrude, rolling her eyes.

'In other words, he slept in,' said Mildred.

'*Again*,' added Gertrude.

'Slept in?' he said. 'I *wish*. I didn't sleep a wink last night, what with the hell-pains in my head. It feels like Mars himself is making war upon my wisdom tooth.'

'Oh, the wisdom tooth again,' Mildred nodded, glancing at Gertrude.

'Funny how that wisdom tooth plays up every time there's a big delivery,' said Gertrude with an accusing look.

'Saw you Miss Mohammed this morning?' he said quickly, as he lowered his humongous sunglasses and cast a sly glance around the island.

He squinted as the blast of bright light exploded on his eyeballs, and the panoply of costly things revealed themselves to him. The sight of that lovely landscape, replete with opulent garments and accessories, and ornamented by great heaps of handsome antiques and curios that were everywhere aglitter, at once lifted his spirit.

They may have been a rude and untutored race, these dread druids, but they certainly knew how to present the product. Crassus himself would gape.

'She's upstairs,' answered Mildred.

'Looking for *you*,' added Gertrude ominously. 'You better go find her, Glenn; she's proper mad.'

'I appreciate the augury, haruspex, but the day of parricide is not yet upon us,' he sighed. 'You are right about one thing, though: she is indeed "*proper mad*".'

He flung his head back and laughed aloud.

Mildred and Gertrude did not fling their heads back, nor laugh aloud. Rather they stood staring at him with a mingled expression of boredom and hatred.

Well, he wasn't having much luck with these women.

He wasn't having much luck with *any* women, for that matter. Emily Brontë had led him to believe that women were just aching for wild, passionate entanglements with tall handsome men. Particularly men who were dark and brooding, and who possessed mysterious, almost otherworldly auras—which he most certainly did.

And yet there he was, dying like a mortal soldier who had engaged a god in combat.

'Your gates 'gainst my force are sturdy, Miss Scragg,' said Caesar, a quizzical look crossing his countenance. 'Why dost thou so oppress me with thine eye? Hark; men's was ne'er so much your enemy as that ague which hath made you lean.'

'What?' said Mildred.

In a profound tone, the general continued.

'Dost thou not think 'tis time we sang in the shop, and went about our functions friendly? Come now! Let's drop war and give ourselves to pleasure on Call Lane—whither we can quaff the Falernian wine, breathe the smoke of sacrifice, and cordax round the compact altar. O thou warrior maidens, vex not my proposal, but rather vouchsafe me friendship, and a doting servant embracing thy knees daily in supplication shall be thy portion.

'And that's a promise,' he added.

The warrior maidens exchanged a glance.

'And what does that mean?' said Gertrude.

'I'm proposing a work night out,' he responded.

'So why don't you just say that, then?' said Gertrude, irritably.

'Yeah, talk normal for a change,' said Mildred, 'you daft twat.'

'I am communicating in a manner befitting Divus Julius,' he clarified, smiling.

'You're being a div?' Mildred quipped.

He frowned and eyed her coldly.

'*No*,' he replied. 'I *mean* I'm Gaius Caesar.'

'You're *gay*?'

'That is what everyone says about him,' Gertrude nodded.

'Now you're being childish,' he snapped.

'Hey, don't shoot the messenger,' said Gertrude with a shrug.

'Anyway, we're not going anywhere with you, Glenn,' said Mildred.

'Why not?' he demanded.

'Because you're a gay div,' she grinned.

Is it any wonder Plato thought retail degrading?

Caesar could feel the angry spot glowing on his brow, under the hefty fringe that was plastered to his forehead by his rather tight-fitting top hat.

He turned to the freestanding mirror and stared at himself in search of the problem. He couldn't find one. Sumptuously garbed in a huge, shaggy fur coat, calfskin leather shooting gloves, the aforementioned top hat and oversized black sunglasses, and with the laughing skull crystal handle of his extra-large umbrella protruding prominently before him (for the folded brolly was wedged up his armpit), and augmented by his late grandad's antique pusser suitcase, he looked like a true man about town, a person of quality. Heathcliff wished he could pull this outfit off.

'You know,' he said, 'other shops in the arcade go out every weekend.'

'That's why I don't work in other shops,' said Gertrude. 'I quite like the lack of a social side here.'

'I have money, if that's the issue?' he pressed.

'Oh yeah, that's just what we need,' sighed Mildred. 'More debt.'

'Who said it would be "debt"?' he grinned. 'What's a few sesterces 'tween friends?'

'We're *not* your friends, Glenn,' Gertrude hissed.

'We don't like you,' said Mildred.

'At all,' added Gertrude.

'But you don't *know* me!' he cried, laughing. 'And I don't know you, really. That's why I think a night out would be beneficial—so we could address these conspectuities we have about each other. Didst thou know it was a practice of the ancient Persians to only deliberate on affairs of weight while drunk—'

'Glenn!' bellowed Mildred, startling him.

'Yes?' he gulped.

'For Christ's sake, take the hint. No one wants to go out with you. You're boring. And annoying—'

'And weird,' added Gertrude.

'And weird,' said Mildred. 'And if you don't piss off, right now—' She raised a bony fist to his short, scraggly beard. 'You really *will* have to go to the dentist. Do you understand?'

A silence enveloped the room.

'DO YOU UNDERSTAND!?' she yelled.

'I do, I do,' he acquiesced with a solemn nod. 'In sooth, I appreciate thine eschewing sweet words.' He mustered his most cheery smile. 'Adieu, gentle queen,' he bid Mildred, nodding. He looked to Gertrude. 'Adieu,' he nodded.

He then strode off with his chin in the air and a bounce in his step, satisfied that he had at least tried.

As he passed under the glass mountain of Verisimilitude Femme, he swallowed. As he walked by Ali and Betty, on beauty, he began sniffing. By the time he had reached the foot of the half-turn oak staircase, he was weeping uncontrollably.

He halted, and stood with his back to the room, his huge furry shoulders heaving. Rage had blitzed his brain and nerves, made balls of his fists. Mayhem was whirling in his eyes.

He was actually beginning to rock with anger.

I.II

Thus, like Alexander the Great returning to the banks of the Granicus, the valiant Caesar makes a second expedition to the savage island.

'O, *Mildred*,' he called across the floor, in a formal voice.

The weird sisters turned their heads, evidently surprised at his unexpected return.

'Oh, what now?' Mildred huffed.

East of the main display he stood, inspecting the glass top of a gilt-frame sales rack from which a row of jade-studded llama-wool jumpers was hanging. His umbrella was still wedged up his pit, the hefty suitcase now on the floor. 'Have you not had time to clean the fixtures and fittings this morning?' he said, peeling off his shooting gloves.

'What are you on about?' she said irritably, as she wiggled clip clopping towards him, her pendant jangling over her abbreviated black dress. 'I did it earlier.'

'So what's this then?' demanded Glenn.

Her eyes flitted betwixt his upraised finger and the glass surface upon which he had run it. 'Your fingerprint?' she said.

'Nay, Miss Scragg!' he corrected, briskly. ''Tis *dust* that pollutes thy domain; a disarray of filth, unsightly and foul. Did Marc Antony and his eunuchs throw a party here? It looks like a fundament exploded!' He slipped his gloves back on and picked up his suitcase. 'I am afraid thou must embark upon a renewed tour of the shopfloor to rectify its squalid state,' he sighed.

'Meaning you want me to go round the shopfloor and do it all *again*?' she said.

'And if you would start as soon as possible, please,' he said in a dictatorial tone.

'No.'

Glenn tottered.

'*No*?' he said faintly. 'What—what do you mean, *no*?'

Defiantly, she folded her snow-white arms. 'Shukeena says you're not our manager and we don't have to take orders from you.'

He shook, as if struck by divine wrath. 'Miss Mohammed said that?'

'Yeah, she did.'

'I see.'

Her maroon-glossed lips curled in a smug grin. Stepping closer, she leaned in, fixing her icy blue gaze on his enormous sunglasses. 'So if you think the floor's dusty—why don't you clean it yourself?' she said. '*Gimp.*'

Caesar's jaw dangled in the breeze blowing in from the Germanicus.

Mars, watch over us.

HUNTER

He observed her departure, clip clopping toward the front, her garish yellow ponytail bouncing with each step. It was as she was about to pass the last mannequin that Glenn emerged abruptly from behind it, blocking her path.

She leapt, a startled cry escaping her lips.

'Your speech sticks in my heart, thou marble-heart'd fiend,' he growled. 'Behold! Thy stance proclaims thou art exempt from Glenn's directives. Forget not my influential friends, nor that *thrice* this morn thou hast profaned the air with the unmannerly argot of the common sea dog. Read you not your employee handbook? "Foul language in a customer-facing environment is gross misconduct—and any employee found guilty of gross misconduct shall be subject to *summary dismissal*".'

A pause.

'Summary means instant.'

Mildred's eyes widened beneath her thick mascara.

'Have you ever tried getting a job when you were sacked from your last one?' Glenn whispered. 'It's not easy, believe me. Now wilt thou give ready obedience and clean this floor?'

She scowled, hatred glinting beneath her penciled brows.

'Yea or nay?' he exclaimed. 'Speak!'

She looked bitterly to the hardwood. 'Yes,' she said through gritted teeth.

'Yes, *what*!?' he thundered, removing his sunglasses, looming over her. It did not escape his notice that Gertrude's rolling eyes were now wide with fear.

'Yes, *Glenn*,' Mildred sighed, her gaze fixed on his elongated, pointy shoes.

His eyes followed the gleaming cascade of her hair and her shimmering silhouette to the cashdesk, whither she reluctantly retrieved the cloth and polish from under it.

She was a terror to all but the best of men, the sales assistant. But that morning her saddle had been emptied, her pride cut to pieces. And now the angry spot was gone and his *dignitas* secure. Caesar coolly restored his sunglasses.

He really was a quite singular manager, young Glenn. An example of excellence, a defender of standards. He was the picture of professionalism. And as he strode to the stairs with his chin aloft and a bounce in his step, the example of excellence was muttering something like, *Yeah, who's the daft twat now, you gobby little bitch.* You *piss off.*

I.III

I ask you now, raw pupils, to purge from your sight the dross and behold with reverie a form divine, the Britannic hero—this godlike youth in glittering armour—so comely never could one imagine the boy came just now from combat.

Glenn wears a black mohair wool suit, a crisp white cotton shirt with laughing skull collar buttons and a slim black silk necktie, all by Nirah Frazar, while his banner, the flamboyant red and white polkadot pocket square, flutters with panache.

It takes great effort to dress this effortlessly.

The black and gold name-badge, proclaiming MENSWEAR MANAGER: GLENN HARDING was gleaming immaculately, while his pointy, glossed plastic black brogues had been polished to perfection—Glenn having raided the stock room for the luxury beeswax after placing his tempest toss'd fur coat in his locker.

'Will Glenn Harding live to see old age, Tiresias?' he queried, in that unexpectedly deep baritone his slender frame didn't seem big enough to produce.

'Yes, if he never knows himself,' he answered.

Glenn flung his head back and laughed aloud.

His face dropped abruptly.

His long, spidery fingers encircled the ornate frame of the massive freestanding mirror, his head emerging as if from a hill fort to survey the expanse below. If Caesar could be shivved in the Senate, and Caligula outside his own palace, it was safe to assume that Glenn could be got in his royal compound, situated as he was in the wild realm of the primitive Brigantes, deep in the Outer Zone. But fortunately, no dissident elements manifested themselves among the throng. His subjects were singing, and there was nothing strange about the sections. The honor'd gods were keeping him in safety, at least for now. He breathed a sigh of relief.

He stepped out from behind the mirror, drew himself up to his full height of five-foot-eleven-and-a-half (although six-foot with shoes and six-foot-three if you counted his colossal upswept hair) and strode imperiously through his kingdom, his shoes padding the kaleidoscopic Afghan rugs zigzagging the labyrinth of treasures.

The long laughing skull pendant under his shirt was tintinnabulating in time with the set of manager's keys on his belt loop, and with his chin in the air and his eyes askance, he watched his triumphal march in the profusion of mirrors. . . .

Lock away your wives, Romans! Here we have our spiky whoremonger, that dashing young rex Britannorum who reduced the Lower World to submission! And he suffered but one reverse in that campaign, a reverse he soon rectified by acquainting the madwoman, Mildred the blonde, with the blade of his broadsword.

Never could he have made that crazy charge without some god behind him.

He could actually feel the hardwood trembling under the wheels of his chariot—which was odd because he had stopped moving. It was as he looked in the mirror that he saw the crazy charge of an overloaded rail coming right at him.

He spun around and shrieked with fright.

I.IV

The rail screeched to a halt, and Glenn gaped as great Wilfred, large of limbs, of giant height, emerged from behind it with a surprised expression on his rough-hewn phizog.

'Whoa,' Wilfred chuckled, fingering back the unruly tresses of his sheeny brown hair. 'Sorry, our Glenn; I wasn't expecting to see you there.'

Glenn took an indignant step back from the rail that was pressing into his breast.

'No, Mr Woods, I doubt you were expecting to see *anyone*, what with your eyes bescreened by that Bachhant hair of yours,' he sniped, as he wiggled his limbs back into alignment with the contours of his tight suit. 'When pray do you expect it will assume a more sensible shape? You look like some penny Gallagher. Ridiculous!'

Glenn delicately smoothed down his own luscious mullet.

'Ay, it's not great, is it,' sighed Wilfred, as he strolled round the rail, muscular frame twitching in his tight white shirt. The top button was undone and his necktie loose, as if to accommodate his sinewy neck. His arms, constructed by Vulcan, looked ready to explode from his sleeves. 'I really should stop cutting it myself—but that would indicate I give a shit about fashion, which, as you know, I don't.' He draped an arm over the crossbar and leaned against the rail—a very casual posture for a man whose name-badge said SALES ASSISTANT. 'No, what I meant was: I wasn't expecting to see you *there*, as I know you like to roll in at midday on delivery mornings.'

Glenn tottered.

'Anyway,' Wilfred continued. 'Just in case you're, you know, *interested* in what's going on with your floor, I've processed the delivery, put out the pre-spring, dressed the mannequins, checked the updates, briefed the lads, done the float, and the figures—month to date and year to date— calculated the ATV, the KPI, the CRN, and the UPT, and I've written out a provisional rota. Oh! And I had Dick dust and tidy everything, while I was rearranging the floor for the new plan.'

Pause.

'And I thank you for your pains and courtesy, Mr Woods,' Glenn smiled, nodding. 'I was intending to do all that myself, but *unfortunately* I had to make an unexpected trip to—'

'The *dentist*,' interposed the sales assistant. 'Yeah, I know the delivery routine.'

Glenn's cheeks reddened slightly.

'Yes, well. It's an ongoing issue,' he murmured.

'Shukeena's looking for you,' said Wilfred, ominously.

'I'm not scared of Shukeena,' he lied.

'Hey, man, I'm just telling you what I heard; it's nowt to do with me.'

Glenn said nothing.

'But back to business,' the horrid giant exclaimed. 'Now that you've finally decided to grace us with your presence, I guess I can leave the floor in your safe hands while I put out these transfer shirts?' He smacked his huge hand on the heaving rail. 'That's unless you want to *help* me put them out?

'It's hard graft—but you'll have plenty of energy after the rest you've had.'

Again, Glenn could feel the angry spot glowing on his brow, under the great fringe that was sweeping majestically across his forehead. He took a deep breath.

'Good Mr Woods, 'tis a worthy deed, and shall become you well, to entreat your captain to soft and gentle speech,' he intoned with a profound face. 'Remember: very few of Caesar's assassins outlived him by more than a year—*or died naturally*. "Is not that he that lies upon the ground? He lies not like the living. O my heart! Is not that he? Nay, this was he, Messala—"'

'Please, Glenn,' said Wilfred, wincing.

'Sorry,' Glenn murmured.

'To be honest with you, mate,' said Wilfred in a low voice, leaning in as a confiding smile broke out unexpectedly across his handsome face, 'I was nearly late today myself. I got caught up in a bit of a brouhaha on Brudenell Road at five a.m., between my mate Bazza and one of the local, er, *street pharmacists*.'

'*Really?*' said Glenn, perversely interested.

'Ay. The story goes that instead of distributing the sniff this fella supplied him with, Bazza, being depressed over breaking up with his bird, had been doing it himself. *Well*. I had to barter the bloke down from slitting Bazza's throat with a box-cutter, to just taking his decks—which did admittedly put a dampener on the house party we were having. And didn't do much to lift Bazza's mood, either.'

'I can imagine!' Glenn replied, unconvincingly.

'He was so shaken up that in the end I had to do a whip around and call the dealer back to give us a few bumps. The thing is, the dealer ended up having such a good time he actually broke out Bazza's decks and started busting out some tunes!'

They both burst into uproarious laughter.

'I didn't want to leave,' Wilfred sighed. 'But I didn't want to miss the delivery.'

There was no missing the meaning look the smiling rogue flashed his manager.

'And you have done your work well, Mr Woods!' said Glenn gaily. 'And, now that you have completed the delivery, and the menial jobs—'

'They're not menial jobs, Glenn, they're management duties.'

'—I can give you an *important* one.'

Pause.

'Go on.'

'Someone needs to go through the department and turn round *every garment* so they all hang anticlockwise.'

Wilfred narrowed his eyes. 'Eh?' he said.

'You heard me.'

'And who's asked for everything to hang *anti*clockwise?' he said suspiciously.

'O, it's come from above,' Glenn said with a sagacious smile.

'London?'

'Not that far above.'

'Shukeena?'

Glenn's face dropped abruptly.

'Shukeena is *not* above me,' he snapped. 'You know very well we are the same level. I mean that it's come from *He who makes the shop tremble*: Mr Mountain.'

'Oh *really*? Then you won't mind if I go knock on Mr Mountain's door and ask him myself, will you? Just to, you know, double-check.'

'My, how mortals take the gods to task,' Glenn smiled. 'If you want to interrupt the governor while he's working, just to question his judgment, you're a braver man than I.'

Wilfred, casting a wary eye over the mazelike fixtures and fittings, fixed his gaze on a green door outlined by a blood-red wall, lurking in the shadow of an imposing suit of armour. He visibly shivered and turned to Glenn with a scowl.

'And you don't think it would be *wiser* for me to get the transfer shirts out first?'

'Nope.'

The sight of Wilfred, gigantic even in the distance, engaged in his low correction, coolled the angry spot on Glenn's brow, doused the burning in his belly. The twelve labours of Hercules? More like the twelve-thousand!

Glenn flung his head back and laughed aloud.

His face dropped abruptly.

Boredom beginning to worm its way through his intellect; ennui enveloping his limbs. Suddenly, he whirled around and bolted off, in the direction of the cashdesk.

He yanked open the chaotic drawer with the idea of at last putting it in order but ah, where even to begin. He was about to slam it shut when he glimpsed it:

The gilt lettering of the black leather manager's folder, twinkling amid the debris.

With great vim he spread it open on the counter. God he looked managerial, standing at the tills, reading the updates. He was an example of excellence, the picture of professionalism. Standards? He doth bestride them like a colossus.

He leafed through the pages, and on locating the latest fax he placed his elbows on the counter, propped his chin upon his bony knuckles, knitted his features into an expression of the most profound and serious study. . . .

He pictured himself naked and bound to a great rock, screaming as a vulture devoured his liver.

He gave his head a violent shake.

Glenn scowled and eyed the folder determinedly.

Come, young Harding, let concentration be your song. Sing in me, Mnemosyne, and through my brain record the story of this black report—thy latest theories in the management of customer relations impart; what lines were launch'd, and what stock from the warehouse did depart! To this tyrannous tome thou must thrust thy head, and augment thy learning with many a new and fascinating fact—beginning with:

The Difference Between Concrete Objections and Vague Objections.

Young Harding had to a take another deep breath.

'"No matter how much we as a company invest in our stores and products",' he said, reading aloud, '"what really makes the difference is the way we—"'

He lifted his eyes and looked enviously to Wilfred, turning garments around.

Suddenly, he made a beeline for the small formalwear section, where he emerged theatrically from a thick cloud of steam. 'Hark!' he exclaimed cheerily, 'Good morrow, mine gifted and treasured formalwear supervisor. How doth thee fare on this fine morn? Pray, as well as thy countenance doth suggest?'

Dick, who was running the steam plate of the garment steamer down the sleeve of a ruffle-trimmed caramel silk shirt, didn't look up from his work.

'What do you want now?' he grunted.

'Nothing!' Glenn laughed. 'Can't I check in on my favourite line report without there being an ulterior motive?' His face dropped abruptly. 'Mate, the manager's report is as dull as Nero's lyre playing— that means it's *very dull*—Read it for me.'

'No.'

'If you don't read it, I'll kill myself.'

Dick shrugged.

'All right. If you don't read it, I *won't* kill myself.'

'Leave it on my section.'

'*Yes*,' Glenn cried with relief, pumping his fist.

'Hold on, geez; where are you going?'

'To get the manager's report.'

'Oh, is that it?' he said, setting his steam plate aside. 'You're just going to ask me for a favour then do one?' Dick laughed, wiped the sweat from his brow. 'The Distant One never changes.'

'Come on, Dick; you know I am a small talk detester,' Glenn pleaded with a smile.

'That's why I enjoy inflicting it on you. And anyway, it's good for you to have a chinwag with me. It's part of my project of making you human. Just as you can learn from me professionally, because I'm the top seller, you can learn from me socially, because everyone knows I've got the best chat. And anyway, we don't have small talk! We have—what's that lovely word you use for it? Ah yes, we have *symposiums*.'

'All right; who's Plato, who's Agathon?'

'Yeah, that's not good craic, geez, I'd retire it from the repertoire,' Dick winced, shaking his head. He loosened his black silk necktie, grabbed his white shirt and flapped it a bit to admit some cool air, the garment stretching round the wide contours of his body. 'So what's new with you, anyway? Still sporting that same barnet, I see? Honestly geez, you look like a cross between Sid Vicious and the Yorkshire Ripper. How long do you spend doing your hair?'

'Not that long,' Glenn responded, his defenses slightly raised.

'How long?' pressed Dick.

'Two minutes,' he shrugged.

'It only takes *two* minutes to make it look like that?' said Dick incredulously.

'*Yes.*'

'So why not take three minutes and make it look good?'

Dick erupted into laughter, so hard Glenn could see his bosom quivering.

Boredom beginning to worm its way through his intellect; ennui enveloping his limbs. . . .

He pictured himself bound again to the great rock as the vulture descended, its hooked beak gnashing, its shadow swallowing him whole—

'So I hear you've been enjoying your winnings?' said Dick.

'My what?' said the Distant One in a vacant monotone.

'Your *winnings*,' Dick said. 'Remember? On Saturday? The 2 p.m. at Catterick? I told you Hemingway's Voices was tasty. Bloody twenty to one. It's free money.'

Glenn, momentarily perplexed, finally grasped the subject. 'O, you're talking about a *horse* race,' he said. 'No, I didn't win anything. I didn't even bet.'

'What? You didn't have a little flutter? I don't believe it.'

'Mr Zabledore, I have never placed a bet in my life. I wouldn't even know how to.'

'So you haven't come into money?' Dick probed.

'*No,*' Glenn snapped, looking irked at his underling.

'Oh,' Dick mused, as an impish grin crept onto his face. 'It's just I heard you've been offering to pay the girls to go out with you.'

A strangled sound escaped Glenn as his face turned a violent red, sending Dick into futher peals of laughter. Glenn stammered, attempting to clarify that he offered to help pay for *drinks*, not to hang out with him. He didn't need to pay *anyone* to hang out with him.

He could feel his neck sizzling under his heavy mullet.

'Pay for their drinks,' cried Dick, wiping his eyes. 'What are you like? I know you're frustrated, but throwing money at that lot downstairs won't help matters. They all hate you! They never even talk to you, willingly.' He leaned in and looked at Glenn with a foul leer. 'And what have I told you? Women are like espresso machines. You've got to learn how to press the right buttons to get what you want.'

'Can I get you a coffee while you work on your metaphors?' Glenn yawned.

'If you're offering, make it a double shot. Actually, scrap that—just bring me Gertrude in that black satin dress. She's steaming enough for the both of us.'

'Dick Zabledore!' Glenn cried. 'Thy *Nuts* magazine words show thee a madman. Be *gentlemanly*. And anyway, thou knowest very well I am an impartial gazer,' he sighed, 'for my true-sweet beauty's heart hath long ago made mine hard.'

'Yeah? Well Gertrude's *dress* has made me hard. And those black satin wedge heels. I'm surprised Shukeena doesn't hang her in the window with the rest of the Must-Have items. Oh! What I wouldn't do to put the *rude* in Ger*trude*—if you get what I'm saying!'

'I think I can just about comprehend your drift, Dick, subtle though it is.'

'Good. Anyway, what you on about with your "true-sweet beauty"? Are you still not over your ex? Geez, it's been years.'

'Eighteen months.'

'Well there you go then, that is years, the way time works in here, where every hour feels like two. You need to get yourself a new bird, our Glenn, forget about your ex. But also forget about Gerty. I've been trying to tag *that* particular garment since before you worked here; and, with respect geez, if *I* can't do it, you've got no chance.'

Glenn stared at the man.

For once he didn't appear to be joking.

Suddenly there was a burst of footsteps upon the hardwood. Before Glenn knew it, the towering Lyndsey was looming over him, with a white merino wool sock dangling accusingly from his fingers.

Bald and with a piercing stare magnified by his pink pince-nez, he was all awkward angles, his long limbs stretched out and gangly. He looked like a reflection in a funhouse mirror.

'Glenn,' he said, his voice dripping with irritation. 'This is a sock. Specifically, it is a *trying-on sock*—new, clean, and belonging *exclusively* to footwear. Why does footwear need its own sock, I hear you ask? Well, as any footwear supervisor of seventeen years' experience will tell you, luxury brand customers, unlike high street ones, care about hygiene, and have concerns about trying on shoes that may have been defiled by some scaly troglodyte who is wont to visit a luxury brand store but cannot afford to purchase anything.

'That's why the trying-on sock is *sacred*. It must remain on footwear *at all times*. To be extra clear, that means it is not to be rolled up into a makeshift football and used for staff "kick-arounds." It is not to double as a duster because the menswear manager forgot to order cleaning supplies—*again*. And it is *definitely* not to be stuffed down the trousers of a certain formalwear supervisor to simulate a bigger. . . . package.'

Lyndsey turned to Dick and glowered balefully at him.

'I have to put in an *order* for these socks, Glenn. That takes *time*; it requires *work*; and I *don't* want to lose this one. I trust I can leave you to communicate this to the rest of the team, as I would hate to have to go over your head—*again*. Thank you.'

With that, Lyndsey spun on his heel, his gleaming size-13 Nirah Frazar galoshes squeaking as he stalked back to his corner, tightly clinging onto his sock.

'And stay out of my beeswax!' he shouted back over his shoulder. 'Wanker!'

Pause.

'*Anyway*,' said Dick abruptly, breaking the silence. 'Nice try, geez, but I'm afraid there won't be any work nights out with this lot.'

'No?' said Glenn absently, slinking off to the nearest freestanding mirror, where he stood puffing up his banner, the flamboyant polkadot pocket square.

'Na,' he sighed, slipping his hands in his pockets and waddling after him. 'I'm afraid we're just going to have to wait for some birds who are more up for it to start in the shop. And, if they're not up for it, well. . . . at least we know you can pay them.'

Glenn choked. At once the rage blitzed his brain and nerves, made balls of his fists.

He whirled round with his right one cocked, ready to twat Dick— only to find that he had already legged it, and that standing in his place was the ladieswear manager.

Glenn screamed.

I.V

He blinked and shook his head.

'Hello, Miss Mohammed!' he said pleasantly, unballing his fist. 'Pray you, my great competitor, trumpet me good tidings, and bring me word how the world goes.'

She scowled up at Glenn.

'Have you been swearing at my staff?' she demanded in her shrill, nasal voice.

Glenn rose from his deferential bow, face slack.

'Huh?'

'My *staff*,' she repeated, flashing him an ugly look that belied her radiant beauty. 'I heard you've been swearing at them.'

'I have no idea what you're talking about,' he replied, after a moment's thought. 'Woman, thou art propounding riddles more difficult than the Sphinx. Speak Celtic!'

'This *morning*,' she said impatiently. 'You swore at Gertrude and Mildred.'

'I most certainly did not,' he said, his confusion deepening. 'Wait, do you mean when I first came in? If it be so, then I am afraid it is on thy own staff thou fatal fury must turn; for it was *Mildred* who swore at *me*. And she called me a gimp.'

'Oh, did she now?' said the blazing-eyed Medusa from whose piercing stares nothing could be hidden. 'And is that because you called her'—she lowered her voice—'a "daft twat", a "gobby little bitch", and told her to "piss off"?'

Suddenly he remembered his triumphant stride towards the stairs (in I.II), muttering maledictions as he passed beauty—within earshot of Ali and Betty. He smiled gaily, as behind his badge his heart winced. 'O, Rumour,' he sighed, 'filling the peace with cries, mixing true and false, taking something slight and swelling it with lies.

'I hate to disappoint you, Miss Mohammed; but while those words *were* used, they were not spoken by me. They were spoken *at* me.'

'So Mildred called *you* a "gobby little bitch"?' she asked with a wry smile.

A pause.

'Yes.'

'Rubbish,' said the Gorgon, with a roll of her lambent eyes. 'You were using foul language in a customer-facing environment, Glenn, which is gross misconduct—and, as you know: any employee found guilty of gross misconduct shall be subject to summary dismissal.'

'Gods that we adore, whereof comes this!' he cried, laughing. 'Mark Glenn; note him: look you how his sword is bloodied, and his helm more hacked than Mildred's. Thou know'st foul language and his verse are no kin together, for there's no man in the world more in love with the body of eloquence. I speak no more than truth.'

'And I heard you've been offering to pay the girls to go out with you.'

He sighed. '*No*,' he said, 'I offered to *help* Gertrude and Mildred pay for their *drinks*—*not* pay them to go out with me. Quite why this offer has proved so impolitic, I have no idea.'

'Well, it makes you sound a bit desperate, don't you think?'

Extremes of horror and love alternated as he held the gaze of those gigantically beautiful eyes, glowering coldly at him from under a hard, razor-sharp fringe. He found himself, as always, oddly mesmerised by the jargogle of her exquisite beauty with the horrid, jewel-encrusted skeleton earrings by Nirah Frazar that danced with evil intent at every movement.

'True gentlemen always throw their money about,' he said in an offhanded tone. 'And anyway, what concern is it of yours how I choose to spend mine?'

'My concern is where the money would come from, Glenn. You know we barely get paid more than sales assistants.'

'Yeah, but the girls don't know that.'

'They do now I've told them.'

Now Glenn really did yell some foul language in a customer-facing environment.

He slapped his hand across his mouth and with horror issued a muffled apology, as the ladieswear manager stood gaping at him with utter despair.

'Is this really my support?' she sighed, skeleton earrings dancing ominously as she shook her head. 'Glenn, if you can't do this job, there's plenty of people who *can*. Don't think I won't lodge a capability concern about you with head office. I don't care *what* relationship you have with Norman—we have to think about the needs of the business.'

'But I *can* do this job, Shukeena. It's just I have a different management style to you,' he reasoned. 'You're like Jove, ruling by the book. But me? I'm Apollo—I *inspire* the stones to move themselves.'

'And this hands-off approach of yours just "inspires" everything into the right place, does it?'

'Exactly.'

'So why is Wilfred turning everything the wrong way?'

Glenn's heart stood still.

'Well, you know what Wilfred's like,' he laughed nervously. 'Always having to do the opposite of what I ask. . . . No! Don't approach him! I'll speak to him myself.'

'See, this is what I'm talking about,' said the bride of Hannibal. 'Don't speak. *Order*. Crack the whip. Stop being a passenger on your floor, and start being a manager.

'Get your priorities in order, Glenn. Because I am *not* having our branch's place on the leader board jeopardised by your laziness and incompetence.'

'My priorities *are* in order!' Glenn bellowed after her, shaking his fist, as she wiggled clip clopping away. He winced as she had to step around the abandoned rail of transfer shirts to reach the stairs.

'My priorities *are* in order,' he warbled.

Down she went, the fourth Fury, to the depths of the cold and joyless region, her form tormenting his eyes with every step until she finally vanished from sight.

Yes, a most singular manager was young Glenn. He was an example of excellence, a defender of standards. He was the picture of professionalism. And for his toils, he was reviled by Mildred and Gertrude, betrayed by Ali and Betty, derided by Dick and Lyndsey, and Wilfred, and, at last, literally threatened by Shukeena. All within the span of a single morning.

He sighed, then strode off with his chin in the air and a bounce in his step, satisfied that he had at least attempted to Romanize these hostile tribes.

But as he passed under the glass mountain of Verisimilitude Homme, his brain replayed the tapes of memory. *You daft twat; We don't like you; Gimp.* As he walked by the main display, he was beginning to mutter and chunter to himself, unable to fathom the audacity of their labelling him *weird*.

Now that you've finally decided to grace us with your presence; Why not take three minutes and make it look good? By the time he had reached the cashdesk, his shoulders were heaving and his fists balled. *And stay out of my beeswax. Wanker!*

He was beginning to rock with anger once more.

'Woe to the hand that shed this costly blood; O'er thy wounds now do I prophesy a curse, that domestic fury and fierce civil strife shall cumber all the parts of the shop; blood and destruction shall be so in use, and dreadful objects so familiar, that managers shall but smile when they behold their underlings quartered with the hands of war,' he vowed with a dark intensity that was awesome to behold, he thought, as he watched his performance in the massive freestanding mirror.

Yet, revenge proved elusive.

Ladieswear was under the protection of Shukeena, and he didn't much fancy another run in with her today; Wilfred was a bit too intimidating to risk further provocation, and Dick's assistance reading the manager's report was indispensable. That just left Lyndsey—but exposing him for foul language in a customer-facing environment risked implicating himself in the clandestine act of dipping into the beeswax.

In the end, Glenn resorted to satisfying his revengeful spleen by pilfering Lyndsey's precious trying-on sock while the man had his back turned.

He then took his morning break with the intention of throwing it in the arcade toilets. But once he was out of the shop the joyful gushing of the fountains, the gentle hum of the morning crowds, and the pleasing feel of the marble underfoot made him forget all about the sock. Instead, he ended up sitting in his favourite seat by the arcade coffee stall, enjoying a rich cream cinnamon latte with no foam and reading Emily Brontë.

As he sipped his coffee through a straw, he was muttering over and over again something like, *I am Heathcliff. I am Heathcliff.*

I.VI

He believes his life is destined to be an epic odyssey. . . .

On reading the line, Glenn couldn't restrain a faint cry of pleasure. He closed his copy of *Advert*, let the hefty magazine fall flat on his stomach.

Crack. . . .

A burst of applause.

'That's me, all right,' he declared, grinning through his Carman Weshirbo facemask. He looked like he'd been hit with a cream pie. 'You heard me, Mac,' he said loudly. 'It's *me* they're talking about. *Me!*'

Pause.

'Mac?'

'Shut the chuff up, Glenn,' a rough voice grumbled from behind. 'I'm trying to watch chuffing telly.'

Glenn, furrowing his creamy white brows, peered back over the sofa arm and beheld the behemoth sprawled athwart the adjacent sofa. It had the remote control balanced atop its ample belly, with one paw clutching a can of Yorkshire Relish, the other busy with vigorous genitalia scratching.

And the name of the behemoth was Jimmy Sandaal, and upon receiving the evil eye Glenn was giving him, he retaliated with a violent wet belch, spraying himself in the process.

He then wafted the effluvium towards Glenn, using the remote as a proxy fan.

Glenn scowled and slumped back into his sofa, the fury swelling in his chest cave. Back when Cerialis was governor, a yob like this would be dealt a sword-thrust straight in the eye and no messing about. His bony fists were clenched and his teeth gnashing.

But as he inhaled the fragrant oils that adorned his body, and his hair, a sense of contentment overcame him, and the Beatitudes whirled in his brain. *Rejoice, Glenn Harding, and be exceeding glad, for great is your reward in heaven.*

Crack. . . .

Another burst of applause.

'Nice pot,' remarked Jimmy. 'Although unlucky about the white.' He sipped his can. 'Eeeeee,' he sighed contentedly, 'shit the bed.'

'How long does this game go on for, Jimmy?' Glenn enquired.

'This one?' Jimmy replied. 'It'll be over in a few minutes.'

'*Really?*' Glenn exclaimed. He breathed a sigh of relief. 'Thank Christ for that.'

'And then, the way it's going, probably another six or seven frames.'

'Six or seven frames?' Glenn said incredulously. 'You're not serious?'

'Of course I am,' asserted the great man-mountain. 'To win, it's best of eleven.'

'Best of *eleven!*' Glenn cried. 'But it's already been on for a fizzing hour!'

'And with any luck it'll be on for at least a few more.'

Glenn groaned with anger and lamentation. He was desperate to work on his drawings, but it was impossible with the events from Eboracum blaring through the wonkbox, and the incessant comments, claps, and crack. . . .

Another burst of applause.

'Ooh hellfire, that's a good safety that,' commented the Leviathan. 'You might want to add a couple of frames to my earlier calculation,' he chuckled.

Glenn gazed up at the green ceiling. Shit the bed, his lips mouthed.

'Shit the bed,' Jimmy sighed contentedly, quaffing his can.

He emitted another wet belch.

Glenn's grimace morphed into a look of abject sorrow, and he cried out with an exceedingly great and bitter cry. Was this the most galling confinement since Saturn's spell in Tartarus? Glenn certainly thought so. A man about town, a person of quality, the Britannic hero, reduced to staying on a convertible sofa-bed in a cramped, cell-like green living room. And while Saturn had to share his space with eleven other Titans, at least there was room in that vast chasm for him to stretch his legs. All Glenn had besides the living room was a narrow green corridor connected to a tiny, blue-tiled bathroom, an equally tiny kitchen, and the behemoth's tiny cell-like green bedroom. And Saturn wasn't expected to pay Jimmy Sandaal rent like Glenn was.

No wonder Glenn hadn't bothered to pay any yet. Jimmy should have been paying him.

'Doesn't he look a bugger,' he heard Jimmy sigh.

'What?' said Glenn distantly. 'Who?'

'Him there. In that bloody Alice band. I mean, he's made some dodgy fashion decisions lately, but he's excelled himself this time. He looks bloody doolally.'

Glenn glanced at the little screen and did a double-take. The man wore an eccentric hodgepodge of formal evening dress and leisure wear, his black bowtie and waistcoat interplayed with long hair and the silly Alice band. It was the sort of look that would get you beaten up on the streets of Leeds, and Glenn couldn't help but be impressed.

'Fashion follows the brave, Jimmy,' he intoned. 'And it's not lost on me that the gentleman whose appearance you are castigating has a wardrobe not unlike my own; is this persiflage your roundabout way of traducing your friend's fashion sense—again? Am I to take it you think that *I* look "doolally"?' he asked.

Glenn wears a fluorescent yellow belted cashmere dressing gown with NF monogram over a purple silk pyjama suit and fluffy teddy bear slippers, complete with gilt laughing skulls embroidered into the fur, all by Nirah Frazar. Headcomb pinning back the hair model's own.

'I wasn't talking about *your* fashion sense, our Glenn,' Jimmy assured him. 'Don't worry, I don't think *you* look doolally.'

'Good.'

'I think *you* look like a twat.'

Pause.

Glenn, knitting his creamy white brows, looked back over the sofa arm and took in his great opposer's outfit at a glance. His ghastly rags were not even worth delineating. He looked like a clothing donation bank that had blown over.

'Very funny, Jimmy,' Glenn sighed. 'I believe it was Johnny Rotten who said of style, "The idea is to lead, not to follow."' He made a point of looking the behemoth's attire up and down, then smiled sadistically. 'Remind me again—what was the most daring fashion decision that *you* ever took?'

'Being seen out with you.'

Glenn choked.

'O, is that right!' he shouted, bolting upright. 'Well, all right—in that case, you won't want to risk being seen out with me on my upcoming work night out.'

'You're having a work night out?' said Jimmy, suddenly interested.

'Yes.'

'What, with them stunners from ladieswear?'

'Yes!'

'Can I come?'

Glenn folded his arms and fell back on his sofa. 'Pluck off,' he said sullenly.

'Oh, come on, mate, don't be like that,' he pleaded. 'You want to bring me along if you're going out with women. I'm funny. I can make them laugh.'

'Thank you, Jimmy, but I am quite capable of making them laugh myself.'

'Yeah, but you want them laughing *with* you.'

'GOD DAMN IT, JIMMY!' he yelled, bolting upright again. 'Why do you think you're the only one who understands comedy? I'm funny too, you know. I made those girls in Revolution laugh, remember?'

'No.'

'Yes, you do. Those two girls from Armley we got talking to. They were asking me about discount at Nirah Frazar, and I said, "We only give discount to friends and family—of course, you can always *become* my friends and family."'

Pause.

'Jimmy, they laughed their heads off at that!'

'Yeah, I bet they did, I was paying for their drinks. Which is *another* reason why you need me with you—my bankcard. Face it, H; you're completely dependent on me! It's actually a bit embarrassing, given that you peddle luxury for a living.'

Glenn scowled at him and slumped back on the sofa, resumed staring at the ceiling.

A pregnant pause.

'Look, mate,' said Jimmy. 'It's not that you're not funny. You actually

34

can be funny, in your own way, but you have to get to know you first, you know? Your humour's very much an acquired taste. It doesn't go over in crowds of normal people. That's why you need *me* with you, to provide the comic relief.'

'And what am I meant to do, if you're being the comedian?' Glenn asked bitterly.

'You can be the straight man,' said Jimmy.

Crack. . . .

'And I never thought I'd say that about *you*.'

A burst of applause.

Glenn leapt to his feet and bolted down the passage, his mullet billowing behind him. And it came to pass that he returned ten minutes later, dressed with aplomb in a vintage grey wool blazer, salmon silk shirt, and a fat green carnation pinned to the lapel, and not even Solomon in all his glory was arrayed like this. Glenn wagged his hips as he strutted the pinewood, in a thick swirl of oil and spices, and on halting in the airless dungeon he made a point of coolly adjusting his headcomb.

'Oh, were you getting changed?' said Jimmy. 'I thought you were just crying again.'

'I am going out,' Glenn announced in a haughty tone.

'Where to?' asked Jimmy. 'Romeez? Ooh, bring us something back, will you?'

'Romeez? Do you not think I'm a bit overdressed for a kebab shop, Jimmy?'

'Not by your standards.'

'If you must know,' Glenn grinned, 'I have a date.'

'Oh, a *date?*' said Jimmy with an upraised eyebrow. 'You've kept that quiet.'

'Well all right, it's not a date, *per se*; I got talking to the girl in Carman Wershirbo when I was shopping for facemasks, and she said that she would be out tonight with friends and that I should come see her.' He slipped his hands into his calfskin leather shooting gloves. 'I wasn't going to go as I'm saving for the work night out, but in the absence of Severus or Hadrian to protect me from thy repeated sallies, a cold, rainy weeknight in Leeds suddenly assumes a more appealing aspect.'

'What's the bird's name?' said Jimmy.

'I dislike this term "bird", Jimmy. It's insulting. The *divinity's* name is Chardonnay,' he said, with a triumphant look. 'Chardonnay Sharples.'

'Chardonnay. . . .' the Leviathan echoed, relishing the name. 'Is she fit?'

'Fit? Jimmy, she works on a beauty counter; she is *unearthly*,' Glenn hymed.

Jimmy took a long gulp of his lager.

'Bring her back here,' he said hopefully.

'I wouldn't be so presumptuous she would come,' Glenn laughed.

'Tell her about your discount for friends and family. That'll win her over.'

Glenn grabbed his extra-large Nirah Frazar umbrella. 'Don't wait up,' he winked, relishing the envy in Jimmy's eyes. He then slammed the door shut behind him.

I.VII

Glenn of course had shit all to do in town that night. He didn't have a date. He hadn't even dared speak to Chardonnay Sharples, never mind ask her out on a date.

He had never been on a date in his life. He'd never asked anyone out, and no one had ever asked him out.

Well, that wasn't strictly true. No *woman* had ever asked him out on a date. Plenty of men had, but men didn't interest him in that way, in spite of the assumptions everyone made about him, and the hateful, bigoted slurs they hurled at him, all through high school and now, on a daily basis in the workplace.

It was a shame he wasn't gay, given that so many of his friends were: James Baldwin, William S. Burroughs, Bret Easton Ellis, Jean Genet, Ernest Hemingway (probably), Charles Jackson, Malcolm Lowry, Christopher Marlowe, Marcel Proust, Gore Vidal, Oscar Wilde. Maybe even the Bard himself.

He had had a girlfriend, obviously. He wasn't that weird. Her name was Peggy—and she was a spirit, yet a woman too. But neither he nor Peggy had asked the other one out. They had simply run into each other in town and one thing had led to another and the next thing he knew, he had a girlfriend. And then, not long after that, he didn't.

'And I awoke and found me here, on the cold hill's side. . . .' he murmured.

Anyway, bollocks to all that. Undettered by the absence of a companion or even a coin to his name, they could all go to hell because he was going to make a good night of it! Thus, from the mists of antiquity he strode, past Leeds General Infirmary and onto upper Headrow, where he emerged into the light of history, his mullet flapping madly behind him. Lo! Glenn Harding, that miserable remnant, the groan of Rome, and of Albion, lingers alone on the steps of Leeds Art Gallery. From under his umbrella he watches abstractedly the endless drizzle envelop the unpeopled piazza, dimly lit in the weak glimmers of lamplight. . . .

Sometimes the gallery had an exhibition that was open till late, where you might see something interesting, and then follow it as it moved from room to room. But no such luck tonight. The lights were off and the doors locked.

He goggled the strange mix of Gothic, Victorian, and brutalist buildings looming over him. They looked as if they had been arranged with all the care of a clothes rack in a charity shop. His eyes surveyed the lions outside Town Hall, marvelled the ancient building's towering columns and immense clock tower. He gave the deserted piazza a scalding look. Don't you know that George the Fifth once walked on this ground? Or that they shot *Billy Liar* here? Or that Glenn Harding has photos of himself and Peggy, frolicking gaily atop yon steps, on a glorious summer's day?

Cast thy sandals from off thy feet, for the place on which thou stand is holy ground.

Possibly that last item, about Peggy, was a bit too obscure for the people of Leeds. But there really was no excuse for not knowing about the King making a royal visit, or their city being the setting for some classic cinema. Easily in the top ten British films—perhaps top three?

Let's argue it later. We'll come back to that one.

And then off he went, the streets unfolding in a further chaos of elegant Georgian and ugly brutalist structures, shoved together. Through the downpour, in the distance, he could discern the hazy outline of Leeds Train Station—where the architects must have high-tailed it out of town after they finished Park Row.

Father, forgive them; for they know not what they do.

And he looked in his fearless habiliments like a man of fashion, the arch enemy of the high street—a latter day Joseph with his tunic of many colours. His garish salmon shirt brought light to the darkness, and Glenn saw the light, and it was good. It was so good that he got distracted and walked face-first into a lamppost.

But the Lord was with the boy, for not even the faintest contusion developed upon his exposed forehead, and our hero had shown his first miracle. He promptly recovered himself, and in an exuberant mood wheeled into the beat of busy Greek Street, bearing a laughing skull for his banner, chanting litanies:

> *He believes his life is destined to be an epic odyssey.*
> *He believes his life is destined to be an epic odyssey.*
> *He believes his life is destined to be an epic odyssey.*

As he strode by the Living Room, he saw the bouncer giving his outfit the once over. The brute's eyebrows practically leapt up into his beanie. Glenn's heart giggled.

O impious pagan! O child of Woden! Friend of the high street—sorry, *mate* of the high street—cast away thy Forkbeard earpiece instructing thee to consecrate thy threshold with the blood of this young prophet, and instead fall to thy knees and pray that thou might receive wardrobe advice from the saintly one.

So spake the holy man constrained by his great humility.

Music was pouring out of the doors, and as he looked aslant at the high darkened windows he could discern the flute players, and the noisy crowd wailing, and though he felt the pull, the wrathful stare of the unbelieving bouncer meant the sharing of his joyful message with the denizens was in nowise a possibility. And that is why the Living Room is a desolation to this day, just in case you were wondering.

The rain intensified, and he could hear it beating against his umbrella—until it was drowned out by the percussive beat emanating from Prohibition. A large bar/club that was always busy, it was darkly lit but with floor-to-ceiling windows so that one could see inside. And in it, as always, behold, the ignorant multitude, the after-work crowd—*the army of the enemy*. And Glenn could see that they were in noisy uproar, those bed-mates of Moloch, all of them demon-possessed and drinking iniquity like water. And they were defended in their perverse lair not by one, not by two, but *three* bouncers, who he knew from bitter experience were exceeding hostile to any male happening to swing by on his own fancying a quick drink inside.

Woe to you who are powerful at wine-bibbing, strong at mixing drunkenness; the day that you fall together into the pit of Hell is near. Howl! Glenn now marching back and forth outside the bar with his long-legged stride, shoes splashing in the road, head erect, shoulders back, up, two, three, down, two, three—combating the heresy of the townie's short back-and-sides, untucked shirt, unbuttoned collar and ill-fitting jeans, drooping ignominiously over formal shoes, with his armour of spiritual warfare. Here is a truthful witness, speaking for all to hear. You are an offense to me!

And the light of his salmon shirt shines before the evil congregation, and they are all amazed, and throng the window, and seeing so many heavenly miracles in one outfit, they begin to question among themselves, saying, 'What new doctrine is this? Get him for us, this modern Alban, this latter-day Augustine, bring him in, so that we might share his wisdom, and be liberated from "the tattered uniform of blandness," as Johnny Rotten was wont to call it.'

But the bouncers took one look at Glenn and laughed at his appearance, prompting his hasty retreat. And that is why Prohibition, too, is a desolation to this day.

Are you noticing a pattern yet?

He turned his nose up at Henry's bar, with its harsh lighting and shabby décor, did the same at Bibi's, a restaurant inhabited by old people, those who were in their thirties and even forties. However, when Casa came into view, he halted.

The sight of the snug bar shut down and steeped in darkness elicited in his entrails a twinge of anguish. An assortment of dreamlike fragments were projected across the massive windows, and he beheld himself frolicking with Peggy atop the yellow sofas, the two of them smothering each other with kisses, their hearts aflame with love—and with a gasp he turned his back to the vision, and bit his fist to stop himself blubbing.

I.VIII

The same Glenn, who had tried to spread salvation on Greek Street, now found himself lurking under the humongous stone bridge down Kirkgate, gazing into vacancy as the raging elements pelted a cadaverous tree that had sprouted up from the cobbles. Dirty rainwater was streaming down the deserted road, swirling and gurgling over the drain, while pancakes of birdshit had made a Pollock out of the lone dry patch of pavement.

His eyes drifted to the stoic face of Leeds Parish Church, rising up behind a swaying congregation of skeletal trees. O Lord, I pray Thee, make prosperous the way in which I am going.

But it was a lost looking figure that stood outside the Loft, the rain bouncing off his umbrella. No bouncers, no queue.

O, ye of little faith. Glenn tried the door.

Locked.

He toddled backwards, onto the empty road, tilted back his umbrella and looked for any signs of life in the arched windows overhead. If they were going to open up any time soon they would have to let him in, just to get things started.

But there was no life up there. Only darkness inhabiting its cavernous confines.

His ears were taking the full brunt of the frosty wind, as his mullet viciously whipped his face. His teeth were actually chattering. Will Glenn Harding live to see old age, Tiresias? Not if he stays out in this all night.

The sky moaned and the clouds wept heavily.

He skulked up Duncan Street under the deluge, surveying the widespread dereliction down that end of the city. For some reason Johnny Rotten was on his mind, and he remembered reading in his book how as a teenager he had skulked up King's Road wearing a T-shirt that said "I HATE PINK FLOYD," and just like that was spotted by Malcolm McLaren, who in turn introduced him to the Sex Pistols—with whom he ascended to Fame's immortal house.

On such timely twists of fate do great revolutions rely.

When did you settle on the brand name, Doolally? While I was walking up Duncan Street one rainy night. I remember I was lamenting my city's lack of an artistic scene, its shunning of any sort of intellectual centre, and I resolved there and then to establish one *myself*. For my store would not just sell sartorial elegance, but also art, books and antiques. And it would have couches to lie down on, and remain open after hours—and *rhapsodes* from far and wide would congregate there to recite and interpret the verse of Homer, the paintings of Bosch, and the long canvas spats with galosh tops of Glenn Harding. But why call it Doolally, Mr Harding? Because, sir, to embark on such an ambitious project was, quite literally, *doolally*. But you succeeded, Mr Harding; so, really, it wasn't doolally at all. Well there you go, it's ironic. It's *funny*. It shows that I have a sense of humour, that I *get* comedy—so you can shut your fat mouth, Jimmy Sandaal, if you're watching this; you don't have a clue! And who is Jimmy Sandaal, may I ask?

Exactly.

Pensive steps past Think Tank, fleeting glances at Milo's, and then, an apparition: Peggy upstairs sitting at a little candle-lit table, in that ravishing black jumpsuit by Nirah Frazar. And he was holding her delicate hand, kissing it, stroking her fingers. And she was—Glenn halted. His eyes were drawn to the shining lights of Call Lane, a beacon rising splendidly from beyond the shattered bus stands and upturned dustbins.

Galvanised, he surged forward, galloping towards it, and within seconds he was striding down the side street with palpable excitement, panting slightly, as he arrived at the pinnacle of the city's fashion conclave—Norman's, a bar so renowned, its name needed no proclamation (literally—the owners didn't even have a sign saying its name). His heartbeats quickened, an involuntary giddiness overcame him as he approached the glass door, a gateway into that haven of red-lit angels, resonant laughter, and wavy snakes of fag smoke he could see curling toward the high ceiling.

'*Yes?*' the bouncer grunted. He looked like Goliath.

'I'm just meeting a friend!' Glenn replied with a crack in his voice. He knew it was over.

'Not tonight mate.'

Glenn goggled him helplessly. 'But, my friend—'

'Piss off,' belched the Philistine with a meaning stare.

Glenn did as instructed, and instead watched the city's number one nightspot from the window of Opporto, a distinctly uncool rock bar across the street from Norman's.

On a worn leather sofa within a dimly lit room, the aroma of melting candles enveloping him, he beheld Norman's coveted red leather sofas, now claimed by the esteemed retinue from Harvey Nichols. Waves of envy lapped over him as he recognised familiar faces—once colleagues—now ensconced in the city's most sought-after spot.

He sighed. They wouldn't remember him, but he remembered them all right. He could see big, handsome, strawberry-blonde Wilbur, who Wilfred always reminded him of; Cecilia, that pretty but very snotty Asian girl who used to pull faces at his daring outfit choices; and Dicky Patton, a boy who had been in Glenn's class at school, and who now wore a moustache and high heels, and had once asked him out.

Many false prophets, and Glenn couldn't help but glare incredulously at the bouncer who knocked him back. *That's* who you let in?

He looked again at Dicky Patton, prancing around, waving his cigarette, amusing them all with his cheap table gibing. . . . Glenn groaned in the spirit, as he turned away from the scene, threw himself off the backrest and sank down into the decrepit sofa.

There was only two ways that a Call Lane bouncer would grant you

HUNTER

passage into Norman's. Either you compelled him by armed force, or you arrived with a train of nymphs so pretty they hypnotised him into opening the door. Ambuscade or trickery, nothing else. And for Glenn, tragically, neither option was a possibility. But O, how he would love to see the face of that heathen if he waltzed up with the girls of Nirah Frazar. O! They would walk through him like a spritz of perfume. Glenn began twirling his scraggle meditatively. And then, once he was in, Dicky would have to acknowledge him. And they would chat for a while. And Dicky would introduce him to the gang. And then he would have an in, he could actually speak to them for once—and who could say where *that* would lead? He knew from listening in on their conversations that they enjoyed a wide acquaintance with the fashion world. O, interested in design are you, Harding? Got some drawings? Well, I know some students at St. Martin's who could put together some prototypes. And Cecilia's cousins have a factory in Bradford. It's wedding stuff mainly, but they could do some lines prêt-a-porter, you know, on the understanding they'd get a cut of the profits. And then at least you'd be in production, have pieces you could sell. And you know that I'm in with the Harvey Nichols buyers? I think if I spoke to them, I could easily. . . .

Glenn's palms were sweaty and his heart was pounding.

He swallowed.

And as the man of fashion, the arch enemy of the high street, beheld his bloodless triumph, his very own Hallelujah Victory, a welling tear fell from his eye. Glenn Harding *for sale*. Stocked in Harvey Nichols. Word of his mighty works spread wide, throughout all the country. . . .

Then the population of Leeds would change its tune about him. O, yes, yes, yes. Already he could see them, their awed expressions, as he stood triumphantly before them, on the steps outside Town Hall, his face shining like the sun, his suit white as the light. Well, people! What do you think of me *now*? Was I right when I said that fashion follows the brave? That the apparel aft proclaims the man? Huh? What's that you say? Speak up, you herd of swine, you brood of vipers, or by God there will be much weeping and gnashing of teeth! And yes, they'll cry, yes, as they fall down full length on the ground, wailing and rending their hair. We're sorry we shunned you, Glenn Harding, and failed to recognise your godlike genius. If anything, you were too good for *us*—what with your fearless habiliments, and your flagship branch of Doolally, which is not so much a shop but a modern day Plato's *Symposium*, the new "Dinner at Trimalchio's". Can you ever find it in your heart to forgive us? *We want to join your entourage!*

And I'll smile. And they'll smile too, out of relief. Arise, I'll say, and do not be afraid. For you have given your account on thy day of judgment, and I am pleased.

And they'll laugh, and I'll laugh too. And I'll kiss each one of them, tenderly, on the forehead.

And then I'll have them whipped to death. And have their corpses hanged from the Call Lane lampposts, as a warning to others.

Glenn found himself staring vacantly at the exposed brickwork.

He quaffed his goblet of tap water and hurled himself up on his soggy shoes.

Outside Norman's, he gazed longingly into the steamed windows. He then looked with undisguised scorn at the bouncer who had obstructed his great stride, who had denied him his timely twist. But when the bouncer looked back at him, he made a swift retreat into a dark and cobbled alley. And it was there, beyond a row of fetid dumpsters, that he saw it—a beckoning portal, free from the scrutinizing gaze of a bouncer.

I.IX

Glenn's discovery of the clandestine bar prompted him to unravel the tenner he pilfered from Jimmy's wallet, while he had been in the act of changing.

'How now, first serving-man,' he bellowed over the monotonous beat, peeling off his gloves. 'One Paint the Town Pink, please—and don't spare the Pernod!'

His excited eyes slyly raked the room. No *rhapsodes*, but plenty of shadowy female forms, their lovely outlines shimmering beneath the frosty, neon-blue glare of the lights.

In a jubilant mood, he perched on a barstool. 'What service is here!'

he exclaimed merrily, as the bar tender slid him his drink. And Glenn left the man some change, for gold and silver was accounted nothing in the days of Solomon. He then flicked back his glossy mane, crossed his legs and sucked his fruity cocktail, relishing the cold tingle in his empty stomach. *Dum dum dum dum dum.* It felt as if the speakers were plugged into his sconce. He took another quaff of the ambrosial drink, and feeling a pleasant glow pervade his spirit, assumed his man about town persona, and swiveled his stool round, offered the room his most smug, conceited smile. A reciprocal smile from a nearby table prompted a quick about-face, and he swivelled back round with his head down.

With his back to the young maiden, he goggled her in the mirror over the bar.

She, an ethereal vision, cast inquisitive eyes at Glenn. He took another quaff of his cocktail, as his eyeballs nervously inspected his neon-lit phizog. His huge forehead gleamed under the lights like one of the myriad bottles bejeweling the wall. And had those ass's ears of his actually grown bigger? Were they inflamed with frostbite? He winced at his terrifying reflection. How did a skinny little body like his manage to accommodate the ears and forehead of a giant? He wanted his *designs* to flout the rules of form and composition, not his person!

He went on revolving anxious thoughts in his brain for so long that by the time he summoned up the courage to smile back at her, his glass was empty and her table vacant. He jerked on his stool. He looked, and behold, his angel was slinking into the hurly-burly of the dancefloor— and 'twould take another cocktail before he could wade into the ranks of that gyrating mob. *Dum dum dum dum dum* went his heart, accelerating as he remembered the generous tip he left the barman. He felt the plastic in his pocket, but didn't dare try any of them so soon after the Christmas splurge.

But the end is not yet.

And so, just like the ancient Britons who used the mountains and caves for cover, and from them launched surprise attacks on the unsuspecting Saxons, he concealed himself deep within the darksome clusters blathering at each other over beers, in the jammed bar next door, intending to return to his angel shortly. Through the smoky fog he crept, slithering between the throngs, until he saw it—the obligatory unguarded pint, plonked temporarily on a shelf outside the door to the gents.

Manna from Heaven.

Now crushed in the crowd of the parlour, he gulped down the beer he had surreptitiously seized then gasped, his features contorting hideously. His belly tried throwing the drink back up, but his mouth caught it and threw it back down. He wiped the spit from his scraggle, waited impatiently, as his eyes raked the row of headless backs hunched o'er the bar, aglow in the smoke-whorled glare of the dangling lightbulbs. And it was hot in the dark, and he could feel himself sweating as he twirled through the clangorous crowd, and a girl's face appeared before him, smirking, and she squalled *Carvalho* in his face, *Ricardo Carvalho*, and he flung his arm around her, and he felt her limbs brace, and he squalled *Jezreel* in her face, *Jezebel Jezreel*, and his spittle flecked her nose, and frowning she wriggled free of him, and his face was pressed against the wall, and he had to push himself off it before twirling away, and the clanging of bells made him jump, and he found himself pinned to a wall that was actually moving, and when he turned to examine this amazing wall he found it had little hands, little hands that were holding a fag and a pint, and a bemused little face that was deliberately avoiding his own, and he leaned into the face and, breathing heavy, sweating, informed it that there was a new artists' settlement in Ambrosia, out on route 11, but shhhh, don't tell anyone, and in trying to tap his nose in sign of their secret understanding he spilt the man's pint, and the man looked pained, and fancying a puff of his fag Glenn tried to take it, but the man admonished him furiously, and Glenn twirled and twirled, and treading on the spot beside a crowded table, peeking at an unguarded pint, he surreptitiously seized it, and he watched Glenn Harding smiling, trying to reason with the woman shouting in his face, and the woman's friends joined in, and it looked like the whole room was against him, and he saw himself sitting defiantly on the cold wet cobbles, and the two bouncers were standing over him and brushing their hands, glowering violently at him. And suddenly there were changes in the air, thunderings and lightnings, as the rain returned and a great windstorm arose, and his hands searched the cobbles for his gloves and umbrella, and to his horror he discovered they were gone, and it was the bouncers who had stolen them, and in a rage he scrabbled to his feet, and on jellied legs he screamed in their faces, about how he would call the police on them, but he had left his Kumquat at home, and the wind was freezing, the plague of hail pelting him, and he watched himself go wobbling down the wet cobbles, head flopping back and forth, and they could all go to hell because he had yet room for six scotches more—but Norman's was shut, and he was remonstrating with the bouncer at Queen's Court, Dicky Patton will pay for him, go tell Dicky Patton that Glenn Harding is outside, and he was saying no, shaking his head, no, and he told him his flatmate would pay the fare, but the taxi driver was saying no, shaking his head, no, and Glenn stumbled up Headrow in the tempest, feet squelching, face dripping, the direful winds blasting him back over Millennium Square, and he was weeping, literally weeping, over his dry clean only shirt, and he would never make it past the Infirmary, and when he made it past the Infirmary he would never make it up that hill, and when he was up the hill, his clothes drenched in rain, and sweat, he fell gasping against the arched oak doors and groped around inside his pocket. Along with his keys, he pulled out the change he kept from Jimmy's tenner, and when he counted it out he realised he had had more than enough for a bus fare, and probably even a taxi.

I.X

Glenn. . . . Glenn. . . . Glenn. . . .

Glenn's eyes parted but darkness veiled them. His legs, reacting instinctively, thrust him off his seat. The crack of his coccyx against the cold, stony floor echoed far above his head, as if he were in the pit of some cavernous dungeon.

'Glenn?' queried the irksome voice, tinged with apprehension. 'Is that you, geez?'

The menswear manager found himself on the floor, one arm draped over a toppled piano stool, fingers clutching a shrinkwrapped garment over his head. Brummell's hard, ceramic body began to take shape before his bulging eyeballs.

'Ay, 'tis me,' he replied curtly, scrambling to his feet. 'What's the noise?'

He smoothed down his mullet, checked the shape of his massive sculpted crown.

Dick, emerging from behind the towering metal racks, grinned mischievously.

'Here he is!' he chuckled, panting lightly. 'What are you doing in the back of the stock room, you weirdo? Everyone's been wondering where you are.' He playfully nudged Glenn. 'We didn't know if you were getting off with your boyfriend again,' he added, nodding towards Brummell, the mannequin.

Dick yelped as Glenn grabbed him by the measuring tape.

'FOR THE LAST TIME, DICK, I WASN'T DOING ANYTHING WITH THAT MANNEQUIN!' he yelled. 'All I was *attempting* to do was move the damn thing out of the way! And I was naked because I was trying on clothes—'

'Geez geez geez,' Dick interjected, giving Glenn's hips a playful squeeze. 'You don't have to explain yourself to me! I know you weren't doing anything with the mannequin; I was *joking*. If you remember, it was *Sheila* who started that rumour. Which was pretty rich of her, given what her and Wilfred used to get up to in here, playing their little games of, "*Here's Johnny*". . . .'

With a grunt, Glenn released his grip on his formalwear supervisor. He then straightened his necktie, wiggled his limbs back into alignment with the contours of his tight black wool waistcoat, for which he had eschewed his blazer. With the crisp white shirt and matching black wool trousers he looked like an utter rake, an authentic English playboy— almost aristocratic. Brummell would be lucky to get off with him.

'Anyway, geez,' Dick said, 'I only came to ask you to put something through on discount.'

Glenn's eyes narrowed. '*Discount?*' he queried. 'What, do you mean you're actually *buying* something?'

'It happens occasionally,' Dick shrugged.

'Not in all the time that I've been here it hasn't. What are you buying?'

'The new marigold shirt, if that's all right with you,' he answered cheekily.

'The new marigold shirt! That's very fancy for Mr Zabledore. Art thou going out?'

'No! Well, yes, sort of. Oh, look, it doesn't matter, geez. I'll get Shukeena to do it.'

Glenn's face dropped abruptly.

'Mr Zabledore,' he said, fastening his eyes on him.

'Glenn, seriously. It's nothing, I swear.'

'Mr Zabledore. . . .' he snarled.

'Geez, it doesn't concern you. Please—'

'DICK!' Glenn screamed.

'A couple of us are going for drinks after work!' Dick cried. 'All right!?'

Pause.

'You mean there's a. . . . *work* night out?' said Glenn tonelessly.

'No, there's not a *work* night out. A few of us are having drinks cos it's payday, that's all. Anyway, look, I'll find Shukeena and ask her to put it through.'

Dick was hastening down the aisle, heading for the lift, when suddenly, impossibly, Glenn materialised from behind a row of garments and blocked his path.

The formalwear supervisor leapt about a foot off the floor and shrieked.

'So there *is* a work night out!' Glenn growled.

'*No!*' said Dick, clutching his heart and glowering up at him. 'I've told you. It's not a work night out. It's just a sort of, I don't know—*mates'* night out.'

'A *work* mates' night out?' Glenn ventured hopefully.

'A mates *from* work night out,' Dick clarified.

Glenn stared searchingly at his underling, his heart thumping in his chest. 'Are any of the girls going?' he asked faintly.

'Well yeah, I think so. . . . Mildred, Betty.' He cleared his throat. 'Gertrude.'

Glenn tottered.

'Anyone from menswear?' he whispered.

'Maybe Wilfred?'

Another pause.

'I see,' Glenn nodded. 'And during which secret assembly was all this planned?'

Dick's cackle echoed around the lofty heights of the old room.

'Secret assembly!' he cried. He grinned, his sharp yellow teeth glinting in the gloom. 'Geez, it was arranged openly, before the morning meeting—right after the Barebones delivery.' Suddenly his face turned serious. 'Oh, that's right. You missed the delivery, didn't you? Because you were. . . . at the dentist again, or something?'

'Carrying out a competition report,' Glenn warbled.

'That's it, a competition report. But anyway, it's just a few of us, not a *work* thing. To be honest, it'll probably be shit!'

'Peace, peace,' Glenn groaned, waving his hands. He stepped aside. 'Pray you, speak no more to me. I will leave all as I found it, and there an end.'

'Good lad,' Dick nodded, waddling off towards the lift. 'I knew you would.'

'One last thing though,' Glenn called after him. 'Who actually arranged the night?'

'Glenn, please don't drag me into one of your shopfloor squabbles,' Dick begged.

'Mr Zabledore!' cried the menswear manager, laughing. 'I'm not going to drag you into anything,' he said innocently. 'I ask merely for information. . . .'

I.XI

Rain had been forecast all week, prompting Shukeena to move the umbrellas to the front. (Always create further selling opportunities.) They now dangled from the mouth of a massive Ugandan rain god facemask, like long strings of slobber, and in this tableau stood Mildred with the cold blue eyes, shining hair and arms of snowy hue, duly marking up the swing tickets.

She wore her signature black leather kneeboots, perched on six-inch heels, paired with a tight, cut-off, sequin-studded black dress by Nirah Frazar, Barebones collection, and it took considerable skill to expose so much flesh while still being clothed. She looked like a mannequin the staff had forgot to finish dressing. It was as she lifted her tag-gun to the last umbrella that an evil sound rose up that was not of this earth.

Hmmmraaah!

Her jewels jingled as she turned her brightly painted visage to ladieswear. It was the midmorning lull, and the floor was quiet but for the low sounds of the plodding, electronic unmusic. The only other people in were Ali and Betty, who were all the way over on the beauty counter, trying the new makeup lines. (Ali trying the makeup on himself, Betty holding the mirror for him.)

She felt the air around her turn cold, which would have been an eerie sensation had she not been standing next to the doors. However, the eyes in the immense paintings adorning the blood-red walls did almost seem to be watching her. . . .

'Nyaaarrgh!' thundered a disembodied voice, making her jump.

She promptly drew back from the rain god and thrust the tag-gun between its hollowed eyes. 'Was that you?' she enquired of the lump of wood, almost hopefully.

'Oh for fu—RAAAAAAAR!'

Her eyes narrowed. She looked over her bare, bony shoulder at a towering row of plush green doors. She crept up to the end cubicle, clip clopping loudly, and cupped an ear to the door. Something was tumbling and thrashing around inside. Something vicious, spitting obscenities that shocked even her. She breathed a sigh of relief.

'Gerty?' she called, rapping on the door. 'Is that you?'

A pause.

'Yeah, it's me,' came a breathless yell from within. 'What do you want?'

'Are you all right in there?' Mildred enquired.

'I'm *fine*,' Gertrude yelled back. 'Piss off!'

But Mildred could hear her panting. She cupped an ear to the door again.

'Hyarrrrrrrrrgh!'

'Mate, you're not going to the toilet in the fitting room, are you? It's bad enough when customers do it.'

Mildred leaped back as the door swung open and Gertrude staggered out, squeezed into a Barebones long sleeve snakeskin print jersey dress.

'Well?' gasped Gertrude, swaying slightly, sweat trickling from her beehive. 'What do you think?'

Mildred appraised the dress. It looked like a python trying to suffocate her.

'That looks *great* on you,' she replied, before giving her head a violent shake. 'Sorry, force of habit. What I meant to say is, you look like *shit*.'

'You what!?'

'Well have you seen yourself?' Mildred laughed. 'It's obviously too tight.'

'This is why *I'm* the style advisor and you're a sales assistant,' said Gertrude curtly. 'Barebones is *meant* to be tight. It's a snug cut, designed to work *with* your body.'

She turned to the floor-to-ceiling mirror and assumed an end-of-runway stance.

Something ripped.

Mildred rolled her eyes. 'I think you should try the next size up,' she suggested, checking the swing ticket. 'Christ,' she choked. 'Gerty, this is a 4!'

'I know it's a 4!' Gertrude shouted back. 'Barebones doesn't go past 4, does it. It's meant to be catwalk style, extreme beauty. Nirah Frazar doesn't want some dumptruck spoiling his beautiful designs, does he? Think about brand image.' She turned to assess her rear. A pair of knickers was poking through the rupture. She stroked her chin contemplatively. 'Hmmm. This one must be faulty,' she said, with a crack in her voice.

'Gerty, you've gone right pale, you know?' said Mildred.

'*Good*. Have you seen the girls in the new *Advert*? Pale is in.'

'Yeah, but you're going paler by the second. Are you all right?'

'It's just my body adjusting to the new cut. Don't worry, I'll break it in.'

The style advisor turned on her heel, placed one hand on her hip, and strode commandingly toward the mirror. Her eyes then rolled back in her skull and she collapsed headfirst into the glass, breaking it.

I.XII

He stood before beauty with his legs spread, arms akimbo, his eyes fixed sternly on Ali—who was murmuring to Betty something like, *yeah, Wilfred knows Derek doesn't he, and he lives by Woodhouse anyway, he can get the goods*.

'So I hear there's a work night out and *I'm* not invited!' Glenn thundered.

The two slender youths stood in mute amazement, sharing an incredulous glance.

'You heard *what*?' said Ali, in his low, husky, docile tones.

'Yeah, you heard *what*?' squeaked Betty, just in case Glenn missed it.

'Whatever in the darkness ye said, in the light shall be heard,' intoned the menswear manager, in a grave and terrible voice. 'And what to the ear ye spake in private shall be proclaimed upon the shopfloor. Dost thou know the policies Nirah Frazar has in place to protect team members from bullying, Mr Hussain?'

A tremor shook the makeup artist head to foot, his pretty countenance slacking.

'Bullying?' the boy choked. 'I don't even know what you're on about.'

'Yeah, bullying? He doesn't even know what you're on about,' contributed Betty.

Glenn ejaculated a jolting, one-syllable laugh. He then repeated it, even louder. Ali and Betty exchanged another glance.

'Come, come, Mr Hussain,' Glenn grinned, flashing his straight, sparkly white teeth. 'Warfare is not for you, child. Your friend Dick has already told me the whole tale! You arranged a work night out behind my back and made everyone agree not to tell me. Now why distort things, when you know well how to be just?'

'Eh!' exclaimed the boy who had Narcissus in his face. 'No, I didn't.'

'Yeah, eh! No, he didn't,' squeaked Echo. She looked hesitantly at Ali.

Glenn frowned. 'So what *did* happen?' he demanded.

'I don't know, do I,' said Ali. 'All I said was I fancied a drink cos it's payday.'

'O! And just like that, everyone's going?' Glenn asked, arching a plucked eyebrow.

'Well, no,' Ali responded. 'Not *everyone's* going.'

The two minxes joined arms, issuing Glenn a united icy stare.

Glenn held up his large, arachnid hand. 'Ali, *seriously*. I'm not bothered about your lack of an invite,' he smiled. 'I *am* bothered by your trying to *hide* a night out from me, but I'll get over it. To be honest, I already have plans tonight! So if you can just tell me where you're going, I'll be sure to avoid it. That way, you won't even have to worry about running into me.'

'I'm not worried about running into you. You wouldn't get in where we're going.'

'Yeah! You wouldn't get in where we're going.'

'What, you mean Norman's?' Glenn scoffed. 'Please, Ali! I'm in all the time—'

'Ergh, we're not going to Norman's! No one goes there anymore.' Ali sneered. 'We're off to LS1.'

'LS-*what?*' said Glenn.

'LS*1*,' Betty squeaked.

'And what the hell is LS1?' demanded Glenn.

'Only the club people in Norman's *wish* they could get into,' Ali grinned.

Pain shot through Glenn's chest, and he staggered slightly, steadying himself on an antique medicine cabinet housing the perfume bottles.

'Where is this club?' he croaked, deathly pale.

The makeup artist provided directions, but Glenn could never remember directions, or street names, or basically anything that was of practical application. He swallowed.

'Take me with you,' he pleaded in a faint, timorous voice.

Ali tilted his head sideways, fluttered his deep lashes. 'But I thought you had plans, Glenn?' he said in a singsong voice. 'Do you want to come now?'

'Like a lusty Moor I'd like to come.'

'Well tough shit,' said Ali coldly.

The next thing Glenn knew, he had the child by his throat.

'PLEASE ALI!' he heard himself scream. 'You *can't* go to LS1 without me!'

'Here, get off me, you prick!'

'Yeah, get off him, you prick!'

'Come on, Ali! You arranged the night—let me come with you! Be rul'd!'

'I didn't arrange it! I just said I fancied a drink cos it was payday! It was *Gertrude* who sorted it—she's the one who knows the bouncers!'

The involuntary moan Glenn emitted sounded like an actor on stage overplaying his death scene. He unhanded the boy. 'So now I have to ask Gertrude?' he said weakly.

'*Yes,*' snapped Ali, indignantly checking his neck in the mirror. His pale-gold skin had turned an angry red round his throat. He looked like he was wearing a neckerchief.

'Although you can't ask her,' squeaked Betty, 'because she's in hospital.'

'*What!*' Glenn yelped. 'What do you mean she's in hospital? Is she all right?'

'Excuse me,' said a voice.

'I'm afraid that's all we have left in that size, sir,' Glenn barked over his shoulder, glaring at Betty. 'What say'st thou to me now, about Gertrude? Speak again!'

'Er, *excuse* me,' said the voice. 'I'm not a "sir", and I'm not asking about "size" either. I have a question about makeup, if you don't mind.'

Glenn grimaced angrily at the woman. She returned him a stare that would give pause to a bouncer. In fact, she looked like she could work the doors herself.

He dragooned a deep breath, inhaled the sweet Verisimiltude in the air.

O Jerusalem, Jerusalem.

'You know, I was here first,' he said grudgingly.

The giantess was unmoved.

'Fine,' he grunted, wheeling round and stamping off. 'FINE!' he yelled.

What more can this hulk suffer? What comes now?

To the field goes he; deep into the heart of the Danelaw, wading in evil. And it came to pass that while fingering apart the belted teddy bear fur coats, in the shadow of the Chinese red lacquer wedding cabinet, he spied it: the sun-bright ponytail of that pallid shade, the original barbarian woman—Charon's *chore*—gliding around amid the innumerable multitude of mannequin and customer heads.

With arms held wide to the heavens that were painted overhead on the high ceilings, Glenn praying to God.

He also prays to Wyrd, the grim force of destiny, just to hedge his bets.

Mildred held a tasselled black leather kilt in front of her, and was looking at it in the adjacent freestanding mirror. The hem hung past the knob of her kneeboots, as she regarded her reflection sternly. She raised the kilt so that the hem was over her knees, but still seemed dissatisfied. She lifted it higher, so that the belt was under her armpits and the hem someplace provocative. She nodded approvingly.

'Good morrow, my Gipton dish!' Glenn exclaimed gaily, emerging from behind the glistering displays. 'How do you, shop-sister! What do you talk of?'

The fierce maid looked at him in the mirror and frowned. 'You *what?*'

'Ah, it doesn't matter,' Glenn dismissed with a flick of his hand. 'So what's all this about Gertrude? The two playthings tell me she's gone to hospital!'

'Oh. She just bumped her head, that's all,' Mildred yawned. 'Be right as rain by tonight.' She hung the kilt back on the feature rail and stiffened.

'Not that anything's happening *tonight*. . . .' she added innocently, finger-spacing the garments.

'The lady doth protest too much, methinks,' he chuckled. 'Drop the charade, Miss Scragg; tales of a work night out have come to my ears, and I know that you are involved in it. However, I also know that, in spite of everything, you aren't going to proceed with such a venture without first inviting thy menswear manager.'

'Oh aye?' she said curiously, peeping back at him over her bare, bony shoulder. 'And why's that then?'

'Because I know that you are, at heart, a good person.'

Mildred responded with a rather nasty sounding cackle.

'Oh,' she said. 'A "good person" am I now? I thought I was a "gobby little bitch" who needed to "piss off"?'

Glenn held his smile, as behind his badge his heart winced.

'Bless those who curse you, Miss Scragg. For, if you greet only your brethren, what do you do more than others? Do not even the tax collectors do so? Be perfect!'

The bare, ivory-white skin on show amid the wide crossover straps beckoned his gaze. The hot shudder that passed through him nearly took out his knee-joints.

With a sigh she whirled round to face him. He quickly lifted his eyes.

'Look, it's not a *work* thing; it's just a few of us going out *after* work. And to be honest, it's not really your scene. Discriminate has a very strict dress code.'

Glenn thought he had misheard her. 'It has a what?'

'A very strict dress code,' she said.

Glenn's eyes narrowed. 'A strict. . . .' He lost the power of speech.

He checked his reflection in the mirror. All right, his face was slack and his mouth open, but from the neck down he looked as if he had been styled by the hand of God.

'*Dress code?*' he blurted out, turning back to her. 'You—you don't think that I—*Glenn Harding*—could pass a dress code?' he asked, almost with awe.

'Well, you do dress a bit like a grandad.'

'Like a *grandad*!?' Glenn wailed. 'Wait, you mean my vintage grey wool blazer? That's not dressing like a grandad. That's dressing like an experimenter with form—like a person who thinks for himself! It's dressing like an *arbiter elegantiae*. And yes, all right, it did belong to my grandad, but that just underlines its timeless—hey, wait a minute; *Discriminate*? I thought you were going to LS1? What's Discriminate?'

Mildred rolled her eyes at the menswear manager.

'You really don't know anything, do you?' she said. 'We *are* going to LS1, grandad. Discriminate is the *name* of the night. It's called that because it's held on the third floor—which is even more exclusive than the first two floors.'

Pause.

'Mildred, I'll cover shifts for you; I'll recommend you for promotion; I'll even give you my staff discount; I will do *anything*. Please. Let me come out tonight.'

She cocked her head and eyed him inquisitively.

'You'll do anything?'

'*Anything.*'

'Okay.' Her lips curled in a cruel grin. 'How about you "piss off"— right now?'

She turned her back on him and resumed finger-spacing the feature rail.

Hamlet, thou art slain.

'Fine!' he barked at her ponytail. 'I don't want to be part of your faction of fools, anyway. Have your fancy night out without me—I won't shed any tears, I assure you.'

He let out a yelp as he tried to stifle a sudden attack of tears, biting his fist as his eyes welled uncontrollably. Then he wheeled round, and with one almighty kick sent the feature rail and it contents crashing loudly to the floor.

'YOU'RE A GOBBY LITTLE BITCH!' he shrieked in her grinning face.

He ran to the stairs, crying hysterically.

I.XIII

Behind him a mounted moose head, of monstrous size, adorned the wine-dark wall. Its vast horns, hard as steel, were all but impaling the low woodbeam ceiling, and with tall Wilfred situated where he was, they appeared almost to be attached to his head. Combined with his square jaw, flowing hair, and fearsome arms, he looked like something out of Norse mythology, sent to wrap the world in war and thunder.

Certainly not the first staff member you'd approach for service.

He was quietly studying a houndstooth print sock when he heard a man whispering and gibbering to himself, his tone alternating between violent rage and manic fear.

'You all right there, our Glenn?' he said, peeping around the mountain of clothes piled high atop the counter.

Glenn jumped. At once he turned beaming to the brawny giant.

'Forsooth! I am reasonable, Mr Woods; very reasonable.'

'Happy to hear it.'

Wilfred dangled the sock before his face, stroking his chin as he tried to decide whether the ribbing was beginning to unravel or the heel prematurely thinning.

Glenn eyed the antique German castle cuckoo clock, to the side of the moose head. It was nearly one, which meant it was nearly time for his ninety-minute lunch hour.

'Will you be long processing the faulties?' he enquired innocently, eyeing the till.

Wilfred looked at the apex of the mountain of clothes, which was at his eye-level, then looked at the menswear manager.

'No, fine,' Glenn nodded. 'It's important we get this done.'

Wilfred stretched apart the heel and pressed his thumbs into it until it split. He then scribbled "torn heel" on the return sticker, slapped it on the sock and tossed the pair of them into the big faulty box on the floor. He cleared his throat. 'The faulties would be done a lot quicker if you could remember to write down the reason for an item being returned, Glenn. You know, like we're *supposed* to?'

'Ah, but still, no one can process a faulty returns pile as fast as you,'

Glenn smiled. 'You're known for it. In fact, of men who now eat bread upon the earth, I hold you the best at completing a task efficiently. I've always said that if anyone wants lessons in performance, they can learn how Wilfred Woods excels them. O! nerve and bone of menswear, hear what thy manager speaks: if my daily report can give immortal life, thy fame shall ever live in the halls of head office!'

'I don't know anything about this night out, Glenn.'

Glenn banged his fist on the counter. 'Don't lie to me!'

'I'm not lying,' he laughed, as he lifted a black blazer from the faulty returns pile. 'You probably know more about it than I do. I know shit-all.'

He coolly ran a massive hand through his rock 'n' roll hair.

'O, come on, you must know *something*,' Glenn said in a pleading voice. 'You know Derek! And you're going to get the goods from him!' He cocked his head, looked at him quizzically. 'What are "the goods"?'

'I have no idea,' Wilfred sighed. 'No one tells me anything.'

'So you're not going to LS1?'

Wilfred spread the blazer out on the counter. 'Not if I can help it,' he replied, as he stood stroking his chin, examining the garment point by point. 'I've never been one for crowd chasing. Crowd *surfing*, yes. But not crowd chasing. How did your competition report go?'

'My what?' said Glenn cluelessly. 'O, yeah. *That*. Er, it went fine, thank you. Very useful.' He then scuttled round the cashdesk and came face to shoulder with Wilfred. 'So where do *you* go then?' he enquired, peering curiously at the daunting prodigy.

'All depends where the tins guide me,' he shrugged. He bent down and began picking at the stitching. 'Could be a bench in Hyde Park, could be the mosh pit in the misleadingly named Cockpit. But most Fridays, I go tattoo hunting in Bar Phono.' He scribbled "loose stitching" on the return sticker, glanced up at Glenn. His eyes glinted through his glossy threads of hair. 'The more writing they have on them, the more likely they are to let you write your name *on* them.'

The menswear manager looked back at him uncomprehendingly.

But then his eyes lit up, as an idea sprouted suddenly in his grey matter.

'Hey, I just realised,' he said, 'I've been paid, too. Why don't I go to Woodhouse and see this Derek chap for you? I can get the goods for everyone!'

Wilfred had to laugh. He rose up, and up, and up, and rested a heavy hand on the menswear manager's bony shoulder. 'Glenn,' he smiled, 'I don't always get on with you, but, for some strange reason, I do like you. And for that reason, I could not in good conscience send you, or your little red pocket hanky there, into the mean streets of Woodhouse.' He then took the black blazer and tossed it into the faulty box. 'If you're that desperate to go to LS1, you need to speak to Cruella,' he advised. 'She's the one who knows the bouncers. Not me.'

'Yes, but she's also in hospital right now.'

'Oh yeah. Good point.'

'Dost thou know what happened to her? Apparently, she bumped her head?'

'She did more than bump her head—she blacked out while trying on one of them Barebones dresses and fell headfirst through the fitting room mirror,' he related with glee. He pulled a pink shell jacket from the faulty pile. 'I always said that bitch had a face that could break mirrors; I didn't know how right I was!'

Glenn cocked his fist and was about to twat the whoreson cur who had insulted the second Helen, but on contemplating his Herculean bulk thought better of it.

Instead, he banged his fist on the counter again.

'So that's it!' he yelled. 'You don't know anything about the night out; Ali arranged it, but he can't invite me because he doesn't know the bouncers; and Gertrude *does* know the bouncers, but I can't speak to her because she's been conveniently rushed to A&E!'

'Glenn,—'

'Again and again, these loathsome creatures press me severely! Asses! Fools! Dolts!' he roared. 'O! I wish all you Romans had only one neck—'

'Glenn!'

'What?'

Wilfred was staring incredulously at Glenn, who was nearly hyperventilating.

'Ali didn't arrange the night out,' he said. 'He mentioned a drink, but it was Dick who arranged it all, and made it a work night out.'

A pause.

'*Dick* arranged it all?' Glenn said in a faint voice.

'Yes!' Wilfred chuckled. 'Who else would it be? Didn't he tell you?'

The menswear manager could feel stabbing pains in his belly. His head felt dizzy. He goggled the formalwear section: Unmanned.

Wilfred spread the pink shell jacket out on the counter. When he looked up to speak, Glenn was already gone.

The struggle was too strong, hateful, and long-lasting, and all length was torture. But if the fatal hour had come, then, like Nero before him, he was going to first watch his servant stab himself in the neck—just to see how it was done.

'Come on, come on,' Glenn snarled, as he slammed his palm impatiently against the button. 'From whence is this lift coming? The Ninth Circle of Hell?'

The lift doors parted to reveal Shukeena Mohammed.

'There you are,' she said gravely.

'O, I don't have time, Shukeena,' Glenn snapped, thrusting an outspread palm in her face. 'I have very urgent business upstairs with Dick Zabledore!'

The skeletons did a hideous little dance as she stepped out of the lift.

'Er, I have urgent business down here, with *you*,' she said with a stern glare.

And such was the power of her dread gaze Glenn at once felt his shoulder blades pinned against the partition. He watched helplessly as the lift doors closed behind her.

'What now?' he moaned.

'Have you been swearing at my staff, *again*? And kicking over my feature rail? And shouting, and doing it all on the shopfloor—in front of *customers*?'

A pause.

'In the words of Solomon—'

'Did you or did you not swear at Mildred and kick over my rail!' she flared.

'I did *not*,' said Glenn. 'What happened was that Mildred swore at me—again—and as I tried to walk away my size 10 shoe *inadvertently* kicked the rail, knocking it over. And then, yes, I hopped around swearing a bit, because I thought I'd broken my toe. Would that you could experience such pain, Miss Mohammed—it's enough to make the cleanest spirit sound severely demon-possessed!'

'Don't even try it, Glenn,' snarled Mrs Pluto, queen of the abyss, host of the House of Death. 'You were upset because you didn't get invited to this silly work night out. Do you really think it sets a good example to our juniors, seeing the menswear manager get so worked up over something so trivial?'

'I'm not upset at all!' Glenn laughed. 'I don't even care about the work night out!' His face fell abruptly. 'Are *you* invited?'

Shukeena wears a thick, fluffy black lambswool rollneck, black leather skirt, black tights and black studded suede ankle boots, all by Nirah Frazar, and there isn't a dress code in the world that would pose problems for her. . . .

Glenn swallowed.

'You see?' she said. 'You're at it again. While Mildred has had to go home early because she was so shaken up by your actions. You made her cry, Glenn!'

'*What*! O, please, Shukeena, don't tell me you believe that. Agod-a-mercy—that rascal was smirking when I saw her! She found it funny!'

'And with Gertrude having a fall I'm down to two members of staff now. I can get by with three, but *two*? On *ladieswear*? It's impossible. And all because you had to come downstairs, uninvited, and upset my sales assistant.'

'All right!' he cried in a strained falsetto. 'I'll apologise to her when she's back. Okay? Now, thou stirring dwarf, leave me in peace and go, while you can, in safety!'

He reached over her and slammed his palm impatiently against the button.

'It's too late, Glenn.'

'Huh?'

'You've been reported. Kicking over the feature rail and shouting in a staff member's face is physical intimidation—which is gross misconduct.'

'What are you saying?' Glenn warbled.

'Oh, I'm happy to let Norman say it.' The Gorgon's maroon-glossed lips curled into an evil grin. 'He wants to see you in his office. *Now.*'

Glenn peered round the partition wall, to that green door outlined by the blood-red wall, lurking in the shadow of the great suit of armour.

A tremor of terror shot through his bowels.

I.XIV

He stood outside the manager's office fearing and trembling. Sickly green fear was tugging at his entrails, and the knocking of his heart was making his pendant tinkle.

O Lord, I pray Thee, make prosperous the way in which I am going.

He rapped on the door.

'Come in. . . .' came a guttural growl from within.

Glenn roused his most charming smile, opened the door. The room was shaped like a shoebox, eight feet wide and about twelve feet long, and as he peered in he beheld Norman, steeped in the half-dark, looming large and burly in his throne. The tremulous light from the shopfloor slapped Glenn's long shadow athwart the store manager, and as his eyes were adjusting he saw something glinting in the murk.

'How does my royal lord!' said Glenn gaily. 'How fares your majesty?—'

Glenn realised the glinting was from the gun Norman had trained on his face.

'*Sterben!*' the store manager shouted. '*Schweinehund!*'

Glenn screamed and slammed the door shut, stood clinging to the suit of armour, visibly trembling.

He was met with a room full of slack faces, gaping him with astonishment.

The office door creaked opened, and Norman poked his grizzled head out.

'Sorry love, I didn't mean to scare you—I was just playing with my new toy!' he laughed. He held the door open. 'Come in and sit down; although you might want to look at our new gold label hipbriefs first— because I do believe you've shit yourself!'

A jellied Glenn staggered into the office, dazed and gurgling.

'They called it the "Trench Broom",' he could hear the store manager bellowing, 'because you could flick it on automatic, point it at a trench and go *brrrrr*! and it'd just sweep away the enemy. And then, when the empty case was ejected, you'd slam the next one in, press the trigger and do it all over again: *brrrrr*! Another one cleared. Eject, slam, fire; eject, slam, fire. Oh! You could go skipping through those trenches you could, slaughtering men like dogs.'

Glenn found himself sitting on an antique steel mill worker's chair, staring stupidly at the long red 9 bored into the handle of the weapon gleaming in his hands.

Norman glowered at him. '*Illegal?*' he said severely. 'No, it's not illegal, you mong. Any citizen judged by the licensing authority not to pose a threat to the public, and who has not been sentenced to a term of imprisonment of three years or more, is free under UK law to acquire firearms and ammunition. Everyone knows that.'

Glenn looked up at Norman. 'Huh?'

'*Exactly*,' nodded the store manager. 'It's *handguns* that are Section 5 prohibited, which is why I no longer have my two .22 pistols, my 9mm Browning, my 357/38 Distinguished Magnum and a Star PD .45.' He shook his head, ran a brawny hand through his dishevelled hair. 'God, I miss those guns. It's not an exaggeration to say I loved them as much as my own children. I loved them more, actually—at least my guns didn't grow up to disappoint me. But as I say, you can still purchase *historic* handguns like this one, just so long as they're *deactivated*. It's a very popular hobby.'

The shock had worn off and Glenn's brain waves were resuming their normal frequency. Mind and senses were in accord again, as he goggled the pistol curiously.

'Really?' he replied. 'So it's legal, then?'

'Totally legal and completely above board,' Norman smiled. His face fell abruptly. 'The only thing that makes this particular one dodgy is that I've reactivated it.'

'You've *what?*' Glenn cried.

'You heard me.'

Glenn's eyes flitted between the complex piece of craftsmanship in his hands and the succession of buttons implanted in the wrong button holes on Norman's shirt.

'But. . . . *how?*' he said.

'With my old pals "Lathe and Miller",' the store manager said in a stage whisper, grinning deviously as he tried tapping his nose. He found it on the third try.

'Do they run a gun shop?' Glenn queried.

Norman thought for a moment. 'Sort of.'

Glenn peered down the muzzle and felt the thrill of fear flow through him. 'And "Trench Brooms" were used in the World Wars, were they?' he asked, curiously.

'Oh, even before that. Churchill had one in the last charge of the British cavalry, at the Battle of Omdurman. Although his will have been a 7.63, obviously. But, yes, he went over this hill and suddenly there were five thousand mad Dervishes coming at him, and he just stood there banging away. He said in his memoirs a whole mass of Arabs just dissolved into fragments. Speaking of which, be careful with that, it is loaded.'

Glenn threw his head back from the muzzle.

'JESUS CHRIST, NORMAN!' he shrieked, as the gun sent a cold shock up his arms. 'Can you put this away, *please?*' he begged.

'All right,' said Norman reluctantly. He took the weapon and, with his shaky hands, flicked it on safety. He then placed it inside the red quilted interior of a small black gunbox and, with a heavy sigh, dropped it in his desk drawer.

Norman, draped in a black Cuban silk shirt, oversized, with all-over white laughing skull print by Nirah Frazar, pairs it with scruffy black chinos and battered black galoshes, origin unknown. He also wears his wedding ring, although he has long since joined the multitude of singletons in the shop.

'Anyway, boy, what can I do for you?' he beamed, his blue, bloodshot eyes lingering on Glenn with an air of curiosity that quickly morphed into suspicion.

Glenn cleared his throat. 'Er, Shukeena said you wanted to see me.'

'Who?' Norman yelled.

'Shukeena,' Glenn stuttered. 'From ladieswear.'

Norman was looking helplessly at him. He turned to the gallery of headshots gummed to a filing cabinet and squinted at them, murmuring her name.

'The makeup artist?' he ventured.

'The ladieswear manager,' Glenn replied delicately.

'Oh, *her*,' the old one rumbled, as suddenly his face grew grim. 'Yes, I remember this business now. My wayward menswear manager!' He scanned the men's headshots and stopped on one of a boy in a brim hat, tilted diagonally over his forehead, fixing the camera with one moody eye. 'You must be Glenn Harding.'

''Tis I,' Glenn nodded.

'Well, Mr Harding, I'm afraid that that young lady has written me a whole list of your misdemeanours,' he grunted. He leafed through the towering stacks of paperwork cluttering his desk. 'Menswear manager, menswear manager—ah-ha! Here we go,' he said, donning a pair of warped spectacles, one lens conspicuously absent. He held the sheet up to the bare lightbulb dangling overhead. 'Liaising with head office!' he bellowed. 'Maximising KPIs! Preparing and conducting appraisals—' He lowered the sheet, looked baffled at Glenn. 'Wait a minute; I thought you were supposed to do this?'

'I think you're reading the manager's duties list.'

'Oh.'

'Look, Mr Mountain, if I can speak: all that happened is that I tripped on the feature rail and knocked it over. O! and I swore a bit

HUNTER

because I thought I'd broke my toe. Now, that considered, can we not see better, and check this hideous rashness? If thou ask me, the real sound is the devilment brewing *downstairs*; for there our bloody sister is bestowed on ladieswear, not confessing the cruel parricide I suspect she is plotting.'

Norman sat up in his seat. '*Drang nach?*' he said, with a spooked look.

'Ay,' Glenn nodded. 'And yes, I have done my work ill, yes, I accuse myself sorely; but, Mr Mountain, I urge thee: do not push out of your gates the very defender of them. Sleek o'er your rugged looks and give Glenn reprieve, and I swear to thee by my badge's awe that I will meet that little Cnut downstairs beard to beard, and discipline thine great opposer soundly—'

'I'm going to have to stop you there, lad,' Norman interjected, waving his ginormous hands. 'I've got a conference call with head office in half an hour.'

'Sorry,' Glenn murmured sheepishly.

'Look, calm yourself down, love,' Norman advised, 'you're not in trouble with me.'

'*Really?*' said Glenn, incredulously. 'Why not?'

'Because I know how stressful retail is, especially on the shopfloor,' he explained with a certain camaraderie. 'Bloody hell, if I were to sack someone every time tempers flared, I'd be the only team member left! Also, if I were to sack you, it'd be me who'd have to go through the faff of finding your replacement, and I've got enough to be getting on with in here—' He banged his hand down on his desktop. Bottles clinked. 'Now, obviously I've got to be seen to take *some* disciplinary action, which is why I'm going to give you an informal stage "improvement note", which is as follows: *stop pissing about*. And now, with that issued, we'll say no more about it.'

'Fine by me,' said Glenn quickly. 'But what if Shukeena wants to take it further?'

'Who?' Norman asked again.

'Shukeena! The ladieswear *manager*.'

'Oh yes! Yes, sorry. Well, I'll just tell her that I've dealt with the matter, and that we won't be taking any further action.'

'And you'll definitely remember?' Glenn delicately pressed.

'OF COURSE I'LL BLOODY REMEMBER!' Norman screamed. 'WHAT THE HELL DO YOU THINK I AM, BOY, SOME SORT OF IMBECILE!?'

'No, no! I was just checking!' Glenn said with obeisance. 'Sorry!'

Norman was leering grotesquely at him. And then suddenly he pulled open a desk drawer and lifted the small black gunbox out of it. He was grinning mischievously.

'Hey!' he whispered. 'Do you want to see something interesting?'

I.XV

Lyndsey was bent down on his bony haunches, contemplating the angle of a white suede wellington boot, when suddenly he felt the hardwood beneath him shaking.

In a moment a moonlike sphere had engulfed him in darkness.

'Well, Lynn, I'm all dressed up and ready for tonight,' came Dick's breathless voice from behind. 'What do you think? Have I got a chance with Gertrude?'

Lyndsey looked back at Dick, who was standing proudly in his new marigold shirt, his blubber stretching the seams to their absolute limit. It looked like a star exploding.

'She's had a bump on the head, Dick,' said Lyndsey. 'She's not brain damaged.'

Dick cocked his head, eyed the footwear section curiously.

'Here, Lynn, what's with the layout? Have you not seen the new plan?'

Lyndsey stood up. 'What do you mean?' he asked, readjusting his pince-nez. 'The shoes are laid out exactly as they are in the new plan. I followed it to the letter.'

'Yeah, you may have followed the *old* new plan to the letter, but Lynn, head office have sent over a *new* new plan,' Dick chuckled.

'A *new* new plan?' The thick rubber soles of his bow-embellished gilt workboots squeaked as he spun around to face Dick. 'Seriously?'

'Yes, seriously! Christ's sake, geez—you're so fixated on your little corner that you never know what's going on in the shop! You better hope we don't get a mystery shopper. Any supervisor who doesn't meet standard has to sit through a performance review—with *Norman*.'

'Please tell me you have a copy of the *new* new plan,' Lyndsey croaked.

'What's it worth to you?' said Dick, grinning from ear to ear.

Lyndsey glowered violently at the formalwear supervisor.

'All right, don't get your knickers in a twist. I was only joshing with you,' said Dick, pulling out a crumpled piece of paper from his pocket. 'Right, first: take the silk running slippers and arrange them so they're parallel; using the six-inch platform derby, the ostrich skin wingtip and the thousand-pound penny loafer, form a line;'—Lyndsey was darting from one side of his display to the other, like a cyclone of shoes ripping through his section—'Then, move the spring-heeled clogs to the top right; place the white suede wellington boots on the middle shelf between the slippers; position the diamond-studded man heels on the top shelf.' Lyndsey was scurrying to and fro, the light from the woodbeam recessed spotlights bouncing off his bald head. He halted.

'Go on,' panted the footwear supervisor. 'What's next?'

'Nothing,' said Dick. 'Your section is sorted.'

Lyndsey was gulping air. 'This is the *new* new layout?' he said, stroking his pencil-goatee thoughtfully. 'It doesn't look right?'

'Really? It is accurate,' Dick insisted. 'Why don't you take a step back?'

Lyndsey skirted the low footwear display table, zigzagged the antique piano stools, back to where Dick was standing, and took in the display as a whole.

The shoes had been arranged to spell out:

TWAT

'DIIIIII-I-I-CK!' Lyndsey screamed.

Dick erupted into laughter as he revealed his real plan—a printout of Lyndsey's staff headshot. The footwear supervisor lunged for him, only to be intercepted by a furious Glenn, bounding between them and forcefully pushing them apart.

'Stop shouting on the shopfloor, you two!' he shouted. 'What's the quarrel now? Peace, you ungracious clamours! Fools on both sides! Ho!'

Dick eyeballed Glenn. 'Sir, you can't speak to us like that,' he protested.

'You *what?*' Glenn barked.

'Yes, if you have a complaint then you must take it to the menswear manager,' Lyndsey asserted. 'Although I do believe that post is currently vacant.'

'For now,' opined Wilfred, swaggering onto the section.

A pause.

'O, I get it,' Glenn groaned, as a black cloud formed on his countenance. 'You yellow dogs, you best o'th'cut-throats,' he snarled furiously, 'you thought I'd never make it out of that manager's office, didn't you? Well, I'm sorry to disappoint you all, but I am *still* the menswear manager!'

'What!' yelped Dick.

'After what he did downstairs?' Lyndsey exclaimed.

Wilfred muttered some foul language in a customer-facing environment.

Glenn's eyes rained arrows on his team.

'Is this *really* my support?' he sighed bitterly. He quietly straightened his necktie, smoothed down his debonair waistcoat. 'Well, clearly I can have no pacts with you,' he growled. 'As between men and lions there are none, no concord between wolves and sheep, but all hold one another hateful through and through; so there can be no courtesy between us. And with that in mind, I think you better summon up what skills you have, for I bring heavy business from Norman. . . .'

A hush fell over the assembled team.

'Which is?' asked Wilfred apprehensively.

Glenn's lips contorted into an ugly smirk. 'A yoking time tomorrow of six a.m.'

The staff screamed.

'Six a.m.!' Dick cried. 'Are you having a laugh!?'

'We can't get in at six a.m., Glenn,' said Wilfred. 'We're going out tonight!'

'I'm not,' said Glenn tersely.

He saw their hearts sink. They stood without a word, their eyes cold as the air-con.

'And don't even think about being late,' Glenn said. 'For I have strict instructions to send any stragglers straight to the office. And you can take your coat and your bag with you, for thy will have thrown away thy badge as 'twere a careless trifle.'

As the menswear manager flounced off the field, his mullet billowing behind him, a heavy gloom passed over the department.

I.XVI

He believes his life is destined to be an epic odyssey.

He believes his life is destined to be an epic odyssey.

He believed his life was destined to be a pointless and uneventful non-story, as he lay brooding on the sofa in Saturn's prison cell, staring up at the green ceiling.

The *arbiter elegantiae* had meticulously groomed his regal upswept crown, was newly clad in his luminous marigold shirt by Nirah Frazar. A pair of black skinny jeans concealed his new gold label hipbriefs, destined to remain undiscovered beneath his impeccable attire.

'And now I'm in the world alone, upon the wide, wide sea: But why should I for others groan, when none will sigh for me?' Glenn muttered in a vacant monotone.

Jimmy, sprawled athwart the adjacent sofa, one paw clutching his glass of whisky, the other one scratching his genitals, turned his face from the wonkbox and looked up at the little arched window. The black night was ablaze with uncountable white flakes, a relentless snowstorm accompanied by howling winds that beat against the glass.

'Shit the bed,' he gasped, acknowledging the ferocity of the storm. He glanced at Glenn. 'I'm glad I'm not out in *that* tonight.'

Glenn moaned.

'You'd *never* go out in a blizzard like this, would you?' the behemoth laughed.

Glenn's countenance darkened. 'Mr Sandaal,' he uttered stiffly, 'I would go out in Noah's *flood* if it meant a night out in the company of Gertrude Ogden.'

'You'd get your hair wet, though. Don't forget, you lost your brolly.'

The remembrance of him losing that exquisite umbrella, along with his gorgeous calfskin shooting gloves, on that merciless and pitchy night (somewhere within I.VII, I.VIII, and I.IX), wrung from the atrabilious menswear manager another moan. He cast a despondent glance at his pointy brogues, now rendered warped and crinkly by the tempest, and moaned once more. He then turned his face to Jimmy.

'Perhaps I could borrow yours?' he proposed.

'Chuff that,' the Leviathan belched. 'If you can't remember a brolly that cost more than a month's rent, what chance has mine got?'

Glenn stiffened at the mention of rent.

'Anyway, it's a moot point, because I'm not going anywhere,' he deflected quickly. 'My Kumquat is never going to ring, and there will be no occasion tonight for Glenn to sport and dance, to toy, to wanton, dally, smile, and jest.' He grimly sipped his whisky, choked as the fiery liquid pierced his throat. 'O, muses!' he wailed dolefully. 'The causes and the crime relate—what goddess was provoked, and whence her hate!'

'If you wanted a drink after work, you could have always come out with us.'

'What, you mean go out on *Greek Street*, with the drones from your office?'

'Yeah.'

'And talk about what, Jimmy? "Renewal premiums", and "mid-term adjustments"? Wow, that'd be a laugh.'

'Well, no, obviously you don't have to talk about *insurance*; you could talk about anything! Arthur loves his books, you know? He's read *The Da Vinci Code*.'

Glenn cried out with an exceedingly great and bitter cry.

Pause.

'You just want to go to Norman's tonight, don't you?' said Jimmy.

'Ergh! I don't want to go to Norman's. No one goes there anymore,' Glenn said derisively. He sipped some more hell-broth and choked, gasping as it set his throat aflame. 'I want to go to LS1!' he yelped.

Jimmy asked where that was. Glenn could only provide vague directions.

'And if we got a taxi down there, would that cheer you up?' said Jimmy.

Glenn scrutinized the behemoth's unsightly attire: a cheap white shirt stretched tight over his rolls of flesh, a dark, grubby tie, a vile grey polyester suit, shapeless baggy trousers and scruffy tan shoes. He looked like the sale wall at Tie Rack.

Glenn couldn't repress a shudder.

'We wouldn't get in,' he answered bitterly.

'All right then, sack off LS1 and bring over that mint sounding bird from Carman Weshirbo. What's her name again, Sade?'

'Chardonnay.'

'That's it. Invite her round. We've got plenty of booze in. She can even bring a mate! In fact, *definitely* tell her to bring a mate. No fat ones, though, obviously.'

It took all Glenn's energy just to muster a response. 'No.'

'All right, fine. Just sit there all night waiting for your Kumquat to ring instead.'

'I'm *not* waiting for my Kumquat to ring.' He looked expectantly at his Kumquat, resting on the coffee table. Nothing. 'I know very well that it's not going to ring.'

Glenn lay pining and praying, dreaming and dying.

'What do you do that always makes everyone you work with hate you?' asked Jimmy.

'What did Ovid do to attract the wrath of Augustus? No one knows.'

'Do you think it's because you act posh and use all these pretentious references, even though you're from Seacroft, literally the roughest part of Leeds?'

Glenn bolted upright. 'I am most certainly *not* from the roughest part of Leeds,' he snapped. 'Yes, I grew up in Seacroft, but may I remind you, Mr Sandaal, that I was born *here*, in this very building? Hyde Hill was a maternity home, remember? *You*, on the other hand, were born in St James's, in the bad lands of Harehills, like every other peasant in Leeds. So, strictly speaking, it's *you* who's from the rough area. O! How it must pain you, my being born in a premium location, a great gothic building with a bucolic backdrop—just outside the city centre.' He smiled conceitedly. '*Seacroft*. What nonsense! Where I'm *from*, is very likely the exact spot in which I am currently sitting!'

'And look how far you've come.'

Glenn's face turned pale.

Jimmy's gibe had thrown him into a sort of trance, conjuring up a mental tapestry of dead-end jobs, debt, and mediocrity that whizzed across his eye-beams, as outside the winds, and the ghosts, and the goblins, were screaming. He blinked and shook his head, gazed vacantly at the Leviathan.

He swigged down his hell-broth, dropped his glass, and with an anguished groan rose to his feet and tottered off down the corridor.

He returned a moment later, enwrapped in his big, shaggy fur coat.

'You're not really going out in this weather, are you?' Jimmy gasped.

Glenn tried to reply but no words would come. He just stood there, stock-still, gaping at Jimmy with a look of horror imprinted on his face.

He gave up. The door slammed shut behind him.

I.XVII

Jesus wept.

I.XVIII

Glenn skulked through the grey, dreary staff room, placed his arm against one of the lockers and, with a low sob, rested his throbbing head against his forearm, careful not to disturb the rigid line of his enormous fringe. He was beginning to slip into the mist of slumber when, all of a sudden, he heard footsteps splashing in the passageway.

'Glenn!' cried Dick, as he came bursting into the room.

Glenn didn't move a muscle. 'Dick,' he growled, 'if this is about me being late—'

'Haven't you heard?' Dick interrupted, in the same hysterical tone.

'Heard what?' Glenn groaned.

The formalwear supervisor made a strangled sound, began to splutter and gurgle. He couldn't get the words out.

Glenn flung himself off the locker, turned furiously on his underling. 'Have I heard *what*!' he shouted. He saw Dick's eyes were welling up, his lips trembling uncontrollably. 'O God, what's happened?' he asked nervously.

'It's Gertrude,' Dick warbled, tears streaming down his cheeks.

'What about her?' Glenn said faintly.

A pause.

'WHAT ABOUT HER!' Glenn screamed.

'Wilfred shagged her!'

Glenn felt his entrails do a somersault. His legs gave out, and he staggered sideways, falling against the lockers. 'Do not abuse me,' he croaked.

'He shagged her, Glenn! Wilfred shagged Gertrude!'

I.XIX

Glenn goggled the hideous mask of tears and snot, sitting across from him in the little brown leather booth. With jangled nerves and trembling heart, he tried to navigate his way through the fog of confusion in his brain, until at last he found the elusory word:

'*How?*'

'How?' said Dick, his voice still hoarse from last night. 'Well, I don't know, do I. I'd prefer not to think about it, to be honest. Hopefully it was only missionary—'

'I don't mean that!' Glenn snapped, banging his fist on the table. 'God mend me,' he groaned, as he writhed awkwardly in his tight trousers. He looked at Dick with impatient eyes. 'I mean how did it happen?'

'Oh right, yes. Sorry geez,' said Dick. He blew his nose on a serviette, slumped back in his seat. Still the table was wedged into his flab. 'Well, for a start she was pissed. They all were, thanks to me getting the rounds in all night. And that wasn't cheap, I can tell you. It's bloody London prices in that LS1. I'm brassic now!'

'Thanks for the rum baba,' Glenn murmured sheepishly, acknowledging his cake.

'Huh? Oh, that's okay. Anyway, so they're all twatted, and then, at midnight, after *hours* of me grafting, joking, entertaining—which is hard work, geez; those kids are *not* raconteurs, believe me—Wilfred makes his big entrance. And of course he's brought the goods, so now they forget about me and they're all over him. Well, next thing you know, he's leading Gerty off to the toilets every two minutes—which I thought was odd, because as recently as the Christmas do she wasn't into the goods at all, was she?'

'I wouldn't know,' Glenn shrugged. He picked up his rum baba, bit into it. 'And I still don't get it, either. I mean, Wilfred said to me that Gertrude had "a face that could break mirrors". He calls her "Cruella"!'

'Cruella,' cried Dick, scornfully. 'You don't believe that shit, do you? It's all misdirection, geez. It's the reason why he was flirting with Mildred and Betty but not Gerty. You see, beautiful women are used to being chased by blokes. It's boring to them. But the man who doesn't chase

79

them—the man who has better things to do—now *he* interests them. If he knows what he's doing, he'll have them chasing him! It's pick-up artist shit, and that's the game Wilfred's playing. Do you understand?'

'I don't understand anything relating to men or women.'

'It's basic human nature, geez. Why do we covet the luxury brand and not the high street? Because it's harder to get, more exclusive. Who covets the one who's easy to get? We want the one who's *hard to get*.'

Glenn was listening with rapt attention. 'Now I understand,' he nodded.

'Yes, he's quite the Casanova is our Wilfred,' Dick continued. 'First Sheila, now Gerty. Who knows, next it might be Mildred, or even Betty.' He reached over and pinioned Glenn's arm, looked him square in the eyeball. 'Or, even worse: Shukeena.'

'Or,' said Glenn, 'even worse than that: Gertrude *again*.'

Glenn had to apologise to the smattering of greyhairs who populated the dark, sleepy café, Dick's blood-curdling shriek having made them all jump in their seats.

'Sorry geez,' Dick sniffed. 'It's just I don't think I could take it again. When I saw that creep getting into a taxi with *my* Gerty, oh. . . . I could have died.'

'Well, I'm glad I wasn't there to see it,' said Glenn, glowering at him.

'Oh yeah,' Dick murmured. 'Look, about the invite. It wasn't anything personal. It's just that I arranged a work night out because I wanted to spend some quality time with Gertrude! And I was worried that if *you* came out, well. . . . you know.'

'You would have had competition,' nodded Glenn with a knowing smile.

'No. I meant that if *you* came out, Gertrude wouldn't.'

Glenn held his knowing smile, as he felt the blood rush to his face.

'I never liked that lad, geez. I always thought there was *something* devious about him. Have you noticed how he's always trying to undermine you? Like doing in an hour all them tasks that it takes you a week to do? Or writing those "provisional rotas", knowing full well you won't change them, because he's put you on all the easy duties, and himself on all the peaks? Do you see what he's doing?'

'No?'

'He's making himself indispensible to the department. And you mark my words: next he's going to make a move on your job.'

Glenn started in his seat.

'Thinkst thou Cassius has a lean and hungry look?' he asked nervously.

'Well, he applied for the job when Sheila left, didn't he? Which is why he hates you. And he knows I put in a good word for you with Norman, which is why he hates me. No, I'm afraid our Wilfred's a threat to *both* of us—and there's no doubt in my mind he'll go for your job once he feels he's got a strong enough case against you. And I know he acts like he doesn't give a shit about fashion, but remember—he said the same thing about Gerty, and look what happened there!'

Pause.

'What are we going to do?' said Glenn tonelessly.

'Let's get him sacked,' whispered Dick, with a dagger in his voice.

'O, I don't know about that, Dick. It's hard to get sacked where we work.'

Dick leaned in. 'Not if you do something to a *customer* it's not,' he murmured darkly. 'That goes over Norman's head, straight to head office. Summary dismissal.'

'But you can't really make someone "do something" to a customer, can you?'

'Oh, there's ways,' said Dick, knowingly.

'*Really?*' Glenn blurted. 'Ah! Then this thou should have done and not spoke on it! In me 'tis villainy; in thee't had been good service.'

'Has Shukeena told you when her next day off is?'

'No. She's stopped speaking to me since I got off with an improvement note for attacking her staff. Why do you ask?'

'Because we need to do it on a day when she's off, so she can't get in the way.' Dick stroked his myriad chins. 'The problem there is, she has a habit of popping in, even on her days off. . . . But I *think* she told me that Friday after next she's out of town.'

'Then God as my witness, that is the day we will deal out doom on this man,' Glenn vowed. 'But I suspect our complot will have to be something especially smart—something *exceptionally clever*—to catch out Wilfred Woods.'

'Hey, this is *me* you're talking to!'

I.XX

Dick and Wilfred stood before the main display on menswear, their attention drawn to the green art deco closet, within which the featured spring sellers were neatly hung. An ostentatious, floral embroidered ottoman sat before it, bearing a mannequin in a green kimono, lost in contemplation. Wilfred, clutching a heavy doorstop, appeared similarly lost in thought.

'So, you want me to take this cast-iron owl's head and place it on top of that rickety old closet, under which *customers* are constantly walking?' he asked.

'And if you could do it as quickly as possible, please,' said Dick.

'*No,*' he replied flatly.

'Eh?' said Dick. 'Why not?'

'Why not?' said Wilfred, his voice hoarse. He looked with bleary eyes at the throngs of shoppers on all sides traversing the sections. 'Because it's going to fall off and give someone an even worse headache than I have right now.'

'Why would it fall off?'

'Because that closet's got dry rot. Look at those brown patches all down the right board. I'm surprised the air-con hasn't blown it over.'

'Oh come off it, geez; that thing's been standing longer than the two of us put together.' Dick leaned over the mannequin, rapped the lesion-riddled panel. 'Look! Solid as a rock.'

With a snap Dick's fist went through it.

'Shit,' he muttered.

'I don't have time for this,' Wilfred croaked, as he plodded back behind the fresh heap of faulty returns, piled high on the counter. He plonked the doorstop behind the sign that read TILL CLOSED –

YOUNG MAN FROM LEEDS

PLEASE TAKE PURCHASES TO LADIESWEAR.

'But head office said they wanted us to dress up the displays!' cried Dick, brushing the splinters off his knuckles. 'We have to do something.'

'I *am* doing something—the faulties. Which I was making great progress with, until you interrupted me.' He lifted a black tasseled leather shirt up from the pile and began to inspect it.

'I wonder if Norman would let us hang his Bavarian police sword up?' said Dick, stroking his chins as he eyeballed the woodbeams over the cashdesk.

'Mate, I *really* don't have time,' said Wilfred weakly. It took surprising effort for him just to rip some flimsy tassels off the shirt breast. 'Pick up's in an hour, and if I don't get these faulties done they'll be cluttering up the stock room all weekend. Shukeena will go mental.'

As Wilfred hunched over the counter, scribbling the details on the sticker, Dick's eyes rolled around the hubbub. At the far end of the department, at the top of the stairs, he spotted Glenn, who was standing in his fur coat and ginormous sunglasses, possibly staring straight at him.

'What now, soft heart?' chided the menswear manager, as Dick came stumping towards him. 'Is the hunt on?' he said, pointing his gold-topped formal day cane to the cashdesk. 'I see a stag, but no arrow in its back.'

'I think our Wilfred was drinking with St Paddy himself last night,' said Dick. 'None of the harassing operations are working. He's not in the mood to do anything, except his faulties—which he's making *rapid* progress with.'

Glenn looked to the great-sized sales assistant, settled behind his shining pile.

'Death to him for whom the hour of death has come,' he intoned gravely, before sucking up some of his rich cream cinnamon latte through a straw. He then shoved his cane under his arm, peeled the plastic lid off his cup, and proceeded to discreetly pour coffee and spume all over the hardwood. He slipped Dick his set of manager's keys. 'Quickly. Go to the utility cupboard, take the mop and hide it downstairs, in the basement,' he instructed.

Dick nodded. He waddled off behind the big partition, keys jangling in his hands.

The menswear manager hurried forward into the fighting line.

'O, Wilfred,' he said, slipping his empty cup in the bin under the cashdesk.

'Oh, what now?' Wilfred groaned, as he rose up, and up, and up, clutching a pair of crinkled gingham trousers.

'Do you know there's some weird spillage at the top of the stairs?' he said, pointing his cane. 'I tell thee what, sirrah: want not a broken neck on thy watch; methinks the floor is *your* responsibility while I'm on my lunch.'

'The floor is indeed my responsibility while you're on your lunch, Glenn; but since your lunch ended half an hour ago, methinks responsibility has transferred back to *you*.'

'O, it looks like it's been there for more than half an hour, all right.'

'Of course it has!' Wilfred grunted, as he threw the trousers back on the pile. He rubbed his phizog wearily. 'Keys?' he said.

'Keys?' said Glenn.

'The mop's in the utility cupboard, Glenn!' he shouted. 'I need your keys to get it!'

With his free hand Glenn felt about his suit, under his fur coat. 'O,' he said. 'Dick had to borrow them for some reason; I think he may have gone upstairs?'

'Forget it,' Wilfred snarled, as he snatched up the crinkled gingham trousers and stamped past Glenn, towards the stairs. There the great lover got down on his hands and knees and actually scrubbed the mess up with the trousers, as the sweat pasted his shirt to his broad, V-shaped back.

"Dirty" wrote the sales assistant on the sticker, back at the cashdesk. 'There,' he panted, slapping it on the soiled trousers. 'Two birds, one stone.'

He slung the trousers in the faulty box.

'Thanks Glenn,' said Dick in passing, panting as he handed him back his keys. 'I'm going back to the fitting room, to see how my customer's doing.'

'Live,' Glenn nodded.

'Are you clowns done with me now?' Wilfred pleaded. 'I'm so busy—'

'*Hey*,' Glenn gasped, lifting his ginormous sunglasses. 'Is that what I think it is?' In three hops he was down the other end of the cashdesk. 'It is!' he cried, holding up a magnificent scarlet tartan wool blazer. 'This is from that limited run Skotch Bottle collection, do you remember? I can't *believe* someone would return it.' With trembling hands he checked the label. He nearly choked at what he saw. 'O my God!' he cried. 'Have I eaten on the insane root, or is there husbandry in Heaven!'

'What?'

'It's a 36, Wilfred! I wanted to buy a 36 at Christmas, but I couldn't find one *anywhere*. To discover one now, on the faulty pile, stands not in the prospect of belief; indeed, it is a favourable omen if ever there was one,' Glenn babbled. He held the blazer up to the woodbeams. 'I hear thee, Fate! And I obey thy call!' He paused for a moment, looked sheepishly at the sales assistant. 'Wilfred; I know you're busy, but. . . . could you find out the barcode for me? I mean, I appreciate we're not supposed to *buy* customer's faulty returns, but we all bend the rules from time to—'

Wilfred snatched the garment from Glenn's hands, and with Vulcan's strength yanked the vents and ripped it right down the back.

A pause.

'No, you're right,' Glenn murmured. 'Best we, er, keep it professional.'

Wilfred bent down, scribbled "weak seam" on the sticker, slapped it on the blazer and tossed it into the faulty box. He wiped the sweat from his brow and, with a sigh, swiped a raven print sweatshirt from the pile.

As he inspected it up and down there was a pained look in his dull eyes.

'Wilfred,' said Glenn.

'*What?*' he replied, with a quaver in his voice.

'Ronnie Colenso is leaving Nirah Frazar.'

Wilfred glared at Glenn through the threads of his hair. His eyes were bloodshot, his face muscles twitching.

'I mention it because it is an unforeseen departure, and thus leaves

85

the company without a visual merchandiser. And that, underling, is where *you* come in.'

The sales assistant was staring expectantly at Glenn.

'To end a tale of length,' he continued, 'it is the menswear manager's pleasure to have a word with Norman on thy behalf. . . . And, from some knowledge and assurance, offer this office to you.'

Wilfred's face fell slack and his mouth open.

'Is—is this some sort of joke?' he said faintly.

Glenn flung his head back and laughed aloud.

'Nay, it's not a joke. I'd go for the job myself, but I can't drive, and, as you know, the main part of the job is driving. And in a flash company car no less—while work pays for your hotels and expenses! Can you believe it? You just swan into each branch, put together the window display, and leave. No customers, no bosses—no stress. O! it's a dream job! Alack, as I have been remiss in my driving lessons, I must reluctantly pass this sinecure on to thee. Here's to thy better fortune and good stars.'

Wilfred eyed the menswear manager suspiciously. 'Is this just because you want to get me off your shopfloor?' he said.

'Does it matter?'

Wilfred fingered back his lustrous hair, considered the question. 'No,' he determined. He swallowed. 'Well, I can't believe this. Thanks, mate.'

Glenn removed his ginormous sunglasses and beamed at the man. 'It is my promise, and it will be kept,' he crooned. 'I'm just going to put my things in my locker; we'll talk about it more anon.'

'Okay!' said Wilfred in ecstasy.

Glenn flicked his mullet, turned on his heel and strode off, swinging his cane.

Wilfred jumped when he heard Dick call his name.

He looked and saw the formalwear supervisor coming his way, joined by one of his regular clients—a very slim, executive-looking gentleman, who was always decked out in the most raffish Nirah Frazar lines.

'Mr Christian here was trying on some things in the fitting room,' said Dick, 'and thinks he might have left his jacket here. You haven't seen it, have you?'

The sight of the man's scarlet tartan wool trousers shook Wilfred to his boots. He looked with horror to the matching blazer, torn and dangling out of the faulty box.

He made a strangled sound and began to splutter and gurgle, as his face turned a deathly pale.

'Is everything all right, geez?'

Suddenly, Wilfred's eyes rolled back in his head and he fell forward, pitching across the counter. He bounced off the faulty pile, slammed his skull against the cast-iron doorstop and was sent sprawling backwards, where he hit the hardwood with an almighty thud, as garments rained down on him.

Stretched unconscious on the floor, spread-eagled under his returns, he looked like a murder victim covered by a police sheet.

And Glenn, who was craning his head round the partition, observing from afar, saw his man down and smiled.

He drew back and slipped through the door marked STAFF ONLY.

SUMMER

II.I

SHE CAST HER EYES ROUND THE ROWS OF DERELICT warehouses looming over her, convinced the boarded-up windows were in some way watching her. Her clip clops were echoing up the enormity of the red brick buildings, alerting the large figure she spied lurking within a disused doorway to her presence.

She *knew* he was pretending not to have noticed her.

None of the brands impinged on her frame of reference. Chunky gold earrings peeping out from under a black wool beanie visor, a fat gold watch; camouflage jacket over a huge navy T-shirt with baggy stonewashed blue jeans; trainers so loud they had to be expensive. He was eating, quite contentedly, from a takeaway box.

'Derek?' she said, her voice puncturing the blue, lulling air.

He stopped forking his box of greasy prawnballs and stared at her.

His dark, handsome phizog was devoid of expression. His wiry black beard, dappled with some sort of beard cream, glinted in the shadows.

'I might be,' he said cautiously. 'Who's asking?'

The voice more than lived up to his ogrelike proportions.

'Gertrude,' she said nervously.

'*Who?*'

'Gertrude Ogden!' she said quickly.

Pause.

'I'm friends with Mildred Scragg.'

'Ohhh,' said the ogre, giving her appearance the once over—the expensive coat, mad eyes, extreme makeup and skeletal body. His eyes also noted the weird scar on the forehead that the poultice of foundation was presumably meant to disguise. 'Yeah,' he nodded, 'I can believe that.'

The style advisor shifted anxiously in her belted black trenchcoat by Nirah Frazar.

'And what can I do for thee, Miss Ogden?'

She glanced up and down the long, quiet road she was standing in, squinting in the glare of the sun. 'That stuff Mildred got for me,' she said. 'I want some more.'

The ogre stared at the jittery woman. 'What?' he said.

'I want some *more*,' she replied, pleadingly.

'More?' he said, in a booming voice that rang up the heights of the old buildings. 'You want some MORE!'

'Please!'

He shrugged. 'Sure, that's no problem. How much do you need?'

'Er, well I went through Mildred's stuff in no time, so. . . . I don't know really. Ten bags?'

As the ogre went about his calculation, she again shifted anxiously in her trenchcoat, glanced up and down the road. She looked over her shoulder, at the blue sign and bright green awning of the Chinese restaurant behind her, and marvelled at how anyone could stay in business in an area as dead as this. She eyed it narrowly, and was beginning to wonder if it really was a Chinese restaurant, and, if not, what they *really* were up to in there. . . . when suddenly the ogre answered her. 'How much!' she said.

The ogre repeated his calculation.

'I didn't realise it was *that* expensive,' she gasped. She thought for a moment. 'Can I not just get some more of them complimentary bags?' she said desperately.

'Complimentary!' he exclaimed, screwing his face up. He forked another bundle of prawnballs into his mouth, peered curiously at the mark on her forehead. 'Was that a *serious* head injury?' he enquired, nodding at her scar.

Gertrude's eyes bulged, as the scarlet overspread her face.

'WELL THAT FIRST ONE WAS FREE, WASN'T IT!?' she abruptly flared, with a ferocity that startled even him.

'Yes, that *first one* was free. Mildred recommending my services to you and all that,' he explained through his mouthful. 'But love, that was an *introductory* offer; I wouldn't stay in business long if I kept giving those out now, would I?'

'But Derek!' she wailed. 'I need *more*. Lots more! You don't understand!'

'Oh I understand, trust me.'

'Well there must be something I can do?' she said hopefully.

'Other than pay me money?' he laughed. 'Like what?'

Pause.

II.II

Glenn wears a black wool beanie hat, a long laughing skull pendant over a skinny black T-shirt with an enormous white laughing skull print, with a 28-waist leather belt with diamond-encrusted laughing skull belt buckle protruding over his skinny bleach wash blue jeans, all by Nirah Frazar, while the pair of shiny white trainers with neon-green detail by Klark Amaba subvert his Nirah Frazar Man motif brilliantly.

Savouring his Paint the Town Pink, Glenn executed a sly pirouette on his heel. Through a rift in the headless forms hunched over the bar he caught sight of his own reflection in the mirror behind it. You couldn't miss him. His visage, resplendent in Starstuff, was shining like a gem, and he gazed approvingly at it. The cascading waves of his mullet enveloped his neck, while the lengthy, choppy side strands gently brushed across his radiant features.

'Sorry, *who* dresses like a grandad?' Glenn muttered disdainfully, surveying the room. Surely not him, for no mere mortal had ever bore upon his person threads so magnificent. He stood as the fulcrum of fashion, the *Advert* ideal—a picture of gay Paree. His ensemble, if anything, served to defy the passage of time, rendering him not only younger but remarkably sexier. In fact, with his lean physique, flat chest, and pert buttocks, he could pass for a member of ladieswear.

'Are you having a good night then, H?' Jimmy yelled in his ear, making him jump.

They were standing together on the upper tier of a bustling bar,

HUNTER

where the clash of guitars was exploding from the speaker just above their heads, shaking the floor.

H, pausing thoughtfully, offered a smile. 'Yes,' he yelled, reflectively. 'Yes, I think—I think I actually am having a good night.'

'Nice one,' yelled Jimmy, clinking his pint against Glenn's fancy cocktail glass. 'And hey, it's a good turn out for your birthday, isn't it?'

'Put on thy boldest suit of mirth, Mr Sandaal, for I hath friends that purpose merriment!' Glenn exulted, casting an approving eye around his impressive entourage. He leaned into Jimmy. 'Who are they all again?'

The behemoth lifted his giant face to the ceiling and sighed what could only have been shit the bed. He leaned into Glenn and yelled, reproachfully, 'Mate, you've *got* to start making the effort to remember people's names. It's rude not to! Now, once more: the lad next to me is Joe Schofield; then there's Oaksey; then the Brandon boys, Harry and Archie; and the lad next to you is Freddie Bramley. Got that?'

'Loud and clear!' Glenn yelled, nodding affirmatively.

'And another thing: if someone offers to get the round in, can you please just have a pint like a normal person? Asking for expensive cocktails is taking the piss.'

Glenn frowned and eyed the behemoth coldly. 'It's *my* birthday,' he hissed.

'Yeah, but they're my mates.'

A pause.

'I shall do't,' Glenn yelled, clinking glasses with the great man-mountain.

'How are you then, big lad?' Joe Schofield yelled up at Jimmy.

'Reasonable, Joe, very reasonable,' Jimmy yelled.

Glenn, eavesdropping with intent, aimed to stay engaged in the conversation. He was determined that from now on he would be more attuned to the affairs of others, and thus focused unwaveringly on Joe, listening with rapt attention.

'Good, good,' Joe yelled. He sipped his pint, took a suck of his tab. 'I see Leeds is still in contention for the play-offs—'

Glenn at once tuned out of the conversation.

'Happy birthday then,' a soft, cheery voice bellowed in his ear.

Glenn wheeled round to face the speaker. 'Thank you, Frankie,' he yelled.

'Freddie.'

'Freddie! Sorry.'

Freddie chuckled. 'Oh, it's quite all right,' he smiled. His eyes combed Glenn's sumptuous outfit. 'Well,' he said, 'I wonder which shop *you* work in. . . .'

Glenn looked agog at the man. '*Nirah Frazar*,' he yelled, his hands guiding Freddie's attention to the myriad Nirah Frazar logos decorating his body.

'I know, mate,' Freddie nodded. 'I was joking.'

'O,' said Glenn. He forced a brief laugh. 'And, er, what do you do? "*Mate*"?'

'I'm a social engagement officer at Ethical North.'

Glenn stared blankly at him.

'We get young people jobs, basically,' Freddie explained.

'O, I see! Interesting,' Glenn yelled. 'What sort of jobs?' he asked, stifling a yawn.

'Media jobs, mainly.'

Glenn stiffened.

'*Really?*' he yelled. 'What sort of media jobs?' he enquired, staring intently at him.

'TV mainly,' yelled Freddie, coolly sipping his pint. 'We just got twelve people hired by YTV, actually.'

Glenn's eyes widened. 'Yorkshire Television!' he cried. 'Now that *is* interesting.'

'It is.'

'You know,' Glenn yelled, after a moment's contemplation, 'there's a lad I work with who's very creative, and eager to start the next chapter of his life. I don't suppose it's worth him sending you his CV? I know he'd *love* to work in TV.'

'Ah, we only work with the socially disadvantaged, I'm afraid. Sorry.'

'O! He's socially disadvantaged all right,' Glenn laughed. 'Don't you worry about that. He's been brought low and made very poor, lately. In fact, he's bloody brassic!'

'Diddums,' Freddie smiled. 'Can he only afford to wear *one* item of Nirah Frazar?'

Glenn looked flummoxed.

And then, suddenly, his countenance darkened, and his eyes flashed with fire.

'So, birthday boy,' yelled Freddie, scrutinizing again Glenn's flamboyant costume. 'Are you seeing anyone? Girlfriend? *Boyfriend*?'

Glenn choked; he promptly showed the man his mullet.

'Jimmy,' he yelled, 'can we swap places please?'

'No,' yelled Jimmy.

Reporting all the details would be tedious, but what Jimmy did do was thrust a pint in Glenn's hand and cajole him further into the smoke-whorled inner circle, where he began to receive instruction in the mysterious practice of the manly confab. They spoke of this and that; football, work—Joe was a temp at Government Office, Oaksey a temp in a different office every week, the Brandon brothers barmen; then there was more football, more birds, indie bands, even more football, even more birds—with old acts of darkness being delineated in graphic and unchivalrous detail. The exact words soon faded into the fog and filthy air, but when conversation swung back to work, and through that career aspirations, something truly memorable was finally uttered:

'H here thinks he's going to be a famous fashion designer,' Jimmy proclaimed, gesturing towards the menswear manager. 'He doesn't have a business plan, or any capital, or a degree—but he *has* drawn some lovely dresses in his sketch book.'

The blokes all fixated on Glenn, who felt the blood rush straight to his face.

'I don't want to be *famous*,' he yelled, grimacing. 'I just want to work for *myself*.'

He tried to explain that Stella Winerack had started on the floor of her council flat—although that was in London, and she knew famous people, so. . . . he trailed off.

With a shaky hand, he swigged his foul pint and groaned in the spirit.

Out of the corner of his eye, while he was still waiting for his face to cool down, he noticed that Joe Schofield wasn't smirking at him like the others, but rather was looking at him almost thoughtfully, as he quietly sucked his tab. 'You want to get yourself down to Business Sense, on Wellington Street,' Joe recommended. 'They do free evening classes for people who want to start a business.'

Glenn goggled him curiously. '*Really?*' he yelled.

'Yep.' Joe took another suck on his tab. 'They teach you how to put together a business plan. Tell you about insurance, VAT, what grants you qualify for. All that shit. I think they've helped a lot of people get started in business.'

'And they do it for *free?*' Glenn yelled suspiciously.

'It's government funded,' Joe yelled. He smiled. 'You've already paid for it. . . .'

Glenn's face fell slack. When Caesar saw the statue of Alexander the Great in the Temple of Hercules, he was overheard to sigh that at an age when the Macedonian had already conquered the world, he himself had done nothing. That scene had been on Glenn's mind all day, being more conscious than ever that time was passing him by, that he wanted to be someone, that he felt destined to be more than just a menswear manager—and then, right on cue, this valuable datum had been delivered to him.

'There's a god behind this plan,' he uttered. 'I *know* there's a god behind this plan.'

And if the gods were smiling upon Glenn, then they must have been smiling on Joe Schofield too, for when he finally looked back at Joe he saw a creature speaking to him so astonishingly beautiful his eyes actually did a double take.

Goddess or girl, he could not tell, but as he beheld her looking up at the boys, chattering happily, her bronze face and throbbing eyes the very bloom of youth, a first adventure of spring, young Glenn knew he wanted to fall down at her feet and worship her forevermore. . . .

The angel wears a loose-fit, black brushed mohair-wool blazer with

YOUNG MAN FROM LEEDS

tight leather trousers, a pink satin blouse and weird, blood-red ballet flats, and a knuckle duster pendant that makes his nerves thrill, as he gapes again that unnatural visage. Her eyebrows are thick, her makeup so stark it looks like war paint. The dark hair she slicks back into a fat ponytail, while the thick hoop earrings shock the eyes with their cheap tackiness—like signing a masterpiece with a primitive X.

Glenn's face had again fallen slack, his mouth hanging open. It was difficult to believe there could be so much going on in the costume of one person, but somehow there was. She was like a one-woman artistic scene, a flouter of dress codes, the *true* arch enemy of the high street. Her presence made him delirious, lifting him to ecstasies. With shaking hands he swigged his foul pint, standing spellbound before her.

Come, gentle Ganymede, play with me; I love thee well, say Juno what she will.

She must have sensed him staring at her, because when she paused to take a sip of her pint, she made a point of looking him full in the face. He tottered slightly, as if struck by an arrow. She took in the outfit of the man of fashion at a glance: the wool hat, the tight T-shirt, the tawdry belt buckle, and the bright neon trainers. . . . and turned her attention straight back to the lads. He felt as if the arrow had felled him.

'Here you go, birthday boy,' yelled Jimmy, swapping his empty pint for a full one.

'Who is that girl?' Glenn yelled in Jimmy's ear.

He gave her one glance. 'Dunno,' he yelled. 'Joe's mate, I guess. Want me to ask?'

'No!' But when Glenn saw his queen was leaving, he felt his stomach lurch. Again, she must have sensed him staring, because she threw him a last fleeting glance over her shoulder, and needlessly his stupid wool hat, before swanning off down the stairs with her attendant train of forgettable male hangers-on, in a swirl of smoke and attitude.

'Where are we going next?' he yelled quickly.

'Home, I hope,' Jimmy yelled.

Glenn nearly dropped his pint.

'*Home?*' he yelped. 'We're not going home yet! It's my birthday!' He swigged his horrific pint. 'Let's try some of the other bars around here,' he belched.

'I've been drinking since one with the rugby,' Jimmy yawned.

Glenn cried out with an exceedingly great and bitter cry.

'All right, none of that!' Jimmy yelled. 'What did we say this morning?'

Glenn sighed that it was his birthday, he was a year older, and he needed to start acting it—starting with his hysterics.

'*Exactly,*' Jimmy yelled. But as he saw Glenn's eyes looking longingly to the doors downstairs, and the night beyond them, he did relent. 'Look, this lot will be off after these; since it is your birthday, I *suppose* I can stay out for a couple more—perhaps at one of the other fine establishments that Headingley has to offer? I know there's a little place called Trio nearby, where all the cool kids go. Fancy giving that a try?'

'You're God damn right I do, Jimmy. And thank you!'

'Okay then,' Jimmy yelled. 'But *only* if you're going to behave yourself. Yeah? No more madness. Be normal.'

'I'll be normal, I promise,' Glenn nodded. 'No more madness.'

'Good man,' yelled Jimmy. 'Shall we go?'

'I just need to run home first and change my outfit.'

II.III

Business Sense, Wellington Street (23.3.■)

> *Get simplex d first (Jimmy steal from work?)*
>
> *Insurance*
>
> *Employer's liability*
>
> *Inland revenue offer free self-assessment*
>
> *Companies house – find out year and returns of businesses*
>
> *Business Balls website – plans, templates, cv*
>
> *BLWY – GRANT FINDER!!!*
>
> *Office of national statistics*
>
> *Brokers – seek out best insurance for me*
>
> *Victoria road, headingley – the rates office, leeds metropolitan council*
>
> *Website (andrew build it for me??), business cards, flyers etc*

Business Sense, Wellington Street (30.3.■)

   SOLE TRADER

   Pay tax on profits of business (gross income all)

   No limit on liability...

   LIMITED COMPANY

   £40 with companies house

   Generic conditions – certificate of incorporation

   £60 with agency

   Become an "employee" (DIRECTOR!!!)

   Pay tax on personal allowance level

   ONLY business assets are liable

   Health & safety

   Employment law

   VAT

   Over £61,000 profit must register for VAT

   Register so that customer (and not me) pays the 17 ½ VAT. . . .

Dick was gasping for breath after the exertion of climbing the half-turn oak staircase. He was wearing a weathered pleather biker jacket of dubious origin, and the stench from his greasy bag of chips was wafting through the department's fragrant odours.

As he stood panting, his small forehead bathed in sweat mingled with gel from his side-parting, he cast his gaze around the room and spied Lyndsey, browsing underwear.

His little black eyes lit up.

'Here, Lynn,' he called out over the floor.

'_Lyndsey_,' Lyndsey grunted, not bothering to look back. 'My name is _Lyndsey_; we've worked together for ten years, Dick; you could at least bother to learn my name.'

'Furry muff; here, _Lyndsey_,' Dick persisted. 'What you sniffing under there?'

'What?' said Lyndsey.

'I said, what you sniffing under there?'

Lyndsey whirled around. 'Under _where_?' he queried irritably.

'*Underwear?*' Dick cried, recoiling. 'Ergh, he's sniffing underwear! And look, it's men's as well!'

Lyndsey's face flushed a violent purple as the handful of customers browsing the quiet department turned and eyed him suspiciously. He looked with horror at the pack of skimpy gold label hipbriefs in his hands and quickly threw them aside.

His heels clacked against the hardwood as he bounded angrily over to Dick, zigzagging the displays and sections. '*Dick!*' he snarled, looming over the formalwear supervisor. 'Will you *please* cease with these offensive insinuations? It's not funny and it's *very* unprofessional!'

'All right, geez! Calm down,' he chuckled nonchalantly between bites of chips. 'It was only a joke.'

'Yes well it's always the same joke, and if you do it again, I'm going to report you to head office!'

'Fine! No more insinuations, I promise. Don't get your knickers in a twist.'

Lyndsey glowered violently at him.

'Oh come on, it's a turn of phrase!' Dick protested.

'*Dick,*' came Glenn's booming voice across the floor. 'Hie thee hither!' he yelled.

'Oh great—*now* look what you've done,' Dick growled, shaking his fist at Lyndsey.

Glenn was standing on front wielding a weighty armful of garments. The swing ticket dangled from the sleeve of the dark overcoat he was enwrapped in, as did another swing ticket from the brown tweed deerstalker on his head.

'Yes, geez,' panted Dick cheerily, as he toddled up beside him. 'How are you? What's bothering the Distant One this fine afternoon?'

The Distant One was contemplating some empty sidebars and forward facers. 'The garments that should be on this section,' he said. 'Whither are they vanished?'

'You mean the new collaboration?' Dick enquired, talking with his mouth full. 'It's still up in the stock room, geez.'

'*What?*' said Glenn anxiously. 'Why is it still up there?'

'Because unboxing the delivery, tagging it up and transferring it to the shopfloor is one of those big, ball ache jobs that Wilfred used to do for us.'

'I see,' Glenn nodded. He grinned. 'So there *is* a drawback to his demise.'

Both burst into peals of laughter.

'Anyway, geez,' said Dick merrily, 'I've gone over on my lunch hour; I better go put my stuff back in my locker—and then have a nap in the stock room.'

'Fare ye well, Mishter Zabledore. If anyone asks for me, I'll be in the fitting room for an hour or two—familiarising myself with last month's lines.'

The triumphant king strode imperiously through his peaceful dominion, his mangled brogues clacking and squeaking against the hardwood. His manager's keys were jangling importantly on his belt loop, as the coins he had won short-changing some cash-paying customers jingled in the royal coffers. In his blazer pocket was Wilfred's name-badge, a trophy he kept as a memorial of the great victory God had given him. Along with Sheila's name-badge, he was building quite the collection!

There was no denying that menswear had become a very pleasant place to work.

In fact, the weeks that followed after Wilfred had been put to death were happier than any previous period on the shopfloor. Normalcy had been restored, and the team reconciled to Glenn's rule. Days were quiet, breaks were long, and his department at last enjoyed that elusive state the ancient Greeks called *Eudaimonia*—the highest condition of contentment achievable for humans.

Sure, Dick and Lyndsey still engaged in the occasional shopfloor brawl, but such roughhousing was the reality of any normal, healthy workplace.

Another good thing about the days being so quiet was that he could employ his energies on his business plan. His lunches were filled with reading and learning, his shifts spent mostly in a fitting room cubicle, sketching ideas on scraps of receipt roll.

However, a hurdle loomed before him—the naming of his shop.

Compared to colourful names like Nirah Frazar, Carman Weshirbo, and Stella Winerack, Glenn Harding seemed incredibly bland. Harvey Nichols, though not overly distinctive, carried an air of elegance and evoked images of London, luxury, and high-end fashion. Glenn Harding, in contrast, conjured visions of Seacroft, smashed up bus shelters, and dog shit on the pavement. Not exactly aspirational.

He knew he wanted it to be more than a shop. Like the one Malcolm McLaren ran with Vivienne Westwood in London in the '70s, which was at various times called Let It Rock, Too Fast to Live—Too Young to Die, Sex, and Seditionaries. The teenage Glenn had been captivated by Glen Matlock's tales of the place in *I Was a Teenage Sex Pistol*. It sounded like a refuge or sanctuary for fashion radicals, drawing in all manner of local characters, art school types, and disaffected youths. A place free from corporate constraints, where they created garments on an ad hoc basis, fostered style liberty, and basically enjoyed total artistic freedom.

It sounded like *Eudaimonia* to him.

Glenn halted. His brain was reeling, as he felt pangs of fear and excitement assailing his belly. *That* was the kind of place he was going to unleash on Leeds. A clothes shop *and* artists' colony. Last exit from the straight world. But translating all these thoughts into a business plan posed a challenge. He might just present Business Sense with a copy of *I Was a Teenage Sex Pistol* and say read that.

Thank God Joe Schofield entered his life.

Without that man, he might never have found his way. He had met *exactly* the right person on *exactly* the right night and said *exactly* the right thing—not unlike the unemployed Glen Matlock mooching along King's Road and walking into McLaren's shop the *exact* moment he needed a bassist for the Sex Pistols. Or like John Lydon going out in his "I HATE PINK FLOYD" T-shirt and being spotted by the one man on earth who could give him the job of being Johnny Rotten. It was the stuff of Jove's scale, life and lucky chance. Changing heavens and smiling fortune. And it wasn't lost on Glenn that it was those Matlock and Lydon books that had initially generated his interest in clothes, and put him on the path that led to Nirah Frazar, and through that Joe Schofield and Business Sense, and now, suddenly, *his dream life. . . .*

And then, just as suddenly, he was dragged back to his rock.

'Er, *Glenn,*' a voice shrilled across the floor, with all the pleasantry of an alarm clock. Glenn whirled around and saw Shukeena standing at the top of the stairs.

'How now, Miss Mohammed,' he called back affably. 'What tidings bring thee from Lucifer?'

Her heels clacked against the hardwood as she hastened toward him, zigzagging the displays and sections. 'I want you in the office,' she declared. '*Now.*'

'Say that again,' Glenn purred, with a dreamy expression on his face.

'This isn't a joke, Glenn! We're having a managers' meeting!'

Glenn looked into the nearby fitting room, saw his reflection in the great mirror with his dark overcoat and armful of garments, winking at him, beckoning him in.

'*Another* managers' meeting?' he said, with a disgruntled sigh. 'Didn't we just have one on Monday? Nothing's changed since then, has it?'

'It's an *emergency* meeting,' she snapped back, her voice becoming even shriller than usual. It actually hurt his ears. 'Can you get a move on?'

'Fine,' he groaned. 'You go ahead. I'll just put this stuff back.'

Off she went, the goddess of fight, heading for the mighty hall of Glads-heim—where danger itself dwelled; Glenn after-eyed her shape in her black belted jersey dress until she disappeared behind a display. He looked again to the fitting room.

He would need an emergency meeting with himself before he went to the office.

II.IV

Shukeena perched rigidly on a steel mill worker's chair, a clipboard resting upon her lap. Norman slouched back in his grand throne, fingers drumming the desk. A faint drip echoed in the half-dark.

They were both staring in silence at the cold concrete floor.

Suddenly the door was thrown open and Glenn came sauntering in, clacking and squeaking. 'Sorry I'm late, I came as quickly as I could,' he said in an offhanded tone. He then sucked some of his rich cream cinnamon latte through a straw. 'O! By the way, Norman, I was watching a documentary the other night about the Gallipoli campaign, and that landing in Turkey that turned into a bloodbath. Apparently, it was Churchill's bright idea. He was lucky not to hang for that one, wasn't he!'

Norman stared blankly at the menswear manager.

'Have we met?'

'Yes,' Glenn answered amiably. 'You hired me, remember? Glenn Harding. I've been working under you for some time now.'

'That's right!' Norman said, laughing. 'Sorry love, a lot of staff members you see. I remember you now.'

The blue bloodshot eyes lingered on Glenn. They looked almost suspicious.

Glenn attempted to exchange a despairing look with Shukeena as he sank down on the mill worker's chair next to her, but she was having none of it.

'Right then,' she said briskly, 'now that Glenn has *finally* decided to grace us with his presence, I can begin. The reason I've had to call this emergency meeting is because of the alarming news that came out of today's morning meeting.'

Glenn and Norman both stared blankly at the ladieswear manager.

She shook her head, lifted her eyes to the ceiling. There she did a double take. In the gloom, she could see mushrooms spawning around the lightbulb hole. She shook her head again, looked down at her clipboard. 'Yesterday ladieswear was up 5%, which is good for this time of year,' she said. 'Menswear on the other hand was down a staggering 82%—which is not only a record low for the branch, but now makes it nineteen days in a row that men's has failed to meet target; which, I believe, is a record for the *company*.'

Glenn choked on his rich cream cinnamon latte.

'Shit,' uttered Norman.

'These figures are *disgraceful*,' said Shukeena. The dragon-headed terror then shifted her dread gaze to the menswear manager. 'Glenn, do you have any explanation for this shocking drop in sales?'

Mouth agape, Glenn made a strangled sound.

'Right, well thank you for that, Glenn,' said Shukeena, 'but I think I have a better explanation.' She leafed through the reports on her lap. 'If you track the figures back, the exact day menswear began its decline was the day Wilfred Woods was sacked.'

Glenn jerked in his mill worker's chair.

'Wilfred Woods?' Norman frowned.

'That sly and constant knave from menswear, Norman,' Glenn quickly interjected. 'Not only did he indulge in a close personal relationship with a colleague, which is against the rules, but he also destroyed the blazer of Dick Zabledore's top returning client. Do you remember, Norman? You physically threw him out of the shop.'

'Oh, I remember that,' Norman laughed.

'There's no proof that Wilfred and Gertrude had any sort of relationship, Glenn,' said Shukeena with a disdainful look. 'And, quite honestly, I find it *disgusting* that a manager is using a formal meeting to spread gossip.' She turned to Norman. 'Wilfred was one of the top sellers in the shop. And he was also the only one on men's who would actually read the updates and communicate the information to the rest of the team.'

'The devil can cite scripture for his purpose,' Glenn intoned.

'As far as that blazer goes,' she said, 'it was an accident. How it ended up on the faulty pile I have no idea, but Wilfred tore it because he couldn't see what was wrong with it. Of course, if the return slips were being filled out *properly* the whole incident could have been avoided. And since returns can only be actioned by managers, maybe Glenn could explain why procedure wasn't being followed on his floor?'

'Wait, I thought we were talking about the drop in sales?' said Norman.

'Yes, let's focus on that,' Glenn nodded vigorously.

'All right, let's focus on that,' she said. 'Men's is below target, it's not meeting standard, and head office are asking questions. Now we can blame the seasonal nature of sales for this recent dip, but if it were to continue, when we have the new gold skull collection out, then I genuinely believe it would put the whole branch in danger.'

'O! do I ever have fair play in your forecasts!?' Glenn protested. 'Calamity is all you care about or see; no happy portents, nothing agreeable ever brought to pass. Of course there was a drop in sales the day Wilfred was sacked, you vision of hell—for that was the day I became short-staffed!'

'Wait, why are you short-staffed?' asked Norman.

Glenn cried out with an exceedingly great and bitter cry.

'*Because*, Norman,' he said through gritted teeth, 'there was a man named Wilfred who worked on menswear; and one day Wilfred saw a blazer on the faulty pile—'

'I KNOW THAT ALREADY!' Norman screamed, smashing his fist on the desk. 'I mean why the hell haven't you hired a replacement yet!?'

'O right, I see, sorry,' Glenn stammered, discomfited by the sudden and unexpected sharpening of the store manager's wits. 'I *have* been looking for one; I just haven't found the right person yet.'

'*Er*, have you been looking?' Shukeena asked suspiciously. 'I haven't seen anyone interviewed. Have you advertised the job? There isn't a sign in the window, or on your floor. I see that old pile of CVs is still there, under the cashdesk. Have you looked through it yet, or phoned anyone about their availability? Because that's what I'd be doing—if *I* ran menswear.'

'I'm going to do all of that,' Glenn said irritably.

'"Going to"?' Norman gasped. He glared incredulously at his menswear manager. 'What do you mean, "going to"?' What *have* you been doing?'

'What have I been doing?' said Glenn stupidly. He shook his head, blew air. 'What *haven't* I been doing?'

'That's not an answer,' said Shukeena quickly.

'Miss Mohammed!' Glenn cried. 'I'm running a department with only two fizzing members of staff. *Two*! I'm doing the best I can!'

His hands were trembling now, and he was sweating under his tightly fitted suit. His eyes were scanning Norman's desk in search of the Trench Room.

'He's all talk, Norman,' said Shukeena. 'He hasn't arranged a single interview, his rails are empty, there's faulties piling up in the stock room, boxes of Homme piled up in the basement—oh, and someone's put a hole in the side of his antique display closet. He's a liability, and it's time we started thinking about the needs of the business—'

'All right, that's enough!' Norman yelled. He groaned, rubbing his face. 'Christ, you four give me a headache.' He glowered at Glenn. 'Now look, boy. I appreciate you're short-staffed and it's having a knock on effect on your sales; but the fact is, you *are* a manager and you're supposed to be able to sort out problems like this. Now the question I have is—and spare me the bollocks, I just want a straight answer—can you get your floor back on track without me having to take drastic action. *Yes or no?*'

'To do this is within the compass of thy menswear manager's wit,' Glenn nodded.

A pause.

'Yes yes I can get the floor back on track,' said Glenn quickly.

'I should hope so,' said Norman with relief, slumping back in his throne. He stared at the boy. 'Honestly love, it's not running through snow in the Ardennes, with bloody Panzers gunning for you; it's a *shopfloor*. It's not that difficult.'

'I know it isn't!' Glenn laughed. He could feel Shukeena glaring dubiously at him.

II.V

Betty, she who was godlike in form and birdlike in brain, was in full flow: 'And I said, I'm not scared of you, Maisy; what are you going to do, start a fight on the street? I said, I'm not bothered, Maisy; my hair's real, yours isn't.'

'*Exactly*,' Ali nodded, his bouncy flue of hair wavering to and fro as he did.

'I said Maisy, you don't have any friends. Daisy doesn't speak to you;

Rosie doesn't speak to you; Elsie doesn't speak to you. Does that tell you anything?'

'*Exactly.*'

'I said Maisy, whatever that bitch told you was all lies. Lizzie's always talking shit about me, she's jealous. If anything, Lizzie is jealous of *you*. I thought, let them two have it out instead. I'll be clever, innit.'

'*Innit.*'

Glenn was slouched at the other end of the staff room table, listening to this dialogue with the sort of pained grimace you might observe on someone who was having a toenail removed. He shook his head despairingly, tuned out the wittering and with a low sigh turned his attention back to the mass of CVs spread out on the table before him. He felt overwhelmed by the size of the task confronting him, much like King David must have been at Socoh, when confronted by Goliath, with all of his six cubits and a span.

I am a highly driven, enthusiastic and hard working professional.

I am a experienced professional with 7 years experience in retail fashion. I excel in customer service and communicating with the public.

I am a hard working, experienced professional with strong interpersonal skills and I strive to achieve my goals. . . .

Glenn wanted to take David's sling and stone and smite his own head.

Restlessly, he turned back to the window, where the sun's broad disk beamed at him through frosted, filthy glass. The joyful hum of the afternoon crowds reached his ears, gave him visions of the street in the sunshine, filled with hustle and bustle. . . .

What about the goals *he* was striving to achieve? The latest was that he had been thinking of christening his shop something like Private Club or Secret Society—names that were inspired by Glen Matlock's book, where he wrote that Malcolm McLaren hadn't sold rubber clothing because he was into rubber fetishism, but because he had a fascination with any and all underground cultures. McLaren, said Matlock, had an ardent desire to be part of *every private club and secret society* in the city. Of course Glenn (Harding) shared the same desire—and now, thanks to Business Sense, he would soon be in a position to establish his own one. Other names in this vein were Bandwagon or Movement—or even Originality—but they, while accurate, felt a bit flat. The grander, more literary names in contention were Neptune's Park and Apollo's Palace of the Sun, but those ones were perhaps a bit too lofty for Leeds. The name Lofty for Leeds then slipped into contention, until his brain while browsing back through the tapestry stumbled upon the scene of his birthday, in II.II, where suddenly the name, the perfect name, the iconic, manifest, apodictic name, shot out and struck him between the eyes, like a stone from a sling:

UNETHICAL NORTH

And just like that, he had a title that encapsulated *everything* his label stood for. A proper underground name—the birth of a movement. The thought transported him into his renegade shop, his sanctuary from the straight world, where he could see himself looming over the action from behind his elevated till, sipping the rich cream cinnamon latte his Saturday boy brought him, as he sat reading a story about himself in the latest *Advert* (titled "And Fruitful Leeds Noble Glenn Rears"). And the story is full of praise for him, and it's raving over the radical innovation that is his custom-made service, where customers bring their own fabric and idea, and his team of tailors in the back room make it for them. Design your own fearless habiliments—we'll do the rest! And don't worry if it's just some rough doodle. This is the *artistic scene*. In here, we have *imagination*. For this is the shop, says *Advert*, that spawned a thousand Glenn Hardings, and sent them out into the world to combat the high street heresy; *an army of such fine taste and piety they refute unbelief and by preaching the word of Glenn convert the heathens to his way of thinking.* Window display: tattered uniforms of blandness being fed into an open fire. (Yes, an actual open fire, in the shopwindow.) Slogan: The idea is to *Leeds*, not to follow. . . .

Glenn chuckled at heart. Enchantment whirled in his eyeballs. And as Ali and Betty's incessant wittering intruded on the scene, a scum-caked staff room window promptly slid down like a shutter, closing off his dream world. He sighed.

He was about to turn back to his CVs when he heard footsteps splashing in the passageway, and all of a sudden Gertrude wiggled clip clopping into the room.

'Shukeena's asking for you,' she said sharply to Ali and Betty. 'You better go down.'

Glenn watched Gertrude watching them leave, and as soon as the door shut behind them, she turned and looked straight at him. He felt his stomach lurch.

'All right,' she nodded—the first time ever that she had spoken to him willingly.

'How doth,' he murmured, looking down at his vast assortment of CVs.

She was arrayed in a high neck, scoop back black cashmere midi dress by Nirah Frazar, adorned with gold and precious stones and pearls. She wore her signature ivory-embellished black satin wedge heels, and when he saw the thigh-high split of her flared midi hem he felt his stomach lurch again. He swallowed.

I am a highly driven, enthusiastic and hard working professional—

'What did you think of Betty in that jumper?' she said, joining him at the table.

Glenn didn't know what surprised him the most. That Gertrude was speaking to him, or that she had a pack lunch in front of her.

'What did *you* think of it?' he said after a moment's pause.

'You can't wear knitwear this time of year,' the style advisor sneered. 'It looks like you're wearing last of sale.'

'That's what I thought.'

She lifted from her pack lunch's leafy contents a miserable looking breadstick.

'Her teeth are bad, too,' she said. 'She needs to get them sorted.'

'That's what I thought.'

He was peering askance at the scarlet woman, who was sat gazing into vacancy, chewing her breadstick. She may have lost some of her mystique with her ill-advised frolics (sweets grown common lose their dear delight), but in the last analysis she was still *Gertrude Ogden*; and her deigning to speak to him was making his head high with excitement, his heart thump. An elated smile grew across his scraggly beard.

'How's it going with your interviews?' she asked.

Glenn's countenance abruptly fell.

'Gertrude,' he groaned, 'if Shukeena has sent you to check up on me—'

'Shukeena hasn't sent me to do anything!' she barked. 'I'm just asking you, aren't I.'

'O,' he said. 'Sorry.'

'What sort of girl are you looking for?' she asked, staring fixedly at him. 'I bet you want some skinny blonde, don't you? Like Mildred. Well, I mean a *young* skinny blonde, obviously. Mildred's got a good body, but her face is getting proper haggard now.'

'It hadn't even occurred to me that I could hire a girl,' he said sincerely.

'Well, you don't want one who's too good looking, cos men get intimidated by them. You want an *average* girl. Then your customers are at ease, and more likely to buy.' With her little fork she fed herself a strip of lettuce, looking keenly at him.

'I see,' he said, his eyes lingering on that little scar grinning through her makeup.

II.VI

It was the hour of unyoking, and the staff were huddled together in their coats and bags, beneath the colossal chandeliers on ladieswear. The lights were off, the shutter down, and Shukeena was clip clopping from person to person, conducting a bag search under the silent gaze of the gods above. *I'd love to work in the flagship store, me; you have to be a millionaire just to shop there. Eh? I don't think so, Ali, why do say that? Cos Glenn told me you need a million quid just to buy a shoebox in London. Oh, do you heck, what are you listening to him for? He's never been out of Leeeeds.*

Suddenly, a burst of clacks and squeaks echoed from above, piercing the chatter. The staff turned to the half-turn oak staircase, where Glenn stood with his legs spread, arms akimbo, and a cocksure grin on his face. He was decked out in a twinkling, almost breathtaking double-breasted black sequin blazer, a black silk shirt, black peg trousers and his warped pointy brogues.

'Ah-ha, the sheep without a shepherd!' he exclaimed. 'Arise, and do not be afraid, O ye of little faith—for Christ and his saints have at last awoken.' He then descended the staircase three steps at a time and strode boldly through the group, clacking and squeaking, as he made crosses in the air and said solemnly to each colleague, 'I am willing; be cleansed. I am willing; be cleansed.' He then made a cross at the room itself. 'I am willing; be cleansed.'

The staff stared at the menswear manager in blank and utter indifference.

'*Er*, Glenn,' shrilled Beelzebub, the ruler of demons, who was then shoulder-deep in Mildred's tote. 'I need a word with you before you leave.'

Glenn, already bent down with both hands gripping the shutter, looked puzzled. 'You need a word with me now? Shukeena, I *have* finished my shift.'

'It'll just be a minute!' barked the devil incarnal. 'Everyone else can go.

'And those of you working Sunday, remember: I want you in an hour early for replenishment duty. Don't forget that if you're going out tonight.'

'No one's going out tonight, are they?' said Mildred innocently, looking askance at Glenn as she dipped under the shutter.

'I don't think so,' said Ali, who was standing outside, under the massive portico.

'What?' squeaked Betty, bobbing under the shutter. 'But I thought we were all—'

Glenn, catching the foul language Mildred employed to tell Betty to shut her mouth, waved his colleagues goodbye. 'Bye everyone! I wish you sport!' he exclaimed cheerily. 'Have an exceeding pleasant night!'

Stepping back, the Lord's Anointed, killer of men and collector of name-badges, found himself alone in the shop with his arch nemesis.

'*Well?*' she said.

'Well what, Miss Mohammed?' he said sonorously. Already the eerie power of her Psiren-like presence was crying beauty to his heart, singing away his mind.

'Are you going to tell me how the interviews went today?'

Glenn sighed. 'Saturday night and you want to talk about *work*,' he said, shaking his head. 'Yes, I think they went well. I certainly met some attractive candidates.'

'Well, let me know who your favourite is, because I want to meet him before he's hired.'

'You're my favourite, Shukeena.'

'It's crucial we hire the right person. And no offence, Glenn, but I don't think on your current form you should be making important decisions by yourself. Do you?'

'Miss Mohammed!' he cried, laughing. 'Have you any eyes? For your information, Glenn, like a latter-day Cerialis, has pulled together the divided loyalties of his domain, and we are enjoying an age of peace and prosperity upstairs.'

'So why was your till down ten pounds today?'

'No idea,' he shrugged. 'But I'll be sure to have words with Dick and Lyndsey when I next see them.'

'Good. Because your till's had *a lot* of discrepancies since you lost Wilfred.'

'Yet must I hear that loathsome name again,' he groaned, heaving a deep sigh. He then looked curiously at her. 'How come you're not going out with everyone tonight?'

She frowned. 'Because I'm *not*,' she replied, slightly defensively.
Pause.

'What does Shukeena Mohammed *do* on a Saturday night?' he

pressed, raptly.

'What?' she laughed awkwardly, pushing past him.

'Can you believe them all,' said Glenn, following her under the shutter, 'leaving the arcade when there's an amazing bar just round the corner, in Harvey Nichols?'

'Have you got your keys?' she asked, ignoring his comment.

'Always,' he answered, suddenly remembering he'd left them by the till.

She locked the shutter as Glenn stood bathed in the variegated sunbeams slanting through the arcade's stained-glass ceiling.

'Yes,' said the Distant One, 'I can't believe they left the arcade, when there's an amazing bar just round the corner, in Harvey Nichols. . . .' He gave his hefty watch a glance. 'You know, I've got a couple of hours spare,' he said, suddenly whirling around. 'The team's gone for drinks. Why don't the two department managers go—'

Shukeena had vanished.

Glenn shrugged. He smiled, then swaggered off in the direction of Harvey Nichols.

II.VII

Ye gods, ye goddesses! How sweet that night! What a pair of spectacles is here!

'He was so shaken up I had to do a whip around and call the dealer back to give us a few bumps,' Glenn yelled. 'The thing is, the dealer ended up having such a good time he actually broke out the decks and started busting out some tunes!'

He burst into peals of laughter, as the girl, called Amor, laughed along with him.

Norman's, the bar so renowned *it didn't even put its name on the door*, was resounding with a cacophony of voices and music. Young faces danced in the red glow of lights, under the wavy snakes of fag smoke curling toward the high ceiling.

On the red leather sofas by the window, once the most prized spot in all of Leeds (and still pretty cool), Glenn sat, bedizened in his black sequin blazer, sipping his Paint the Town Pink.

'Is that jacket Nirah Frazar?' yelled Amor.

'Nay,' Glenn responded. 'This belonged to my grandad, Stanley Harding, who wore it in his days as a Leeds club turn in the 1950s. So you see, the urge to shepherd the city's fashion crowd is in my blood.'

'Okay,' she yelled. 'Yeah, I thought it looked a bit unusual for Nirah Frazar.'

Glenn switched to a serious tone. 'Have you read Plato's *Euthyphro*?' Alas, she had not.

'Okay, well in it, Socrates is found guilty of not believing in *the gods in whom the city believes*,' Glenn elucidated. 'He is a lover of enquiry, and as such asks too many questions, which gets him in all sorts of bother—and that's *exactly* what I am trying to achieve with this blazer, and, ultimately, with my shop, Unethical North. I believe it's high time someone asked questions about the way people dress around here, and challenged the untruths of the high street.' A pause, pregnant with meaning, hung in the air. 'Although obviously I hope that Leeds doesn't kill me for it, like Athens did Socrates!'

He erupted into peals of laughter.

'Wait, you've lost me,' yelled Amor. 'I thought this was a job interview for Nirah Frazar. Am I being interviewed for Unethical North now?'

'No. This is the second round *group* stage of the Nirah Frazar interview process,' Glenn yelled. 'Unethical North is the forthcoming clothes shop and sanctuary for style schismatics that I intend to open in Victoria Quarter, when I complete the various business classes and consultations I'm currently attending.'

'*Right*, I'm with you now,' Amor nodded. She sipped her gin and tonic. 'Although you never mentioned a second round group interview,' she yelled curiously. 'You just said after our interview you'd call me if I was successful.'

'Successful in advancing to the second round,' Glenn clarified, smiling pleasantly.

'Okay,' she nodded. They both then sipped their drinks in unison.

'You see,' he yelled, 'it's quite a specific team member I'm looking for.

My last sales assistant was such a dissentious rogue that it's imperative that I—*we*—hire someone with whom I can be more than just a boss. I need someone with whom I get along; with whom I can be a *friend*. I have to think about the needs of the business.'

'Well, I'm always looking for new mates,' laughed Amor.

'As am I,' Glenn chuckled, 'as am I.'

He noticed that his Kumquat was quivering on the low glass table. He looked down and saw that Jimmy was calling him. He turned it off.

'Anyway!' Glenn yelled. 'Next question. Same as the first one: single or double?'

The sun's rim dipped down behind Call Lane, as night descended on the city. Uncountable cliques of half-gods and deities—forever coming, going—filled the crushing half-dark; a feverish mass of nymphs, satyrs, and fauns shouting, drinking, and gyrating, as an old soul number—with sped up vocals and a new electronic beat—shook the walls and jiggled the brain. And as the thronging queues outside the window veiled the street, and a thick cloud of smoke, with elbows, hips, and buttocks poking out of it, drifted ever more intrusively into the seating area, Glenn found himself pressed right up against Amor, in whose ear he was yelling.

'Apparently it drew in all the local characters, art school types, disaffected youths et al, all of them just wanting to hang out there, as if the shop was its own standalone scene, a self-contained little world; and *that's* exactly the kind of place *I'm* going to unleash on Leeds. The city has been crying out for it for years—and yet much I marvel that I cannot find no steps of men imprinted on this path.'

Amor was looking thoughtfully, dazedly at him.

'You're handsome,' she yelled, slurring.

'I know I'm striving for a prize that's great, but fortune rejects the prayers of the halfhearted.' He turned his face, looked curiously into her large, bleary eyes. 'Have you read Gibbon's heptalogy of—'

Amor leaned in and started kissing him.

The shock, like an electric current, blitzed his brain and nervous system, snapped the antenna of his senses. His bulging eyes stared wonderstruck at the girl feeding him kisses. He then gently pushed her off him.

'Was it bad?' Amor gasped, a vulnerable note in her voice.

'No,' he yelled breathlessly, 'it was. . . . wonderful.'

'Then what's the problem?'

'I don't want you to think *this* was my motivation for inviting you to the interview.'

She rolled her eyes. 'Oh, come on, mate,' she yelled. 'Holding a job interview in a bar on a Saturday night? It doesn't take a genius to figure out what you're up to.'

'What am I up to?' Glenn enquired.

'You wanted to pull me,' she replied.

'I most certainly did not!' Glenn retorted, aghast.

Amor stared incredulously at him. 'Then what did you want?' she demanded. She had really sobered up now.

'Well, to be honest with you, I just wanted a night out,' he yelled, slightly embarrassed. 'But the issue is a man can't get in anywhere cool if he doesn't have a woman with him! And I don't know any women who want to go out with me.'

She stared at him, mouth agape.

'Oh,' she responded, with her hand on her heart, 'that is—that is so *sad*.'

Glenn flinched. 'Well, no, it's not *sad*,' he yelled, slightly defensively. He could feel the blood rushing to his face. 'I didn't want you to feel *sorry* for me! I just don't get out much. At least not with people.'

'Do you not have any mates?'

'Yes, I have mates! Well, I sort of have mates. I have *one* friend.' Glenn sipped his cocktail, brooding. 'But we don't have much in common. Which is a bit of an issue because I live on his sofa.'

'So you didn't want to hire me, you just wanted to. . . . hang out with me?'

'Oh no, this is *genuinely* an interview, unorthodox though it is. And I am *genuinely* looking to hire a sales assistant.'

'And it's just a coincidence you wanted to advance a girl who looks like me?'

'Well, no, there's already girls who look like *you* at work, but they are obdurate, flinty, and hard as steel, and I think if I introduced you into the store it would really take them down a peg or two. In fact, I know it would!'

'So you're not just sad and lonely, you also want revenge?'

'I mean. . . . that's giving thy worst of thoughts the worst of words, but, basically, yes. And I just wanted to set that out before we proceed any further.'

'Thanks, Glenn. I really appreciate your honesty.'

'Not a problem. I am a lad determined to be more attuned to the affairs of others! Now, where were we?' He leaned in, puckered his lips.

His eyes opened. 'What's wrong?'

'Don't take this the wrong way, mate, but you seem like a bit of a loser.'

'What? Wait, where are you going now?' he cried, as she stood up and grabbed her handbag. 'Are you *leaving*?'

'Yeah. Thanks for being so honest, Glenn. Oh God, I'm so glad I didn't sleep with you.'

'Were you going to?' he called after her, as she headed for the doors.

'Yes.'

'*Shit!*'

And so the hero Jason gained the Golden Fleece. And then he lost it. And then he walked all the way back to Hyde Hill because he couldn't afford a taxi, and that was because his purchase of the gold lambskin card-case with black laughing skull insignia by Nirah Frazar had all but wiped out his plastic for the month.

He found the keyhole on the third attempt, and on opening the door felt his heart sink when he beheld the lights off and the flat empty.

'When, in disgrace with fortune and men's eyes (and women's— *especially* women's), I all alone beweep my outcast state,' he croaked feebly, 'and trouble deaf heaven with my bootless cries, and look upon myself, and curse my fate.'

A huge and terrible silence was hiding under the hum of the small electric heater.

He slipped off his mangled brogues and padded down the corridor, vanishing into the murk. He emerged from it a moment later with a bottle of Jimmy's gin. He pulled the strap of the sofa-bed, converting it into a bed, and spread-eagled himself upon it.

Running his large, arachnid hand along the cool, empty bedspace beside him, he looked upward to the little arched window, where he held the moon's blank gaze.

'O thou cursed moon that hast no care of me, shall I abide in this dull world without a friend forever?' He swigged from the bottle. 'Is't Glenn's fate never to share his bed with another?' A tear then trickled down his cheek.

Suddenly, the ground began to tremble, and he bolted upright as the door burst open. The behemoth then lumbered into the flat, wheezing and grunting, reeling to and fro until he saw that Glenn was up and managed to steady himself. He stood wobbling dangerously over the menswear manager, his eyes in orbit as he wagged his finger and tried to explain something of vital importance about Chelsea, but he had drunk so much he had lost the function of human speech, and instead he just made a series of primeval noises, before having to sit down on the bed to catch his breath. Chelsea he grunted again, something about Chelsea, as he turned his great girth and, in need of a rest, collapsed back on the bedspace beside Glenn. In a moment he was snoring.

Glenn looked with disgust at the mocking moon.

II.VIII

Business Sense, Wellington Street (27.4.■)
BREAKING EVEN.
At break-even point, total sales equal total costs – fixed costs fully covered, no profit or loss. (Point where total revenue matches both fixed and variable costs)
Desk Research – trade mag
Primary – talk to people, questionnaires, time people walk by, dress sense etc
"Do you spend a lot on clothes?"
What label, how much etc
"Is there anything YOU want?"

Glenn couldn't decide what vexed him more. That Ali was wearing short shorts, or that the girls all seemed to be excited by the fact Ali was wearing short shorts.

The makeup artist was on beauty, bent over the bed of creams and powders as he touched up his face in the mirror, much to the delight of his train of tender maids—Gertrude, Mildred, Betty, some female customers they seemed to be friendly with—who were slapping his pert buttocks, pinching his bare legs, to a symphony of squeals, giggles, and cries, and comments like are you sure you're not putting on weight you fat little bitch.

Unmarked by the doors, Glenn stood gaping the base scene with his mouth open.

The sight infused in his heart an ardent yearning for bevies of beautiful women to entangle *him* in fondle and frolic, like they did that o'errated boy. (Why chase Ali, when a man as straight as Circe's wand is standing right here?) He felt like Odysseus, tethered to the mast of his ship as they sailed by the thrilling Psirens.

He lifted his ginormous sunglasses, squinting in the golden light that illuminated his black-streaked eyebags. Ali wears a black polo with gold laughing skull logo, laughing skull pendant, short shorts, black cashmere socks and lacquered black leather loafers, all by Nirah Frazar.

At the sight of socks with shorts, Glenn recoiled. And yet it was the menswear manager whose dress sense was forever being mocked?

Never mind break-even point; he felt like he was at breaking point.

Glenn surveyed himself in the freestanding mirror. All right, his black wool suit looked a little rough round the edges, what with the constant daily wear, and his new black silk shirt was stained and smelt of gin because he could not afford the trip to Stitches to get it dry cleaned. And yes, his crown and mullet had grown a bit out of hand, because he could not afford the trip to Fez at Haircuttery to get that sorted either. And as for the shoes, well. . . . they'd been a write off since I.IX, with one sole now actually beginning to part from the upper.

But *still*. At least he wasn't wearing short shorts.

He sighed, donned his sunglasses and went skulking off towards the stairs, squeaking and slapping. As he passed by beauty, he made a point of looking directly at Ali's shorts and socks and tutted loudly. When they didn't notice him, he resorted to ejaculating a piercing, one-syllable guffaw that echoed round the room. That got their attention all right. The look they returned him was not dissimilar to the one Glenn later gave himself in the fitting room mirror, a sort of loathing mingled with desparate frustration, as he contemplated the ensemble he was wearing: a black polo, black short shorts with black socks and lacquered black leather loafers.

He goggled with disbelief his knobbly knees and pale, skeletal legs.

This was not a look that was going to bring women squealing and giggling to him. They might point and laugh at him, or even scream and run, but not squeal and giggle. He turned a dark, disliking eye on the short shorts. O disloyal thing, that shouldst repair my youth, thou heapest ten years' age on me!

But what if he wore the short shorts *over* his trousers? A fearless experiment, never before attempted; fashion pushed forward in a truly heroic work!

Ah, what hopes delude thee, thou miserable man. As he sighed, and his eyes began welling, an unwelcome rapping on his cubicle door disrupted his introspective moment.

'What now?' Glenn warbled.

'Geez,' came Dick's voice, 'sorry to bother you. I'm afraid there's a customer who's unhappy with the service on menswear, and she wants to complain to the manager.'

Glenn groaned because of his bondage, and he cried out in anguish.

'Geez?' said Dick.

'I'm *busy*, Dick,' he snarled. 'Tell her I've gone out. In fact, no—if she doesn't like the service up here, tell her she can piss off. Tell her she can piss *right off*!'

A pause.

'Er, she's standing right next to me, geez.'

Glenn grimaced.

II.IX

'I'm afraid I just don't understand you, boy. I don't understand you at all. I just—' but his voice trailed off. He cocked his head, casting a dubious, searching look. 'Is there something *wrong* with you?' he asked seriously.

Glenn, perched at the foot of Norman's throne on one of the mill worker's chairs, held his head in his hands.

'Norman, I *didn't know* that woman was a mystery shopper,' he said. 'Perhaps if head office had warned me that one was coming, I could have been better prepared!'

'You don't pick and choose who you're going to give good customer service to, Glenn,' Shukeena cut in, seated beside him. 'We should be treating *every* customer as if they were a mystery shopper.'

He lifted his face from his hands. '*Every* customer?' he cried, laughing. 'We'd never get anything done!'

'You *don't* get anything done, Glenn, that's the point,' replied the mighty mere woman, the ravenous vulture, Cain's wicked offspring. 'And the disaster zone that is your floor failed the visit *long* before that poor woman had the misfortune of speaking to you. First line of the first page of the employee handbook: *Staff must deliver a customer experience that is extraordinary*. Do you really think you delivered a customer experience that was *extraordinary*?'

'There's an argument that I did,' Glenn shrugged.

Shukeena turned and glared at him. 'This is *serious*, Glenn.'

Glenn returned her glare and growled, 'I'm being *serious*, Shukeena.'

'Nothing's changed since our emergency meeting, Norman. The new collaboration *still* isn't out; his faulties are *still* piling up in the stock room. Oh, and all those Homme boxes are *still* cluttering up the basement. Quite honestly, I've seen mannequins more active than Glenn.' She then looked at him with disdainful eyes. 'How are you getting on with your vacancy?'

'O, how many more times, Shukeena!' he howled. 'I'm *trying* to fill it. But it's hard finding the time to interview people when you're as short of people as I am!'

'You've had weeks to do it,' she replied pointedly.

'Well I'll need at least a few more.'

'How are you getting on with the Thank You card?' Norman enquired.

'The *what* card?'

'You must be joking,' gasped the great lady of the undergloom.

'I'm not joking, woman! I don't have a clue what you're talking about!' Momentarily struck dumb, Glenn stared blankly now at the store manager, now at Shukeena. 'What, are we really doing thank you cards now?' he asked incredulously.

You might not remember this, but back in I.V Shukeena while chiding Glenn for some offence said words to the effect that she would be willing to lodge a capability concern about him with head office, *regardless of what relationship he had with Norman*—implying that she felt her boss had a certain rapport with the menswear manager that made disciplining him problematic. But to look at Norman's countenance at that moment was to confirm that any fondness the old sack of wine may have felt for his erstwhile Saturday boy had now met death's embrace. In fact, Glenn was startled by the sheer darkness of the scowl the store manager was directing at him—and the beastly way his neck was corded and his eyelids twitching. Smoke was curling from his ears, while his brawny hands were shaking even more than they normally did. And while Glenn's business classes were progressing nicely, they were not progressing so nicely that he was going to be accessing one of their amazing grants any time soon. For the first time ever, the vital necessity of his Nirah Frazar job began to dawn on him. At once a clammy sweat broke out under his tight clothes, and he began to tremble with fear.

'What's really going on, boy?' Norman growled, glowering inquisitively at him. 'Is there something *missing* here?' he said, his voice rising.

'There's a lot missing from his department,' Shukeena quipped.

Norman flashed her a ferocious look. She at once dipped her head.

'Nothing's going on,' Glenn insisted, nervously.

'Is there something *we're* not doing? Or are you just not big enough for the job?' Norman continued. 'Why is everything such a *struggle* for you?'

'I don't know,' Glenn replied, his voice wobbling.

'I've been *very* patient with you. I've given you *every* opportunity to redeem yourself. You promised me you would get your floor back on track, but instead you're *still* not meeting target, you *still* haven't hired a new sales assistant, and evidently you're *still* not managing your staff—your footwear man didn't want the mystery shopper "messing up his neat displays", while your formalwear man was actually *asleep* on the divan!—and to top it all off, you're telling customers to "piss off"? What do you think Nirah Frazar should tell *you* to do right now?'

'To stop pissing about?' Glenn said hopefully. 'And issue me with another informal stage improvement note?'

Norman was shaking his head.

'Not this time, boy,' he said. 'I'm afraid your behaviour has not gone unnoticed.' He turned to his chaotic desk and began fumbling through his correspondence. 'It seems your unprofessional, twisted, possibly illegal antics are no longer a mere Nirah Frazar Leeds matter. In fact, they've gone all the way up the line. Read this!'

'Wait, what's the matter?' Glenn croaked, taking the formal looking letter Norman handed him. 'Why tender'st thou this paper to me, with a look untender?'

He held the sheet up to the feeble light. When he saw the HOUSE OF COMMONS logo, it felt like terror itself punched him in the stomach.

'"Dear sir,"' he read aloud with a quaver in his voice, '"in reference to your offer of military service in the event of North Korea engaging the Western hemisphere in thermonuclear war—"'

'Shit, not that,' said Norman, quickly snatching the letter back. 'This one!' he said, thrusting a print out from head office into Glenn's hands.

Glenn's eyes zigzagged the text. '"Head office is taking the mystery shopper incident *very seriously*,"' he read aloud, breathlessly. '"The unusual activity on menswear has been under investigation *for some time*. . . . Mr Harding is to be issued a *stage 1 verbal warning*. . . . with any further action *pending the result of the investigation*. Ciao, head office".' Glenn looked up from the sheet of paper. His face was the same colour as it.

'Pluto and Hell,' he gasped. 'I'm being investigated!'

Shukeena flung her head back and laughed aloud.

'O damn'd paper! Black as the ink that's on thee!' Glenn cried, as pangs of fear ran through his heart. 'Norman! Tell me it's not that serious,' he begged. 'They only fire people for gross misconduct, which is *instant* dismissal. If they wanted to get rid of me, they would have done it already? Wouldn't they?'

'Perhaps,' Norman shrugged. 'But you're a senior, unbelievably, so they probably have to follow procedure with you, to give you half a chance.'

'Phew.'

'And then they'll sack you.'

Glenn screamed.

II.X

Glenn was at the tree trunk coffee table on front, standing behind the portable table, on which he used the folding board to fold shirts from the huge heap of items that had been piling up on the display for weeks. The task was a formidable one, what with his hands trembling and his knees knocking. He was so filled with terror he could *feel* the worry beating in his brain, the dread gnawing perpetually at his entrails.

Shukeena had loaned him Betty shaped by Heaven, fairest of unearthly nymphs. She was stood nearby, applying the garment steamer to last month's new collection.

The work was slow and tedious to the point of torture, and as Glenn endeavoured to fold his umpteenth shirt, and considered the sheer number of garments that still needed folding, he felt his spirit stultify and his muscular control momentarily flag.

And *still* he needed to find a new sales assistant!

Behind his big fringe, and even bigger forehead, his mental organs were grinding feverishly, as a multitude of peccadilloes flashed upon his inward eye: Bullying Mildred; kicking over a feature rail and swearing at her; taxing the tills for coffee and bus fare; putting Wilfred in the dust. And that was before you got to his ignorance of updates, poor timekeeping, and his abusing of the interview process to force cool people to hang out with him. Just how far back did the investigation stretch? What did they know? And why couldn't he just do his job like everyone else did?

Why *was* everything such a struggle for him?

Betty wears a black one-shoulder alligator skin dress with laughing skull pendant and black mesh leather ankle boots by Nirah Frazar, and standing there in a whirl of steam, with her scraped back brown hair, and her splendid beauty intensified by the artisan Ali's rich palette and bold craftsmanship, she bewrays nothing of the minimum wage floor-dweller in form. No, she is pure *Advert*—a supermodel being paid huge sums to hype the new Nirah Frazar collection in a major campaign. *Eudaimonia* in heels.

O, happy shall he be whom Betty loves.

In fact, one look at her and a man could forget all his troubles, lift his drooping thoughts. Idle fantasies began to addle Glenn's brain.

'Are you getting on all right with your job, Miss Holroyd?' he said pleasantly.

'Yes,' she squeaked absently.

'It's a rather quiet afternoon on menswear, isn't it?' he said.

'Yes,' she squeaked absently.

'Still, that's a good thing, I suppose. It makes replenishment a lot easier, wouldn't you agree?'

'Yes,' she squeaked absently.

A pause.

'There's a black hole at the centre of our galaxy that scientists think is as heavy as three million suns. Do you have any opinions as to what might be inside it?'

She closed her eyes and wailed, 'How *long* do I have to stay up here!?'

Glenn choked at her insolence. Had he not been under investigation, he might well have kicked over her garment steamer and sworn in her face. Instead, he sighed, and answered: 'Until I find a new sales assistant.'

'And how long will *that* take?'

'O God, don't you start too. It will take as long as it takes.'

'But why did it have to be *me* who got sent up?' she sobbed.

'I know'st not.' But it was a damn good question. Surely a demonic, half-mad Fury like Mildred Scragg would have been a more disruptive weapon to deploy on Glenn's beleaguered department, rather than the cold but ultimately pliant Betty Holroyd? What was Shukeena thinking? She clearly hadn't been reading her Sun-Tzu.

He was brooding over the matter when suddenly the gold skull of the pink polo shirt Betty was steaming winked at him. 'Miss Holroyd,' he said.

'What?' she squeaked absently.

'The gold skull collection *is* the new collection, isn't it?'

She stared at him. 'Are you joking?'

'Just answer the question,' he said briskly.

'Yeah, it's the new collection.'

'And the new collaboration? Whereabouts is that?'

A pause.

'Do you really not know?' she squeaked.

'O, Sodom and Egypt, Betty! Of course *I* know! I'm just seeing whether *you* know. Read you not your employee handbook? *Managers should regularly test staff members' product knowledge.* All right? Now where is the new collaboration? Answer me!'

'*Here,*' she squeaked with wide eyes, pointing the steamer at the pink polo shirt.

Her answer wrung from Glenn a prolonged and weary sigh. '*No,*' he said in a strained voice, 'that's the new *collection.* I'm asking about the new *collaboration.*'

'The new collaboration *is* the new collection.'

'The new collaboration *is* the new collection?'

'*Yeah.*'

'Yes, it is. Exactly.' Glenn gazed into his thoughts, with his finger to his chin. 'But wait, I read in *Advert* that Nirah Frazar was collaborating with Sammi de Hun? This collection looks like the same one we've been flogging all year? What's different?'

'It's got a gold skull instead of a white one.'

He cocked his head, looked quizzically at her. 'What? So Sammi de Hun with all his genius did nothing with this collaboration except change the colour of the logo?'

'*Yeah*. That's what makes it so genius.'

'Right, now I get it. . . .' he nodded. 'Er—I mean *you* get it! Well done. O! And one last thing: this "Thank You card",' he said vaguely. 'What's that all about?'

'Are you still testing me? Or do you really not know?'

Glenn stared at the girl. His eyelid was beginning to twitch.

'The idea,' squeaked Betty, 'is that, "With special offers, no credit checks, and a guaranteed four-figure spending limit, it's not so much a store card as it is a *thank you card*—to our loyal customers, with love from Nirah Frazar",' she recited with effort.

'But why does Nirah Frazar need to do it?'

'Because the new collection is twice the price of the old one.'

'O, we're lending customers the money so they can buy it?'

'Yeah. But you knew that already.'

'Of course I did.' He picked up the Thank You card signage Betty had placed on the tree trunk table, narrowed his eyes as he read the small print. 'But it does seem a rather obvious swindle though. I mean look at this interest rate! How many of these things have you managed to flog?'

'None. I'm the only one on ladieswear who hasn't been able to sell one.'

And *that* explained why Shukeena had supplied him with Betty.

Sun-Tzu himself could have learned a thing or two from the ladieswear manager.

After this, opened Glenn his mouth and cursed his job.

The conundrum of the unsellable collection, unworkable staff, and odious card prostrated him psychologically. He felt like Pompey at sea, 'twixt Caesar on one shore, Ptolemy the other—and black doom whichever course he chose.

Norman was right—he wasn't big enough for the job. His eyes welled.

'Glenn?' said a husky, docile voice suddenly.

'*Ali?*' Betty squeaked. Her little face lit up as she cast aside the garment steamer, jumped for joy, and wiggled clip clopping towards him with her arms outspread. 'Oh my God, I've missed you!' she squeaked, hugging and kissing him.

'Yeah, I've missed you too, babe,' Ali yawned, absently patting her hips. He looked over her bare, ivory-white shoulder, to the menswear manager. 'Glenn, can I get the mop? Some woman saw the price on handbags and threw up.'

Glenn strove to speak but shock had tied his tongue. The metamorphosis he had witnessed Betty undergo was worthy of Ovid—from cold, loveless queen to love-sick teen in the blink of an eye—and he goggled her with his mouth open.

He groaned in himself, as his blood chafed and his heart grew sick.

'*Glenn?*' said Ali, looking at him expectantly. The makeup artist was arrayed in the pink polo shirt, laughing skull pendant, those absurd black short shorts, cream socks and lacquered black leather loafers, all by Nirah Frazar/Sammi de Hun, and, such was the foppery of the gods, *this* was what Betty threw herself upon.

Forget people who were socially disadvantaged—Glenn was *divinely* disadvantaged. He lamented over this lamentation of his life, as his visage grew dark as hell-black night, and a tear of anger trilled down his unkissed cheek.

He stood stock-still, as the boy wherein false destiny delights, the favourite of the Fates, shook himself free of Betty, walked up to him and boldly plucked the manager's keys right from his belt. 'I'll be back in a sec,' he said coolly to Glenn, jingling his keys in front of his eyes, upon which mayhem was whirling.

'When are you back downstairs?' Ali called over to Betty, as he strutted off.

'Ask him,' she squeaked sullenly, jerking her head at Glenn.

But he disappeared behind the partition without asking Glenn anything.

In the blink of an eye Betty morphed back into her cold, loveless queen, as she stared darkly first at Glenn, then at his department, before closing her eyes and emitting a moan that seemed to come from the very bottom of her four-inch heels.

At that instant Glenn's heart grew hard and pure frenzy filled him. He could feel his veins sizzling with hate. Then, bent on destruction, and bulging with rage, he went marching behind the partition, squeaking and slapping—where he discovered the makeup artist with the utility cupboard door open, peering into the half-dark.

Ali screamed as Glenn shoved him into it, followed him inside and slammed the door behind them. He then locked it shut. . . .

II.XI

'And then what happened?' asked Jimmy. He was eyeing Glenn almost suspiciously.

The menswear manager looked shamefaced. He said something inaudible.

'You *what?*' said Jimmy, straining his ears.

Glenn banged his fist on the bar. 'I SAID I—' He promptly lowered his voice, leaned into the Leviathan. 'I *said* I asked him for some style advice,' he muttered. 'And don't you *ever* make me say it again!' He shook his head, sipped his Paint the Town Pink. 'I may be a lover of enquiry, Mr Sandaal, but having to consult that female wanton boy on matters of wardrobe was truly a bitter pill to swallow. It very nearly made me doubt my status as the city's most stylish man.'

'What did he say?'

'He said—not in these words—that if I wanted radiant nymphs to amuse me with attention and harlotry like they did him, I would have to vary up my costume a little.'

'Not *more* spending?' the behemoth groaned.

'Have the air of wealth, if not the account,' Glenn intoned. 'You know, Julius Caesar himself accumulated great debts while trying to establish his name. In fact, he was so profligate he was in the red by thirteen hundred talents before he enjoyed any public employment! So really, I'm in good company.'

'Didn't he get stabbed to death?'

'Yes,' said Glenn, after a moment's pause. There was a spooked look in his eye.

Jimmy quaffed his pint. 'Oh, that's what I meant to ask you: it's Wednesday night; why aren't you at Business Sense?'

Glenn coolly sipped his cocktail. 'Because I no longer attend their classes.'

'What! But why? I thought you enjoyed going there?' He quaffed more beer. 'You've been obsessed with that place for months,' he belched.

'Ay, but I lost interest when I learned that I don't qualify for a grant.'

'Eh!? *You* don't qualify for a grant? But you haven't got a pot to piss in!'

'*Peace*, Jimmy,' Glenn growled under his breath. He used the mirror over the bar to steal a nervous glance at the room last sighted in I.IX. There was a small, weeknight's smattering of female forms shimmering under the neon-blue glare of the lights, but thankfully none of them seemed to have heard the behemoth's booming voice. 'Thou doth not need to speak of my vagabond state to all of Leeds, you know? I don't qualify for a grant because, in their view, I'm not *disadvantaged*,' he said quietly.

'Not disadvantaged? But you live on a *sofa*,' said Jimmy. 'If it wasn't for me, you'd be out on the street!'

'I know.' Glenn sipped his Paint the Town Pink and sighed. 'I tell thee what, Jimmy, it's a scandal the way Business Sense doles out those ducats. "Not disadvantaged"? I'm disadvantaged by the fact they consider me not disadvantaged!'

'I guess they have to give grants to people who really would put the money to good use. You'd probably spend it on chuffing. . . . magic beans or something.'

'If they were printed on a silk shirt, absolutely.'

'I don't think Business Sense is your problem, Glenn.'

'Well either way, I told them to go preach on a pole.'

'Right,' said Jimmy, nodding. He looked like he had shooting pains in his head. 'So you won't be starting your own business then?'

'To do so stands not in the prospect of belief.'

'Well,' Jimmy sighed, 'at least you have your job!'

'Probably not for much longer.'

Pause.

'What have you done now?'

Glenn told him about the mystery shopper incident, and his stage 1 verbal warning.

'Shit the bed,' was all the behemoth could say.

'I probably will, once head office completes their investigation,' Glenn nodded. 'But at least I had the good sense to buy a new suit before they could sack me.'

Jimmy nearly spat out his beer.

'You bought a new *suit*?!' he cried, staring with amazement at him.

'Yeah,' Glenn shrugged. 'So what?'

'With what money did you buy it? The only card you have that still works is your debit card, and there can't be enough in *your* bank account to pay for a designer suit?'

'There isn't. And by the way, that debit card doesn't work anymore either; but it doesn't matter—because I bought it with our new store card!'

Jimmy stared at his tenant.

'You—you signed up for your *own store card*? Mate, are you out of your chuffing mind? Store cards are worse than credit cards!'

'Ah, but you see, Jimmy, it's not *really* a store card. "Because with special offers, no credit checks, and a guaranteed four-figure spending limit, it's more like a *thank you* card—with love from Nirah Frazar." Quite frankly, I'd be mad *not* to sign up for it.'

'Did it cross your mind that you should try settle some of your existing debts, before creating new ones? Christ, you haven't paid off your old suit yet!'

'Ay me!' Glenn cried, banging his glass down on the counter. 'Dost thou *drink* tears, Mr Sandaal, that thou provokest such weeping? What may a heavy groan advantage thee? Jimmy, for God's sake, not even Seacroft Job Centre would send a man to work in my old suit. I honestly think it was harming my sales!'

Jimmy had to take a long swig of his pint. 'Go on then,' he sighed.

'Let's see it.'

'See *what*, you great steaming heap of excrement?'

'What the chuff do you think? This amazing new suit! Where is it? In that trunkcase or something?'

Glenn stared incredulously at the man. 'Jimmy—I'm *wearing* it.'

The behemoth gaped the tightly fitting black wool suit Glenn was wearing.

'But—but that's the suit you *always* wear,' he choked. 'Isn't it?'

'Wrong as usual,' said Glenn, heaving a deep sigh. 'My old suit was standard white skull line. This one is *gold* skull. Plus, it has Sammi de Hun's name on it!'

Jimmy looked the suit up and down. 'Where?'

'On the inside label.'

'And is that white shirt different too?'

'Of course it's different. Look—' He pulled aside his silk necktie with zeal. 'Covered plackets.'

'And the tie?' Jimmy grimaced.

'Sammi de Hun's name on the back.'

'The shoes?'

'Sammi de Hun's name on the in-sole.'

'Oh God.'

'And his name on the belt, socks, and skimpy hipbriefs.'

The Leviathan took a long, long swig of his beer.

'Glenn,' he said, 'we need to have a serious discussion about your spending.'

'No we don't.'

'You're not thinking about the future.'

'I never stop thinking about the future.'

'Yeah, I know you want to be this famous fashion designer, but you *need* to have something to fall back on. I'd like to captain the Leeds Rhinos! But until I get the call, I've got my underwriting.' The great man-mountain was looking almost pleadingly at Glenn. 'Mate, you *have* to be realistic. You don't have any *training* in fashion design; you don't have any *knowledge* of fashion design; you don't know anyone who *works* in fashion design. Shit the bed—you don't even have a *degree!*'

'A degree,' Glenn scoffed. 'Did Franz Kafka's law degree teach him how to write *The Metamorphosis*? Or Vincent van Gogh's theological studies train him to paint *The Starry Night*? Jimmy, if a man's calling is *art*, then, when the hour is come, the talent that has been gestating all the long years shall at last reveal itself—whether or not St. Martin's College has issued him with some silly piece of paper. A *degree*.' He flung his head back and gave a jolting, one syllable guffaw. 'Who needs one? Once you've made something of yourself, the universities give you them for free!'

'GLENN!' yelled Jimmy. 'Your "art" has to date produced a grand total of *one* notepad filled with crude and very shitty-looking doodles. So, given your output, trying to compare yourself with these genius, one-in-million talents isn't just delusional—it's *retarded*. Now if I were you, I'd stick to the day job, consolidate my debts, apply for council housing as a matter of urgency, and, with all due respect—*grow up*.'

Pause.

'Right,' Glenn said in a low voice. 'Well, I thank you for that honest-true assessment of my circumstances, Mr Sandaal; forsooth, no one could ever accuse you of beating about the bush!' He turned his gaze to the mirror over the bar, sipped his cocktail. 'Yes, perhaps the quality of my pencilled figures has hitherto been somewhat "*shitty-looking*". And I suppose it could be argued that my having ambition is—what did you call it? Ah yes, "*retarded*". Really I suppose I should just abandon this mission of mine, and resign myself to the day job. Perhaps it is time I did, as you say, "*grow up*". And I will grow up. O yes! I'll grow up all right. In fact, you know what? I think I'll grow up right now.'

Glenn gave a little chuckle.

'GROW UP LIKE THIS!' he shrieked, as he leaped to his feet, threw his glass high over his head, and was about to bring the base crashing down on Jimmy's skull when, suddenly, a goddess materialised between them.

'Hi,' she said.

Glenn stood paralyzed. 'How doth,' he nodded breathlessly.

The young woman was imposingly tall and exceptionally beautiful, and Glenn had beheld her many times before, behind the beauty counter in Carman Weshirbo. For it was none other than Chardonnay Sharples.

'Chardonnay,' she smiled.

'I know,' he replied. 'Er—I mean, *Glenn*,' he spluttered. When he saw her outstretched hand, he remembered his own were still in the air. He hastily put his glass down on the counter. 'Nice to meet you,' he said nervously, as he shook her delicate, buttock-soft hand. He could tell she didn't recognise him, in spite of once serving him.

'*Chardonnay?*' blurted Jimmy. His baffled eyes darted back and forth between the pair. 'Hang on, don't you two already know each other—'

The look Glenn shot him said it all. Jimmy groaned, turned back to his pint.

'I couldn't help overhearing you shouting about your new suit,' she said, 'and I was impressed by the way you wear it.' She eyed the gaudy red and white polkadot pocket square bursting from his breast pocket. 'And I just *love* your funny choice of accessories, which are obviously ironic.'

'Er—'

'Are you a model?'

'No.'

'Have you ever *thought* about modeling?'

'No.' He then remembered that he thought about it all the time. 'Wait, yes.'

'*Cool,*' she grinned. 'I'm a brand ambassador for Carman Weshirbo, which gives me the opportunity to do a few other things in fashion—including street spotting for the "Trend Setters" section in *Advert*. I was wondering if you'd be interested in modeling?'

'In—in "Trend Setters"?' said Glenn in falsetto.

'Yeah,' she nodded, smiling. 'I think you could be in "Trend Setters".'

'"Trend Setters" in *Advert*?' he said, somehow reaching an even higher pitch.

She laughed a beautiful laugh. '*Yes.*'

She wore a gold sequin chiffon dress by Carman Weshirbo and

her ash-brown hair was fastened back by a gold headband, the garish colour contrasting her radiant skin sublimely, and her pulchritudinous features, awesome in green eyeshadow and pink lipgloss, would send Paul Gauguin scrambling madly for a blank canvas—would make Ali Hussain throw up his hands and say, *I have nothing to add here*.

'And you really think I could be a model?' Glenn said, his voice tinged with awe.

'No,' she smiled. 'I *know* you could be a model.'

'Shit the bed,' was all the behemoth could say.

II.XII

Ask and it shall be given you; knock, and it shall be opened unto you. Glenn simply yanked up the shutter, bobbed his head under it and strode gaily into the shop.

The bizarre scene he encountered stopped him in his tracks.

A section of ladieswear had been cleared of gondalas, and in their place was a line of antique piano stools, borrowed from footwear and arranged in a semi-circle. The team was sitting on them, while the menacing figure of Shukeena Mohammed loomed over all on the elevated platform outside the fitting room cubicles. She was standing behind a lectern, and in her hands was an immense black folder.

Glenn lifted his colossal sunglasses and goggled the scene with amazement.

'What the hell is this?' he said. 'A congregation of the Church of Satan?'

'I'm afraid we're not open yet, sir,' said Shukeena, squinting at the rakish silhouette drenched in the dazzle of sunlight. 'You will have to come back at nine.'

Glenn chuckled as he lowered his sunglasses. 'Thou villain base, know'st me not by my clothes?' he smiled, flashing his white teeth. He left the shutter up and swaggered toward the staff with his shoulders back, pelvis pressed forward, as his heels clacked sharply against the hardwood. ''Tis I, your kinsman and devoted shop-husband,' he exclaimed. 'Beowulf is my name, and a nobler sir ne'er liv'd 'twixt sky

137

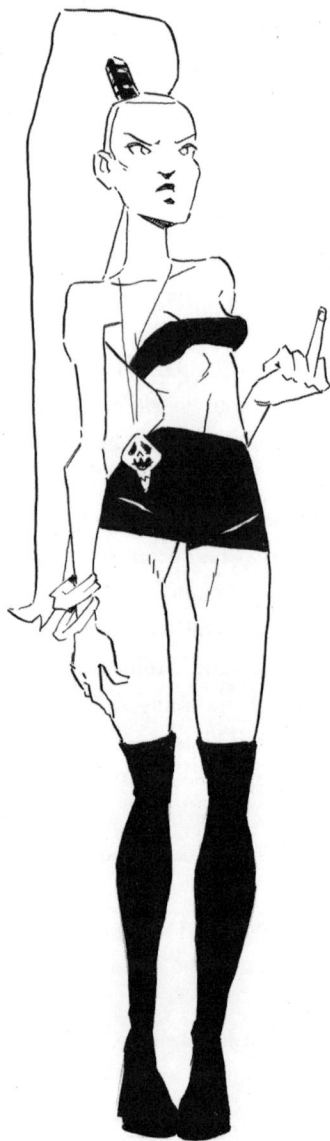

and shopfloor.'

Shukeena gaped at him with her mouth open. 'Glenn?' she said faintly.

'That's right, Miss Mohammed,' he beamed. 'It's me, Glenn—and I have come to work *early*.'

A collective gasp rose up from the team.

There was a loud thud—Shukeena had dropped her folder.

'What's with the funny walk, Glenn?' asked Lyndsey. 'Are your shoes too tight?'

'Funny walk?' Glenn repeated, smirking. 'It's called a *catwalk strut*, Mr Fryer; and it's how *we* models walk to make an impression on people. O! That's right—'twas my day off yesterday. I haven't had chance to avise you all of my news yet, have I?'

'What news?' said Dick, looking back over his fleshy shoulder. 'And why do you look different? Have you had your barnet chopped or something?'

'There's nowt different about his appearence,' Mildred piped up. 'We're just not use to seeing him at this time.'

'No, there's definitely *something* different about him,' squeaked Betty curiously.

'Oh my God,' gasped Ali, 'he's had cosmetic surgery!'

Through all this Gertrude was oddly wide-eyed and jittery, wiping her nose as she regarded him intently. 'No, you idiots,' she blurted, sniffing. '*Look at him*. He's dressed head to toe in the new gold skull!'

Another collective gasp rose up from the team.

'Well spotted, Miss Ogden,' Glenn nodded. He then catwalk strutted round to the front of the shining synod, so that he stood between them and the ladieswear manager. 'Yes, I look different because I am now clothed entirely in the new Sammi de Hun collaboration—and I feel like a new man!'

'Good for you, Glenn,' said Shukeena, crouched down and gathering up her papers. 'But I *was* in the middle of the morning meeting, until you so rudely interrupted—'

'Piss off!' Mildred rudely interrupted. 'How can *you* afford a gold skull suit? Managers barely make anymore than we do!'

A vainglorious grin broke out over Glenn's scraggle. 'By signing up for the new store card—' He thrust an outspanned hand in Shukeena's face. 'I call it a "*store card*" because with special offers, no credit checks, and a guaranteed four-figure spending limit, really it is *I* who should be sending a thank you card to Nirah Frazar—which brings me back to my news. . . .'

The team were all awed and silent, sat stupid with surprise.

'Go on,' said Dick curiously.

'I was out in Boutique the other night in my handsome robes, where I got scouted by a particularly well-connected street spotter,' he grinned excitedly. He paused for maximum effect. 'And she intends to feature me in next month's *Advert*!' he exclaimed.

The shop erupted with such ferocity the windows almost shattered.

'Oh my God!' Ali cried amid the garboil. 'Glenn's going to be a model!'

'He's going to be famous!' squeaked Betty.

'He's going to be minted!' said Mildred. '*Bastard*!'

'What can be avoided, whose end is purposed by the mighty gods?' Glenn sighed.

'Perhaps I've misjudged this store card?' said Dick thoughtfully, rising to his brothel creepers. 'I think I might sign up for one myself.'

And then Ali stood up. 'Me too.'

And then Mildred stood up. 'Me three.'

'Me five!' squeaked Betty.

'Me *first*,' Gertrude snarled, rising to her soaring six-inch heels. 'I need a store card more than any of you—I'm the pissing style advisor!'

There was a tense stare off between the staff.

And then a stampede. It sounded like the thudding hooves of horses upon a plain, the hardwood shaking as they went bounding as one across the shopfloor and crashed into the cashdesk, where, in a din of shouting, and shoving, and elbowing, they battled like Grecians and Trojans over the store card application book.

'Well, thanks a lot, Glenn,' said Shukeena, turning darkly on the menswear manager. 'First you interrupt the morning meeting, then you completely *ruin* it!'

'Yes! Thanks a lot, Glenn,' bellowed Norman, as he stumbled in and steadied himself on the lad. 'You've only been in two minutes and you've already bagged us *six* new store card applications. Head office are going to love this!'

'Just doing my job, boss,' Glenn fawned.

'Yes you are, boy, yes you are,' said Norman with ardor. He then pointed sternly at Shukeena. '*You* could learn a lot from Glenn.'

There was a loud thud—Shukeena had dropped her folder again.

II.XIII

Glenn rubbed his aching jaw. His mouth was actually sore from smooching so much. Ask and it shall be given you; knock, and it shall be opened unto you. Walk blindly into the staff room and Betty Holroyd shall invite you out to lunch with her. How good the food in the Conservatory bar is he couldn't say, for, during his time there, he had feasted solely upon the numinous, fairylike face of Betty, who had thrown herself upon him. That feast, however, was a true gastronomic delight, a culinary experience of the highest order—a dish fit for the gods!

It was a taste of *Eudaimonia*.

Was there ever man had such luck? All of a sudden, it was Glenn who was the shop's fresh ornament, his upcoming *Advert* shoot giving him all manner of admittance and opportunity to friend. Betty had hurried him to a sofa in a shadowy alcove, wanted to know all his news; and after he had told her, he asked why she was so besotted with Ali who would never love her; said that she was too beautiful even for a beauty counter, and that she would be better off pursuing someone with a brighter future than a paltry makeup artist. And then after having explained what the word paltry meant, he told her that she could have any man she wanted (except Ali), and, before he knew it, she had entwined him in her arms and launched her lips onto his.

How far he had come from the beardless boy who needed to down five cocktails before he could summon up the courage to kiss Peggy! Now the shop's chief flower was begging *him* to be her boyfriend, but he had wisely avoided giving her a straight answer, his thinking being that one of those intense, Emily Brontë type entanglements he once dreamed of could risk taking up too much of his time, obstruct his once-in-a-lifetime chance at being a model.

Like Heathcliff, he could not allow fleeting passions to derail him now. For just as that dark soul had sacrificed love for revenge, Glenn would sacrifice love for ambition—and if he broke some hearts along the way, so be it.

He strutted through his domain with his shoulders back, pelvis pushed forward, deftly using the profusion of mirrors to steer clear of any customers. His eyes noted that his new cover staff, the gloomy Gertrude, kept stealing sly glances at him whenever his back was turned. Did even the icy heart of the impregnable style advisor pant and quiver for him now? Her looks transmitted to him speechless messages: that she regretted persecuting him, and secretly wished it was *her* who was being seduced by a famous model in a romantic, underground bar. . . .

Well, dash her. She should have thought about that before playing the two-backed beast with Wilfred Woods. Gertrude was yesterday's news now. Betty was today's.

And Glenn Harding was tomorrow's.

But was this all some pure frolic of luck? Had he simply blundered into his big opening? He found himself standing in the fitting room, where he began pacing back and forth in front of the mirror, staring fixedly at himself. The chance counsel with Ali; the synchronicity of the store card, the gold skull collection, and his new suit; and the right bar, on the right night, at the right time, with exactly the right words to catch Chardonnay's ear. And that bar he discovered one night all those months ago when he was out on his own—having told Jimmy that he was going on a date with who?

Chardonnay Sharples!

This was not luck. This was High Providence. A complex succession of improbable incidents, and all it needed was one of them—*just one*—to be withdrawn and he would have missed his chance. He halted. His eyes were wide, and he could not repress his shiver. But as he remembered his recent excursion to Leeds Museum, and his reading about Brigantia, the ancient goddess who views the north of England, and who gives what fate she pleases to adventurous men, he began to suspect that it was her who had been conducting the cosmic circuit in his favour, lighting his path and guiding him down it. It seemed a reasonable enough theory to him. And as the sheer enormity of these celestial manoeuvres began to dawn on Glenn, he closed his eyes and gave a joyful cry. Suddenly he had realised that he was indeed destined for greatness—that it was his turn to ascend to Fame's immortal house. . . .

As he opened his eyes, he saw himself levitating in the mirror.

And then, before he could comprehend the situation, he was floating up past the woodbeams and through the stock room, watching with wonder as the stained-glass ceiling of the arcade shrank rapidly between his loafers. Like a rocket he was shooting into the air, going higher and higher, until suddenly he felt the spikes of his hair pierce the atmosphere. In a moment he was suspended godlike in the infinite, swimming in the cosmic bliss, his rakish form silhouetted by the sun's broad disk.

And then he lowered his gaze and looked, and behold—the Earth itself had stopped to admire him, its lidless blue-green eye bulging in its deep black socket.

Glenn looked furtively over each shoulder and unzipped his fly.

He began to relieve himself, and as he micturated, gravity took its hold on the stream and it began to gather pace. Soon it had reached dangerous speeds, puncturing the mesosphere and crashing into the skies with an almighty boom, transmuting into a sort of golden laser beam as it hurtled straight for London—and before Glenn knew it, he was pissing on St. Martin's College from the greatest possible height.

It hit the ground like whipping razorwire, sluicing great swathes of students in one fell strike, spilling their entrails out onto the pavement. A shriek of panic! A scene of terror! Flailing javelins of deadly effluence that sluice the retreating clique of Russell Group rejects and drench the campus in a grotesque mixture of piss and gore. Study this, you creative poseurs! Take that, you privileged idlers! Bolts of liquid lightning from outer space, shattering your skulls—*the first original concept ever to enter your stupid heads*!

'Hi,' said a voice.

Glenn shrieked with such fright he nearly fell over.

'Sorry! I didn't mean to sneak up on you,' she laughed.

'Chardonnay,' he said breathlessly. 'What are *you* doing here?'

'I came to exchange something,' she said, producing a crystal-embellished leather shoulder bag from her Nirah Frazar shopping bag. 'I got it home and realised it's been splattered with. . . . well, I don't even know what that is. It looks like vomit!'

'Weird,' was all that his amazing, highly original mind could muster for a reply.

'I see you're wearing that same suit again,' she said.

'Huh?' Glenn shook his head. 'O yes. Well, you know me, Miss Sharples,' he smiled suavely. 'I'm just trying to bring some style and elegance to my small city.'

'Your fly's undone.'

He jerked spasmodically. '*Shit*,' he muttered as he zipped himself up. 'Sorry.'

'I can't wait to see your other outfits, on the shoot,' she said.

'Other outfits?'

'Then afterwards we can go for cocktails in LS1 to celebrate.'

His eyes bulged. '*LS1*,' he gasped. 'You can get *in*?'

'Of course I can get in,' she laughed. 'Can't you? Oh and then after that we can go back to the hotel and you can get your stuff, or. . . . whatever,' she added casually.

Glenn stiffened.

Suddenly her cross-bag whistled. She produced her Kumquat and, having to take the call, pecked him on his cheek and wiggled clip clopping away, talking business. She wore a silk crepe shirt by Carman Weshirbo, a short black leather jacket by Ubiquity and U monogrammed leather cross-bag by same, with black super skinny jeans by Elf X that accentuated her long legs. His eyeballs were almost leaping after her.

I can't wait to see your other outfits, on the shoot.

HUNTER

He turned back to the mirror. There was a grave, panicked expression on his face.

Then suddenly, a cubicle door was thrown open, and a customer stepped out holding a pair of gold label jeans.

'Ah!' said the man. 'Do you know whether—'

'I'm afraid that's all we have left in that size, sir!' Glenn barked, as he swatted the jeans out of his hands and went storming out of the fitting room with his shoulders back, pelvis pushed forward.

II.XIV

The business card she had slipped him that night in the bar simply read

UNCORRUPTIBLE MODEL MANAGEMENT
Your face. Our skills.
Chardonnay Sharples, Company Secretary

Glenn was reclining in the little green dungeon at Hyde Hill, enrobed in his belted, fluorescent yellow cashmere dressing gown with NF monogram. A towel was wrapped round his head, and his smooth skin was drenched in an abundance of oil and spices. He had been reading the luxurious cream coloured card all evening, while relishing the sensation of its dimpled texture against the pads of his pinkies.

The model frowned and eyed the Leviathan coldly, who was stretched athwart the adjacent sofa, chewing his pencil as he studied the smallprint of the store card contract.

'Well, brute?' he grunted impatiently. 'Speak to me thy thinkings, as thou dost ruminate, and give thy worst of thoughts the worst of words.'

'All right,' he said. 'You're totally spent up on your store card.'

'*What!*' Glenn shouted. He jumped up and in two strides was standing over Jimmy. 'I can't have spent it all? Hey! What are those big numbers you've scribbled down there? Is that my backlog of rent? I've told you, I'm going to pay you!'

'No, Glenn. That figure there is what you'll owe them this time next year, if you don't settle your account in full—which you can't afford to do—and instead opt for the monthly minimum payment—which you can barely afford to do.'

'O no.'

'And this figure here is how much you'll owe in two years.'

'*Jesus.*'

'Ah, it's not that bad—when you consider what you'll owe in three years!'

'HELL AND NIGHT!' Glenn yelled, staggering back. He then screamed.

'I didn't even realise this level of interest was legal,' remarked Jimmy. 'Shit the bed, H, you should *never* have signed up for this store card. What were you thinking?'

'For the millionth time, *dad*, I needed a new suit for work. And now I need a new wardrobe for my photo shoot. And if I can't produce one, very quickly, then I will have no option but to go seek some ditch wherein to die!'

'Not until you've settled your debts with me you won't.'

'I'm serious, you block! This is a once in a lifetime opportunity! It's a plot twist straight out of a bad TV show—and yet it happened! It actually happened! And I would be *mad* not to seize it now with both hands!'

Jimmy was staring up incredulously at Glenn, who was now hyperventilating.

'How much do you need?' he asked.

'A few grand.'

Jimmy had to laugh. 'Mate, as an underwriter, I can assure you that no one is giving a man with your credit rating a few quid, let alone a few grand. You're what's known in the business as a *bad risk*.'

Glenn felt as if he had been struck by the bolt from a crossbow. Clutching his heart, he collapsed back on the sofa-bed. 'Don't say that,' he choked. 'Don't you understand how important this photo shoot is to me? That this is my one chance to escape the straight world? Jimmy, this could change my *life*!'

'Glenn,' said the behemoth irritably, 'nobody forced you to spend all your money. And then to spend everybody else's money. Look, it's this idea that you're always "a few grand" away from sorting yourself out that got you into this mess in the first place.'

'I know, I know, I know—but Jimmy: this time I *really am* a few grand away from sorting myself out!'

Jimmy rolled his eyes despairingly. He put aside the contract, rose to his feet and, with a huff, waddled off down the corridor.

'Lend me the money?' Glenn begged. 'Please? *Mate?*'

Jimmy slammed his bedroom door behind him.

The menswear manager was left to brood in the pinkish balmy twilight. He watched himself doing so, glowing spectrally in his luminous robe, in the little curved black screen of the wonkbox. His heart felt sick, horror swelled his brain. He looked desperately to the little arched window. Whither goest thou, kind star?

The sky was growing darker.

II.XV

Is Stella Winerack selling her one hundred thousand pound bangle cheap? Will Nirah Frazar become the most important woman in fashion—despite being a man? And have you smelled Klark Amaba's musky wood? Glenn was hunched over the cashdesk with his head propped on his fist, leafing through the latest *Advert*. He turned the page and was confronted by the golden smile of Jack Bragg, festooned in a lion print cardigan intermingled with a dirty denim jacket intermingled with a transparent plastic hooded top, all by Donna Tefes.

Bragg had once worked in the arcade, in the Leeds branch of the Saville Row tailor Maden & Ireland. He had in fact measured a teenage Glenn for his first suit. However, during a lunch break on Briggate, he had been spotted—and now, a short time later, he had become the literal face of a major autumn/winter campaign!

Glenn groaned in the spirit, as agonising waves of envy lapped over him.

He furiously poked out Bragg's eyes with his pen, and then mutilated his groin for good measure. He then tore out the page, screwed it into a little ball and threw it on the floor. He then collapsed onto the cashdesk and wept.

'Glenn?' a voice interrupted.

'I'm afraid that's all we have left in that size, sir!' snarled the menswear manager, bolting up with his teeth bared.

He discovered Lyndsey looming over him, with a white gold skull shirt in his hands.

'Er, no, Glenn; I think we *do* have more of these shirts, actually,' said the footwear supervisor. 'Can you run upstairs and get a size 16 for this gentleman, please?'

'Do your legs not work?' Glenn frowned.

'I have a *customer* on footwear already, Glenn!' Lyndsey retorted with annoyance. 'And I need to go back before he starts touching everything, and messing up my displays,' he added in a low voice.

'Dick will be back from lunch in twenty minutes?'

Lyndsey exchanged glances with the customer standing on the adjacent formalwear. The man was staring indignantly at Glenn, who now remembered that he was under investigation. He kicked the door open and stamped furiously into the half-dark of the stock room—where the sound of a woman screaming stopped him in his tracks.

His heart came down off the roof of his chest cave when he saw a familiar face.

'Hell and night, Gertrude!' he said breathlessly. 'I wasn't expecting to see anyone up here! What are you doing?'

Gertrude, also clutching her heart, glared violently at him. 'Having the shit scared out of me, thanks to you! Do you always come bursting in here like that?'

'The lift wasn't working—' He noticed the empty rail shoved between the lift doors. 'O, well that explains that then. Why didst thou jam the lift?'

'No reason,' she answered with a quaver in her voice.

Glenn tilted his head sideways, eyeing the style advisor suspiciously. Her gold skull draped black satin jersey dress was hung up on the racking, and she now wore a gold skull draped white satin jersey dress that looked slightly distorted on her, and he could see hanging out from under it the hem of some snakeprint number.

And, dangling out from under that, were the black tassels of another dress.

'You're *stealing*,' he gasped.

'No, I'm not,' she said innocently.

He stood gaping in wonder at all the layers of clothing she was wearing, and the torn underwear boxes encircling her feet. She had on so many pairs of bras she looked like she had boobs now. He gave the girl his sternest look.

She instantly burst into tears.

'All right, I *am* stealing! But it's not what it looks like! Please Glenn, don't report me! I—I can explain!' Then, in redoubled peals, she cried almost to roaring.

Glenn could not help but grin from massive ear to massive ear. (She hath despised me rejoicingly, and I'll be merry in my revenge!)

'What's to explain, O thou contaminate of ruffian lust?' he laughed. 'To Nirah Frazar thou art a traitor. Read you not your employee handbook, O thou Priapic priestess? *Thieves will be prosecuted to the full extent of the law.*'

'But I'm not stealing stuff for myself; I'm selling it for drug money!'

Glenn's eyes stretched. 'You're a drug addict, too?' he gasped. 'O Miss Ogden, how the mighty have fallen.' (This just gets better!)

'I am *not* a drug addict,' she snarled with an upraised finger. 'I'm only on the goods to lose weight. I need to fit into the Barebones collection.'

'You're taking *drugs* just to drop a dress size?' he said dubiously.

'It reduces your appetite,' she explained. 'It's how Mildred's managed to stay so skinny all these years—even after having a kid. Do you know how shit it felt to be the only girl in here who couldn't fit into a size 4? I'm the style advisor, Glenn—it's my job to make *other* girls feel like shit!'

'That's still no excuse for stealing,' Glenn intoned.

Gertrude used her forearm to wipe the black streaky tears defacing her cheeks.

'I know it isn't,' she sniffed. 'But it's just so *easy* to steal clothes in here.'

'What?'

'You take them from the box before they've been processed and hide them under your uniform,' she snuffled. 'It just gets reported as "lost in transit".'

'And with the garments hidden under your uniform, you can easily get around Shukeena's nightly bag search,' said Glenn thoughtfully.

'*Exactly.*' She burst into more tears. 'Oh God, what have I done? I've been such an idiot! An idiot who's going to get sacked! And *prosecuted*! And all because I wanted to show off. . . .' She looked at him fearfully. 'So what happens now?' she gulped. 'Oh shit. Are you—are you gonna take me to the office?'

A pause.

Glenn was staring at the style advisor, meditatively twirling his scraggle.

II.XVI

Incompetent, Shukeena had called him! Delusional, Jimmy had claimed! A total psycho, said Peggy! And yet there he was, the man of the hour, dressed with bravura in a salmon pink bomber jacket, cream velour Pluto print sweater, oxblood rumpled pantaloons and lacquered black leather loafers, all of it Nirah Frazar gold skull, and no man in Leeds had ever bore upon his shoulders gear so magnificent—or expensive.

'The apparel aft proclaims the man,' as Hamlet would say, and as Glenn did say, to the snappy figure swaggering down the street beside him, reflected in the blue-tinted windows. He was in an exalted mood that evening, with a stupid, dreamy smile glazed across his face.

His photo shoot was fast approaching, and how very Hardingesque he was looking these days!

Hardingesque. adj. Of G. Harding (19▪—), English fashion designer, or his philosophy. An ensemble so courageous it confuses the multitude. *Hollywood star makes bold statement on red carpet in Hardingesque number, tops Worst Dressed List.*

He gave BBC Yorkshire a lingering look, before shimmying into the jangling hot salsa beat of a converted warehouse bar. He espied the enormous outline of the behemoth's back and in five long, commanding strides was standing beside him.

'*Well*,' he grinned, showing his beamy bright teeth. 'What do you think?'

Jimmy looked his idiosyncratic outfit up and down.

'Did you lose a bet with Elton John?' he belched.

'Very funny,' Glenn yawned, straddling the barstool next to him.

He sipped the Paint the Town Pink that was waiting for him on the long, bright red counter. 'I thought you would be happy that I showed up on time for once?' He smirked. 'That I managed to. . . . *steal* away early?'

'More time for drinking I guess,' the behemoth remarked, clinking Glenn's glass.

'Yes,' said the menswear manager, 'anything less would be a. . . . *criminal* waste of a Saturday night.' He was shaking as he tried to contain his laughter.

'You don't need to keep dropping these hints, Glenn; you've already told me about your new career in shoplifting.'

'O yes, sorry.'

'You want to be careful with that stuff,' Jimmy warned, in a tone so serious it bored Glenn immediately. And shite and onions, if he wasn't wearing a T-shirt that said on it MY OTHER T-SHIRT IS A VERSACE. On a Saturday night in Leeds, no less!

'He that is robb'd, not wanting what is stoln, let him not know't, and he's not robb'd at all,' said Glenn absently. 'You know, Jesus Christ himself stole an ass.'

'I'm not even going to comment on that one. Look, Glenn, you can't keep doing this without someone noticing it. These people aren't stupid.'

'Have you not met Norman?'

'The last thing you need is to be unemployed with a criminal record. Shit the bed! Aren't you on your first warning? And under investigation?'

'*Yes*. But, conversely, I'm also top store card seller *and* employee of the month!' He sipped his cocktail and smiled. 'The Lord—and *Brigantia*—will not always chide; nor will He—or *she*—keep anger forever. Jimmy, listen: when you had me as doomed as Adrastus, what happened? Chardonnay. And when I needed a new wardrobe, and was without means to acquire one, what happened then? I go upstairs at the *exact moment* Gertrude is there, plundering the stock like a mad Pict. Do you see what I'm saying? Every time, in the hour of need—I get *exactly* what I need. How charmed a life can one man live!? Do you not think that these could *perhaps* be portentous things? That there might—*just might*—be some special providence in *my* preservation?'

'No.'

Glenn held the man's gaze a moment. He could feel his spirit stultify, his muscular control momentarily flag. He turned his attention back to his cocktail and sighed.

There he was, with his mind ascending the summits of the loftiest mountains, sharing ideas prophetic and magical, yet Jimmy could not lift his dreamless, sublunary brain out of the quotidian existence—and sitting next to him, Glenn was struck by the same cultural divide that Glen Matlock experienced when the Pistols played Leeds in the '70s. In his interactions with the locals the southerner soon realised their problem wasn't the government not giving them their fair share of money, but rather God not giving them their fair share of brain cells. And though Glenn himself was a Leodiensian, he realised then that he had *nothing* in common with these stones, these worse than senseless things, and he could not get his face in *Advert* quick enough—and escape them all forever.

Christ these people up north really are a bit thick! as Matlock said.

Glenn was irritated now. He felt restless, his eyes raking the room. The denizens made for a depressing sight. It was an older crowd, people in their thirties, content to just sit around and talk, listen to the music. His gorgeous apparel was wasted on them. There was a burning in his belly, and his bone and sinew yearned for action.

Through the windows the city centre was beckoning him in, calling for his cameo.

'Where are we going next?' he asked, interrupting whatever it was that Jimmy was wittering on about. Something about a woman, possibly his mother.

'Oh, I'm not spending another Saturday night being dragged round every bar in Leeds,' Jimmy groaned. 'What's wrong with this one? We've got a seat. It's quiet!'

'*Exactly.*'

'Glenn, I'm telling you now; nothing you can say is going to convince me to move from this barstool, all right? So give up.'

'I'll invite Betty and tell her to bring some mates?'

'All right, let's go.'

II.XVII

Of course, Glenn wasn't *really* going to risk any further romantic moments with Betty, or his reputation in the shop, by being seen out with a fat pisshead who wore novelty T-shirts. He simply pretended to message her, then subjected Jimmy to another Saturday night being dragged round every bar in Leeds, while maintaining the ruse that she was going to reply any minute with the details of her whereabouts.

However, Betty really did seem to be slipping through his tentacles. Since that heavenly lunch hour in the Conservatory, he just hadn't been able to secure a sequel. First, Shukeena, having caught wind of their amorous play, ensured they were scheduled for separate lunch breaks. Then, to make matters worse, he couldn't ask her for drinks after work, as he didn't have a ducat to his name. He grew so mad with yearning to hold that majestic body again that on the day of his big shoot he waited until he saw her going on lunch and immediately changed the time of his own to coincide with hers.

He was then subjected to an infuriating lunch hour, being dragged round every shop in Leeds while Betty sought a shoe she didn't know the name of and couldn't describe. In the end there was only enough time for her to grab a panini and run back to work, with only the most paltry, unfulfilling peck on the cheek for him.

Devastated, he tried lifting his spirits by taking a seat at his favourite coffee stall in the arcade and watching the pretty people as they went by. And dressed in his splendid three-piece suit by Sammi de Hun, sucking his rich cream cinnamon latte through a straw, the style grandee went completely unnoticed. . . .

Ah well. He had been noticed when it counted. And they would all notice him, once his face was in *Advert*. That evening he would be with Chardonnay, in the deluxe room she had booked them, in the classy, four star Marriott Hotel. He could *feel* the next chapter of his life fast approaching, as pangs of nervous optimism ran through his vitals.

All the many checks he had met with whirled through his brain: Peggy's dumping him; work's excluding him; the warnings, investigations, bans, bans, bans. The colossal proportions of his debts. In spite of the incommunicable pain they had caused him, they had all served as steps that had brought him to this momentous day.

Were they really portentous things? Might there be some special providence in his preservation? He gazed at his hefty, gold moonstone-studded watch. At his lowest point it had stopped, literally the last thing the cash-strapped menswear manager needed at that moment. But at what time had it stopped? 8 p.m.

And at what time was his photo shoot scheduled for tonight?

8 p.m.

His hands began to tremble.

'A *thief*?' he gasped. 'Working in the shop?'

'A *thief*,' Norman affirmed. 'Working in the shop.'

Glenn regarded Norman with amazement. He made a point of showing the same amazed face to Shukeena, who was sitting next to him in a black pleated silk top with plunging neckline, black leather pencil skirt and black crackled calfskin ankleboots, all by Sammi de Hun, and his look of amazement was, for a moment, authentic.

'But I thought there were rings of shoplifters working the arcade?' Glenn said. 'How do we know the thief works on menswear?'

Pause.

'Er, we *don't* know that the thief works on menswear, Glenn,' Shukeena clarified. 'No one's mentioned menswear.'

'Sorry!' Glenn laughed nervously, 'I meant to say the *shop*, not menswear. How do we know that he works in the *shop*?'

Shukeena peered curiously at him.

'We don't know that it's a *he*,' she remarked. 'We haven't said whether the thief is a man or woman.'

'Right,' Glenn warbled.

'What *do* we know?' Norman enquired.

'I'm glad you ask,' she said. 'So, the other day, while I was passing through men's, a customer asked me for a different size in a gold label black leather shirt. He'd been told that it was "all we had left in that size". I knew that it wasn't, but when I went up to the stock room to get it, I found it had disappeared with no record of a sale. At first I thought a customer had stolen it—until I started investigating.'

Glenn winced at the word 'investigating'.

'I kept checking the stock room,' she continued. 'Obviously I couldn't go up at the same time as Glenn, because one manager always has to be on the floor, but I noticed the strangest thing was happening—gold skull garments were going missing *even in the short amount of time between my visits.*'

'That is strange!' added Glenn with a crack in his voice.

The middle managers jumped as Norman pounded his mighty fist on the desk.

'Thieving bastard!' he bellowed. 'I can't believe my own staff would steal from me! Do we not pay them enough money!?'

'Speaking of money, I've calculated how much has been stolen,' Shukeena said.

'It won't be that much,' said Glenn dismissively. 'I *assume*,' he hastily added.

Norman's colossal hands gripped the arms of his chair so forcibly they began to turn white. 'Go on then,' he urged anxiously. 'Hit me with it. Is it five hundred? Six? Don't say a grand!'

The ladieswear manager paused for maximum effect—and then gave a figure that made even Glenn's eyes stretch.

Norman jerked himself to his feet with his mouth open.

'*WHAT!*' he screamed. 'I'VE GOT TO TELL HEAD OFFICE WE'VE LOST *HOW* MUCH!? FORGET PROSECUTING THE

BASTARD—I'M GOING TO *KILL HIM*!!'

'I think we should call the police right now,' Shukeena solemnly proposed.

Glenn's heart stood still. 'Whoa! The *police*?' he said. 'Slow down, Shukeena! What can the police do *now*? The stock's already stolen! And he—*or she*—is hardly going to nick anything while the bloody rozzers are in.' Glenn pulled at his collar to cool down. It felt very hot in his tight fitting suit, especially with the scoop neck canary yellow sweater he was wearing underneath his shirt. 'No, I think we've got a better chance at catching the thief by just biding our time, and monitoring the staff until we catch them in the act. Has no one read *The Art of War*? You win with *strategy*—not the sword!'

'It's not neccessary to catch them in the act, Glenn,' said Shukeena dismissively. 'The police will have more than enough evidence to work out who's responsible.'

'Evidence!' Glenn cried, laughing. 'What evidence? The garments are already gone, Miss Mohammed! And, with all due respect, it's not like they're going to start dusting for fingerprints over some silly stock theft.' He swallowed. 'Are they?'

'They don't *need* to dust for fingerprints,' she said. 'They only need to look at what's been stolen.' She referred to the notes in the folder on her lap. 'The items are generally the louder designs from the menswear gold skull range—always in a size small, usually skinnyfit, with a 32 inside leg. That pattern would suggest a male staff member; but Lyndsey's too tall, and Dick's too fat.'

She then turned to Glenn and gave him the glare of all glares.

'Interesting!' he nodded, a rivulet of sweat trickling down his forehead.

Norman sank back in his huge throne, frowning under the feeble office light. 'So,' he said, mulling it over. 'It seems we're looking for a slim male, of average height, odious character—and an *extremely* camp dress sense.'

Glenn nervously dabbed his forehead with his gaudy polkadot pocket square.

II.XVIII

Mascara-streaked tears were cascading down Ali's powdered cheeks.

'But I haven't stolen *anything*!' he protested. 'I've got the receipts for all my clothes!'

'Look, no one's accusing you of stealing anything,' said Norman, looming over the makeup artist with an accusing gaze. 'But come on. Size small, skinnyfit? As Glenn says, who else could it be?'

Glenn avoided Ali's outraged stare, withdrawing into a shadowy corner.

'But I don't even *go* to the stock room!' Ali insisted. 'All my stuff is kept under the beauty counter.'

Norman snorted. 'A likely story!' he replied contemptuously. He then turned his back to confer with his middle managers.

'Well?' Glenn whispered, stepping forward. 'What do you think?'

'I think this is a joke,' Shukeena whispered back. 'He obviously didn't do it.'

'*He?*' Norman interjected, looking over his shoulder. 'You mean that's a *bloke?*'

Glenn eyed the clock on the wall. It was nearly six and still they were no closer to a resolution. 'No,' he whispered impatiently. 'I mean, what do you think about my suggestion, that we suspend Ali now and continue the investigation in the morning?'

'We are *not* suspending anyone from my team, Glenn Harding!' Shukeena whispered angrily. 'Ali is under *my* watch all day; he hasn't stolen *anything*.'

'So who has?' Norman demanded.

Shukeena rolled her massive eyes. 'Oh, come on, Norman! Size small, skinnyfit? We all know who fits that description.'

Glenn tightened, as she stared him point-blank in the face.

'Bay not me, Miss Mohammed, I'll not endure it,' he growled threateningly. 'I recall Sheila throwing around a lot of reckless accusations, too—she ended up fighting so many harassment cases she could barely find time to write a rota.'

'Oi! What are you two on about?' said Norman. 'Do you know who the thief is?'

The two middle managers were locked in an intense staredown. . . .

And it was Shukeena who blinked first.

'I don't know, Norman,' she said. But then her glossed purple lips curled into a cunning smile. 'But I *do* know that none of us can leave until we've caught the thief.'

'No!' Glenn screamed.

Norman looked agog at the menswear manager.

'Are you all right there, boy?' he asked.

'No,' Glenn laughed, 'there'll be. . . . no need for that. Wait here! Methinks that I can draw a confession out of Ali.' He whirled around and in two long, commanding strides was straddling the mill worker's chair next to the makeup artist.

'Mr Hussain,' he said in a severe voice, 'are you or are you not the stock thief? Be simple answer'd, for we know the truth.'

'You know I'm *not*,' he snuffled.

'There's no one else it could be.'

'Yes there is. *You!*'

Glenn jerked in his seat.

'Ingrateful fox! Hold thy tongue, O thou squeaking Cleopatra boy, or I shall forget myself!' he snarled. He leaned into his ear. 'Mate, listen to me,' he murmured. 'You can still get a job in retail with a criminal record, you know? How do you think they staff those discount designer outlets?'

'But I haven't done anything!' Ali wailed.

'I'll give you a great reference if you say you did.'

'No way!'

Glenn eyed the clock. Past six. 'Please, Ali,' he begged.

'Piss off!'

'Ali.'

'No!'

'You're only going to make things worse for yourself.'

'I said no!'

'Confess!' Glenn screamed. 'Or the devil damn thee, thou cream-faced loon!'

Ali made a strangled sound.

'Stop it, Glenn!' Shukeena yelled—as Norman had to jump in and prize his hands off the child's throat. 'WE CAN'T MANHANDLE THE STAFF, YOU MORON!' the store manager screamed. 'WHAT THE HELL DO YOU THINK YOU'RE DOING!?'

'Well, I told him he was going to make things worse for himself.'

'All right, everybody,' exclaimed the ladieswear manager in her severest shrill. 'I know it's past seven and you all want to go home, but I'm afraid you can't. In fact there's a good chance we'll be spending the night here. Quiet—all of you! I've called this emergency team meeting to find out once and for all who the stock thief is. Now they can do the decent thing, save everyone a long night and own up now—' She directed an accusing stare at Glenn, who was standing next to her, avoiding her eyes, alongside Norman, on the elevated platform outside the fitting room cubicles. The team was all sitting around on the antique piano stools. '—or they can be a coward, keep quiet and let everybody suffer. It's completely up to them. Either way, *no one* is leaving tonight, until the thief comes forward.'

There was a light jingling of pendants, as staff looked round the room, shooting accusing stares in every direction. Gertrude looked worriedly at Glenn, who was looking worriedly at the antique Dutch grandfather clock.

Shukeena, catching his eyeing of the clock, allowed a faint smile to seep out onto her otherwise cold phizog. 'And to be clear,' she continued, 'I can wait *all night*. I haven't got anywhere to be, believe me.'

Glenn's heart felt sick; horror swelled his brain. He glanced down at his beloved name-badge, glinting on his breast.

He thought of Chardonnay and her golden smile.

He thought of *Advert*, and himself in it.

He thought of Chardonnay's hotel room—and himself in that as well.

Menswear has been under investigation for some time. . . .

Nothing in his life had ever mattered more than this photo shoot. The sequence of events that led to it would never be repeated. And to miss it would be an insult to Brigantia, who engineered the whole thing, and would put him in her bad books for all eternity. He looked at Shukeena, whose jewel-encrusted skeleton earrings were leering monstrously at him. If anyone was the embodiment of the straight world and everything he longed to escape, it was her. She was more handbooks and harangues than she was human, and even if he got away with the stock theft, and somehow survived the investigation, she would never leave him alone. The truth was, he didn't belong on a shopfloor. He wasn't a menswear manager, any more than he was a businessman. In fact, the only part of the job he liked was the dressing up, which was further evidence that modeling was his *true* calling.

He closed his eyes, took a deep breath. Now was the time! This was his moment! Cross that little bridge, Glenn Harding, for immortality lies on the other side of the Rimini! Be as great in act, as you have been in thought. . . .

And they were going to sack you, anyway.

Glenn stepped forward and raised his hand.

As a collective gasp rose from the staff, Gertrude opened her eyes, saw everyone staring at Glenn, and quickly dropped her hand.

'I knew it!' Shukeena exclaimed triumphantly. 'Go home, everybody; we've—*I've*—caught the stock thief!'

He smiled. 'O, sorry, Miss Mohammed,' he said, 'I'm afraid I'm not the stock thief.'

'*What!*' she said.

'I just wanted to announce that I am tendering my resignation.'

'WHAT!' said Norman and Shukeena in unison.

'You heard me,' said Glenn. 'I am terminating my contract with immediate effect. Which means that I am no longer an employee of Nirah Frazar, which means that no one here has any authority over me, which means that I am free to leave—and I intend to exercise that right at once. So, fare ye well, friends, and think of the world!'

He was heading for the door when suddenly it felt as if he had snagged his sleeve on a forward-facer. He was strutting so fast his arm nearly popped out of its socket.

He looked back and beheld the ruddy complexion of Norman staring back at him.

'O, Mr Mountain,' he said gaily. 'Sorry! Where are my manners? Thank you for everything—working with you has been a holy pleasure. Now if you don't mind, I'll make the doors fast and be with a new job straight. Well may you prosper!'

A pause.

'Norman, please let go of my arm.'

'Sorry, boy, but I'm afraid I can't let you go.'

'Norman, I'm flattered! But it really is time for me to move on to pastures—'

'No, no, don't worry about that. It is with regret that I accept your resignation and will be seeking your replacement immediately, but, you see, while we suspect someone of stealing, we *do* have the right to hold them until the police arrive.'

The colour drained from Glenn's face.

'So I've quit my job and I still can't leave?' he croaked.

'That's about the size of it, yes.'

Glenn could see Shukeena grinning at him. He glanced to the clock, then to Norman, who was gazing at him almost sympathetically.

'Sorry again,' said the store manager.

'It's all right, Norman, I understand,' Glenn sighed, nodding solemnly. 'And now that I am an ex-manager, I suppose I should go sit down and await my fate.'

'That'd be best,' said Norman, releasing his viselike grip.

He watched Glenn go skulking off, past the main display, in the direction of the team. He then watched as, in a flash, Glenn spun on his heel and went bounding round the other side of the display, where he vaulted the front table, yanked up the shutter—and legged it out of the shop.

II.XIX

'*Glenn!*' said Chardonnay, beaming. 'I was beginning to think you weren't coming!'

'I believe in the trade it's called being fashionably late,' he panted breathlessly.

She laughed a beautiful laugh. 'You're learning!'

He wore a skinnyfit psychedelic print velour sweatshirt with blinding, lime-green skinny jeans pasted to his body with sweat. His old pusser suitcase was so stuffed with outfits it looked ready to burst, and the heavy suitbag he was heaving over his shoulder contained even more of Sammi de Hun's divine booty.

'Come in then,' she smiled, kissing his cheek. 'We have a lovely room.'

'All right!' said Glenn with a crack in his voice.

He swaggered into the ritzy, dimly-lit room with his shoulders back and his pelvis pushed forward, still catching his breath.

Sure enough there was a white screen set up in the corner, with a spotlight standing next to it and a very expensive camera resting on a plush red leather wingchair. He had crossed that little bridge, all right. And the cultural divide, and pretty much any other metaphor he could think of. And at the sight of the kingsize bed, half-screened by the heavy curtains of the ornate four-poster frame, his eyes ballooned.

He turned to Chardonnay, a helpless look in his eyes.

She was wearing a short, bright red ruffle dress by Anglophonia, and when he saw the long legs his heart leaped into his mouth. She was in red leather heels and overtopped him a good couple of inches, and her hair was pinned down by a huge crystal hairclip on which was written, honest to God, the words DO IT NOW.

'Shall we get started then?' he said faintly. He could hear his voice wobbling.

'Let's sit down first and go through the plan.'

'The plan?'

She took him by the arm and led him round the massive bed, to where three wingchairs had been arranged in a circle.

In one of them was a man, sitting quietly in the glow of a desklamp.

'*Who's this!*' Glenn cried.

'Glenn, this is Lyndon. He's the director of Uncorruptible Management. Lyndon, this is Glenn.'

Lyndon half-rose to his feet. 'Hello Glenn,' he smiled, holding out his hand.

Glenn ignored his hand, staring instead at his bald mazzard and beige clothes.

'I didn't realise there would be someone else here,' he said, in a severe tone.

'Lyndon takes clients through the business side,' Chardonnay explained cheerily. 'I do the shoot.'

'Business side!' Glenn exclaimed in falsetto. '*What* business side? I didn't come here for a business meeting!'

Lyndon settled back down in his seat.

'Well, we have to work out what we're doing with you,' Chardonnay laughed. For the first time her amiable smile dropped, and she looked at him sort of quizzically. 'Why, what did you think was going to happen?'

'I didn't think *anything* was going to happen!' he replied defensively.

Then suddenly his bulging suitcase popped open, spilling out onto the carpet a mass of clothes. On top of the pile was a ladies gold skull see-through lace thong and bra—in Chardonnay's size.

Glenn's whole head flushed a violent purple.

'Why don't you take a seat, Glenn,' Chardonnay advised, stiffly.

A jellied Glenn dropped his suitcase and suit bag and quietly did as instructed. He was in a daze.

'The three-star is our basic plan,' he could hear Lyndon saying, in a stentorian voice. 'With that you get your ten twelve-by-eights in a plastic sleeve and a set of ten business cards. Four-star is fifteen twelve-by-eights in a special deluxe leather zipped folder, plus your negatives and a set of fifty business cards. The five-star is our premium plan, and that gets you twenty-five sixteen-by-twelves, each one embossed with the Uncorruptible Model Management logo, the deluxe leather zipped folder, all your negatives, one hundred business cards, a limited edition Uncorruptible Model Management ballpoint pen and, best of all, you'll be featured in our exclusive *Book of Faces*, which will be seen by all of our agency contacts in London.'

Glenn looked down, discovering the *Book of Faces* was somehow in his lap. He began to leaf through it, expecting to see comely boys and unearthly nymphs, but found only goblins, potbellies, and greybeards.

'They're all *great* plans,' Chardonnay enthused, 'but if you *really* want to improve your chances of being seen, then the five-star is your best bet.'

She slid a clipboard with a contract on it over the book.

'Chardonnay,' Glenn croaked.

'Yes babe?'

'I thought you said you could get me in *Advert*?'

'I said I *think* you could be in *Advert*. And I still do! But we won't know for sure until we try, will we?' She tapped on the contract with a pen.

Glenn scanned the figures quoted next to the various plans. They wouldn't look out of place on a Nirah Frazar swing ticket.

A long, drawn-out and dreadful groan escaped his lips.

'What's wrong, babe?' asked Chardonnay.

He looked up. Lyndon was staring coldly at him, while Chardonnay was leaning in, holding her smile. You could puncture the tension with the pen she was holding.

'This is a scam, isn't it?' Glenn sighed.

She drew back. 'A *scam*!' she gasped. 'Do you mind? I'm a trained photographer! And Lyndon here's a successful businessman!'

Lyndon was still staring coldly at him.

'I quit my job for this,' Glenn said faintly. He rose to his feet, as the book and clipboard fell to the floor. 'O my God, I quit my job. . . . What have I done?'

'You've done the right thing, that's what you've done!' she replied. 'Come on, Glenn! You can't back out now.' She picked up the clipboard and held it out to him. 'Are you going to sign or what?'

He glared furiously at the woman.

'CHARDONNAY!' he yelled at the top of his lungs. 'I QUIT MY JOB, YOU STUPID BITCH!! AND FOR *WHAT*!? TO HAVE MY PICTURE PUT IN YOUR DOMESDAY BOOK OF ENGLAND'S *MUTANTS*!'

And then he screamed. And screamed again.

And then he was gone. His brain was blank, wiped clean by the calamity. He staggered back and fell against the wall, sliding down it until he lay splayed on the floor, with his head still upright, propped grotesquely against the skirting board.

Pause.

'Is that a yes or a no?' asked Chardonnay.

II.XX

Dear Mr Mountain,

Please treat this message as confirmation that we have reviewed the recent series of claims against Mr Harding, and have come to the following decision(s):

> *A) Head office finds Mr Harding's snobby and contemptuous manner to be in keeping with Nirah Frazar's prestigious, luxury brand image.*

We will not be taking any further action against Mr Harding.

Ciao,
Head office

AUTUMN

III.I

"THOU SHALT COVET THE SUMMER SALE" WAS WRITTEN in large gold letters on the shopwindow, and when a woman passing by with her young son caught sight of the display she came to an abrupt halt, gaping at it with astonishment.

A mannequin, adorned in a lightweight cream linen suit, sported a massive beard. It stood atop a small hill of glinting gold and silver watches, and in its hand a hefty tablet of Commandments listed the latest items to go into sale. At the foot of this sparkly hill, a huddled ring of mannequins, clad in horrid rags, awaited guidance. Behind them rose a carved oak display rail featuring the Commandments: silk shawls, jackets, jeans, cashmere socks and so much more.

As a scowling girl sprang up from the ragged mannequins, the mum and boy gasped.

Gertrude stood scrutinising the guide Ronnie Colenso drew up, oblivious to the big skeletal hand emerging slowly from behind the purple curtain.

With theatrical flair, the curtain was thrown aside, revealing the fulcrum of fashion, arch enemy of the high street, the city's most eligible man, Glenn Harding, standing behind it. He swanned into the window display in a thick swirl of Finite, clad in a pink polo shirt tucked into his signature tight black wool trousers and lacquered black leather loafers, all of it, naturally, gold skull.

'How doth!' he exclaimed with bonhomie, stroking his mullet.

'Oh no, not *you* again,' Gertrude groaned. 'What do you want now?'

'I have come down to the people, so that I may speak to them,' he intoned, his baritone stately.

'And say what?'

He held up some signage. It said:

STAFF WANTED. APPLY WITHIN.

'Oh my god, *finally*,' she sighed. 'How long has it taken you to get that sign up?'

'Not long,' he said defensively.

'They should be advertising for *your* job,' the style advisor chided. 'I still can't believe Norman let you back in, after what you did.'

'Head office investigated me and elected not to take any further action, Miss Ogden. Now why don't you follow their example, and thy threatening colours wind up?'

'I didn't mean your investigation; I meant all the clothes you nicked.'

'O yes; *that* little snafu. Well, the police couldn't have timed the arrest of that organised ring of shoplifters any better,' he said, with relief. 'And the fact they were Eastern European was all it took to convince Norman that they were the real culprits.' A smile of triumph broke over his scraggle. 'Anyway! Of course he took me back; it's not like he was going to find anyone who loves Nirah Frazar more than me—or who knows more about the brand than I do. He was actually happy to see me!'

'Is that why he put you on a stage 2 written warning?'

'All that matters is that I still have my badge,' he said with an airy indifference. 'Although, yes; I suppose there are *some* parallels between the document I was made to sign, and that evil Charter the barons forced upon the good King John,' he mused. 'But, cut out my tongue, if I may keep mine eyes, and all that.'

Gertrude shook her head. 'I had such a good thing going in the stock room,' she said bitterly. 'Now they watch us every second of the day, thanks to you. Prick!'

Glenn eyed her lily-slim figure, and the Barebones black sequined bodice she wore, with a long laughing skull pendant, black silk crepe trousers and black mesh leather ankle boots. The beehive was sculpted to perfection, and under the spotlights, and the sunshine streaming in through the shopwindow, her person glimmered so impressively you

forgot all about her little scar.

She quite literally dazzled the eyes.

'Miss Ogden!' he laughed. 'What need you be so boisterous-rough? You wanted to fit into the Barebones collection, and, evidently, you achieved your goal.'

'So?'

'So end thy ills 'gainst our shop, thou irregulous devil, and quit while y'are—'

Suddenly, Glenn froze. He was distracted by the woman who had been pressed up against the window, steaming the glass as she stared open mouthed at the luxurious garments on display. She had turned and began tottering towards the doors as if in a trance—leaving her little child behind.

'Have you seen this?' said Glenn, incredulously.

'Seen what?' said Gertrude absently, staring at Ronnie Colenso's guide.

Glenn pulled the curtain aside and pushed the display door slightly ajar so he could peep into the shop.

'Seen *what?*' Gertrude grunted, walking up to Glenn and peering over his shoulder. All she saw was Betty in her gold skull black mini dress, laying out jeans on the front table. Her pleated skirt was wide and swishing, and as she bent forward, the milky-white haunches on display looked like pieces of the finest polish'd ivory.

'Oh, are you perving on that little mess again?' she groaned. 'You're obsessed!'

'What?' said Glenn. 'Away, envious rascal! I am watching *this* character.'

Gertrude's eyes followed Glenn's finger away from Betty, to the middle-aged mum, now twirling along in the deep pools of gold cast by the chandeliers.

'Oh, whatever!' she scoffed. 'You love Betty. You want to go out with her!'

'Staff are forbidden from engaging in close personal relationships upon pain of *death*,' he said with asperity. 'As Shukeena made sure to remind me, after those dissentious rumours about Betty and me started flying about.'

The style advisor reached past him and yanked the door shut.

'What was that for?' he cried.

'Because I can see why Betty begged Shukeena not to put her on men's anymore. The way you men all gawp at her is pathetic!'

'Do I detect a note of jealousy?'

'*Me*? Jealous of *that*!?' Gertrude gave a single, piercing shriek of a laugh. She glared disbelievingly at Glenn. 'She's *short*; and she wears open-toe sandals without doing her nails; and do her handbags *ever* match her outfits!?'

Glenn cocked his head to one side and peered at the style advisor.

'Wow,' he grinned. 'Are you sure it's the *men* who gawp at her?'

A pause.

The boy outside watched as the angry-looking woman grabbed the big tablet of Commandments and chased the scared-looking man around the display, swinging for his head. He appeared to be screaming, *Watch the hair! Watch the hair!*

He still had his STAFF WANTED sign in his hand as he escaped through the door.

III.II

The world-candle burned in the sky, casting an infernal heat upon the city. Great armies of Saturday shoppers surged up and down the high street, releasing into the air such a cacophony that walking among them, oppressed by the heat, disturbed by the din, Glenn felt like a Crusader from the twelfth century, questioning whether this really was the Asiatic shore he had arrived upon, or rather the banks of the Acheron.

The intense heat made every step a labour, especially for Glenn in his impeccably fitted clothes. His suit jacket's sharp cut was wedged into his armpits, the pink polo shirt clung to his back with sweat, and the blazer felt like a stack of hot towels on his shoulders. He was worried the muggy air might warp his mullet.

Jingling in his chain armour, with a heavy longsword in his scabbard, he proceeded to ride his horse up the broad, sloping thoroughfare of Brig-market, as the roaring babel of his great army signaled the hour of death for those heretic dogs that had occupied the surrounding territories.

Remember your duties, lads. Protect the Church. Defend the oppressed. Advancing as one we shall bring light, learning, and civilisation to these savages in the straight world.

This one's for you, Jesus.

Thus, he embarked on his campaign, recapturing Leeds, unmanning Sheffield; in York he made the Ouse turn red. The rolling hills of the Pennines were within sight, Manchester quaking in its boots, when suddenly King Glenn the First, heir of Hellas, saviour of Rome, menswear manager of Nirah Frazar, opted on a whim to turn into Queen's Arcade—at which point he heard a familiar voice. Glenn! she said excitedly, grabbing his elbow. He wheeled round and beheld her beautiful face. O, hello Peggy. Where have you been hiding? she asked. Nowhere, he said. I've been missing our little cashdesk chats; are you not coming back? I doubt it, Peggy; that manager said he'd never hire me again. Oh no! Then how am I going to see you?

Exiting the arcade, the massive face of Victoria Quarter loomed. Glenn looked left and right, then back up the arcade. Nothing. Evidently, it was not Brigantia's will that he regreet her today, and he sighed resignedly. He took a right, went up Albion Place, turned onto Lands Lane and went again down Queen's Arcade, but still to no avail.

He knew for certain now it was not Brigantia's will that he regreet her today, and he would just have to respect her divine decision.

He repeated the circuit one last time, just on the off-chance Brigantia had changed her mind, walking extra slowly so that Peggy could catch him up if she needed to, but still nothing. Definitely not Brigantia's will. Also, he knew that Peggy was studying at Newcastle now, so a chance run in with her in Leeds city centre was admittedly unlikely.

No, she was as hard to get as a grant from Business Sense, or a feature in *Advert*. As elusive as a second lunch hour with Betty—or a new source of credit. Peggy didn't give out second chances as easily as Nirah Frazar did.

Jewels being lost are found again, never; 'tis lost but once, and once lost, lost forever.

Glenn expelled another sigh.

Loafing towards Thornton's Arcade, with an idea of staring at the sandwiches in the sandwich shop, he witnessed something that made his eyes to do a double take.

He halted suddenly, stood on the street with his mouth open. He lowered his gigantic sunglasses and looked over them.

The sight that met his eyes shook him to his black lacquered leather loafers.

Standing in Moon, the little shoe shop, in her hot makeup, loose-fit black blazer, and black leather trousers, was that fashion visionary from Headingley who had bedeviled him on the night of his birthday, a good twenty cantos back.

'Well, I'll be hanged,' he gasped. 'It's—' He realised he didn't know the angel's name, and his brain reeled at the name-badge he could espy fixed to her lapel.

He remembered her disappearing act that night, and how he had gone running round Headingley like a madman in search of her. But now, a chance sighting had opened a door to her world.

He looked with exultant eyes to the azure sky, mouthed a noiseless thank you.

Glenn scuttled into the coffee shop next door, sank down in a comfy chair upstairs, so he could try composing himself and figure out what to say. He peeped over the armrest into the drab, pale blue arcade outside. From up here he could see into Moon through the side window that ran the length of the little unit. And lingering in the gap between displays, standing back from the tumult, was the enchantress, looking very bored and almost surly.

He plonked his gigantic sunglasses on the table, gazed upon her brilliance.

The pulled-back hair and voluminous ponytail cascading down her back caught his attention. The sleek leather trousers and the unconventional blood-red ballet flats fascinated him. He appreciated every aspect of her presence, felt positively inspired by her costume. She was in Leeds but not of it, her look more like that of a great artist. Yes, it was her creativity more than anything that excited him—although admittedly there was a subtle allure emanating from the gentle curve of her buttocks beneath the blazer.

He would *have* to go in and say hello, if only to compliment her on her fashion genius.

But that was rather a lot to hurl at a stranger.

Perhaps he could first name drop Joe Schofield to elicit a conversation, then build gradually toward his hero-worship?

What to do, what to do. As he reached for his glass of tap water, he noticed his hands trembling. He put one hand to his chest and felt his heart thumping dementedly. Pulling out his small vanity mirror, he examined his flushed face and sweaty forehead. He glanced at his shoes. They could do with a polish.

With a twinge of relief, he decided to postpone entering Moon to another day when he was better prepared. He was much too giddy, his nerves too jangled, to approach her at that moment. Also, his outfit wasn't ideal, and he didn't want to risk a repeat of his birthday. O! He hadn't forgotten her looking his misjudged costume up and down, or that last wicked glance she had thrown his woolly hat, as she walked away with her friends. He had misfired that time, but he would not misfire this time.

The skilful warrior's energy is like a drawn crossbow; his timing like the release of a trigger.

My hour is almost come.

III.III

Having discovered the enchantress's place of work, Glenn passed the remainder of the afternoon in a mad, gleeful daze. Only later, in bed, did the revolving door nature of retail impress itself on his thoughts. And as a deep sleep fell upon him, lo, he slipped into a horror of great darkness, tormented by nightmares: she might quit her job over trifles, or get fired for some minor transgression, or simply disappear. He awakened in a violent sweat.

Later that day, when he sank into his big comfy chair and saw she wasn't at work, he screamed. Perturbed to the point of illness, he brooded for hours before concluding that today must be her day off, and that she would surely resume her station on the morrow.

The morrow was his day off, but he went into town in his full suit and name-badge anyway. When he saw that she *still* wasn't there and realised he had lost her forever, he decided to throw himself off Leeds Bridge and let the River Aire swallow him up.

But the next day she *did* resume her station, and he breathed a massive sigh of relief.

'Well, well, I suppose I'm in your world now, angel,' he muttered.

He shook his head. Christ, he was sounding more like Morrissey by the day.

Perching himself on his big comfy chair, with a dreamy smile glazed across his face, he cast an admiring gaze toward her and her now familiar costume, which was evidently her uniform, and which Glenn had cunningly mirrored by intermixing his silk salmon shirt with his black suit. I title this piece: "Conversation Starter".

But Glenn did not go in and start a conversation with her. Instead, he remained perched on the edge of his seat, hesitating.

Armies prize high ground, shun low; they esteem yang, avoid yin.

The wise general is a Lord of Destiny.

With trembling hands, he retrieved his grandad's pocket watch. His fifteen-minute morning break was almost over. And it really was fifteen minutes, too; he couldn't take long breaks anymore, due to his signing a piece of paper guaranteeing he would behave himself. (In fact, the stage 2 written warning had reduced him to manager in name only, but more on that later.) He glanced furtively over each shoulder, extracted his grandad's Royal Navy hipflask, put the neck to his lips and quaffed Jimmy's rum.

He made a strangled sound.

Observing a lull in the shop's activities, he faced a crucial decision. Engage the little visionary in conversation now, while the floor lay quiet, or risk her being dispatched on a break, forcing him to postpone his move. The sweltering day exacerbated his indecision; he felt clammy in his wool suit, wondered whether he might be better off waiting for tomorrow. He sipped his tot thoughtfully. Yes, why now? She doesn't look as if she's going anywhere. Throw all your force into the fray for some gain, and you still may fail. No, we must prize the high ground. Esteem the yang. Not just blunder in unprepared—

Glenn saw a tall, handsome man approach her about a shoe, and they began *laughing together*. He put away his hipflask, threw aside his glass of tap water and bolted off, descending the stairs three at a time.

He tripped over the threshold and stumbled into Moon, panting. A huge display rack bisected the floor, and to the left of it, on the women's side, some faceless male staff member was serving a customer. To the right he saw her, the enchantress, alone again, and outlined by the drab blue arcade. She was gazing into space, and his heart burned as he beheld her.

Mistress, please: are you divine or mortal?

He looked darkly at that arrant knave he had seen preying upon her with his seedy enquiries, saw that he was off browsing the full price. I know your game, mister.

Glenn drew himself up, assumed a charming smile and strode the length of the shop, swanning straight past her. He stood at the upper end of the room, unimpressed by the staff's failure to greet a customer. He strode back down the length of the shop, making a point of passing her slowly. He stood at the front with his back to the shop, staring out onto Briggate with a disgruntled look upon his face.

Abate, sweet fugitive; turn thy beauteous head, and with kind regard a panting lover view!

'Thanks,' a ridiculously deep voice called out over his head. He looked back and saw the tall, handsome man smiling as he departed the shop. 'Bye,' she replied, flashing a smile at him. Her voice sounded like music in Glenn's massive ears, and weakness seized his knee-joints.

The skilful warrior's energy is like a drawn crossbow; his sneaky sip of tot like the release of a trigger. He stamped right to up her and yanked up the first shoe in reach.

'Do you have this in a 10?' he enquired.

She stared blankly at the shoe, then at Glenn.

'We don't do 10s in ladies' shoes,' she said in her lilting voice.

He winced when he saw the blue satin pump in his hand. 'No, I didn't think so,' he murmured, shoving it back on the shelf. 'I was asking for. . . . my flatmate's sister?'

Her attention captured, a terrifying silence enveloped them. She was regarding him dubiously, almost knowingly, just as she did that night in Headingley. But the rum had buoyed Glenn, instilling strength at his fated moment, and he met her intimidating stare with a carefree smile. 'Nice outfit,' he commented, nodding at their matching attire.

She looked him up and down. 'Thanks,' she said absently.

The socially proper response would have been, *Thanks, you too*, with a nod and a reciprocal smile, but there was no warmth in her, it seemed, only attitude.

'Where's that top from?' Glenn enquired.

'I made it,' she responded.

'You *made* it?' he blurted involuntarily.

'Yep.'

He goggled the weird viscose-like fabric, and that unnerving knuckle duster pendant. 'Talent in handicraft *and* a clever mind,' he nodded, smiling. 'You are a modern day Athena.'

'I don't know what that means, but. . . . okay.'

'Did you make that cool pendant as well?' he asked, as he remembered to read her name-badge. '*Henrietta*,' he added, with supreme relish.

'No,' she smiled, 'I got this in Berlin. I was—'

'*Berlin!*' he blurted involuntarily.

She lifted a thick eyebrow. 'Yep.'

Pause.

Well, his pointless interjection had derailed that prospective paragraph from her. And now he had to think of something—*anything*—to say about Berlin, and quick.

'She's a scratty little mess, with a shit personality, and I don't get what all the fuss is about.'

'Me neither,' Dick chimed in.

'The way you men all gawp at her is pathetic; I don't know what you see in her.'

'I don't gawp at her,' said Dick, picking out an S from the trolley of size cubes between him and Gertrude, and clipping it onto the hook of a clothes hanger. They were working through a gondola of unsized gold skull leather biker jackets. 'I think she's boring,' said Dick. '"Boring Betty", I call her.'

'She wears silver jewelry with *gold* belt buckles. I mean, would you dare!'

'Never,' Dick concurred, glancing down at the claret nails peeping out of the slinky, snake effect leather sandals and rolling an M in his fingers.

'I can't believe anyone would think she's pretty. I mean she's sort of cute, I guess. But novelty-cute. Like a handbag dog.'

'We just need to remind Leeds that Gerty's still here,' mused Dick, ogling her rather obscenely. He grabbed an L.

'Yeah,' Gertrude nodded. 'Let's make this night out a big one. Like old times, as you were saying—Oh wait; I don't know if I can. I think I'm working Sunday.'

'Oh, I'm sorry—I thought I was talking to Gerty. Any idea where she might have gone, *Boring Betty*?' Dick taunted.

Gertrude retaliated with a dark scowl.

'I meant that I don't know if I can. . . . even be bothered going to bed!' she clarified.

'Now *that's* the Gerty I remember! And don't worry; there'll be plenty of time for bed. But if it's 'owt like the old work nights—there won't be any sleeping going on!'

YOUNG MAN FROM LEEDS

'Yeah, don't know about that, mate,' she said. 'But I'm going to wear that Barebones sheer dress, make sure everyone's looking at me. It's completely see-through!'

Dick gave a yelp. He was brandishing an XL.

III.IV

Glenn stepped out of the shop and into the dazzling sunbeams slanting through the great glass ceiling. The air was balmy and still, accompanied by the gentle babble of the nearby fountains. Breathing in the heady melange of aromas wafting from the numerous perfumaries, he felt even more intoxicated than he already was.

Is this happening?

Can this be real?

O, it was real, all right, and he rubbed his hands and cackled with glee. His crown was sculpted to perfection, his mullet straightened to within an inch of its life. Decked out in his three-piece suit, he looked almost as if he were manager of the whole arcade, rather than that one little room, where he had been denuded of all but the tiniest of managerial decisions.

As he turned the corner, there she was, at the little coffee stall, bathed in a golden cone of sunlight. She sat on the same high stool, at the same table where he had once sat, alone and despondent in II.XVII. But now, *she was waiting for him.* The glory of the image almost overwhelmed him.

And the Lord delivered the elusive one into the hand of Glenn Harding.

'How do you, Miss Payne,' he exclaimed, his voice trembling slightly.

He could feel his heart thumping against his hipflask.

'Hello,' she replied warmly, in that lilting, musical voice.

He removed his huge sunglasses, plonked them on the table. 'I see you're wearing that *same* outfit again,' he grinned.

'Yeah,' she said, without even a glimmer of self-awareness.

He ordered the drinks using the note he had shook down Dick for—a

179

rich cream cinnamon latte with no foam and a straw for him; a black coffee for her—and his hands were shaking so violently he nearly spilled the drinks down her while placing them on the table. He inhaled deeply, tried to calm himself.

'So! Henrietta,' he said, mounting the high stool across from her. 'Let's get started.' He cocked his head to one side, peered inquisitively at her. 'Tell me *why* a prestigious, luxury fashion brand like Nirah Frazar should hire *you*?'

Her eyes narrowed. 'Um, because you said you'd give me a job?' she answered.

A pause.

'O yeah,' Glenn murmured sheepishly, 'I did say that, didn't I.'

'It surprised me a bit. I was talking about good places in Europe for vintage shopping, and you just blurted out that I should work for you.' She slurped her black coffee. 'To be honest, you sounded a bit desperate.'

'What, desperate to meet you for a drink?' Glenn laughed, blushing slightly.

'No, desperate to get a new sales assistant,' she clarified.

His face dropped abruptly. 'Right,' he nodded.

Suspicion flashed in her eyes. 'This *is* a job interview, isn't it?' she questioned.

'Of course it's a job interview!' Glenn cried, laughing. He sucked his rich cream cinnamon latte with no foam through his straw. 'I genuinely need a new sales assistant, and have done for some time.'

'I don't know anything about men's fashion,' she warned.

'Neither do the customers,' he said seriously.

To his surprise, she burst into laughter, and the tension coiled within him at last began to unwind. 'Anyway!' he said, retrieving from his blazer a document with great brio. '*This* is the CV of Henrietta Payne,' he beamed, unfolding it on the table.

'It is.'

Glenn's eyes raked the text he had read a hundred times, learned word for word: her birthday, address, jobs, grades, awards. Her atrocious spelling and syntax. 'What are all these prizes for textiles and design?' he asked curiously.

'That's what I do on the side. Make clothes, create patterns and all that. I'm going to study textiles at Manchester Uni.'

'O,' said Glenn, surprised. 'You're going to university?'

'Yeah.'

'When?'

'September,' she replied.

'*Next* September?' he asked, hopefully.

'*This* September.'

His heart winced. 'That's quite soon,' he said after a moment's thought.

'How come you're not at university?' she asked. 'You're very young.'

'I don't want to get into debt,' he said with a straight face.

'Fair enough,' she nodded.

'Do you really want that massive student loan?' he pressed. 'Why not work for Nirah Frazar and start earning?'

She laughed. 'I want to do more with my life than work in a clothes shop in Lee—' She stopped herself, but the sentiment lingered in the air: Retail workers were failures, trapped in dead-end jobs that no one with ambition would ever aspire to. No one wanted to be Glenn Harding. He held his affable smile, as he groaned in the spirit. 'I think I'd rather just work for *myself*,' she answered diplomatically.

'With a degree in textiles?' Glenn said with a hint of malice. 'Doing what?'

'I'm going to be a fashion designer in London,' she said matter of factly.

A pause.

'Yeah, that does sound better than working in a clothes shop,' he conceded.

'Yep. So even though, like you say, you get into debt, I still think uni's worth it for the skills you learn, the contacts you make, and where it takes you in the end.'

'Well, it sounds like you've got it all figured out,' he said tonelessly.

'Except what I'm doing before I leave for uni,' she winked.

YOUNG MAN FROM LEEDS

Rarely did job interviews see the interviewer yearning to swap places with the interviewee, but trust Glenn Harding to find himself in such an extraordinary scenario. Before him sat a woman with clear aspirations, destined for significant achievements. In the current trajectory of his life, Glenn's sole claim to fame would be that he once interviewed Henrietta Payne. How he envied the clarity of her vision, the precision with which she outlined her goals. Behind his forehead, a grim tapestry swiftly unfurled, displaying to him the succession of wrong turns he had taken that had lead him, inexorably, to this dead end. For years, he had immersed himself in the pages of *Advert*, reading the reports of London Fashion Week over and over, and dreaming of one day being part of it. And now, in a rather surprising twist of fate, he found himself in the presence of an individual he intuited would inevitably emerge as a key player in those very narratives.

He fell into a trance, where he beheld the unbridgeable chasm between Leeds and London Fashion Week stretch out before him— and then stood mesmerised by the sight of Henrietta Payne effortlessly soaring over it.

Her coattails flapped in the wind as she ascended to ever greater heights on her amazing voyage, and Glenn began to focus intently on them. Indeed, they might be the most important coattails he had ever seen, or would see, in his life. . . .

As the vision abruptly receded, Glenn found himself back in the arcade—where the fashion designer was staring at him through his own gigantic sunglasses.

'Are you all right?' she said, grinning.

She looked funny and adorable, and the act seemed to him almost romantic. Seated there, rapt in concentration, he watched as she audaciously seized his cinnamon latte, threw his straw on the floor and swigged from his cup. The nymph's conduct was a bit familiar for a job interview—and he was loving every second of it. It seemed every passing moment only deepened his enchantment with this unorthodox woman.

'Miss Payne,' he sighed, his adoring eyes resting upon her heavenly face.

'What?'

'You don't know anything about Nirah Frazar, do you?'

'Nope.'

'And I guess you're only in Leeds till September?'

'If that.'

A pause.

'Henrietta, do you even want this job?'

'Not really.'

'You're hired.'

III.V

Glenn was perched aloft on the main display, reclining in the antique Moroccan throne, reading Henrietta's CV with one leg slung over the armrest. He was so absorbed in the text he didn't even hear the beast ascending out of the bottomless pit.

'*Er!*' she erupted violently. 'Could you come down from that display, Glenn?'

Normally he enjoyed a bit of light sparring with the manslayer before acquiescing to her instructions, but with him now being on his stage 2 written warning he thought it best to comply immediately. (Plus she was wearing her tight blazer with nothing underneath again, and he was powerless to resist her orders on such days anyway.)

'Ah, hie thee, gentle shop-wife,' he cheerily exclaimed, stowing the CV within his waistcoat before leaping to the floor. 'What good love may Glenn perform you?'

'Have you forgotten something?' she enquired with an abominable glare.

'Erm,' he said cluelessly. 'O! Hast thou servant been slack in his homage? Sovereign of Egypt, hail!' he said, genuflecting before the boding bird, pressing a chaste kiss upon her petite hand. 'Thou lays most lawful claim to this floor, and Glenn is fain to confess thy greatness. Forsooth—I am thy servant.'

'What did I ask you to do last week?' she said through gritted teeth.

Glenn remained on one knee, clasping her hand with a lost look on his face.

'I don't know,' he murmured.

'*To put up your staff wanted sign!*' she screeched. 'For God's sake, Glenn, why haven't you done it? I put the thing in your hand and *watched* you go into the window display. Don't tell me you lost it like you did your manager's keys—'

Glenn leaped to his feet smiling.

'O, wait! No, Shukeena, don't worry about that—we don't need the sign anymore. For you will be pleased to know I have hired a new sales assistant!'

Pause.

'You've *what?*' she exclaimed.

'She's working her notice now, and she starts next week,' he gleefully announced.

The slack expression on her face morphed into a hideous scowl. 'You had no right to go over my head, Glenn!' she hissed. 'Have you forgotten the terms of your rehiring? Norman made it *very clear* to you that you had to run *all* major decisions by me—'

'Shukeena, don't worry; you will *love* her,' he insisted. 'I know I do.'

'Oh really?' she said dubiously. 'What's her experience like?'

'Great! She's got loads of it,' he said, reaching inside his waistcoat and whipping her CV out. 'Have a look for yourself.'

Shukeena scrutinized the tatty sheet, her brow furrowing beneath the brutal fringe. 'She's had six jobs,' she observed.

'Exactly.'

'In two years?'

Glenn swallowed nervously. 'Just shows how in demand she is.'

'I'm not happy about this,' she said, shaking her head.

'O, you weren't happy when I didn't have a sales assistant, and now you're not happy that I've hired one; methinks you might just be an unhappy person!'

Upon seeing her stomp off toward the office, CV in hand, Glenn's belly contracted.

'Shukeena, she'll be on menswear!' he exhorted.

'And she'll be covering on ladies in the run up to Christmas,' she called back over her shoulder. 'Well, I am *not* having this stupid girl on my floor.'

A big arachnid hand flew over her shoulder and gripped the doorknob tightly.

'Can we not sort this out between us?' Glenn implored. 'Why bring Norman into it?'

She fixed her gaze on the door. 'Let go of the doorknob,' she threatened.

'No.'

The fire-eyed Gorgon looked back and stared up at him.

Glenn fell to his knees before her and interlocked his fingers around her dinky waist. 'All right! I admit it, I thought you probably wouldn't approve of her!' he confessed. 'But if you remember, Norman told me that my instincts were so poor that in future I'd be better off just doing the *opposite* of whatever my gut feeling was—which is *exactly* what I did here! In the integrity of my heart and the innocency of my hands I have hired Henrietta, and I would appreciate it if you didn't tell Norman—'

'Tell Norman *what*?' thundered Norman from behind.

'Ah, Mr Mountain! How doth!' Glenn sputtered nervously, rising so abruptly he fell against the rusty suit of armour. It clanged. 'How are you?'

'I'm fine,' Norman replied defensively, his broad, simian figure looking fit to burst from his grubby camouflage jacket. 'Why do you ask? And what are you doing outside my office? Look, if this is about that Trench Broom, I found it in the street. I'm handing it in to the police today—'

'No, no,' said Glenn quietly, waving his hands, 'it's nothing to do with that.'

'Phew.'

'Norman,' Shukeena interjected, 'Glenn has taken on a new sales assistant without consulting either one of us, as were the strict terms of his rehiring.'

'What?' Norman exclaimed, fixing his gaze on the menswear

manager. '*You've* hired someone?'

'Yes,' Glenn admitted with a gulp.

'But aren't you that boy who's on his stage 2 written warning?' he said severely.

'Yes,' Glenn replied in a timid voice.

'That incompetent cretin I said would be better off doing the opposite of whatever his instincts told him?' Norman bellowed.

'That's me,' Glenn winced.

'And what do your instincts tell you about this girl?' he demanded.

Pause.

'That she has a bad attitude, she won't do a good job, and you'll all hate her.'

Shukeena shook her head and looked despairingly at the store manager.

'She sounds *great*,' said Norman, nodding approvingly. 'Hire her.'

Their ag'd father then forcibly pushed past them, stepped inside his office, slammed the door behind him and locked it shut.

Shukeena shook her head and looked despairingly at the menswear manager.

Glenn rubbed his hands and chuckled with satisfaction. 'Better luck next time, my darling demon,' he smiled, pinching Henrietta's CV from her hands.

'This isn't over, Glenn,' she said ominously. But then suddenly her face softened. 'What's a "Trench Broom"?'

III.VI

It was time for Lyndsey's lunch, and he arranged the antique piano stools in a line so that footwear was inaccessible. He used to seal the section off behind heavy-duty tensa barriers, until Norman banned him from doing so and locked them away in the basement. But Norman had long ago ceased to monitor his activities, and Glenn had never started. He left his section secured and set off briskly for the staircase.

It was then that he saw it: Dick's Kumquat, left out on the formalwear section.

Lyndsey peered through his pince-nez, to the tree trunk table. He could see the sweaty back of Dick's tapered white shirt, stretching over his rolls of fat as he put on another performance for Gertrude, trying to amuse her with his foole act.

The footwear supervisor scurried sideways and snatched up the little gizmo.

There was no pin and in a second he was whizzing through Dick's private world, skimming short messages, long call logs and small fuzzy photos. He selected the video tab. There were no words to describe what he saw.

His phizog darkened, and he turned his back to the department and crouched down behind a row of pinstripe linen suits. With his heart racing and his hands trembling, he connected the Kumquat to his via Forkbeard and pressed send. The video's journey through the ether felt like forever. . . .

In ninety seconds it was done.

He left Dick's gizmo where he found it and walked through the shop in a daze. In his somnolence he brushed past Shukeena, who was clip clopping through menswear.

'Er, Lyndsey, do you know where Glenn is?' she enquired curtly.

'Don't care.'

She glowered under her sharp fringe, as she watched him totter off unsteadily to the stairs. She then forgot all about him, as her eye-beams swept the floor in pursuit of the elusive menswear manager. They settled on the entrance to the fitting room.

Suddenly there was a rapping on Glenn's cubicle door.

'Whatever it is, Dick, I don't give a shit,' he growled. '*Seriously*. Pluck off!'

'It's me, Glenn,' Shukeena sighed.

A pause.

'Ah, Miss Mohammed!' Glenn's voice cried gaily. 'How do you, my good lady? How goes the world?'

'Can you come out, please? I need a word.'

'Erm—I don't think you want to see me *now*, Shukeena; I need a

HUNTER

minute.'

'I don't have a minute, Glenn. Can you come out *now*?'

'Very well. . . . you asked for it!'

The lock slid aside and the door swung open. Glenn stepped out and stood before her in nought but a skimpy pair of shocking pink gold skull hipbriefs.

Her eyes protruded as she beheld the tall, uncommonly smooth-skinned boy looming over her. His bone-white body was all trim and sinewy, and gleaming like a mannequin. The lean stomach looked like the result of a thousand daily sit-ups, although in reality it was just a byproduct of youth, poverty, and starvation.

'Don't say I didn't warn you!' he chuckled, noting her double take down below. 'Thy business?'

'I wanted to talk to you about your holiday,' she said, her voice vaguely flustered.

'My holiday?' he yawned, ostentatiously stretching out his taut body, flexing his little biceps. 'I don't think I've taken any holiday?' he said.

'*Exactly,*' she stated. She was beginning to collect herself again. 'I was on the phone with head office and the subject of your annual leave just happened to come up. . . . Do you realise you didn't use any last year?'

Nothing registered in Glenn's eyes. 'So?'

'So you *have* to use your holiday, Glenn. It's a legal requirement.'

'Right,' he nodded. He still looked a bit lost. 'How much do I have?'

She rolled her eyes. 'We get four weeks holiday every year,' she said briskly.

'Four weeks! Wow, that's good. I look forward to using it.' He withdrew into his cubicle and tried without success to close the door. His face appeared in the crack.

'Miss Mohammed, I can't close the door with your foot in it,' he giggled. Suddenly, his expression turned serious. 'Unless you want to come in?'

She stared in his eyes. 'I don't think you understand what I'm saying, Glenn. You also have this year's allowance, remember?'

'What, so I can have an *eight week* holiday?' His little black eyes lit up. 'Well, in that case I might just book off all of December and January and actually celebrate Christmas and New Year for once. Splendid!'

'No, Glenn, it doesn't work like that. You'll have to stagger this year's holiday, like you're supposed to. But we need to sort out last year's immediately.'

He squiggled his brow. 'Sayst thou?'

'Head office wants you to take your four weeks off—starting tomorrow.'

'Tomorrow!' he choked. 'But I can't start a four week holiday tomorrow; Henrietta's starting!'

'Don't worry, Glenn; I'm sure she'll still be here when you get back.'

Glenn burst out of the cubicle.

'But Shukeena! We're too busy for me to take four weeks off now—it's the sale!'

'We'll be even more busy next month with the remerchandising and the stock take.' She then rubbed her hands and chuckled with satisfaction. 'I told you this wasn't over.'

'Usurping Mohammed!' Glenn thundered. 'Unnatural queen! Malice is the sin most hated by God—and I beg Him you shall receive your just deserts!'

'Enjoy your holiday,' she smiled, turning and clip clopping away, the thick gold zip down the back of her tight black felt skirt wagging to and fro.

Barefoot, he pursued her, halting at the fitting room entrance.

'Yes! Avaunt, thou hateful villain, and get thee gone!' he cried, shaking his fist. 'With fire and sword, Glenn follows thee at thy four-inch heels, thou dwarfish whelp of Hell!'

Standing with his little chest heaving madly, he realised the room had fallen silent, as a multitude of faces stared at him. His stage 2 written warning obliged him to show them his most charming, personable smile, instead of what he wanted to show them.

He turned and went flouncing back to his cubicle, slamming the door behind him. Then, with eyes red as fire, he unsheath'd his sword and cleaved a psychic image of Shukeena Mohammed into pieces.

III.VII

A sound like a wet slurp woke Jimmy up. He opened his eyes and saw that the green wall was so bright that the blinds had to be open, and he wondered drowsily how that could be. He lifted his face from his pillow and squinted at the door.

It was open.

He felt his heart spasm, and with a squeak of springs he sat up and saw it: A spectral figure looming over his bed in nothing but a headcomb and underpants, gawping blankly at him through a hideous black facemask.

'Morning,' said Glenn in a vacant monotone.

'Shit the bed, our Glenn!' Jimmy gasped, recoiling and clutching his chest. 'What the chuff are you doing in here?'

'Admiring the view,' he said with detachment, nodding his head at the mental hospital that overlooked Hyde Hill, and was the main view from Jimmy's bedroom. He knitted his crusty brow. 'Or at least I was, until you interrupted me.'

Glenn slurped his Irish coffee from Jimmy's Leeds Rhinos mug.

'Hang on, isn't it Saturday today?' the behemoth queried.

'Yes,' said Glenn. 'So?'

'So shouldn't you be at work?' Jimmy enquired, wiping his eyes and checking the bedside clock. 'It's 10 a.m.!' he gasped. 'Oh, chuffing hell, Glenn; don't tell me you've been fired?'

Glenn elucidated how Pharoah's dread decree had exiled him into outer darkness for twenty-eight days and twenty-eight nights.

Jimmy breathed a sigh of relief as he slumped back in his bed.

'A month off, ay?' the underwriter mused with envy. 'What are you going to do with it?' he yawned.

'Dunno,' Glenn shrugged distantly. 'Dost thou have any suggestions?'

'You could always go on holiday?'

They both broke out into uproarious laughter.

'Seriously though,' Jimmy continued, 'have you any plans today?'

Glenn slurped his Irish coffee, stared abstractedly through the warped metal slats. 'None at all,' he sighed, shaking his head.

'Are you all right today? You seem like you're away with the fairies again.'

'Ha, you're not far wrong,' Glenn admitted, a wry smile breaking upon his facemask. 'You must forgive my being distant, Mr Sandaal, but, to paraphrase Gide after he met Wilde: *Since Henrietta, I exist only a little.*'

'Fair enough,' Jimmy yawned.

'Did I tell you she's going to Manchester Uni?' Glenn queried.

'Yes, you told me,' Jimmy replied, his eyes closed.

'Did I tell you she's going to be a fashion designer?'

'Several times,' he said. He grinned. 'Have you shown her your sketch book?'

'*No,*' Glenn grunted.

'Okay.'

Pause.

'Ah, Henrietta; mine sweet and up-locked treasure. What is thy substance? Whereof are you made?' He slurped his Irish coffee. 'Jimmy, do you know what Plato said about the contrasting loves of Common Aphrodite and Heavenly Aphrodite?'

'Nope. And with a bit of luck, I'll never find out.'

'Basically, there are two discrete categories of love, which for the purposes of this talk can be defined as the love I felt for Peggy and the Nirah Frazar girls, and the love I feel for Henrietta Payne—'

'*Glenn*,' the behemoth interposed.

'What?'

'I've just woken up.'

'I know you have, Jimmy. I was here; I saw it.'

'No, look—' Jimmy's eyes were now wide open, and staring at the green ceiling with a distinctly freaked out look. 'Glenn; we need to talk.'

Glenn's countenance abruptly fell.

'"Glenn; we need to talk" is what Peggy said to me,' he cried, aghast. He shook his head. 'O no you don't, Jimmy; not again!' he warbled.

'No, mate, it's nothing like that; calm down.' He sighed, rubbed his eyes wearily. 'Look; it's just that when two people live together, they can start to, you know, get on each other's tits. And. . . .'

Glenn slurped his coffee, stared at him through his demented mask. 'Go on.'

Jimmy stared at the mini wonkbox atop his empty bookcase, by the door.

'Just say it, Jimmy!' Glenn cried, laughing. 'I'm a grown man; I can take it.'

Jimmy looked him square in the eyeball.

'All right. You promised on your birthday you were going to chill out a bit, and stop with all the madness, but you haven't. You've got worse. You brood and obsess *all the time*. You get yourself so worked up it's unsettling to be around you. You're unhinged, unpredictable, violent—'

Glenn threw his drink in Jimmy's face.

'DIE!' he screamed.

He ran from the room with tears running down his cheeks—running like the water he could hear running, behind the bathroom door. He rapped on it.

'I'm in the *shower*, Glenn,' called Jimmy's voice irritably. 'I needed to wash my face, funnily enough.'

'Yes, sorry about that, Jimmy,' Glenn winced. 'But I think you're right. I do brood. And I have been obsessing and getting worse,' he said diplomatically.

'Right?'

'I have suffered some unlucky hits lately, but it's not like it's the end of the world. I mean, blood of Hydra, I'm *young*! And I have my whole life ahead of me. I shouldn't be letting things get on top of me, the way I have been doing.'

'I agree.'

'It is bitter and irksome that I am a manager and must be over-rul'd—but that's why I think, on reflection, a break will probably do me good. I need some time away from the stress of that shopfloor. I need some time to *myself*. And I tell thee what: I'm going to enjoy it. No more unhappy Harding.'

'Good for you mate,' Jimmy said, with relief. 'That's great to hear!'

Glenn turned from the bathroom door and strode decisively down the corridor. In the living room he stood in his skimpy hipbriefs with his legs spread, arms akimbo.

The green walls looked back at him blankly.

Pause.

A key turned in the lock, and the door thrust open. Jimmy stood there in his Leeds Rhinos top, jogging bottoms, and trainers, gripping the handle. In his other paw was a takeout coffee, and wedged under his arm was a shrinkwrapped broadsheet containing an innumerable multitude of bonus magazines and supplements.

'Glenn,' he said, without any warmth in his voice. 'You're still here.'

Glenn lay slumped across the sofa, staring at the ceiling with a glazed look in his eyes.

'Yes,' he answered, in a vacant monotone. He was still in his underpants.

The behemoth dipped his head under the doorframe and lumbered jiggling into the room. He plonked his keys and wallet down by the

Gametraption II, on the wonkbox stand, and used his hind feet to slide off each battered, dirty trainer.

'I thought you'd be out, clothes shopping or something?'

'Can't afford to, now I'm paying off my store card,' he sighed. 'And *you*,' he added darkly.

'Oh, right.' Jimmy sank heavily into the other sofa.

Glenn gazed absently at the Leviathan as he set his coffee down on the coffee table, tore open his stash, and carefully spread the various parts out in front of him.

'Anything that'd interest me?' the menswear manager enquired.

'No,' Jimmy replied flatly. He sighed. 'You know,' he said, assuming an upbeat tone, 'it's a gorgeous day out. Why don't you go read a book in the park?'

'Because I've already read everything.'

'I don't think you've read *everything*, Glenn; there's new books being published every week.'

'New books can kiss my arse.'

Pause.

'Jimmy?'

'*What?*'

'What subject did you study at university?'

'You already know what subject I studied, Glenn. Economics.'

'And did that get you the job you have now?'

'It helped.'

'What would I need to do to go to university?'

'You would need to re-sit your GCSEs, go back to college, complete your GNVQ, attend some open days around the country and then apply where appropriate.'

'Do you think I could do that in a month?'

Jimmy stared at him.

'But I thought everyone could go to university now!' Glenn thundered.

'Everyone can,' said Jimmy. 'Except *you*.'

'I am tied to the stake and must stay the course,' he nodded solemnly. 'O immortal powers, that know the painful cares that wait upon my poor distressed soul—'

'RIGHT!' said Jimmy, rising to his feet. 'That's it!'

'Where are you going?' said Glenn, with a perplexed expession.

Jimmy was scooping up his things, slipping his trainers on. 'I'm off to the park.'

'Shall I come with you?'

Jimmy slammed the door so hard Glenn's framed "no further action" letter fell off its hook and hit the pinewood with a crack. He could hear the behemoth descending the winding stairs, three at a time. He was practically running.

He slammed the great door so hard it shook the walls of the ancient building.

Glenn slumped back in his sofa, resumed staring at the ceiling with a glazed look—until his eyes were drawn to the wallet Jimmy had forgotten to take with him.

III.VIII

For many hours he roamed about the city.

As much as he wanted to, he could not go into work on the first day of his annual leave. To do so would make it look like he didn't have a life, and nothing could be further from the truth because in fact he had a very rich life. Instead, he slipped into the shade of his favourite coffee shop.

'A glass of tapwater?' the barista asked.

'No, today I will have whatever the most expensive coffee on the menu is, please.'

'Is that in or out?' she asked.

'I will have the coffee *in* the mug, please.'

She didn't laugh at his joke, but still he let her keep the change from Jimmy's fiver; for Glenn was a good man, generous as Timon. He sank down in his old lurking place, the sweet aroma emanating from the enormous mug making him feel dizzy.

Clusters of vibrantly attired teenagers crowded the tables, imbibing hot chocolates and milkshakes, laughing and shouting over the loud pop-rock music. The din was quite hideous and as he pricked his ears, he heard one table talking about exams, another one talking about horses; at another table a girl was discussing her symptoms.

Reclining in his chair, he blew air. So, this is what people did with their Saturdays.

They just came out and met each other and sat around and talked.

He peeped over the armrest into the arcade outside, looked into Moon. He amused himself thinking of all the customers who would be horrorstruck that day to discover that their sweet up-locked treasure had been taken from them, stolen in the night!

But then his face dropped abruptly, and a pang of fear ran through his heart.

He was worrying about what his colleagues might be saying to Henrietta about him, what embarrassing stories they could share. How they never invited him on work nights out, and how he was so desperate that he once offered to pay Mildred and Gertrude to go out with him. And then there was his announcement that he was going to model in the next *Advert*, which was out now—without him in it. He bit his fist as he cringed with shame. And there were all the warnings and tellings off, and the various other strange stories circulating about him in the shop: him and Brummell, the mannequin, in the stock room for instance. He didn't know whether the one about him and Betty in the Conservatory would mitigate the damage, or merely reinforce the image of him as a loosed madman with Priapus in his trousers.

He sunk a straw into his mug and sucked. The concoction tasted like hot liquid sugar. He pushed it aside and reached inside his blazer, produced his hipflask.

He swigged the rum and soothed his jangling nerves.

He also had to worry about what Henrietta might say to them. It was obvious that his little fashion luminary was blunt to the point of rudeness, but he hoped that she had the sense not to turn her nose up at the brand in front of the team the way she did with him. *But Shukeena, I told Glenn in my interview that Nirah Frazar was a load of old bollocks, and he said it was fine!* Another pang of fear ran through his heart.

God, how stupid he felt, getting himself so deeply in debt for a brand that fashion students didn't take seriously. And nearly getting himself arrested for stealing so much of it. He sipped his rum and stared forlornly into space, shaking his head.

The feeling of rum sloshing around in his empty belly reminded him of the other note he purloined from Jimmy's wallet. The room he strode into was long and narrow, its green walls festooned with football memorabilia that meant nothing to Glenn. However, the passionate cries of the opera singer, which were playing at full blast, were those of the divine Freni, and her rendition of "Si Mi chiamono Mimi" from Puccini's *La Bohème*, performed with the Berliner Philharmoniker. A spellbinding recording that Glenn was wont to play over and over in the flat, full blast on his Nakamichi SoundSpace 1, driving Jimmy and the neighbours potty.

Already he felt more at home here than he did at Hyde Hill.

'What you like!' screamed a voice from behind the counter.

'Pardon?' said Glenn, momentarily discombobulated.

'What you like what you like!' the banshee wailed, waving a ladle at the trays teeming with delicious food that were set out behind the glass counter.

'O, I see,' he said, feasting his eyes on the steaming piles of fresh pasta and pizza slices, the stacks of bread and ham, the lashings of mozzarella and chopped tomatoes. 'What thinkst thou, mine Italian dish?'

'Ah!' she screamed, confused.

'What wouldst thou recommend?'

'Ah! Ah! Ah!'

'Excuse me,' Glenn called to the young help down the counter. 'This lady appears to be having a fit. Please call an ambulance.'

The girl slinked down the counter. 'He's asking what you *recommend*, Rosa,' she said slowly and loudly in the old girl's ear. Her eyes grew big, and she nodded fervently. She fixed her demented gaze on Glenn. 'Ees all good!' she screamed, with a flail of her arms.

'Thank you, very informative,' Glenn nodded. He ordered spaghetti and meatballs.

She scraped up a dollop of spaghetti and slapped it on a plate with two meatballs.

Glenn cocked his head, looked at her quizzically. 'You surely get more than *two* meatballs?' he laughed.

'Ah!'

'I want *more* meatballs, Rosa. A *lot* more meatballs. Por favor!'

'More!' she screamed. 'You greedy boy! Greedy!'

'Money is no object,' he said egotistically. But when she told him the price his eyes bulged. He gave her Jimmy's twenty. 'Keep the change, mi amore,' he crooned.

She waved him away and shoved his plate into the microwave.

He felt drained, as if he had just finished a meeting with Norman. Sinking down in a chair at the back of the room, he contemplated the pictures of the illustrious patrons who had eaten here, wondering if any of them had had to wrestle a few extra meatballs out of the old ghoul's claws.

The buzz of the room and the thrill of the music lifted him, but as he gazed at the crowded tables of boyfriends and girlfriends, husbands and wives, babies and grandparents, over the empty chair that was sitting across from him, he groaned in the spirit, felt the great waves of envy lapping over him.

But, lo, by the door he spied a newsrack, and at once he was weaving through the busy tables towards it. Scanning the titles, he opted to grab the one the behemoth read, as he always seemed to be clued up on current affairs.

Ping!

She shoved his dish in front of him, on top of the broadsheet that was so broad the page edges dangled over the sides of the table, and he threw himself into his lunch with gusto.

The hard-won meatballs were sumptuous, the flavoursome sauces exploding in his mouth with every bite, and truly he was an outcast from life's feast no longer. He lifted the plate off the table to flick through the paper: PM demands public sector shakeup; social change static; civil liberties risk; Eurosceptic fury; new horror in Middle East—Glenn felt his eyelids growing heavy.

He jumped when he saw a pair of beady peepers hovering over him. 'How doth?' Glenn said hesitantly.

The old man smiled under his bushy white moustache. 'You like a young man?' he said, with an enigmatic waggle of his eyebrows.

Glenn looked at him sideways. 'I beg your pardon?' he said in a faint voice.

'You like a food young man?' he said, smiling warmly.

'O, do I like the *food?*' Glenn said. He ejaculated a jolting, one-syllable laugh. '*Bellissimo!*' he cried, kissing his fingers. 'Caligula himself would be sated!'

The old man gave Glenn a strange look as he shuffled away.

The bon vivant loafed along under the pretty columns and balustraded balconies, revelling in the sensation of a full stomach. He gripped the narrow trunk of a tree and swung himself around it, before continuing on his way. A fat crow scuttling along atop the portico of the Conservatory bar, squawking incessantly, drew his attention to the stairway that led into the underground bar. His brain at once conjured up the image of that other time he tasted the ambrosia, when he had gorged on the lips of Betty shaped by Heaven. He then remembered how he had let her get away, and as the gloom passed over him, and he felt himself plunging into darkness, he heard what sounded like a stack of papers slap against the floor.

'You could've just said no thank you,' complained a gravelly voice.

Glenn looked down and beheld the figure crouched down and picking up his stack of *Big Issues*, strewn over the pavement.

'I beg your pardon?' Glenn said, in a faint voice.

'If you didn't want one, you could've just said no,' said the homeless man, gruffly.

'It was an *accident*,' said Glenn in a hurt voice. 'I was miles away.'

The man rose up with his magazines, glowered horribly at the menswear manager.

'It was deliberate,' he said, 'you twat.'

Glenn's countenance darkened.

'What means this scorn, thou most untoward knave?' he said in a withering tone. 'Avaunt, thou public commoner, and get thee gone; I cannot brook thy sight!'

'Do you think you're better than me?'

Glenn laughed in the man's face.

Then, he walked away.

'Let's hope you never end up homeless, our kid,' said the man, calling after him. 'I'll remember you. The lad who dresses like a queer.'

That one brought Glenn to an abrupt halt. Not only did the remark have the ring of a threat, but it was also a slur and exceedingly ill-timed, coming on a day when he was already regretting all the years of investment in Nirah Frazar, and worrying if today's headcomb/boxy grey vintage wool suit combination even worked as a look.

Rage at once blitzed his brain and nerves, made balls of his fists.

'You spoke heart-wounding words, Iros,' Glenn growled darkly, turning round with his fist cocked. 'You shall be answered.'

The man made as if to lunge at Glenn, who promptly screamed and reeled back, fleeing the scene. He sprinted up a long, deserted backstreet, hurdling the binbags piled up against the succession of overflowing dumpsters, as massive steel vents roared at his head, impelling him to run faster. Suddenly, feeling sick from running on a full stomach, his pace began to slow, and he was forced to lunge sideways into a cobbled alleyway—where he fell against the wall gasping.

His heart was thumping as he sank down on some huge paving slabs and stretched his legs over the mossy cobbles, almost dead for breath.

He checked his watch, saw it was 8 p.m. and wondered what time it really was. His pocket watch was at home in his waistcoat. Was it early noon? Late noon? *Still morning?* Well, what did it matter.

It was eerily quiet. He had to strain his ears just to catch the distant drone of Briggate. He wiped the sweat off his forehead and took a great swig from his hipflask.

So, this was where Glenn Harding had ended up. This was the extreme that Jimmy Sandaal had pushed him to. Thoughts of Henrietta's purposeful life only seemed to accentuate his own lack of direction, and, O, how he envied her knowing exactly what she wanted to be—and, more importantly, knowing precisely *how* to make it happen.

Why did he have no direction?

When did he lose his way?

He wondered if Miss Potteridge, his English teacher, still thought about him. She would rave over the short stories he wrote in English lessons, photocopying them and pinning them up in the staff room. And teachers Glenn had never met would walk up to him and compliment his writing, praise his talent like he was some sort of prodigy. Soon he was being booked to write comedies for the morning assembly.

Was that it?

Was *that* his peak?

Being a twelve-year-old literary celebrity?

His face turned pale. He tilted his head back, jiggled the last drops down his throat. He wiped his mouth, felt disappointly steady. His liver was as cool as the shade.

The food must have deprived the tot of its potency, and as he felt inside his pockets, and realised that *once again* he had spent up and left nothing for emergencies, he began to panic. His plastic was dead and he'd mulcted Jimmy's money-bags. He couldn't access the work tills because he was off work, and he couldn't go in on the first day of his annual leave because it would look like he had no life.

A long, impecunious month stretched out before him, and his head sank despondently between his knees. He thought he might just drink himself into stupor at Hyde Hill—but then Jimmy would be back by now, and he had already warned Glenn not to empty his drink rack again. He cried out with a great and exceedingly bitter cry. O Lord! Why standest thou afar off? Why hidest thou thy self in times of trouble?

Father! If thou be willing, remove this cup from me!

Then, as he began to weep, a gleam of bright light blinded him. The sun was peeping over the top of the building, its hot rays shining directly on his face. He felt the hard slab against his mullet and realised he was on his back, staring at the sky.

Suddenly, he heard footsteps—growing louder. He turned his face and looked.

The elderly man passing by glanced into the alleyway and saw him there, sprawled on his back with his hipflask in hand. Glenn at once bolted upright.

'Spare change?' he said hopefully.

Fear flashed athwart the old man's face, and he stared ahead, quickening his pace.

Glenn scrambled to his loafers and lurched unsteadily toward the backstreet, clinging to the small handrail over the steps at the foot of the alley. He peered around the corner and watched the old man go, his eyeballs fixed on the greyhair's pockets.

It was a long backstreet. Deserted, with plenty of doorways. It would be nothing at all to do it. How far was he willing to go?

He wiped his mouth. . . .

Come on, man! Jean Genet would have done it without a second thought.

A pause.

He couldn't do it. He slunk back into his alleyway, head bowed and sober.

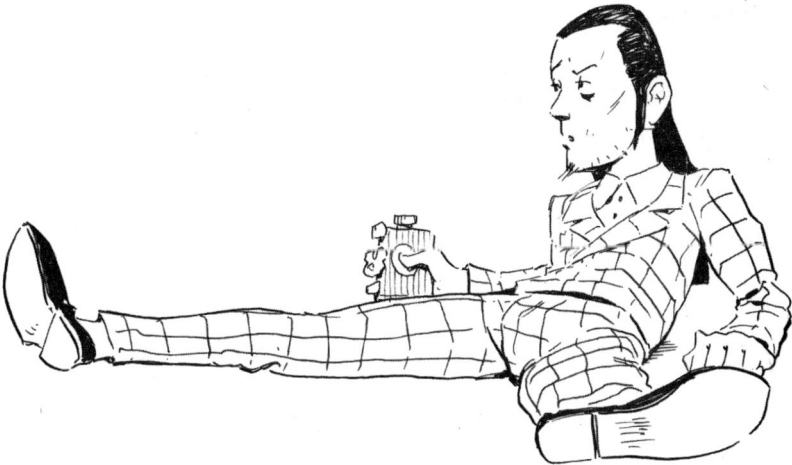

The more he thought about it, sitting there on his slab, the more his going into work on the first day of his annual leave seemed like a great idea. For one, he wanted to see Henrietta again, and it was perfectly reasonable for the man who hired her to come in and check on her on her first day. Also, he needed to raid the cashdesk, and the fact it would create a discrepancy on the till on a day that he was *wasn't* working meant that dipping into it wasn't just a luxury—it was a strategic *necessity*.

He put away his hipflask, and with renewed vigour rose to his feet and dusted down his salmon shirt and old suit. He did a little dance on the cobbles.

'Are you beaten yet, rock?' he giggled. 'I'm not!'

He burst out of the alleyway and marched up the backstreet, humming Puccini.

III.IX

The vision that arrested Glenn's stride was his own countenance mirrored in the reflective finish of the shirt hanging proudly in the shopwindow. Intrigued, he entered, scuttling to the dim recesses of the back room, where the solitary rail of menswear was located. Lifting the garment before his phizog, he beheld a distorted reflection—a skull-like head against the shadowy shop interior and the vivid red and gold backdrop of the arcade. The scene looked like one of Edvard Munch's nightmarish works.

In fact, if Knut Hamsun had set one of his novels in a clothes shop, they would have used this image as the cover.

Glenn became ensnared in a vortex of wordless contemplation. . . .

Suddenly, a second skull-like head materialised beside his. 'Glenn?' it uttered.

Glenn shrieked with such fright he nearly fell over.

'Oh my God, how tense are you!' she laughed.

'Gertrude, you scared me,' he gasped. He returned the peculiar shirt to its rail. 'What are you doing in here?' he asked curiously.

Gertrude lifted a pencil eyebrow.

'*Shopping*. What do you think?'

'O yeah. Fair enough.'

Gertrude, eschewing her usual beehive, had her hair back in a big knot, and wore a black boob tube paired with tiger-print short shorts and black leather sandals, all by Nirah Frazar. The absence of heels brought her eye-level, for the first time ever, below that of Glenn's, somewhat mitigating her intimidating presence.

'Are you off today?' Glenn enquired, almost involuntary.

'Yeah, I'm in tomorrow,' she replied.

He lifted his colossal sunglasses. 'You look so different when you're not in work,' he observed in a tone of wonder.

She lifted her colossal yellow sunglasses by Stella Winerack. 'You don't,' she laughed, looking his outfit up and down. 'Seriously, do you not have casual clothes?'

'I do, but I'm afraid to wear them out because they're all stolen.'

'Oh yeah. Well, maybe you should buy some today, so you don't look so overdressed on your days off!'

'There's no such thing as "overdressed",' Glenn asserted, lowering his sunglasses. He turned to a massive mirror, smoothed down his boxy old suit. 'Casual clothes are for casual people. Some of us, however, prefer to bring a little style and elegance to our small city. . . .' he added egotistically.

'Do you know you've got shit all down your back?' Gertrude asked.

'*Tits*,' Glenn muttered, as he tried to inspect his mossy blazer in the mirror and wipe it down. When she helped him with her free hand it felt like Cupid's love-darts perforating his body. His knee-joints grew slack.

'Thanks,' he mumbled. 'Well, anyway. 'Twas nice seeing thee, Mistress Ogden.'

'Where are you off now?'

'To work.'

'Oh, I need to go in and check the rota,' she said. 'What are you doing?'

'Er. . . . I am *also* going in to check the rota,' he lied.

'You won't be on the rota, Glenn; you're off for the month.'

Pause.

'I can still look at it.'

'Fair enough,' she shrugged. 'Can I come with you?'

Glenn looked at the woman with disbelief.

'Can you *what*?'

III.X

They waltzed into the shop looking like Oscar and Constance Wilde gracing at a soirée, and the sight of them together shook Mildred to her knee-boots.

'Now then, Gerty,' she said bemusedly, her gaze oscillating between Gertrude and the menswear manager. 'Do you need any help today?' She leaned in. 'Like, *psychiatric* help? Seriously. Why are you out with that gimp?'

'Mate, I'm *fine*,' Gertrude replied tersely. 'We just ran into each other in the arcade. And then *he* asked if he could come with *me*,' she added in a low voice.

Gertrude elbowed the peroxide one aside and, accompanied by Glenn, sauntered deeper into the bustling department. They looked as one to beauty, where Ali was standing between the legs of an older lady, applying his magic arts upon her brow.

He glanced up, saw the two of them together and gave such a start his conjuring wand lost control. The lady looked back to see what had startled him. The slashing brow cut across her forehead gave her the most shocked expression in the room.

Glenn, noticing all the attention they were getting, began to revel in it.

At the base of Finite Mountain, they encountered Betty, enveloped in a sweet cloying mist, holding a tester bottle and test strips. She was wearing her gold skull black mini dress again, with the pleated skirt wide and swishing, accentuating those legs that looked like smooth white marble.

'*Whatttt!*' the fair youth squeaked. 'Are you two together?'

'We're *out* together,' Gertrude shrugged. 'So what?'

'But are you an item?' squeaked Betty.

'Oh my God, what is this, Twenty Questions?' Gertrude laughed. 'Get a life!'

'I was just asking,' Betty squeaked, looking injured.

'We just ran into each other in the arcade,' said Gertrude, swiping the tester bottle. 'And then *he* asked if he could come with *me*.' She spritzed herself down, then looked at Betty as if a thought had just occurred to her. 'Oh, that's right; *you* used to be into Glenn, didn't you?'

'No.'

'Sorry, I probably shouldn't have said that, should I? That *Glenn* asked if *he* could come with *me*; don't be jealous, though; nothing's happening.'

Betty looked perplexed. More so than usual. 'I'm not jealous.'

'*Yeah right*,' she said, handing back the tester bottle and strutting off triumphantly.

Glenn, momentarily diverted from the painted goddesses on the shopfloor, looked to the painted gods overhead, remembering that his beloved Henrietta was upstairs.

And his beloved cashdesk.

Making a beeline for the staircase, he collided with what he assumed was a stray child. 'O, sorry Shukeena!' he laughed. 'I didn't see you down there.'

The blazing-eyed Medusa's gaze was cast upward, glaring holes in him.

'Can we talk somewhere *privately*?' the Gorgon said through gritted teeth.

'Nothing would make me happier,' he said sincerely.

The ladieswear manager led him behind the four-leaf Persian screen at the back.

'What's going on between you and Gertrude?' she demanded.

'And what's that to thee?' he replied, grinning as he removed his immense sunglasses. He was quite enjoying the hysteria his encounter with Gertrude had incited. 'Why may not I demand of thine affairs, as well as thou of mine?'

'This isn't a joke, Glenn; do I need to remind you what the employee handbook says about relations between staff?'

'Staff are forbidden from engaging in close personal relationships on pain of *death*,' Glenn recited with asperity. 'I *know*, Shukeena. You told me in no uncertain terms after those silly rumours about Betty and me started flying about.'

'So why are you out with Gertrude if you know better, Glenn? Managers cannot appraise, promote, or manage *anyone* with whom they have, or have had, a personal relationship. It's a conflict of interest!'

'Mate, she's your staff; I'm hardly going to be appraising her any time soon.'

'No. *All* my staff are technically your staff because, thanks to the mess you've made of your department, I have to lend you one every week as cover.'

'And little vantage do I reap thereby; don't think I haven't realised that you send me whoever your lowest seller was the previous week. You're using my floor as a form of punishment!'

'And it's done *wonders* for my sales,' she smiled.

Glenn's face fell. '*Listen*, thou little valiant, great in villainy,' he grunted. 'There is no conflict of interest because Miss Ogden and I are just *friends*. If you could stop thinking about work all the time, just for once, you might have realised it.' He slipped his immense sunglasses back on and smirked. 'Who knows—you might even make some friends of your own?'

Shukeena stood speechless.

'There you are!' said Gertrude, popping her head round the screen. She then saw Shukeena—and the look she was giving her. 'Hi Shukeena,' she added nervously.

'Sorry Gertrude, I didn't mean to stay here prating with my gentle shop-wife,' Glenn smiled. 'Come! Let's away to menswear.'

Shukeena clip clopped out from behind the screen and watched them ascending the stairs. 'See you tomorrow, Gertrude,' she said, with an ominous undertone.

Gertrude shivered in her skimpy clothes, but she soon warmed up, entering the dense steam of the sunless menswear. Dick, wielding the garment steamer, was duly attending to the backlog of Sammi de Hun suits.

When the formalwear supervisor looked up from the white suit he was steaming, and spied Glenn and Gertrude wading together through the turbid mist, his eyes grew big and he made a strangled sound. He stood stock-still, as the wrinkles on the suit seemed to depart the fabric, travel up his arm via the appliance and appear one by one upon his darkly corrugating brow. He then caught a whiff of smoke and heard sizzling.

When he saw the black mark seared into the white fabric he gave a great roar of anguish—which Glenn ignored, being quite accustomed to hearing weird sounds from that side of the shop.

'Are you going to check the rota then?' asked Gertrude.

'The what?' said Glenn. 'O yes! The *rota*. Erm—let's just see who this is first,' he said, eyeing a strange shape approaching, that looked sort of like a cross between Henrietta and Dick. . . .

Henrietta, bearing an obese bundle of garments that had been piling up for weeks on the fitting room rail, emerged from the mist. Upon catching sight of Glenn, she halted abruptly and dropped the load all over the hardwood in front of him.

'Glenn,' she said, elevating her thick eyebrows in surprise. 'I wasn't expecting to see you today.' Her gaze flitted between him and the scantily dressed style advisor.

'Just came in to do a few managerial things,' he said coolly, taking in her outfit with a swift glance. Shukeena had dressed her in the double-breasted wool-twill blazer with big gold skull buttons, matching pressed crease cropped trousers and red slingback crocodile skin pumps. Ali's hand had graced her face with one of his masterworks, and with jewelry being outside the uniform allowance, the symbolic knuckle duster pendant still hung round her neck, plunging into the exposed cleavage.

'How are you finding it?' Glenn asked, his voice suddenly wavering.

Henrietta crouched down, swiftly gathering the clothes. 'What I expected,' she said. She stood up and stared at Gertrude.

'Have we met?' the style advisor asked, looking puzzled.

'Nope,' Henrietta replied.

Glenn promptly introduced them to each other.

'Oh, *you're* the new girl?' said Gertrude, lifting her oversized sunglasses to assess her. Not remotely threatened, she nodded. 'Fine.'

The new girl looked at Glenn and smiled. 'Well, if you need any help—just ask,' she said with mock subservience.

'Actually,' said Gertrude, '*I'm* the style advisor in here, so if he does need any help, he can ask *me*.' She glanced at Henrietta's knuckle duster pendant and frowned. 'But when I'm back, we should definitely talk.'

'I'll look forward to it,' said Henrietta indifferently.

Glenn watched her wiggle off with some regret.

'I know I told you to hire an average girl,' Gertrude whispered, 'but I didn't think you'd take it *that* far. She looks like something out of *The Muppets*.' She glanced over to footwear. 'Lyndsey, hi!' she cried, smiling as she swanned off for a gossip.

Glenn turned and cast longing glances at his sweet fugitive, returning garments to their rightful displays and sections.

She was performing her menial task with the sort of easy equanimity that only those who know they are merely passing through a workplace can pull off. His adoring eyes lingered on her heavenly form, more awesome than ever in her new, snug-fitting attire.

He was about to approach her when suddenly a steam plate was thrust in his face.

'Oi!' Dick panted, waving the steamer he had dragged with him, hissing and spitting. 'What's going on here? You never told me you and Gerty hung out!'

'Dick, please,' Glenn cried, evading the jabbing weapon, 'we're just friends.'

'"Just friends"!' Dick scoffed contemptuously. 'Like any girl can be "just friends" with you. Or boy, for that matter. Don't think I didn't see you following Ali into the utility cupboard that time. You're a creepy man, Harding. A *very* creepy man!'

'Dick, will you please stop pointing that thing in my face?' Glenn snapped, yanking the iron from his hand and hanging it back on the rod. 'It's dangerous!'

'As are *you*,' Dick growled. 'You *know* I like Gerty. I liked her before you even worked here. And it was *me* who got you your job—and this is how you repay me!'

'Dick! On thy life, no more!' Glenn warned with an upraised fist. 'If you must know, we just ran into each other in the arcade. It's completely innocent—'

'I have powers,' blurted Dick.

'*What?*'

'You couldn't get rid of Wilfred without me; but I could have got rid of him without you,' he said with a roguish smile, revealing his sharp yellow teeth. 'And I can get rid of you, too. . . .' he added menacingly.

Glenn goggled his sweaty underling in astonishment mingled with fear.

'Eh?' said Gertrude as they strolled through the busy arcade. 'How?'

'He didn't say,' Glenn replied, a spooked look in his eye. 'Honestly, I don't know what's got into him. Well, I do know; he has a demon and is mad.'

'I think *I* know what's got into him,' she grinned. 'I'll tell you when we sit down. Lyndsey has sent me something I have to show you!'

He halted like a model reaching the end of the runway.

'Sit down?' Glenn choked.

'Do you fancy cockails in Harvey Nics?' she asked, turning to face him.

She was illuminated in the all-enclasping radiance of the sunbeams, and he stood stupefied by the majesty of the vision. An angel of God, descending Jacob's ladder.

'You—you want to go for drinks with *me?*' he said, his voice growing tremulous.

'Yeah,' she shrugged. Her countenance fell abruptly. '*Why?* Don't you want to?'

'Of course I—' But then he remembered his reason for his going into work in the first place. The various skirmishes with Shukeena, Henrietta, and Dick had made him forget all about his till tribute. He cried out in pain.

'What's wrong?' said Gertrude.

'I can't,' Glenn moaned. 'I just remembered. I, er, left my card-case at home.'

'Oh, don't worry about that!' she laughed. 'I've got money.'

Oscar and Constance waltzed into the Harvey Nics bar with their arms entwined.

So, this is what people did with their Saturdays. They just came out and met each other and sat around and talked.

And it was *paradise*. . . .

III.XI

It was only as he stretched himself out the boy realised the scale of the bed he was lying in. His limbs, fully extended, failed to reach the edges. The duvet felt thick but soft, as did the pillows his sconce was enmeshed in. With great effort he lifted his head, saw an immense telescreen affixed to the wall at the foot of the bed. To his right, a door; to his left, a towering black wardrobe. The absence of windows left him clueless as to the time or his location, and when the effort of lifting his head proved too much, he dropped back into the pillows and gazed at the elegant ceiling downlights.

Confused thoughts pounding inside his throbbing skull.

And then suddenly the door was thrown open.

Reader, judge for yourself how Glenn felt as he peeped over the duvet and beheld the shimmering form of Gertrude Ogden emerging from the bathroom, with one towel wrapped round her body and another one wrapped round her head.

As Betty might say: *Whattttt*!

He lay there in awe, looking agog at this impossible plot twist.

'Oh, you're awake then?' she grinned, slinking up to the lofty black wardrobe.

Glenn responded with an unintelligible gurgle.

He coughed to clear his throat. 'Morning,' he said, nervously.

He watched her slide open the wardrobe door and stand before it, stroking her chin contemplatively. The hanging space was deep and in there he could see them all: the draped black satin jersey dress; the high neck, scoop back black cashmere midi dress; the black sequined Barebones bodice and black silk crepe trousers. . . . There was even the legendary gold sequin mini dress, with its daring cut-out detail at front, that she wore to the Christmas do.

All his old enemies, together in one place. He shivered with fear under the duvet.

'Did you sleep well?' he croaked, searchingly.

'With your snoring?' she said. 'Did I heck.'

'I was snoring?' he grimaced.

She whirled round, smiling. '*Yeah*. You sounded like a dying animal. I tried nudging you, kicking you, turning you over. Nothing would shut you up!'

She then needlessly indulged herself in an impression of him. It didn't so much sound like a dying animal as it did the noise Edward the Second must have made when the red-hot spit corkscrewed his nether eye. The thunder of Hell's eternal cry.

He warbled an apology and retreated under the duvet.

In his horror, he must have slipped back into unconsciousness, because when she sat down on the bed and drew back the duvet to look at him, her beehive was erected and her cherubic features doubly beautified by Dirty Look. Her ears and wrists jingled with glimmering gold, and the laughing skull pendant hung from her flawless neck.

The Nirah Frazar character who had chased him around the shopwindow, trying to brain him with the tablet of Commandments, was back—and the effect was terrifying.

'Hello,' he said with a quaver in his voice.

'What are you doing today?' asked the rouge-cheeked youth. Her white teeth were sparkling, and her breath smelt fresh and minty.

'I'll go home, don't worry,' he whimpered, keeping his head turned away, conscious of his crusty eyes and chaotic hair. He hoped the sweet waves of Finite lapping in the air were masking the whiff of his rancid morning breath.

'You don't have to go home if you don't want to,' she said.

'*Whattttt!*'

Her face fell abruptly. 'Don't you want to see me tonight?' she snapped.

'*Yes,*' he cried. 'I do. I definitely do!'

Her glossed waxy-red lips curled in a smile. '*Good.*' She turned from him and slipping on some black suede pointed ankle boots, began fastening the buckles. She wore a black gold skull metallic-weave pencil-style silhouette midi dress with a racy cut down the neckline and right up the side hem. He stared in amazement.

More confused thoughts pounding inside his throbbing skull.

'By the way—I've got like a hundred missed calls from Dick,' she laughed. 'I forgot about the work night out. Oh my God—imagine if he knew about *this*!'

Glenn bolted upright. 'Gerturde, remember what Shukeena said about relationships between staff,' he warned. 'Take heed o' the foul fiend, or you'll get us both fired!'

'Oh, shut up,' she said, grabbing her keys. 'I won't say anything, don't worry.'

She then leaned over, grabbed him by the scraggle—*and kissed him.*

Swooning at the sweet taste of her soft lips, he sprawled back in the upholstered kingsize bed and lay there in a catatonic trance, smiling deliriously at the ceiling.

Odysseus at last sleeps in luxury.

Her walk-in power shower felt like some tropical waterfall, and he must have spent an hour in there luxuriating in the shattering blast of the hot water, lustrating himself with her range of premium toiletries. He forgot to close the door, and returned to a bedchamber enveloped in steam. Wiping the condensation from the mirror, he contemplated his reflection. He applied her cream concealer to disguise his gruesome eyebags, then soused himself in her many delectable fragrances.

He whizzed through the tapes of memory in search of the missing scenes from the previous night but found nothing, not even a single blurry vignette. He cursed his brain for failing to record the all-important material. That useless organ, in its time, must have glutted his thoughts with a million fictive scenes starring Gertrude Ogden; and then, when at last, impossibly, he experienced the real thing. . . . it missed it.

His brain deserved the pain it was in, and it was with great reluctance that he took the painkillers Gertrude left out for him on the bedside table.

Hobbling into the living room in his skimpy hipbriefs, expecting to find a poky cell with some dreary view of Beeston (for that was where her confidential staff file said she lived), what he saw instead made his eyeballs fly out of his face on stalks.

The whole of the far wall was one long window, and through it, not a single building was in view—just a clean, naked blue sky adorned with the sun's broad disk. He rushed up to the glass, wiped the steam off it.

His face fell slack.

Leeds itself was spread out beneath him, so far below it made him feel dizzy. He looked straight down and beheld the River Aire meandering along between his feet.

That's when it hit him, like a thunderbolt from Jupiter. *Gertrude lived in River Tower.* He goggled her apartment with his mouth open. It was clean and spacious, with a black leather sofa, a low glass coffee table furnished by fashion magazines, and a big telescreen fixed to the wall. Cactus plants were dotted around, while the white walls were bare but for the odd picture, thick blocks of colour, bold but simple—Rothko type rubbish, but all right in here. In the far corner there was a compact kitchen, white and sparkly, with a liquor corner that he decided he was not going to explore just yet.

God, he felt far from Hyde Hill up here.

And farther still from the slums of Seacroft.

But how could she afford it? She made even less than him! A quick rifle through her statements stuffed in a kitchen drawer revealed that she couldn't afford it, but her dad could. Reading between the lines in the various Christmas and birthday cards in the same drawer, he learned that Mr Ogden was an absent father who ameliorated the effects of his nonattendance with acts of largesse, such as covering her rent.

Glenn shook his head, blew air. Pangs of love undulated through his bosom, and he forgave her at once for the pretty wrongs she had enacted with Wilfred Woods.

He opened the huge windows, letting the warm summer breeze blow gently through the whole apartment. He stood sternly surveying the dark city.

The pain of those below us here drains the colour from my face for pity.

There was a little dining table by the kitchen, and there he gorged himself on a banquet of milk and honey, quails and manna, and freshly ground coffee, while Debussy serenaded him from the radio.

His metamorphosis from outcast of life's feast to Lord of the Feast was worthy of Ovid, and as he gazed upon the luxurious contents of the apartment, outlined by the awesome expanse of the sky, a grin crossed his scraggle.

As exiles went, there were worse places a man could be engaol'd while he waited the three lagging winters it took for a certain student to graduate.

Topping up his hipflask with vodka from liquor corner, he resolved to do something nice for Gertrude, like taking her out for lunch. His being penniless was of course an impediment to such a gesture, and indeed a humiliating circumstance which he must hide from her at all costs, and rummaging through every drawer, cupboard, and handbag in the apartment in search of money proved futile. (Look, it was her dad's money really, and Glenn fully intended to spend most of it on Gertrude, so what harm was he doing?)

While heaving up her mattress, a small envelope fell out that was filled with colourful pills with funny little faces on them. Down the old grey windowpane wool blazer they went.

Alas, the only hard cash Glenn Harding could access was on menswear, and that meant he would have to go back to the shop and make another attempt on his tills.

He vowed not to let anyone get in his way this time.

216

HUNTER

III.XII

He bounded excitedly up the stairs only to come to a sudden halt at the top. What he saw on his department nearly made him fall back down.

His kingdom restored to its former glory, shining magnificently.

The fixtures and fittings were adorned with the new autumn/winter lines, and the mannequins were no longer naked but rather decked out in the most beauteous livery. The woodbeams were wiped down, the dead lightbulbs in the spotlights replaced, and the hardwood polished. A fine cloud of Finite gave the golden air a glistering sheen.

He spied the massive, mounted moose head over the cashdesk. Its vast horns were sparkling and the thick cobwebs cleaned off its face. It looked more presentable than some of his team members. He gasped as he saw the beast turn its nose up at him.

With shaking hands, he took a long quaff of his hipflask.

He had to swiftly screw it up and shove it back in his blazer when Henrietta emerged suddenly from the labyrinthine displays. When she saw him, she stopped her step.

'Back again?' she observed. She smiled knowingly. 'You can't stay away.'

Glenn gaped at her with wild amazement.

'Where is that *shirt* from?' he gasped, jerking his head at the draped, see-through silk blouse she wore tucked in to her black gold skull trousers, with the slingback crocodile skin pumps. You could see the black bra, and while he would have thought this a fashion faux pas, the fairylike youth was so rich in charms she more than got away with it. The taut, slender body he glimpsed underneath made his entrails squirm. 'It doesn't look like Nirah Frazar,' he choked breathlessly.

'Good,' she said. 'It's Harvey Pandit.'

'*Who?*' He goggled the weird external red label protruding from the side seam.

'You wouldn't know him, he's not in *Advert*,' she said, a grin creeping onto her face. 'A bit like *you*,' she added, knowingly.

'And Shukeena lets you wear it at work?' he said quickly, changing the subject.

'She's not in today.'

'O, right.' He frowned. 'Wait, if Shukeena's not in today, who's managing?'

'Glenn,' she said shortly, 'I've got a customer waiting—I'll see you later.'

'All right,' he nodded, after-eying the groove of her back through the transparent top as she slipped through the STAFF ONLY door.

A jellied Glenn tottered wobbling through the quiet floor, dazed and gurgling. He soon snapped out of it though, when he beheld the main display: Brummell had been moved from the stock room and stood atop the platform sporting an electric blue wool-twill suit, canary yellow shirt, and paisley print silk cravat that was simply revolting.

The next thing Glenn knew, he was furiously undoing Brummell's belt buckle.

'Do you need any help there, sir?' said a voice that spoke in a stately accent.

'Yes,' Glenn grunted. 'You get the left leg, I'll get the right, and on my word—pull; don't worry about ripping the fabric.'

'Would you like to try on a pair of these trousers, sir?' the voice enquired.

'Eh?' Glenn's face registered his disgust. '*No.*'

'Right, well in that case, I must ask you to stop—customers are discouraged from disturbing the displays for reasons of health and safety, you see—'

'*Customers?*' Glenn ejaculated. He turned sternly on the man, who was smiling at him in kind reproof. 'I am not a customer, thou beef-witted fool; I am the *manager.*'

Smelling the drink on Glenn's breath, the man lifted his head and looked down his nose at him. 'Er, no, sir;' he replied, 'I think you'll find that *I'm* the manager.'

Glenn lifted his humongous sunglasses, knitted his finely plucked brows.

'What? No you're not, mate,' he replied, raising his voice. '*I'm* the manager.'

'No, *I'm* the manager.'

'No, *I'm* the manager!'

'No, *I'm* the manager—' Suddenly, the man stepped back from Glenn, who was right in his face. 'Oh, wait,' he laughed. 'You must be Glenn Harding?'

'Ay, geek, that is my name.'

'Right!' he said. 'Sorry! Glenn—*hello*. I'm Sylvanus; I'm covering your holiday.'

'Covering?' said Glenn suspiciously. He ignored the man's outstretched hand.

The mustachio'd cover manager had black, slicked back hair and a goatbeard flecked with ginger. His face was clean and his physique trim, and he was sporting the same ghastly outfit Brummell was wearing. When Glenn looked down and beheld the bright orange perforated rubber clogs, he could not repress his shudder. He had never seen a more ridiculous example of Nirah Frazar Man (outside of his old self), and standing in the presence of such a specimen he could see now why fashion students like Henrietta didn't take the brand seriously.

'Yes, covering,' said Sylvanus, withdrawing his hand but holding his smile. 'Anyway. A pleasure to meet you.'

Glenn grunted in reply. He then lowered his humongous sunglasses.

'By the way, I hope I haven't stepped on any toes with my tidy up?' Sylvanus asked. 'I just couldn't work with the floor in that state. It looked like the Third Battle of Ypres in here!' he chuckled.

'The *what?*'

'The Third Battle of Ypres. It was a particularly sticky battle in—'

'Yes! I know perfectly well what the Third Battle of Ypres is!' he barked. 'I just can't believe that anyone would employ such a recondite reference on a shopfloor in *Leeds*. Why, man, thy pretensions are outrageous!'

The cover manager held his polite smile as he flushed a violent crimson.

'Right. Well thanks for the feedback, mate; I'll bear it in mind,' Sylvanus nodded, as his eyes narrowed darkly. 'Oh, and by the way,

Glenn, while I have you here, there was one other thing I wanted to ask: it seems like a lot of the pound coins in your float have been swapped with buttons; do you have any idea how that could be happening?'

'I'm sorry, but I can't be expected to answer questions while I'm on my holiday,' Glenn said with a dismissive flick of his hand, as he quickly scurried off.

'Oh. Hello,' said a strangely subdued Dick, looking up from the suit he was ironing, as Glenn came groping through the steam. 'Hey listen, about yesterday. I'm sorry. I've spoken to Gerty, and I realise now you were telling the truth. There's nothing going on between the two of you—'

'Dick, Dick, Dick,' Glenn interrupted. '*Peace*—or I shall cut out your tongue. Now, that bold fellow yonder: who is he, and what the hell is he doing on my shopfloor?'

'Who, Sylvanus? He's from the Manchester branch, geez. He's your cover manager. Sylvanus Burras-Peake's his full name.'

'Burras-Peake,' Glenn gasped, peering back over his shoulder. The cover manager was doing Brummell's belt back up. 'You mean he's got a double-barrelled surname?'

'Yeah!' Dick chuckled. 'Quite cool, isn't it? Brings a bit of *class* to the floor.'

'I'm going to pretend you didn't say that,' Glenn growled.

'What's up with you today? Oh, look, if this is about the work night out last night, it was totally unplanned, I swear! Plus, Glasshouse isn't really your scene—'

'Mr Zabledore, I don't give a tinker's curse about your stupid work night out; just tell me whether that smiling rogue is going to be training Henrietta? Speak truly!'

'Well obviously he's going to be training her, geez. That's his job.'

And God raised up another adversary against Glenn.

'Do you not like him or something?' said Dick. 'Geez, he's a nice guy! And he's got such a *way* with people; you should see the birds when they're around him—he's got them giggling like schoolgirls. Even Shukeena! I mean, I didn't even think she was into blokes, until I saw the way she is around *him*. I tell you what, I'm glad he's going to be tied up with Henrietta all month, because I would *not* want a handsome, charismatic guy like that spending time with Gerty. . . .

'Do you know,' Dick continued, 'that he even helped me? Yeah, I've had a bit of a rough twenty-four hours, and I *really* needed the support of my manager—'

Glenn turned and quickly scurried off.

III.XIII

O, full of careful business were his looks, as he sat at a table by the balcony, in the Harvey Nichols restaurant, revolving in his brain thoughts of Henrietta and that see-through top working their spell on Sylvanus—while that scoundrel's caddish charms worked their spell on her. He grimaced, as sickly green fear tugged at his entrails.

Also, he had forgot to tax the treasury, *again*—so Gertrude had to take him out, *again*.

'So apparently, yeah, Ali was in the staff room, taking a picture of himself on his Kumquat,' she was saying, her fork poking at her salad starter, 'when Mildred walks in and shoves her Kumquat in front of his face, and he says, "You twat, I had my eyes just right," and she says, "Your eyes will never be right after you watch this".'

'Okay,' said Glenn in a vacant monotone.

'So she Forkbeards him the video, and then he shows it to Betty (your friend), but Shukeena catches them, and she forces Ali to play it for her; but she doesn't know what she's looking at, she thinks it's like bread being kneaded or something.'

'Okay,' said Glenn in a vacant monotone.

'And then Dick comes back off his break, and he's excited about the night out, and he sees Ali and says, "Hey, Ali, it's the big one!" and Ali says, "It wasn't when I saw it"—and everyone pisses themselves. Except Dick, who doesn't get it.'

Glenn sipped his Paint the Town Pink. 'Okay,' he said in a vacant monotone.

'So Shukeena plays it to Norman in the office, and she goes, "What do you think?" and he goes, "Well, what can I say? The man's damn good—she's obviously enjoying it," and Shukeena goes, "*No!* I mean what do you think of staff sharing videos—'

'Wait,' Glenn interjected, looking quizzically at her. 'How would you know what Shukeena and Norman were saying to each other in private, in the office?'

Gertrude lifted a pencil eyebrow. 'Because she *told* me. Duh.'

'She *told* you? What, you mean you have actual conversations with Shukeena?'

'Of course I have actual conversations with Shukeena. Why wouldn't I?'

'Because, Gertrude, she is the Queen of Hell, the face of Dis, the Empress of the Universe of Pain—and no love toward others in that corpulent bosom sits! Do you not remember yesterday? She was angry at you just for walking in the shop with me.'

'Oh, she's fine now. I told her that we just ran into each other. She's my friend!'

Glenn started violently. 'She's your *what?*' he said in a faint voice.

'My *friend*. Why? What's wrong with that?' she said. 'I like Shukeena.'

Glenn excused himself and went to the toilet, where he swigged from his hipflask. 'Do you speak to her every day?' he enquired, teetering back to his seat.

Her countenance fell abruptly. 'Well, I was in the middle of a story but all right,' she huffed, 'let's just talk about what *you* want to talk about.'

'Great, thank you,' Glenn said. He leaned forward, turned a sidelong glance at her. 'Does Shukeena ever tell you things that *I* say to her?' he probed

'She tells me *everything* you say to her,' she said with a knowing look.

'O no.'

'Oh *yes*. And I'm surprised you've never asked her out. You obviously fancy her.'

'Gertrude!' he cried. 'I hardly think that Shukeena wants *me* to ask her out,' he said, laughing. His face fell abruptly. 'Does she?'

'I don't know, Glenn. Would you like me to ask her for you?'

'*No.*'

'Why not? She is single. You and her would make a good looking couple, actually. You should go for it.'

He eyed the woman suspiciously. He didn't understand quite what she was doing, but he could sense himself walking into something that would make the Third Battle of Ypres look tame by comparison. (Whatever the Third Battle of Ypres was.) He drew back. 'Thank you, Gertrude, that's very considerate of you, but if you want to play matchmaker I'm afraid thou art too late. You see, I've already met someone.'

'Oh really? Who's that then?'

'A style advisor,' he said suavely.

'A style advisor?' she said, nodding. 'And what's she like then?'

'What's she like?'

'Yeah. Describe her to me.'

Glenn had to dip into the *Sonnets*. It did the trick. Let the Immortal One sue him.

'Oh, shut up,' she said, smiling as she looked down at her food, blushing gaudy red. 'Get another drink,' she told him.

'Er—remember, I haven't gone home to get my card yet,' he said delicately.

'I *know*. You get it. I'll pay.'

He gazed in wonder upon the girl, who had inherited all of her father's generosity.

Neither now nor later did Wilde allow his uncertain future to interfere with his present enjoyments. Glenn signaled to the waiter and ordered another cocktail.

III.XIV

He stood sternly in his headcomb and skimpy hipbriefs, cooling himself with his oriental hand fan. His eyes rambled the sprawling penumbra of black and red rooftops, located the arcade. They settled on what he was reasonably certain was the roof of the shop.

He could feel every nerve and fibre in his body pulling him towards it.

'You tread upon my patience and shopfloor, Mr Burras-Peake,' he intoned gravely. 'O, let the hours be short, till fields and blows and groans applaud our sport.'

He then turned his pert buttocks on the city and pranced over to the dining table, where he sat down in front of Gertrude's instrument. He cracked his knuckles and wiggled his long, pianist's fingers. He looked out at the endearingly empty sky, then turned his attention to the blank page on the little curved screen before him.

And for this cause awhile we must neglect our holy purpose to Jerusalem.

He took a deep breath and began hammering at the keys. After a short, intense burst of activity he leaned back and gasped. He reviewed the fruits of his labour:

EXT. LEEDS. DAY.

He looked to the clock: ten a.m. He twirled his scraggle meditatively, tried to think of an opening line. He looked to the clock again: eleven a.m.

In the kitchen he poured himself a cup of sack.

A difficult business, this writing. And yet the twelve-year-old version of him had excelled at it! Surely that astounding talent was still somewhere inside of him, lying dormant. But how to rouse it?

He sank down on the sofa, chugged his mug thoughtfully. *I have little or no inspiration or imagination and work very laboriously. Chance furnishes me with what I need.* So said James Joyce. And if a man like that could struggle, then Glenn had no reason to be discouraged by his slight muse. He sloshed back some more sack, gazed at the awesome sky.

He waited patiently for Chance to furnish him with some material.

'Why are you writing a script?' she asked abruptly, over the jabbering telescreen.

He discovered himself sat up in bed, resting his throbbing skull against the huge grey upholstered headboard, while Gertrude with her hair down was all entwined with him under the duvet, gazing up at him through those gigantically beautiful brown eyes.

'Because I want to do more with my life than work in a clothes shop in Leeds,' he sighed, after a moment's thought.

'*Yeah*,' she said. '*I* want to do more with my life than work in a clothes shop in Leeds, too.' She squeezed him tightly. 'Let's go somewhere and do something completely different!' she said with sudden giddiness.

'Patience, thou young and rose-lipt cherubin,' Glenn chuckled. 'All things in time. First things first: what news from the field today? Anything interesting happen?'

'Dick told me that you fancy Henrietta, and that's the only reason you hired her.' She stared upward at him. 'Is that interesting?'

'No, Dick playing mind games with you is *not* interesting,' he stated flatly. He began stroking her hair with his big, arachnid hand. 'He's just trying to find out whether something happened between us that night you were a no-show at his drinks.'

'Glenn, something has happened between us every night for the last fortnight now.'

'Heard you nothing of that mad fellow of Manchester? My usurper?'

'You mean Sylvanus? No, not really. Although I think he's disappointed with Dick's work. It's like he can't sell anymore, since everyone saw that video. He's proper depressed, and it's affecting menswear's figures.'

'Good.'

'*Glenn!*'

'Is Sylvanus still training Henrietta?' he asked in a casual tone.

'Aw, you always ask about Henrietta. It's so nice you worry about her, even when you're off work.' She squeezed him tightly. 'So there is a warm heart hiding somewhere in that cold, loveless chest!'

'But seriously, is he still training her? Do they spend a lot of time together?'

'They're together all day; you know what training's like. It seems to be going well, they're always laughing. I think they've, like, bonded over the fact they're both new.'

'That's great news,' he warbled.

'I wonder if they're shagging yet?' she said. 'Oh my God—wouldn't it be dead weird if they were in bed together right now, talking about *us*? Ha, ha, ha!'

Glenn's face turned pale.

He emerged from the bathroom a moment later with a clammy sweat on all his limbs. Gertrude was sitting up in bed, gaping at him in wonder. 'Are you all right, babe?' she said anxiously. 'You just shot off!'

'Sorry,' he said breathlessly, slipping back under the duvet with her. 'I think all that wine may have caught up with me; I suddenly felt a bit sick, that's all.'

'Aw, my poor piss head,' she smiled, coiling her limbs round his person again. She began smothering his face with kisses. 'Are you all right now?' she asked.

'Never felt better!' he replied, staring up at the ceiling downlights with an anxious expression.

III.XV

ENTER Len Farthing.

Glenn stared at the blank page. His fingers hovered over the keys in anticipation of what his protagonist would do next. He checked the time on his gold moonstone-studded watch, now ticking again thanks to Gertrude getting it fixed for him. Twelve o'clock. He had been waiting for Len Farthing to spring into action for three hours now, but all he seemed capable of doing was standing stock-still like a mannequin.

Could Len check the time? That wasn't very interesting.

Glenn checked the time. One o'clock.

His Kumquat whistled. She had also topped up his gizmo, and now all day long he was subjected to a steady stream of written ambassages from her. No risk of a slight muse or scanty output with that girl. Her daily word count surpassed his.

Glenn swigged from the chunky bottle of mezcal he had asked Gertrude to get him. He felt his body convulse, and he let out a long, beastly growl. Come now, O Brigantia! Come now, Geoffrey Chaucer! O Muses, O masters of the highest school, Dante, Henrietta Payne, and Miss Potteridge too! Pass not away, I pray thee, from thy servant, but rather sing in him the story of these non-adventures and lift them into some great song of gain. Don't let everything be such a struggle for me.

He looked back to the blank page with an expression of supreme determination.

'Evening, babe!' said Gertrude, dumping the keys on the sideboard.

Glenn was lying helpless on the pinewood, in his skimpy hipbriefs, staring at the ceiling with a glazed look in his eyes. He had an empty bottle of mezcal in his hand.

'Hello,' he answered, in a vacant monotone.

'I've got a present for you,' she said, as she clip clopped his way.

'Mezcal?' he said hopefully. His heart sank when he saw the Nirah Frazar bag.

'No,' she said, standing over him smiling. She was wearing a stunning strapless black jumpsuit from the gold skull line. 'The knitwear came today,' she said elatedly, pulling an item out of the large gold bag. 'What do you think of *this*?'

Pause.

'Shall a man put on a woman's garment?' he asked incredulously.

'It's *not* a woman's garment,' she said sternly. 'It's a knee-length *polo*.'

He looked up through blurry eyes at the piece. It was a polo, all right, but lurid scarlet and spangled with sequins. It was so long the hem almost touched the floor.

Glenn didn't know what the turnaround was between death and the crematorium, but if he wore this out on the streets of Leeds he would soon find out. It was dangerous.

'Have you any eyes?' he sneered. 'I don't wish to wear *any* Nirah Frazar, least of all an item that was so obviously misplaced on men's. O fatal shirt, alas, alas I say.'

'Nirah Frazar's boyfriend was just snapped wearing this in Milan!' she flared.

He glared upward at the woman.

'And so what if it is a dress? That weird singer you like wears dresses.'

'Eh? Who?'

'You know, that singer. You're always playing his albums, doing my head in.'

'O, you mean David Bowie.'

'That's him! He can wear dresses, but you can't?'

'Yeah, I'm not sure I'm as cool as David Bowie,' Glenn said with a wry smile. His face turned serious. '*Yet.*'

'So what do you like then, if you've gone off Nirah Frazar?' she sighed, dropping the dress back in the bag. 'Grotty old suits from a hundred years ago that stink of shit?'

'Those,' he nodded. 'And Harvey Pandit.'

'Who?'

'You wouldn't know him, he's not in *Advert*. Which, by the way, was the reason why I opted *not* to model in that pabulum publication,' he claimed with a straight face.

'Fine,' she said with annoyance. 'Oh, and by the way; you know how you want interesting stories from the shop? Well, Dick told me an interesting one about you today. A *very* interesting one.'

Glenn was lying prostrate in bed, his face buried in pillows, as Gertrude in her silk nightie sat on top of him, massaging his back and shoulders with aromatic body oil.

'Go on,' he said sleepily. His eyes were closed.

'He told me you felt up Ali in the utility cupboard.'

Glenn's eyes abruptly opened.

He explained that he had been in the utility cupboard seeking *style advice* from Ali—although in truth that was only marginally less embarrassing than feeling him up.

'Ah, it's all right, I believe you,' she said. 'To be honest, I think Dick was just trying it on cos of what happened earlier: so he'd been trying to get a mannequin into this shirt right, but the arms were stiff and he got all red in the face, sweating and grunting and that, going, "Come on, come on—nearly there", and so Lyndsey said, "Uh oh, he's at it again", and Mildred said, "Quick, someone give him a camera phone!" and everyone pissed themselves laughing.'

'Some good dialogue there,' said Glenn, thinking out loud.

'So Dick goes mental, pulls the arm off the mannequin and starts attacking it with it. But then Sylvanus jumps in and calms him down, and says, "The best seller in the north is better than this." He tells him he shouldn't let people get to him, that he had nothing to be ashamed of, and that they were all just jealous of him. He said, "Dick, all that video shows is that it isn't just *customers* you're great at servicing".'

'That's a brilliant line,' Glenn warbled.

'Anyway, Dick likes that idea and he's been a lot better since. Oh, and I think they're going to get revenge on Lyndsey somehow.'

'This is shaping up to be a roaring second act,' Glenn exclaimed enviously. 'They've got an "A" and "B" storyline in play—both of them solid.' He gazed into his thoughts. 'I wonder what the denouement will be?'

He yelped as he felt her nails sink into his flesh.

'Sometimes I think you're more interested in that shop than you are in *me!*' she shouted at his mullet.

'I cannot conceive you?' Glenn cried, looking back with a startled expression.

'You're always asking about Henrietta, and Shukeena, and Sylvanus, and Dick—you never ask me how *I* am!' she said tearfully.

'But I already *know* how you are, my little rose-bud—I *live* with you,' he explained in gentle tones. 'I ask questions about those shop characters merely as research for my writing.'

'Well, you seem more interested in your writing than you are in me,' she sulked.

'Gertrude, I am *not* more interested in my writing than I am in you; I am interested in you both *equally*.'

As Gertrude bawled in the bathroom, Glenn stared at the locked door, his belly twisting. Ye gads, was history repeating? He never set out to make anyone miserable, but somehow, he always did.

He had always been drawn to ill-fated romances in novels, but living one was a different matter entirely.

Still though, he couldn't deny the utility: these storms were great for his writing—even if they were nightmarish for his life.

O, Emily Brontë. If you were alive, you would understand Glenn Harding!

III.XVI

'Vat the bloody hell have you done. Oh my God. Vat have you done to him.'

'I've let him know where he stands.'

'Vat.'

'He's been hitting on you all day and I'll be damned if I stand by and take it.'

'Vat are you talking about. Did Rick not tell you ze reason vee split up.'

'Whatever the reason was, the guy blatantly wants back in.'

'Heez gay.'

'You what.'

'Heez gay. Heez just broken up viv his boyfriend. I thought you knew.'

'Boyfriend.'

'Heez a friend, you fool. Nothing more. And now you've. Pause. Zis is madness.'

'I'm sorry. I didn't know. Catherine.'

'No. Don't touch me. Get avay from me.'

'James backs away, realising his folly. Catherine. Catherine. Please, Catherine.'

'Just go.'

'But.'

'Go.'

'He turns despondently from the chaotic scene as pigeons scatter wildly into flight. They ascend high above the square. Above a scene of the upmost tragedy. . . . *Fin*.'

The boy looked up from his script with a tear in his eye.

A sudden burst of applause made him throw the papers into the air and shriek.

The girl, sitting on the bench, saw Glenn clapping his hands behind the thick bushes, under the shadow of an enormous tree, and gave a moan of horror.

'Bravo!' Glenn gushed, still clapping. 'O thou star-cross'd lovers, take a bow!'

'What are you doing in the *bushes!*' spluttered the gangly, awkward boy, whose gaunt phizog was turning as red as his hair.

'Enjoying the show,' Glenn answered amiably, as he stepped out from the foliage onto the grass, resplendent in his silk salmon shirt and antique suit, with stray leaves and petals resting on his headcomb. Muck blotted his loafers.

'You vere spying on us from ze *bushes?*' said the rather hard-faced girl, aghast.

'Not spying. *Observing,*' Glenn clarified. 'You see, I am a writer too.'

'A *writer?*' said the girl. She and the awkward boy exchanged a glance.

Freckles gave a sullen huff, crouching down to gather up his pages strewn across the pavement. His whole head had flushed a violent crimson.

'That's right,' Glenn nodded. 'And may I say, from one artist to another, that was a *beautiful* scene. O! Heminges and Condell would envy such verisimilitude!'

'You like my script?' the boy stammered, his eyes fixed to the ground.

'O, not at all,' Glenn laughed. 'I meant the clear sky, the breeze rustling the leaves. The pleasing smell of the wet grass. And the sight of two people alone in such a secluded spot, as the timorous inaction of the boy who brought the girl here expresses some eternal truth about the impotence of the socially inadequate male. 'Tis no mean feat to arouse pity in your audience; and you, sir, achieved it tenfold!'

Glenn brushed the twigs and leaves off himself.

'As for the script, methinks the writer should have his fingers broken,' he added.

'Come on, Annie,' the awkward boy grunted. 'Let's finish this at mine.'

'Can I come with you?' asked the flâneur and critic hopefully.

He watched the pair sloping off down the path, the boy walking stiffly in his drab jacket and ill-fitting jeans, the girl peering back curiously at him over her shoulder.

'It's never going to happen without my help, mate,' Glenn called after him. 'I have mezcal!' he added, waving his hipflask in the air. 'Please? I am much alone.'

Glenn watched them pass through the gates and dissolve into the elegant Georgian buildings enclosing the sleepy square.

Sighing, he unscrewed the hipflask, smelt the contents lovingly. So you want to be a writer, my friend? Well, you crossed paths with the great Len Farthing, and you chose to leave him behind. You abandoned him when he needed you—and he will *never* forgive you for it.

One day you will study his words and, hopefully, learn how to write. And dress.

'So you know how Lyndsey loves his shoes, right? He's dead proud of his section?' (Gertrude was in full flow.) 'Well, cos Dick's sales have been down, Sylvanus came up with this idea of setting the shoes out in a path that leads to Dick's section, like, *Follow your feet to formalwear*; so Sylvanus told him he could take as many shoes as he wanted. Well obviously, Dick just raided it, and when Lyndsey came back and saw all his empty shelves he turned white as a sheet and screamed, "I'M NAKED!"'

Glenn was spread-eagled on the pinewood, in only his hipbriefs.

'So,' he croaked, 'this storyline that began with the footwear supervisor circulating a video of Dick naked, ended with him losing all his shoes and crying, "*I'm naked*"?'

'Yeah!' she laughed, taking off her shoes. 'Kinda weird when you think about it.'

Glenn lifted his throbbing head, stared incredulously at her.

'"Weird"?' he said. 'No, it's not "weird", Gertrude; it's the resolution. It's an utterly *perfect* reversal of fortune.' He sat up. 'It's *textbook*,' he said, almost with awe.

'It was proper funny,' she said absently, slipping off her jumpsuit.

Glenn lifted up his voice and wept.

'This is good as well though!' she insisted. She was now sitting in front of the instrument in her leopard print silk robe, drying her hair with a towel. 'I like it.'

'It's no Dick and Lyndsey, with their five act, four hook drama, complete with snappy dialogue and working one-liners,' he sulked. 'Why the hell can't they put on a show like that when *I'm* at work? I could use the raw material!' he shouted at the ceiling.

'Glenn, seriously; stop it with the shouting. The neighbours have complained to the building managers.'

'Sorry.'

Gertrude resumed reading his script. 'So who's this annoying bimbo, Ermentrude, meant to be?' she asked.

'No one,' he replied. 'I've told you, it's all made up.'

'But it's not all made up though, is it. Len Farthing is obviously you.'

'Len is not me!' he cried, laughing. 'He's more of a Homeric, Virgilian type hero. But with the good looks of Absalom, and the wisdom of Abraham.' He twirled his scraggle meditatively. 'Actually, maybe he is me?'

'And why do Len and Rick care so much that Ermentrude got with Wilbur? I mean, why would *anyone* care what she does? She's an absolute *bitch.*'

'The art of our necessities is strange, that can make vile things precious,' he said with an air of profundity. 'To be honest, I was hoping *you* could give *me* some insight, what with your superior understanding of these things the gods call *humans.*'

'Oh, babe, please; not more questions. I can't answer them. You're the one writing it; you tell me.'

'So you have no insight as to what Shukira might to do when she finds out Len has been switching coins in his float for buttons?' he asked hopefully.

'No! How would I know? To be honest, I don't even get it. I mean I think it's good and that, because *you* wrote it and I love you, but it's not really my thing.'

Glenn sat up. 'Sorry,' he smirked, peering over the sofa backrest. 'Did you say that *art* isn't your thing?'

'Not *art*. You know what I mean. I'm not into this stuff. Writing and that. Fiction. I'd rather talk about *us*, than some made up story that never happened.'

'"Never happened?"' Glenn took a swig of his mezcal, shuddered slightly. 'Gertrude, writing is the dramatic *imitation* of action and life,' he belched.

'Oh, so it *is* real now? It's not fiction after all?' she said, her voice rising.

'It's both! It's truth dressed up as fiction. To quote Paul Gauguin, "Because your canvas is smaller than nature, you have to use a greener green. That is the truth of falsehood". And yes, all right, he was talking about painting, but you can apply what he said to writing. A writer is a portrait-painter whose *words* are his brush strokes.'

'Oh, shut up,' she groaned, rolling her eyes. '*Geek.*'

Glenn choked.

With that one word, he found himself abruptly transported back to the school bus, where rolled up tickets were being pelted at his head while he was sat minding his own business, trying to read his book. When he turned his shocking, acne-riddled face, and saw the projectiles were being thrown from the back seat by girls who looked like Gertrude, for the amusement of ruffian boys who looked like Wilfred, he felt his veins sizzle with hate.

'I am *not* a "geek",' he snarled. 'I am a man with an enquiring mind who enjoys *learning*. Here! Let me use an analogy that even your feeble brain can comprehend: Fiction is nonfiction in the same way that a face with makeup on it is still a face. An artist employs artifice to make real events from his life dramatic, just as you employ paint to make yourself look less ugly.'

A pause.

'Where are you going now? O, Gerty, do not flee in tears again! I *really* need to know what you think's happening between Sylvester and Helena!'

As she lay howling in the bedroom, the red mist lifted, and he felt instant remorse. Heathcliff slumped back on the sofa and emitted a weary sigh.

He then swigged the remnants of his hell-broth, convulsed violently and growled.

III.XVII

LEN: Because I want to do more with my life than work in a clothes shop in Leeds.

Gertrude had bought a printer, and now he could hold his opus in his hands, read evocative phrases like this on the physical page and positively delectate in them.

He sipped his Irish coffee, read the line again. *Because I want to do more with my life than work in a clothes shop in Leeds*. He bit his fist and his eyes began to mist.

And God saw everything that he had made, and, behold, it was good. It was very good.

Suddenly, our humble rhymer heard footsteps in the corridor.

They were feet that shook the solid ground of his apartment, the stride of a man of mountainous dimensions, a total monster, and he knew at once it was coming for him. Could the elevators accommodate a Cyclops? It sounded like Polyphemos himself had come to suck the meat off Glenn's bones. Or even worse: Jimmy had come to collect his rent. Hast thou found me here, O mine enemy?

He looked to the door and, sure enough, the steps came to a halt outside it. When the monster rapped on the door, Glenn felt a spasm in his entrails. He held his breath and kept as still as a corpse, as the silence screamed in his ginormous ears.

The monster knocked again, with such force that in fright Glenn dropped his script.

'Hello?' boomed a voice, so deep he felt it reverberating through his very core.

Trembling, Glenn pulled the door ajar, leaving the chain secured, and peeped through the narrow crack. He looked up, and up, and lo, a single eyeball was staring down at him, from under a black beanie visor tilted to one side to obscure a monstrous visage. Chunky gold earrings glistened in his ears, while the navy parka looked vast enough to accommodate an army of Glenn Hardings.

'What do you want?' Glenn demanded with terror in his voice.

Polyphemos looked him up and down. A mass of black hair was

pulled back in an Alice band, while the loosely tied belt of the ladies' leopard-print robe barely concealed his naked body. 'Who are you?' he asked with amazement.

'Who are *you*?' Glenn retorted.

'I asked you first,' said the menacing creature. The walls shook when he spoke.

'Look! Just give me the letter or parcel will you, and be on your way. I'm a very busy man,' Glenn insisted with asperity.

He could smell the booze on Glenn's breath. 'I just came to see a friend,' he said.

'A friend?' Glenn laughed. 'You have no friends here, I assure you!'

'Is Gertrude not in?' he ventured.

Glenn's demeanour turned cold. 'No. I am afraid my *wife* is at work.'

The single eyeball bulged. 'Wife!' the Cyclops gasped. 'Gertrude's *married?*'

'Yes, she's married! So what do you want with her? Thy story quickly!'

'No, nothing! It's just the other week she said she was off today, that's all. I guess I got my days mixed up. . . . But I never knew she was married. Wow!'

The Cyclops shot Glenn an admiring glance. 'You're a lucky guy.'

''Tis true.'

'What is it you do, bruv?' the ogre enquired. 'If you don't mind me asking?'

'I am a writer,' Glenn answered imperiously.

'Coooool. *Very* cool,' Polyphemos nodded. 'I write sometimes.'

'*You* write?' said Glenn dubiously.

'Yeah. I did a writing course at the Playhouse. I was mentored by this dude who writes soaps and plays and shit. My play went down pretty well actually, they were chasing me for a while. I really should get back in touch with them.'

Glenn stared incredulously, mouth agape.

'The Playhouse, you say. . . . Don't move!' He shot off but was back in a moment. 'If you have tears,' he exclaimed, 'prepare to shed them now.'

'What's this?' asked the Cyclops, taking the jumbled mass of papers.

'A script?'

'A "script"?' Glenn mused. 'Well yes, all right, I suppose you *could* call it a "script". But I think a more accurate description would be canticle, or magnum opus, or simply—*epic*,' he proclaimed, with a sweeping gesture of his hands.

'Okay. And you're calling your epic *That's All We Have Left in That Size, Sir?*'

'That's just a working title,' Glenn grimaced.

'Sweet,' Polyphemos chuckled. 'Hey, what's your name bruv? You haven't put it on your script.'

'My name?' Glenn deliberated. 'Nohbdy,' he answered, after a moment's thought.

'Nohbdy?'

'Nohbdy.'

With that, he slammed the door in the Cyclop's face. Suddenly invigorated, he returned to Gertrude's machine and sat pounding the keys like a virtuoso, and lo, like the young Jerry Lee Lewis Nick Tosches described in *Hellfire*, he hammered away at the instrument now standing up, now sitting down, playing with his hands, playing with his feet, interspersing the performance with 360-degree spins, each time his fingers finding the exact place they left off and seamlessly resuming the riff. It was safe to say no writer in history had ever dared to work a keyboard the way Glenn Harding was doing. He was actually sweating!

'We should go on holiday,' said an alien voice abruptly.

Glenn didn't drive, but he could hear the wheels of his inspiration come screeching to a halt—*eeeeek*! He looked up, was startled to find himself wrapped in twilight.

'Huh?' he grunted. He saw Gertrude peering at him over the sofa backrest, outlined by some weird, sun-baked imbeciles jabbering nonsense on the telescreen.

'I said, *we* should go on holiday.'

'O,' he said. He paused a moment. 'Why?'

'Why!' she laughed. 'I don't know, babe; because it would be nice to go somewhere different?'

'All places are alike, and every earth fit for burial,' he intoned solemnly.

Gertrude goggled the blank face of her boyfriend despairingly.

'You never leave Leeds, do you?' she sighed. 'Do you not think that's a bit sad?'

'Socrates never left Athens, and I hardly think it impeded his march to immortality. Do you?'

'I don't know, maybe he should have gone to Barcelona once or twice, then I might actually have heard of the little twat.'

Glenn held the moon's blank gaze. He could feel his spirit stultify, his muscular control momentarily flag. His High Verses had been scaling the Helicon, soaring through Heaven's air, only for this bookless neanderthal to drag him back down to earth to discuss a holiday that really she only wanted to go on because she was bored.

Glen Matlock was right. These people up north really are a bit thick!

'Holidays are a waste of time and money,' Glenn said dismissively. 'They are but a fading tan, a blurring memory—and the only thing you bring back from them is your empty money-bags. And the deep sadness that you're *here*, instead of there.' He swigged his bottle of hell-broth, convulsed slightly. He belched a beastly growl. 'The world is but a thoroughfare of woe—and we are pilgrims passing to and fro!'

Pause.

He peered at the sofa out of the corner of his eye. She was staring at him silently, with her mouth open and her face ashen. She looked almost disturbed.

She switched off the telescreen, rose slowly to her feet, and tottered off to bed.

Alone again, the animation returned to Glenn's fingers, and suddenly he found himself pummeling the keys in the silvery moonglow.

III.XVIII

It was the style advisor's day off and she answered the door in her unstylish lounging attire. Sunshine and the awful sound of the gabbling telescreen filled the corridor.

'I thought I kicked you out?' she said, looking at him with loathing eyes.

'No one's perfect,' Glenn retorted. He then pulled out from behind him the prettiest, most humongous bouquet of flowers Leeds Market had to offer. 'Except me.'

She looked at him with her mouth agape.

With Gertrude snoring in bed, Glenn plonked the prettiest, most humongous bottle of mezcal Harvey Nichols had to offer on the dining table. Liberated from the Leviathan, and the bondage of rent arrears, payday was once again a day to be enjoyed, and with money to burn, and High Verses to craft, our humble rhymer sat down at the machine in his skimpy hipbriefs and cracked his knuckles, wiggled his fingers.

Abruptly, the earth shook.

'I *like* your script,' Polyphemos boomed enthusiastically.

'You do?' Glenn's voice softened.

'Yeah,' he said, pulling the pages from his parka. 'My girlfriend works in retail and the shit you describe is *exactly* what she goes through; I think you've really captured that *world*. Oh, and I love that moron menswear manager who thinks he's smart.'

'Er—'

'All I could think of while reading it was how much it reminded me of Bottom's play in *A Midsummer Night's Dream*. Do you know what I mean? It's just proper mental.'

'Right. Thank you. . . . I think,' Glenn nodded. 'Do I give it to the Playhouse?'

Frowning, the Cyclops shook his head. 'Don't give it to them. This is a TV show.'

'*Is it?*' Glenn said. He looked amazed. 'I thought it was a play?'

'This has TV written all over it. Get it finished and send it to the Writers Room.'

'The *what* room?'

'BBC Writers Room. It's this department at Television Centre where the public can send their scripts. If they like your idea, they make it!'

Glenn snatched his script excitedly and slammed the door in the ogre's face. . . .

'You're dressed like you're going to work?' he belched.

'I'm going *out*,' she replied, with a note of exasperation.

Two Gertrudes were standing over the great TV writer, who was spread-eagled on the pinewood, in his skimpy hipbriefs, drenched in an alcohol sweat and panting fitfully.

'Where to?' he gurgled, squinting at the four alluring legs bestriding him. The twins were decked out in matching black hotpants and short leather jackets.

'How many times have I told you? To *LS1*. It's Sylvanus' leaving drinks.'

'Leaving drinks? But he can't be leaving already? He's only been here a week?'

'He's been here a *month*, you piss head! And I thought you wanted him gone?'

'Well, yes, but. . . . *I* wanted to get rid of him. Or at least have some dramatic final showdown with him. Otherwise, I won't have any material to wrap up my second act!'

'Oh my God, are you still going on about that *script*!?' she shouted.

'Gertrude, get me dressed,' he trilled feebly. 'I believe I can put Hector down!'

'It's not a big one; he's working in our branch tomorrow. We're just doing his leaving drinks tonight because they've booked his train for six tomorrow. He's only going for one—then he's taking Henrietta to the Marriot to discuss her career or something.'

'The Marriot?' he cried. 'That's a hotel!' he yelled furiously.

'I *know* it's a hotel. It's where they put him while he's working here.'

'But how can Sylvanus help her career? She's going to uni in Manchester soon.'

'Oh, is she now?' said Gertrude, peering at him thoughtfully. 'Well, Shukeena doesn't know that. Actually, it's probably why he wants to sneak her off and talk to her in private. He'll be offering her a part-time job in Manchester.'

'He'll be offering her more than that,' Glenn growled. 'Well I won't stand for it! Staff are forbidden from engaging in close personal relationships on pain of *death*,' he said gravely. 'O Brigantia aloft, let him be humbled, brought down at my hands!'

'I swear, you're more interested in that shop than you are in me,' she said bitterly.

'Gertrude! Don't leave me like this!' he spluttered. Rolling over onto his front, moaning, he watched the blurry twins clip clopping to the door. 'I love you?'

The door slamming felt like a broadsword striking his skull—the deathblow. Life and spirit ebbed from the broken boy lying still upon the pinewood, as the shadow of doom shrouded his body, and darkness veiled his eyes.

Fin.

However, the draught merely induced a deep sleep that resembled death, and when he heard a girl whistle his eyes opened. At the sight of the upturned empty bottle of evil, his belly shuddered. Sprawled face downward on the ground, he lifted his throbbing head, looked cockeyed and dribbling to the window whence the whistle had come.

And lo, it was Brigantia herself, benched on a golden cloud in the starry darkness, her sunny locks framing her phosphorescent face! And she was downgazing Glenn with a smile, whistling suggestively at him, but also pointing to his Kumquat:

> Dick tried it on wiv me.
> had 2 tell him abt us.
> hes gone mental.
> do NOT come!!! Xxx

But Henrietta! But Sylvanus! But the BBC! But Dick! But—Brigantia stretched out her hand over the sky, pointed eastward, and said to him, in breathy tones, *Ultimate excellence lies not in winning every battle but in defeating the enemy without ever fighting.*

I see it this way, and the outcome is apparent.

Glenn didn't have a clue how long mezcal had been around, but he knew for a fact that no man in history had ever drunk a whole bottle of the stuff and looked as erect, sturdy and cogent as he did at that moment, only a short time later.

He had in effect drunk himself sober.

Walking in an effortlessly straight line through the whorling fog, he felt like Charles Jackson after the doctors pumped him full of paraldehyde, or like Malcolm Lowry after a month's drying out in Bellevue. Bite back your spleen, Bacchus! For this has been willed where what is willed must be—and is not yours to ask what it may mean!

Never could he have made this crazy charge without some god behind him.

The thunder of war drums split the air, cannon balls fired through the night sky, as he that was dead shimmered through the tumult and combat, o'er a bloody field, along an internal balcony and past a great chandelier, to the spot destiny had assigned him.

'Where is that *shirt* from?' she gasped, goggling the astounding garment tucked into his vintage tapered grey trousers: Vincent van Gogh's "Self-Portrait dedicated to Paul Gauguin" as a boxy silk shirt, vivid green and with the painter's haunted red phizog gigantic to one side of the chunky wooden buttons.

'O, methinks you know, Miss Payne,' he yelled playfully, as he plonked four pints down on the low glass table, sat down beside her on the long banquette. He proudly displayed the external blood-red label protruding from the side seam.

'Harvey Pandit!' she yelled. But her joy quickly morphed into suspicion. 'You didn't just buy this because I said I liked him, did you?'

'No,' he answered sincerely. (For it was Gertrude who had bought it for him, as a surprise, going all the way to Manchester on her day off just to track one down.)

Shukeena must have been in today, because Henrietta was arrayed in her gold skull double-breasted blazer and matching cropped trousers uniform. He regarded her with some awe, and when he glimpsed that little knuckle duster resting atop the cleft of her bosom he felt like Dante in the Purgatorio, after he stared too fixedly at Beatrice's beauty and got blinded by the light.

`He had to blink and quickly shake his head.

'I bet you're glad I saved you from a night in LS1?' Glenn yelled. Glug, glug!

'I am,' she yelled, nodding. Glug, glug, glug!

'That's why I messaged you. I had a feeling you wouldn't be seen dead in there.'

'Full of twats,' she yelled. Then she grinned. 'I bet *you* love it in there.'

'I've never been in,' he answered truthfully. But he chuckled inwardly at the insult. He was flattered that Henrietta thought he could get into LS1. Glug, glug!

'What is it you wanted to talk about?' she yelled.

He explained that he just wanted to know how her first month in the shop had gone.

'It was all right,' she nodded, as his eyes swept the swarty scene, where throngs of men both old and young roamed round and round in the thick smoke, as the floors vibrated with the hypnotic riff of some rolling synth. 'About what I expected.'

'And why did you want us to meet in a gay bar?' he yelled, with a puzzled look.

'Because I like gay bars. They're the only places I don't get pestered by creepy guys.'

'But, just out of interest, it definitely is *guys* that you like?'

'Yes,' she yelled, lifting a thick eyebrow.

He breathed a quiet sigh of relief. 'Okay.'

'Just out of interest, it definitely is *guys* that you like?' she grinned.

'Very funny, Henrietta.'

'Thought I should check, see if I could play matchmaker,' she yelled. 'Sylvanus does fancy you.'

Glug, glu—Glenn nearly spat out his beer. '*What?*' he yelled.

'Yeah, didn't you know? He's gay. He likes you.' Glug, glug! 'Well, no, he doesn't like you; he thinks you're a complete knob. But he does think you're good looking. "The good looking wanker" he calls you.'

Glenn shook his head. 'No.'

'No? What do you mean, no?'

'There should be nothing improbable among the actual incidents,' he yelled. Glug! 'A love rival turning out to be gay is the sort of lazy, hackneyed reversal an AmDram hack would employ. It shows a lack of invention; it's not *believable*.'

'Wait, "love rival"?' she laughed. 'Who are you two meant to be fighting over?'

'Erm—whomever Sylvanus *thinks* I like in the shop and wants to snatch from me,' he prevaricated nimbly. 'Study Aristotle, then you'll see.' Glug, glug! 'A likely impossibility is always preferable to an unconvincing impossibility.'

'It's more believable than you and Betty,' she said disparagingly.

'That actually did happen!' Glenn yelled. He stared at her. 'You don't believe me?'

'Na.'

'Why?'

'One: she's out of your league.' Glug, glug, glug! 'Two: she's in love with Ali.'

Glenn banged his fist on the table with annoyance.

'One: empirically she isn't.' (*'Empirically!'* laughed Henrietta.) Glug, glug! 'Two: you can love and want somebody while having a brief sojourn with somebody else.'

The cherubin screwed her face up. 'Sounds like an "unconvincing impossibility" to me, mate,' she yelled. 'What would Aristotle make of it?'

'He would be fine with it!' Glenn snapped. 'Odysseus, while pining for Penelope, interrupted his *Odyssey* to stay in the sea chambers of Kalypso; so you see, there *is* a literary precedent.' Glug, glug! 'You don't like it, take it up with Homer,' he choked.

'Do you know Betty was crying today?'

'Why, because she got off with me?'

'No. Ali said he wasn't coming to the leaving drinks because he had a date and she just burst into tears. It was so sad. But then everyone started joking about how his date was probably with you, and that sort of lightened the mood.'

He dispelled for the umpteenth time the Ali rumours.

'They're the weirdest group of people I've ever worked with, anyway,' she yelled. 'I'm glad it's my last day.'

Glug, glu—Glenn spat out his beer, all over the table.

'Are you all right?' she yelled, knitting those thick, sensuous brows.

'Excuse me.' He stumbled back, now sweating profusely, and plonked four more pints on the wet table. He sat down heavily beside her. 'Say that again,' he warbled.

She explained that she had done a month, been paid, and was going to Manchester early. 'No point doing another two weeks here, then quitting and not getting paid.'

'But I was hoping *we'd* get to work together,' he yelled. 'At least for a little while.'

'Are *you* going to pay me?' She grinned. 'I've heard you have form in that area.'

He debunked for the umpteenth time, through clenched teeth, that ridiculous story.

'*Whatever*,' she laughed, as he felt the rage beginning to bubble up inside him. He knew that Lord Rumour had been speaking to her, stuffing slanders in her ears, and he realised now what an almighty blunder it had been to introduce her to his work colleagues who all despised him. It was not the sort of unwise decision that sets up a story; it was one that ended a story before it had started.

'So that's why you weren't bothered about seeing Sylvanus tonight? Because you're leaving?' he croaked.

'Yep. Had enough of those Nirah Frazar twats,' she yelled. 'I thought I'd have a change and see this Nirah Frazar twat,' she grinned.

He blinked. 'So you're not even going to work for Nirah Frazar part-time?' he yelled.

'Na. I need to concentrate on my studies,' she yelled. 'Or else I'll end up working for Nirah Frazar *full-time*,' she grinned.

His lip quivered.

'But I will need a job at Christmas, so listen out for any temp gigs in the arcade,' she yelled. 'With those ears, you'll definitely hear—'

'NO MORE OF THIS, FOR GOD'S DEAR DIGNITY!' he screamed.

Upstairs in the unisex pissoir. Enter GLENN, *who paces the long, dimly-lit room gnashing his teeth, lamping phantasmal opponents with his fists. He is foaming at the mouth.* Fie, lifeless picture, cold and senseless stone! Away thou made-up villain! O thou odious Harpy, contenting but the eye alone, avoid! Halting abruptly, he whirled round to face the cracked mirror over the sink. Silhouetted by the starry night, gigantic and silent, he beheld the gashes that bloodily did yawn upon his face. He wiped his mouth, shook his head forlornly. What is this castle call'd that stands hard by? Dick Lionheart himself couldn't take it!

His liver felt hot, his love palpitant. His pounding heart was making van Gogh's face convulse. And the more he gazed at his shirt, a change seemed to come over it. Animation began to swirl in the portrait's eyes, and suddenly it turned, looking straight at him.

Glenn gave a shriek of terror. He blinked and shook his head, but then saw that Vincent's gnarled hand had risen up and was twirling the ginger beard meditatively.

To his amazement, the image then spoke, propounding the following riddle:

Tell me, what creature whilst none the wiser, gave to Glenn a style advisor?

'I thought you'd left!' Henrietta barked at him with annoyance, as he reeled back to the sofa. 'I was about to go.' 'O, sorry, I would hate to have left and deprived you of the opportunity to inflict on me yet more of your scathing satires, Lucilius!' he heard himself shouting. 'Why not take your gibes to LS1? Thy harsh rude tongue will be more musical to that ghastly crew!' he screamed. 'All right, calm down mate,' she laughed. 'Kill her!' his shirt cried. 'Did you do *any* work while you were being paid for that job that *I* got you? Or did you just stand around rubbishing me all day?' 'Glenn, it wasn't *me* talking about you! They were. They talk about you *a lot*. . . .' 'O, so that's why you've hardened your heart to me? Because they've made you hate me?'

'No, quite the opposite, actually. I *like* the fact you don't fit in. . . .'

How quickly Dame Fortune changes sides.

He stared back with wide eyes as Henrietta enwrapped him in her arms and abruptly started kissing him. 'All right, maybe I have missed you a *little* bit,' she reluctantly confessed.

'*Really?*' he slobbered back, in ecstasies. He closed his eyes with pleasure, feeding deliriously on her kisses—and when he looked again, behold, she was actually stretched on her back upon the banquette! No woman nor work of art, no picture or line of literature had ever been more pleasing to his eyes.

He was paralyzed with fear, but she reached out and yanked him down to her lips. 'I love you!' he exclaimed. 'Yeah?' she said, still feasting on his face. 'Marry me!' he slobbered into her mouth. 'You want to *marry* me?' she laughed. 'Yes!' he slobbered, 'I want to go to Manchester with you! And London! I want to work in fashion!' 'Concentrate on this,' she slobbered, while directing his hands under her blazer, where he began reconnoitring the sumless treasures it hid. 'At least go out with me?' he pleaded. She laughed at him again.

He sobbed noiselessly in her mouth. But then:

'*Come upstairs,*' she grunted.

They were about to leap up when Glenn started at the sight of the diminutive figure standing over them. 'Betty!' he blurted. 'What are *you* doing here?'

She replied something inaudible. Amid the thunderclaps crashing in the air, her little voice was drowned in the cacophony.

'*Eh?*' he yelled, rising to his feet and straining his ear to her mouth. He could just about discern her saying she was bored at the leaving drinks and had gone off in search of Ali. Now, Henrietta began hitting him in the leg. He glanced back and saw her, still sitting on the banquette, arms folded and looking up at him with her face screwed up, angrily mouthing something. 'Sit down, sit down,' Glenn instructed Betty. When they sat down, he turned back to his angel. 'What were you saying?' he yelled.

'What are you doing?' Henrietta yelled.

'Talking to Betty,' he yelled, gesturing at her.

'What does she want?' demanded Henrietta.

'I don't know yet!' Glenn yelled. 'I think she's—' Now Betty was tugging at his sleeve, saying something inaudible. 'Hold on a second, Henrietta,' he grimaced. He leaned into Betty, cupping his ear to her mouth.

He could just about hear her asking him whether this was the only gay bar in Leeds.

'No, there's also Queen's Court, Blayd's Bar, the New Penny, the Bridge,' he yelled. His brows knitted. 'I don't know why I know so much about gay bars in Leeds.'

Glenn yelped as he felt a sharp elbow in his ribs. 'What was that for!'

'Aren't you going to tell her to piss off?' Henrietta yelled. 'I thought you were having a night out with me?'

'I *am* having a night out with you!' he cried. 'I'm just dealing with this situation—' Now Betty was gibbering in his ear again. 'One second, Henrietta!'

Turning back to Betty, he could just about lip read her question about which gay bar he thought Ali was most likely to be drinking in. To his horror, he could see her lip beginning to quiver. 'I don't know, Betty,' he yelled, patting her hand apologetically. 'Huh?' It sounded as if she was asking him to come help her find him. Suddenly an arm threaded his and yanked him back toward Henrietta.

'All right, I take back what I said about you two,' Henrietta admitted grudgingly, looking upset. 'Now tell her to go away.'

Glenn couldn't believe what was happening to him. Aristotle certainly wouldn't have believed what was happening to him; but by God, it was happening. And Glenn, ensnared in a Charybdis and Skylla conundrum, torn between appeasing Henrietta and tending to Betty's delicate emotional state, remained paralyzed.

Oddly enough, in the earlier tumult upstairs, in the unisex toilet, with Glenn reeling from the multitude of heart-wounding words Henrietta had thrown at him, he had found solace in the spectral counsel of Vincent van Gogh, who suggested he employ Betty as a device to bring Henrietta down a peg or two. Of course, he was never going to take life lessons from Vincent van Gogh (Glenn might have been stupid, but he wasn't insane), and he dismissed the wacky scheme out of hand, preferring instead to lock himself in a cubicle and vent his frustrations by weeping into his hands for twenty minutes. However, sitting 'twixt the cherubs now, and observing the evil looks Henrietta was giving Betty, supernal in a black tube top, white shorts, and dinky sandals, all of it gold skull, Glenn found a bizarre coherence in the Dutchman's logic.

'*Well?*' Henrietta yelled.

Glenn, about to respond, suddenly found himself enwrapped in Betty's arms, who began pulling at him, pleading with him, babbling God knows what in his ear.

Powerless, he watched Henrietta, on the verge of tears, stand up and totter away, looking almost pitiful with her makeup a mess and her uniform dishevelled.

To complete the nightmarish unreality of the scene he found himself in, he only seemed to regain the function of speech once she was already dissolving into the smoke.

'She's crying about *Ali*!' he screamed after her in vain. 'It's Ali she likes, not me! Henrietta!'

By the time he had calmed Betty and ran out onto the busy street the fashion designer was of course long gone. He then duly toured Betty around every gay bar in Leeds in search of Ali, predictably failing to find the makeup artist. He ended the night sitting on the curb outside the New Penny, beside Betty, eating a McDonald's in silence.

And Heathcliff thought *he* had woman trouble!

III.XIX

'It's not going to work,' the behemoth opined.

'It *is* going to work,' Glenn said through clenched teeth, his voice painfully hoarse. 'It's called *Forkbeard*, grandad. Just hook Gerty's little gizmo there to your ear and I'll be able to listen in and feed you the lines. Jimmy, we can get this man sacked!'

'But I don't want to get him sacked. He hasn't done anything to me.'

'He's done plenty to me.'

HUNTER

Jimmy sipped his hot chocolate. 'Like what?'

'Increased sales on menswear; brought the floor up to standard; ensured there were no discrepencies on the till. Seriously, Jimmy: if I don't have his blood today, Shukeena will have me resign my badge, and maketh usurping Sylvanus manager!'

'But I thought you wanted to beat him without fighting? Sun. . . . Fu, and all that.'

'That was when I thought he was interested in Henrietta. But I realise now that his interests lie. . . . elsewhere. Look, it doesn't matter! I need a satisfying resolution to this saga, and the only one I can think of right now is to put that man down.'

'Why not team up with Dick again?'

Glenn banged his fist on the table. 'Because we're not on good terms at the moment!' he shouted. 'Jimmy, please, there isn't time for exposition. We need to act *now*!'

Jimmy contemplated the spouting blue fountains. 'What's in it for me?' he probed.

'I'll pay you all that rent I owe you?'

The Leviathan stared at him.

'We'll have a night on the town with Gertrude?'

Jimmy still looked hesitant.

Glenn heaved a heavy sigh. 'I'll stop wearing this twatty headcomb.'

III.XX

HELENA: Oh my God, what the bloody hell have you done to him?

LEN: I've let him know where he stands.

HELENA: What?

LEN: He's been hitting on you all day and I'll be damned if I stand by and take it.

HELENA: Hitting on me? Did Sylvester not tell you the reason we split up?

LEN: Whatever the reason, the guy blatantly wants back in.

HELENA: He's gay!

LEN: You what?

HELENA: He's gay! He's just broken up with his *boyfriend*. I thought you knew.

LEN: Boyfriend?

HELENA: He's a friend, and cover manager, nothing more. And now you've. . . . This is madness!

LEN (*approaching her and attempting to hold her*): I'm sorry. I didn't know. Helena.

HELENA: No, don't touch me! Get away from me!

LEN (*backs away, realising his folly*): Helena. Helena! Please!

HELENA: Just go.

LEN: But—

HELENA: Go!

LEN *turns despondently from the chaotic scene as customers scatter wildly from the menswear department—the scene of the upmost tragedy.*

Gertrude looked up from the script with a puzzled expression.

'Well?' asked Glenn. 'What do you think?' His eyes were wet with tears.

'This isn't what happened,' she asserted.

'It's an impressionistic rendering of the contretemps,' he explained. She stared at him.

'It's made up,' he sighed.

'I know it's made up, Glenn, I was *there*. I just don't get why you've made it seem like you got the better of Sylvanus, when he got the better of you.'

'He certainly did *not* get the better of me!' Glenn barked, jerking upright. He yelped in pain. 'I was hung over, that's all,' he murmured, still sore. 'I wasn't at my best.'

'And you didn't knock him out either. Your stupid mate went up to him with the Forkbeard earpiece in and asked to try on a pair of trousers; Sylvanus said our trousers don't go past 38, and your mate said he was in. . . . in. . . .'

'Insinuating.'

'*Insinuating* that he was fat just because he's a 52-inch waist, and that he was appalled and wanted to lodge a formal complaint about him with head office.'

Glenn was staring at her from over the sofa backrest.

'Yes. And?'

'And then you ran in, saying, "I was just passing by and heard the commotion, what's happening?" and your idiot mate, cos he still had the earpiece in, repeated, "I was just passing by and heard the commotion, what's happening?" and that's when Sylvanus and Shukeena clocked on to what you were doing, and said it was outrageous that you were trying to get a manager fired. And you said it was outrageous that a manager had tried to sneak the new girl off to a hotel bar behind his employer's back, but he shouted at you and said you had alcohol on your breath and that you should go home, and you went bright red. It was a bit cringey to be honest.'

'The campaign was beginning to descend somewhat into farce, yes.'

'And then Dick ran up and said that you've got room to talk, having personal relationships with loads of colleagues, and he shouted, "All the problems in this shop start in Glenn's trousers, and it's about time someone did something about it!"—and then he rammed the garment steamer between your legs.'

'Ah, kill me with thy weapon, not with words!' Glenn exclaimed. 'My breast can better brook thy dagger's point than my ears can that tragic history. Gertrude! You surely don't expect me to conclude my great epic with the image of me lying on my back, holding my genitals and screaming in front of the customers?'

'It would be funnier than this ending.'

'*Funny*? He could have scarred me for life! I'm lucky I got away with a "superficial epidermal burn". I tell thee what: it's a good job they made trousers so thick and coarse in my grandad's day.'

'I bet you're dreading going in on Monday, after that spectacle?'

'I am *not* going in on Monday,' he shuddered.

'*What*? You have to! Or menswear won't have a manager.'

'Gerty, you heard what the doctor said. I have to rest my injury and keep all movement down there to a minimum. Face it, woman: I'm going to be on your sofa, indecent and indisposed, for at least a fortnight. See how my sword weeps!'

'But they'll sack you and bring Sylvanus back!'

'He said very clearly, *no tight clothing*. What can I do? Tight clothing's all I have!'

Pause.

It was a long walk for Glenn through ladieswear on Monday morning, and a very long fortnight, wearing that lurid scarlet knee-length polo, with its twinkling sequins, and its skirt that flapped with every humiliating step.

To drown out the jests and laughter, he hummed "The Man Who Sold the World". Gradually, he might have even found a measure of liberation in the billowy grace of his skirt. However, the tale of those moments would forever remain unwritten.

Fin.

WINTER

IV.I

SO WITH THIS GENTLEWOMAN SIR GLENN WAS A MONTH and more, and there they found the many strange adventures and perilous ye have heard to-fore; and whatever else happened after Dick brent the kingly manager with the garment steamer the tale maketh here no mention thereof, for it would be too long to tell of all that other business that befell them. In fact, the only relevant plot point from this period was the rather ghastly episode where Gertrude was taken to, of all things, a care home; but it was difficult for Glenn to say exactly what happened there, because at the time he was so wrapped up in his own broils that the incident sort of snuck up on him.

Basically, the story went that one night, while staying at her mum's, Gertrude sloshed back a cocktail of vodka and sleeping pills. The ominous sheets of Somnus and Mors beckoned, but fortunately providence intervened when her mum discovered her. After the paramedics employed the trusty stomach pump, she was was whisked off to hospital, where she stayed for the appropriate length of time (one night), before being transferred to a sort of special home—probably not unlike the one overlooking Hyde Hill.

If Glenn had been merely unpopular in the shop, his reception after this near-fatal night was similar in character to that which would be accorded a murder suspect. His very presence on the floor invoked in his colleagues an atavistic abhorrence mingled with horror. It was yet more evil luck, another blast of adverse winds, for the boy the mob had been shunning since at least high school, if not earlier. It was one thing to be unpopular; he had long since come to terms with that. But to be censured like the blackest devil out of hell? It grieved him sore.

Alone in her apartment, which seemed twice the size without her in it, and not in a good way, he took solace in mezcal, which seemed to quieten the castigating voices.

Driven by a fervent desire for redemption, he threw himself into writing, pledging that any profit reaped from its acceptance would be faithfully transferred to Gertrude.

The solitude he experienced in this period, an unintended consequence of being a pariah, an outcast from life's feast, at least enabled him to make progress with his great work. Joyce had seethed with jealousy over Proust's set-up at the Étoile, his cork-lined idyll a palace compared to the hovel the Dubliner had to work in. Indeed, Joyce had wondered whether he would complete *Ulysses* at all, trying to write in such claustrophobic conditions, and with the great flood of visitors forever distracting him. The thought gave Glenn a sort of bittersweet appreciation of his own Proustian set-up, in room 28 of the Dolorous Tower; and every evening he would sit at the instrument and make music, sighing contentedly as he continually reshaped and expanded his canticle.

[*Solemn music.*]

However, amidst this productive if lonely time, a subtle disquiet began gnawing at his head, troubling his breast. The view of the heavens outside his window, growing increasingly black and unsettled, seemed to hint at looming dark clouds on his horizon. Nights found him standing by the window, cocking a suspicious eye at the city, revolving in his brain formless thoughts of a heavy reckoning, some future strife, a day of doom, lying in wait for him, lurking somewhere deep within those mazy streets.

But which street was it? And what form would it take when it emerged from the shadows? He could not repress his shiver.

O good ground be pitiful, and hurt me not!

A more tangible item that dominated his thoughts and actually did have a clear form (and a very pleasing one at that) was Henrietta Payne. The vivid memories of that mad, magical night in III.XVIII replayed incessantly on his inner eye—the sight of her face pressed up against his, the vision of her surrendering herself on the sofa. Yet the dreamy recollection darkened when Betty intruded on the situation, not only ruining his chances with the ponytailed one but perhaps ruining his life. He had so nearly secured his future, so nearly gained entrée into London's fashion scene. And now his beloved Master, his sweet guide, his tutelary goddess, was gone—and would not respond to his written ambassages, no matter how many of them he sent her (now well into double figures). But our desperate young poet was *determined* to get his little Virgil-Beatrice hybrid back. His future literally depended on it.

What he needed to do was run into her by chance (or the appearance of chance). He knew he could win her over again if she saw him in person. The main obstacles were that she now lived in a different city (a city twice as big as Leeds), he had no idea what places she frequented there, and, even if he did, he had no one to go with him. Jimmy was the nearest thing he had to a friend, but that troglodyte had no energy or desire to do anything but drink in the Library (their local; not an actual library), and to propose something different, adventurous, or spiritually edifying to him, such as exploring a different city, was to be looked at like you were trying to entice him into a gay bar.

And given that Glenn's best bet at running into Henrietta was on Manchester's legendary gay scene, the chances of Jimmy going with him were virtually nil.

Standing by the window, quaffing mezcal, he marveled at the unnumbered rooftops beneath him. A city of 700,000 people—and not one of them wanted to be his friend.

He shook his head in disbelief. Yes, the artist must stand apart from the multitude; but for Christ's sake, could he not have at least *one* mate!?

Driven to extremes, on nights he was too drunk to write, he embarked on nocturnal excursions through Leeds, venturing into unfamiliar territories. Cloaked in his grandad's black trench and tatty trilby, he prowled under the eerie streetlights of Chapeltown, fixated on a specific house—the bright red one that bore Henrietta's address.

His intentions were noble (if you considered art noble, which he did). He was not trying to glimpse Henrietta, who he knew was out of town. He was hoping only to catch a glimpse of something, *anything*, that would help him understand what inspired such a singular creature, what influences shaped her fascinating vision.

He did wonder, the nights he was lurking there, whether he was breaking some law. But what difference did it make? He couldn't stop himself even if he was. He did know the intensity of his love, and the inquisitive behaviour it spawned, was an unattractive quality to some, perhaps even frightening. But it was this percipience that separated him from the madmen.

And there was *nothing* wrong with what he was doing. For heaven's sake, a century from now, that house would be a museum! People would flock from all corners of the globe to marvel at it. Guided tours would lead visitors right into her bedroom, where they'd gawk at her first sewing machine as if it were a holy relic. There'd even be a gift shop, where you could buy Henrietta Payne key rings, coffee mugs, and tote bags. And when you looked at it that way, you had to admit that his being there now was just another example of Glenn Harding's knack for being ahead of the curve.

It was testament to his peculiar talent for seeing value where others saw none.

Plus, Glenn knew there was a literary precedent to his behaviour. Dickens had David Copperfield constantly prowling Norwood Road in search of Dora; Proust described his solitary pilgrimages hoping to spy Mme Guermantes; and Martin Eden kept nocturnal vigils outside his beloved Ruth's house, in a passage that surely inspired Glenn to do the same. And just as Eden would hide under a dark tree smoking countless cigarettes, Glenn would conceal himself in the alleyway behind Henrietta's house quaffing mezcal. (Here walk I, in the black brow of night, to find you out.)

However, he could not escape the stark reality of the deprivation surrounding him—some of the houses on her street were boarded-up! And the succession of sirens would chill his blood. He wondered what people would think, were something bad to happen to him on one of his nocturnal adventures. They'd wonder what on earth he had been doing in such a place at such an hour. He found the idea almost intriguing, until it would occur to him that Henrietta would misinterpret what he had been doing, and he felt so ashamed he would at once withdraw. On dire terrain, do not linger.

Each time, he vowed never to return, aware of the dangers of his actions. Yet, he remained ensnared in the world of that wanton ambling nymph. He could not escape it. As Heathcliff said, 'Be with me always— take any form—drive me mad! Only do not leave me in this abyss, where I cannot find you.'

A plan began to spawn in his brain.

IV.II

Liberated at last from the Leviathan's oppressive demands for rent and back-rent, the King found his money-bags unexpectedly plump for this time of month. Thus, he resolved to pay a visit to the divine Fez—artist and sculptor—on Boar Lane, to have his blemisht crown restored. Fez's hands, as always, felt like warm sunbeams on a dreamy summer's day, and Glenn stood before the dirty mirror, admiring the masterpiece. The spikes stood mightier than ever, the fringe flowed with effortless grace, and the side threads and glossy mullet framed his visage and neck with ostentatious splendor.

High majesty looked like itself again.

Suddenly, the toilet flushed, and Glenn watched in the mirror as Ali emerged from the grotty cubicle, decked out in a baggy, brushstroke-print silk shirt that beautifully contrasted his striking grey eyes.

'How now, my pretty knave,' Glenn exclaimed amicably. 'How dost thou?'

'What are you doing?' said Ali with a startled look.

'Waiting for thee,' said Glenn flirtatiously in his lowest basso, trying to coerce a reciprocal smile out of him.

Ali frowned. 'I can smell alcohol on your breath,' he said, cautiously sidestepping Glenn to wash his hands.

'Twas even more tense than usual betwixt Glenn and Ali, because their respective absences from Sylvanus' leaving drinks, combined with the sighting of Glenn in a gay bar, and the makeup on his shirt when he finally returned home that night, had filled the shop with yet more dissentious rumours about the two of them.

It may even have driven Gertrude to her breaking point.

'Never mind my breath, I want to show you something,' Glenn replied, elevating his eyebrows naughtily. 'But I can only get it out in the privacy of the toilets.'

'Oh my God,' said Ali. 'You actually are mental.'

'Feast your eyes on *this*!'

Glenn produced a tatty flyer from his blazer and handed it to Ali.

'"*Scream Queen. . . .*"' Ali read aloud, his brows knitted. '"*A spine-chilling night for gays and ghouls. Embrace the horror this Halloween—on Canal St.*" What's this?' he questioned.

'Canst not read? It's a new gay club that's opening in Manchester this Halloween. And if you read the other side, you'll see that it's a pound a pint and students get in *free*. O Mr Hussain, hark what I shall say to you: the place will be teeming with pleasant fruits and princely delicates that night; I'll bet every student in the city will be there!'

'And?' said Ali.

'And we're going.'

'I am not going anywhere with *you*,' Ali scoffed, tossing the flyer aside.

'Why not?' Glenn demanded.

'Because you're a twat! You tried to get me sacked for *your* stock theft! And it's your fault Gertrude tried to kill herself! Ergh, I'm not going anywhere with you. I hate you. *Everyone* hates you. You're a dick!'

'Mr *Hussain*!' Glenn said in a hurt voice. 'How darkly and deadly dost thou speak! Yes, all right, I have at times done my work ill, and yes I accuse myself sorely; but, Sweet Saint, for charity, *forgive and forget*.

'Ye should give mercy unto them that ask mercy—for a knight without mercy is without worship,' he added with an upraised finger, in an avuncular tone.

'I'm not going to Manchester with you, Glenn.'

'O yes you are,' Glenn assured him.

'Why am I?'

'Because, O mine small herb, I know thee better than thou weenest.'

'Eh?'

'Tell me, Ali, why art thou single?'

'I don't know.'

'Thou must have a theory?'

'A what?'

Glenn sighed. 'A *theory*. An idea, a guess as to why you're single.'

'No.'

'Do you want to know what I think?'

'No.'

'You work with ladies all day on ladieswear; you serve ladies all day on ladieswear; and at night you go out with ladies from ladieswear—to bars where the men are only interested in the ladies from ladieswear.'

'So what? I don't like gay bars.'

'Of course you don't like gay bars.' Glenn grinned. 'You're terrified of them.'

Ali pulled a face. '*What?* No I'm not!' he spluttered, averting his eyes.

'Come on, Ali. You don't know how to speak to men! It's why you hide behind this bitchy persona, with all your little put-downs. It's a defense mechanism.' He chuckled. 'No marvel you've only been on *one* date in *all* the time I've known you.'

Ali lowered his gaze significantly.

Glenn leaned into the makeup artist, rested his big, arachnid hand on his shoulder. 'O thou sweet prince, squandering thy golden prime,' he said in tender tones. 'I'll bet when you're in those straight bars on a night, surrounded by damsels, all you really want to do is slip out and go meet all those strong fair knights nearby. . . . but you *can't*. Because you've no one to go with, and you're scared of men.

'Ah, well-a-day,' Glenn sighed. 'Why should our young Endymion pine away?'

'But why do *you* want to go to a gay club?' Ali asked quizzically.

'Why do you think?' Glenn answered with a cryptic grin.

'But—but you're going out with *Gertrude*,' Ali gasped.

'So? Edward the Second was married to Isabella; Richard the Second to Anne.'

'I don't know what that means.'

'It means that a man can have more than one *queen*,' Glenn smiled. 'Now come on, Ali! Cometh with me to Manchester—and I shall show you within Halloween night the highest adventure that ever any knight saw. . . .'

Glenn gaped the unnumbered tiny rooftops outspread beneath him.

A city of 700,000 people, and now only 699,999 of them didn't want to be his friend.

The numbers were still dire. But at least they were moving in the right direction.

Yes, today had been a triumph, and tonight the lights were dimmed, the mezcal poured, the spirits high. Glenn was lying back on Gertrude's sofa, resplendent in a skimpy pair of gold hipbriefs, twirling the cold wet glass on his flat, hairless stomach.

An electric bass was being picked, a set of drums rapped. Horns and trumpets were sounding some weird but glorious fanfare; a fanfare for Glenn Harding thought Glenn Harding, whose face was aching from smiling all day.

Set out on the coffee table were his most precious possessions: Sheila's name-badge, Wilfred's name-badge, a set of Gertrude's name-badges from the high street phase of her retail career, Henrietta's CV, her staff photo, and the name-badge he had deftly pinched in III.XVIII, when she let his hands run free over her body.

Glenn quaffed his mezcal, smiled vaingloriously upon his treasures.

'My son, to be not quite so great would be better,' whispered the sinister figure that was hovering by the door.

'Fie on thee, devil; thou speakest cowardly!' Glenn answered with annoyance, although without looking back, as he preferred not to lay eyes on the dreadful shape.

The thing called itself Mr Hyde from Hyde Hill, and it had by hap come to lodge in the Dolorous Tower, and was discernible only because it wore a long black coat and an old black hat and insisted on speaking.

'Faith,' Glenn said, 'some certain dregs of conscience are yet with me; but I may not now turn again for shame, and what adventure shall fall to me, be it life or death, I will take the adventure that shall come to me. Now pray! Forbade me til anon.'

Pause.

Glenn gulped as he glanced back at the door.

The ghoul had vanished.

IV.III

Under the skeletal branches of a bare tree on Sovereign Street, up to his ankles in dead leaves, he raised the large envelope up to the glare of the streetlight for one final glimpse at the meticulously inscribed address:

WRITERS ROOM
BRITISH BROADCASTING CORPORATION
GRAFTON HOUSE
379/81 EUSTON ROAD
LONDON
NW1 3AU

He had slapped all six of Gertrude's first-class stamps on the envelope. And, with an unsual stroke of prudence, he had put down Hyde Hill as the sender's address.

I spoke to him and told him I was an artist myself, though not a very successful one.

The postbox stood solitary, a lone senitel before a vast gravel car park, beyond which were the great red brick arches of the train station stretched across the horizon. He observed a train departing, wheezing slowly into the night. Headed to London?

He brought the envelope to his lips, kissed the BBC's address. It then disappeared into the postbox's maw with a cathartic slap. He expelled a contented sigh, its vapour whirling before his eyes. He then expelled a long, mezcal-infused belch.

My flesh shall dwell in hope, because thou will not leave my soul in Hades.

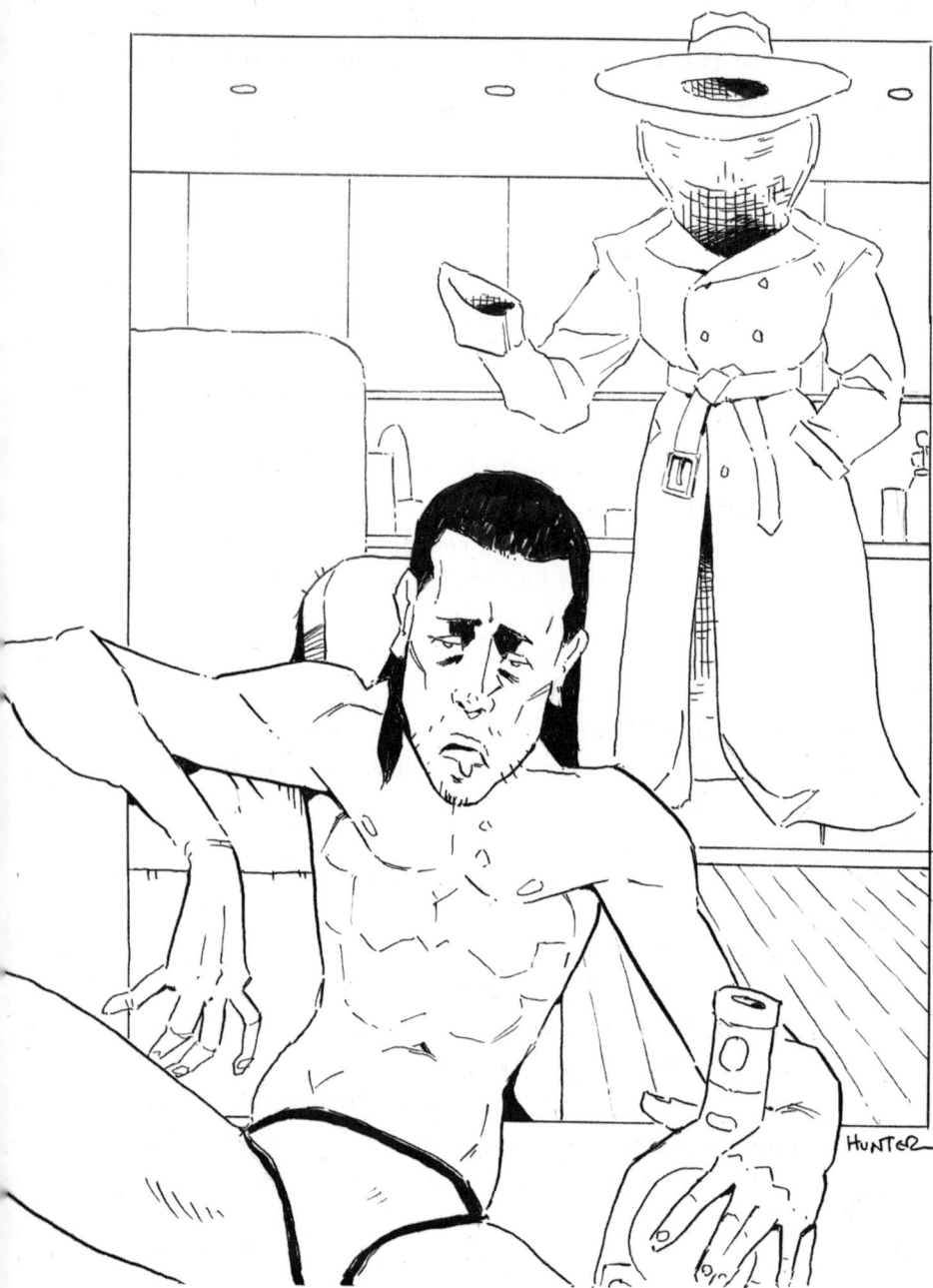

The air was raw, the roads hushed. Alone in the moonglow, he contemplated the cosmos. Echoes of Stanley Harding, that doleful tenor, resonated in his enormous ears. Ah, Grandad Stanley! A man more handy with a pen than most, proven in his haunting memoirs, that little book in which the sweet poet was still alive, and able to recount to Glenn, always in good humour, the many tragic events of his short life.

I asked him if he minded if I got up and sang. By all means, he said.

Sing in me, Grandad Stanley! Don't pass me by, Thomas Malory! Let my opus fly on thy immortal breath and drop into the right lap at the BBC. O Lord, let these same sparks gaze back at me, quaffing cocktails on the rooftop bar of some private club in Soho. Let me pass the final stage, from bad fortune to good, and end this epic.

And at that moment, it happened. The earth shook and trembled, the foundations of the great arches of the train station stirred and trembled; and he looked, and beheld his good stars rising in the firmament. The Hardings were out tonight! And the Haighs! All of them together! And they were saying to him yes, this time yes—and he could feel in his bones that *this time* he would be big. . . .

But before any of that he would first have to take up evil instead of good; desire darkness instead of sun; welcome Satan instead of light. First, he would have to go to Manchester.

THE DEVILS' REVELLING NIGHT

Soon came Halloween, and by adventure Glenn and Ali located Scream Queen, not on Canal Street as advertised but rather round a corner and down a dark alley. The façade of the old building seemed to pulsate with an otherworldly presence, and spraypainted in jagged black letters on the rust-red wall, Glenn read the cryptic covenant:

Whoso pulleth this quene oute of alle the lusty knyghtes in this halle
is rightwhys kynge of her herte and shalle have ado with hir

or words to that effect. The sight was as pleasing to him as Paradise was to Adam, but as they staggered up to the velvet rope they discovered, lurking under the massive stone doorway, out of the drizzle, two dread monsters blocking their path.

'—and I said, "Listen, love, if I liked your boyfriend I'd have taken him off you",' Frankenstein's Creature was telling Count Dracula, in his sandpaper voice.

'What's o'clock, lads!' Glenn exclaimed with bonhomie. 'Be we too late? Brief, good sir, for I am in haste, ho!'

The monsters looked straight through him.

'Have you got ID?' the Count grunted, eyeballing the babyfaced Ali.

Glenn looked with fear at the makeup artist, convinced he wouldn't have any ID and that *this* would be the stumbling block the laughing gods had planted to intercept his high quest, just as he reached the very threshold of Fate.

But he did have ID—a driving licence, no less—and Glenn breathed a sigh of relief.

'I have my ID too,' Glenn proffered, flashing them his provisional.

The monsters stamped a huge QUEEN on his hand and tossed him into the lobby. Ali too got the stamp but was allowed to swan in under his own steam.

'I like you, lads,' Glenn shouted back merrily. 'About your business straight.'

He saw them turn their heads and eyeball him as the huge doors swung shut.

The grim, dimly lit lobby vibrated fiercely, and as the menswear manager looked to the black door that led to the club his belly began fluttering. He turned to Ali, who was at the cloakroom counter, handing his purple glossed-shell puffer jacket by Sammi de Hun to Pennywise the clown.

He was grieved sore by the makeup artist's so-called "costume". All he had on was a laughing skull pendant over a baggy off-white vest, with his crepe black wool trousers with tapered ankles and gold python textured trainers. Glenn shook his head. 'Who have you come dressed as, exactly? Ali Hussain?' he joked.

'I'm a vampire, aren't I,' said Ali, pointing to his makeup.

'O, is that meant to be *blood*? I thought you'd smudged your lipstick on my hipflask,' Glenn said, as he removed his huge fur coat. 'You look like you're dressed for work!' he said with a great guffaw.

'*You* look like *you're* dressed for work,' Ali shot back at Glenn, who was wearing a black tie with his grandad's boxy old grey windowpane English wool suit.

'Nonsense!' Glenn cried, laughing. 'Look at my face, Ali; it's painted *white*. And I've got a pencil moustache now. And my hair's brylcreemed back.'

'You don't look like Gomez Addams,' Ali retorted.

'I bloody *do* look like Gomez Addams. I look like the *original* Gomez Addams, that Charles Addams drew, in his illustrations for the *New Yorker*—which, by the way, were published *decades* before all those execrable film and TV adaptations. Honestly, Ali; you know nothing of Art Nouveau-inspired American illustrators of the 1930s!'

Pause.

'He's so gay, isn't he?' Ali said to Pennywise.

The clown nodded, as he took his huge fur coat.

Then was Gomez wroth, but Ali grabbed him by the arm and led him through the black door, into a dark passage, where suddenly the thumping beat grew louder, and the muffled chorus of guttural shrieks made their hearts beat faster in their chests. In a frenzy of excitement, they threw open the doors and strode into the club.

It is no easy undertaking to describe the bottom of the universe, but I'll give it a go.

They stood on the brink of a narrow landing, overlooking a deep dungeon that was rimmed by a stony wall that rose up so high, and into such darkness, that the topmost point could not be sighted. The only light came from the red glare of an LED-lit dancefloor, on which a great throng of supernatural beings were engaged in an orgiastic dance, gyrating to a monotonous beat, over which the last line of the chorus of "Monster Mash" was repeated continually at short intervals.

'So this is Scream Queen. . . .' Ali yelled with wonder.

'Yep,' yelled Glenn. He sighed. 'Right, we've seen it now. Let's go home.'

'*What*! I'm not going yet. We just got here!'

A bitter groan burst from Glenn's lips, as Ali grabbed his hand and led him towards the bar, first descending the jagged, snaking staircase that was wedded to the wall, before cutting through the filthy fry. He was cursing continuously as he went.

Glenn had assumed Scream Queen would be some cool, contemporary club. A place in which Manchester's healthy supply of fashion students could feel at home. Instead, the premises looked like Goya's lost Black Painting, and as his eyes swept the denizens, there was not a woman to be seen, never mind a goddess like Henrietta Payne.

Ali turned from the bar, shoved a G&T in his hands. After all the mezcal, the cocktail tasted like a soft drink. It went down in one gulp.

'Have you heard from Gertrude?' yelled Ali. They were on the dance floor now, Ali dancing, Glenn standing perfectly still but for the odd quaff of his hipflask.

'No.'

Ali stared at him.

'Do you love her?' he asked.

'Do I *what* her?'

'Do you *love* her?'

'Ali, it's difficult to engage in a serious conversation with someone whose gyrating their buttocks on a dancefloor.'

'You didn't answer the question.'

'Do I love her? Yes, but. . . . Well, it's difficult to explain. Are you familiar with the tale of Odysseus, Penelope, and Kalypso?'

'Oh, don't start with all that shit. Didn't you know she was ill?'

Glenn eyed him irritably. The vampire seemed determined to suck every last drop of blood out of this subject. 'To my everlasting shame,' he replied, 'I had no idea.'

'You couldn't see she was doing drugs and going through stuff?'

'No.'

'*No!*'

'I accuse myself sorely, Mr Hussain.' He quaffed his hipflask. 'Believe me.'

'You should be ashamed of yourself!'

'Ali!' Glenn yelled. 'Thinketh thou this damsel was the truest lady living? She hath been the destroyer of *many* a good knight before Glenn; and though my heart mourneth sore the sickness of her, as I shall answer to God, she never had no villainy by me.'

'You what?'

'O, forget it. I'm going for a peregrination,' he barked with annoyance.

'I think the toilets are that way.'

Thus, he rode the rim of the desolate pit, his heart torn in his breast. He reached reflexively for his hipflask, but on finding it empty his strength feebled, and he waxed passing faint. He groaned with anguish, tabulating the exorbitant cost of this pointless expedition. (Dante and Virgil may also have journeyed to the depths of Hell—but they didn't have to pay TransPennine Express prices for the tickets.)

'Are you not bored yet?' Glenn yelled, returning to his dance partner. 'Come on, Ali! Let's get a Phaecian bark out of here.'

'Shut up and take this,' he yelled, slipping something into his hand.

'What is it?' Glenn asked, peering suspiciously into his palm.

'It doesn't matter. Just take it, it'll cheer you up. You're doing my head in!'

At the bar, Glenn turned his back to the mute Michael Myers who served him, and used the double gin and tonic to wash down Ali's unholy drug. He stared expectantly into the chamber of horrors, but the vision looked exactly as depressing as it did before.

He downed the double gin and tonic he bought for Ali, but still nothing.

And with this, let us turn from the sight of the abyss, and slip into the pissoir.

Glenn, alone in the murk, staring into the mirror, was trying to decide whether the pencil moustache improved his face or merely aged it, when suddenly he saw something that made his heart jerk in his ribcage.

Wilfred Woods, standing in the far corner, staring at him.

'Wonder of wonders! *You?*' Glenn gasped. He whirled around beaming. 'And what adventure brought *you* hither, mine hardy, stout-resolved mate?' he asked cheerily.

He kept his balled fist concealed in his pocket.

'Recoil at the horrible terror,' Wilfred intoned, 'as the enemy of God screamed songs of despair, his cries of defeat—as this captive of Hell found his wounds fatal.'

'Huh?' said Glenn. 'I mean, I know the words, Mr Woods—but thy employment of them here is obscure to me.'

Glenn winced at the word *employment*.

'Thus he must wait for the Day of Judgment,' said the brute, advancing on Glenn, 'smeared with his sins, to learn his doom—'

'—from the God of Glory,' Glenn nodded, looking up at him with astonished eyes. 'I know. Fair knight, what will ye with me? Will ye joust with me? Dear friend, hark! 'Tis a quarrel most unnatural, to be reveng'd on him that loveth thee!'

The horrid giant stopped and loomed over him.

'There is no easy way to flee from one's fate. . . .' he concluded ominously.

'All right,' Glenn gulped, his voice shaking. 'I see well I must have ado with you. But, before we start, let me say one thing—' His sucker punch missed Wilfred by a mile, and the momentum sent him spinning into the toilet door.

Screaming, Glenn yanked it open and fled into the club.

He concealed himself amid the demons on the dancefloor, where he cowered behind the massive, V-shaped back of a suited up Patrick Bateman, peering around his hulking arms and spying on the dim outline of the toilet doors.

Suddenly, the banker and serial killer looked over his shoulder.

'*Jimmy*!?' Glenn gasped. '*You're* in a gay club!?'

'Ah, how cautiously a man should breathe near those who see not only what we do, but have the sense which reads the mind *beneath*,' the behemoth yelled.

'What!' Glenn yelled in perplexed astonishment.

'Still?' Jimmy groaned. 'Still like the other fools? Then I shall select the simplest words that need be from now on to make things clear to your dull intellect.' He whirled round and yelled in Glenn's face: 'WOE TO YOU, DEPRAVED SOUL! AND BURY HERE FOREVER ALL HOPE OF PARADISE!'

Reeling backward, Glenn bumped into some diminutive figure. Wheeling around, he saw the red coat of that spavined ghoul from *Don't Look Now* and braced himself for Shukeena's face. When she pulled back her hood to reveal the face of Dick Zabledore, he screamed.

'Truly poor are they who whine and fret, and covet what they cannot hope to get,' warned Dick with an ugly leer. 'Learn repentence, geez— ere the devil get you!'

Glenn, pacing backward into the stew of dead souls, didn't take his eyes off Dick.

'Remember, our Glenn,' the formalwear supervisor yelled after him, 'madness when it takes a fellow lasts longer than drunkenness!' He raised a pint to him and grinned. 'Jealous folk are dangerous, you know. . . .'

'O thou false knight and traitor unto knighthood,' uttered a demonic rasp in his ear, 'who did learn thee to distress ladies and gentlewomen?' Glenn turned his head and came face to face with Regan from *The Exorcist*. Her eyes were dead and her skin green and puffy, and she wore her lank, matted hair in an awesome beehive. '*Gertrude?*' he gurgled.

'And because ye would not abide and help her, ye shall see your best friend fail you when ye be in the greatest distress that ever ye were or shall be,' she grinned.

Her black teeth made the chill blood in his veins run backward.

'Will all ye have ado with me at once!' Glenn shrieked, mad with terror. 'If I be so disgracious in your eyes, let me march on and not offend ye!'

Thunder clapped o'er the monotonous beat, as the voices of the damned rose up in a deafening scream. The bowels of the old building were growing unbearably hot, and wading blindly through the rank air, sweat trickling down his face and back, Glenn felt as if he was swimming in a witch's cauldron. 'Ali!' he screamed, beginning to panic. 'Ali! Ali! O! There you are, Ali!'

'Oh, what now?' Ali slobbered irritably, looking as sweaty as Glenn. He had folded the beastly Leatherface in his arms, who had him up in the air, pinned against the wall, as if hanging from a meat hook, as they mauled each other with kisses.

'Is that stimulant of yours *meant* to conjure up fatal visions?' Glenn yelled.

'I don't think so?' said Ali, still necking the monster. 'Why, what did you see?'

'The sins of the past, in a medley of annoying voices.'

'That's not my stuff. I think that's you.'

'O, so they're merely symptoms of my o'er-fraught head? Okay, well, that's a relief,' Glenn nodded. His face fell. 'Wait, *is* that a relief?'

'Glenn!' Ali barked. 'Go get the round in and stop being annoying.'

'All right.' Glenn still felt shaken as he threaded his way through the satanic throng, but on arriving at the bar was cheered to observe behind it a quasi-familiar face.

'Hello Fester!' he yelled, grinning. 'Two double gin and tonics please.'

'What did you call me?' replied the bartender.

'Fester!' Glenn smiled.

The bartender stared blankly at him.

'I'm *Gomez!*' he chuckled. 'And you're Uncle Fester.' He gulped. 'Aren't you?'

Pause.

'So he wasn't Uncle Fester?' said Ali, dribbling into Glenn's fur coat.

'No,' answered Glenn bitterly. '*He* was a very humorless woman.'

Glenn was piggybacking the inebriated makeup artist up the deserted Canal Street, under the heavy downpour and roaring thunder. The cold winds blew hard against them, and he struggled to see as the rain lashed his massive sunglasses unmercifully.

'I was having such a good night,' Ali slurred, exhausted. 'I *knew* you'd ruin it. . . . Just like you ruin everything. . . . I don't know how you do it.'

'I do seem to share Poe's facility for making enemies,' Glenn mused.

HUNTER

'Tell me, Ali, are you familiar with a writer by the name of Rufus Griswold—'

'Oh, shut up, Glenn. I've drunk too much. I feel sick.'

'We'll get you a bottle of water at the station, don't worry. You won't be sick.'

Glenn felt Ali's body contract, and the next thing he knew a jet of vomit had shot down his front. He halted, looking with horror at his plastered fur coat and loafers, his jaw dangling in the tempest.

'Sorry,' Ali dribbled.

Before he could respond, a second burst of puke exploded from Ali's mouth. Glenn promptly threw the makeup artist off him, who hit the cobbles with a horrific crack. The shriek echoed up the heights of the vertiginous buildings surrounding them.

'Oof, sorry Ali!' Glenn grimaced. 'Did I drop you on your coccyx?'

'No, you prick,' Ali cried, writhing in pain. 'You dropped me right on my arse!'

Thus endeth this ignoble and gloomy canto entitled The Devils' Revelling Night, *which canto was reduced into English by a Leodiensian, unemployed.*

IV.V

[*The* Ghosts *vanish*. King Glenn *starts out of his dream.*]

He found himself wrapped in the warm caress of Gertrude's colossal bed. He closed his eyes and breathed a sigh of relief.

However, the tranquility was short-lived, as all of a sudden a bevy of cannonades began firing upon his skull.

His mouth felt dry and there was the oddest taste clinging to the back of his throat. (No doubt the pernicious effects of mixing mezcal with all that gin and tonic.)

Rising unsteadily from the bed, he hobbled into the room. Standing in his skimpy gold hipbriefs, he cast a saturnine look over the city. It was a dark morning, the streets wrapped in a thick blanket of fog. It looked as if Leeds couldn't be arsed getting out of bed either. In the kitchen, he grabbed a four-pint bottle of full-fat milk and began swigging it. He lowered the bottle, wiped his mouth with his forearm and sighed wearily.

O sweet Lord, when shall this sorrow leave me?

His quest had failed, and he realised now the only prospect of seeing his Master again was when she returned for Christmas and New Year.

Other than that, he had no real objectives.

His script had been posted. It would now be in Television Centre, but at the bottom of some towering pile of scripts that all needed to be read.

All of a sudden, he found his hopes and dreams were stasis, the two main threads of his epic suspended for the time being. The double story had stopped.

He did feel almost relieved at this reprieve from the incessant action.

What next? Next was a massive bowl of granola, with full-fat milk, a topping of finely diced fruit and an indulgent trickle of honey.

Now what next?

He already knew the answer. The only way to make it through the slow hours, to that dateless day when he saw Henrietta again, or received word about his script, was, unfortunately, to shift his focus back to the day job and, specifically, his shopfloor—and the concomitant everlasting fight with Shukeena.

He groaned because of his bondage, and his headache, and he cried out in anguish.

Machiavelli was right. Those who go from being private citizens to princes soley through Fortune do so with little effort, *but they maintain their position with a great deal of it*; although they have no difficulty on the way, all their difficulties arise when they have arrived. He nodded, looking far away into the troubled heavens. He had waltzed into his manager's job, all right; but it was with awesome difficulty that he held onto it.

Of course, Machiavelli *also* said that princes become great when they overcome the obstacles that confront them, and therefore Fortune, especially when she wants to make a new prince *great*, causes enemies to appear for him and has them undertake campaigns against him, *so that he may have cause to overcome them and to climb up higher on the ladder which his enemies have brought him.*

Glenn liked that interpretation. Fortune wanting to make him great and all that. Certainly, she hadn't scanted him enemies, giving him all the incidents he needed to elevate his script and make it great. But that was done now, and it was time for a new approach in the shop, if only to calm things down a bit and make his life less stressful. He knew he must turn his back on his old ways, and lead his principality out of all the disorder, broils, and disturbances that dominated the Middle Part of his epic.

And it could be done.

He had executed the recent stock take and remerchandising without issue. Plus, he still had Dick on his team, having opted not to report him to the police for attacking him with the garment steamer, as Dick was his best seller and he couldn't afford to lose him; and, in fairness, and as Dick had reminded him, Glenn had been guilty of physically assaulting him on multiple occasions.

Now they were even.

'Enrich the time to come with smooth-faced peace, with smiling plenty and fair prosperous days,' he croaked hoarsely. 'God say amen.'

As he was about to enrich himself with a full English, the front door was thrown open, and in walked Gertrude, festooned in a huge black fur coat and an enormous pair of black sunglasses, dragging a two-wheeled suitcase.

'*Gertrude!*' he rasped, surprised. 'Thank God you're back! How are you feeling?'

Removing her sunglasses, Gertrude glared at him.

'Yeah, I'm feeling a lot better, actually,' she said briskly.

'O, good!'

'At least I was—until I heard my boyfriend was *gay*.'

'O, no.'

'Oh, yes,' she nodded. 'So you *were* in that gay bar, cheating on me with Ali, when I was at Sylvanus' leaving drinks!'

'We've had this discussion, Gerty. I was at that gay bar with *Jimmy*.'

'So why was there makeup on your shirt then!' she screamed.

'I've told you, that makeup was mine!'

'Well yeah, all right, that is believable; but I know for a *fact* you told Ali you were gay, and wanted to go to some gay club with him, while I was in that home.'

'What makes you say that?' Glenn asked innocently, twirling his Gomez moustache. He was wondering why Gertrude was staring at his hand, until he remembered the massive QUEEN stamped on it. He quickly folded his arms.

'I—I can't believe it,' she said, shaking her head. 'I *loved* you!' she sniffed. 'But you were just. . . . using me.'

Her bottom lip was beginning to quiver.

'Gertrude, don't worry, it's not what you think. Our relationship is a conflict of interest, remember? And I'm already on my second warning. So, I thought that if I told Ali I was gay, he would inevitably blab it about the shop—which, evidently, he did—and *that* would throw Shukeena off the scent.' He toddled over to the style advisor and wrapped her in his arms. 'Obviously, I didn't expect my little lie to make it all the way to *you*, in a home, but, ultimately, that's all it is. A lie.'

She peered at him through wet, brooding eyes. 'Really?' she snuffled.

Glenn stepped forward, gave her a reassuring hug and smiled. '*Really*,' he said, looking her straight in the eye. 'And I've never done anything with Ali, I promise you.'

A pause.

And right on cue, Ali toddled out of the bedroom, in nothing but a skimpy pair of white hipbriefs—grimacing as he rubbed his buttocks.

'Argh, my arse is killing me,' he said bitterly. 'Thanks a lot, Glenn!'

He jerked on the spot when he saw Gertrude.

'Oh! All right, Gerty?' he stammered.

The style advisor was stood stone still, her jaw dangling in the air.

Glenn couldn't help but marvel the scene unfolding before him, staring with horror now at Ali, and now at his girlfriend. 'I—I can't believe I'm about to employ such a hackneyed phrase,' he said, almost in awe. 'Gertrude—this is *not* what it looks like.'

IV.VI

'Come on, mate,' Mildred offered in soothing tones, enveloping her in a comforting hug—the only source of warmth in the otherwise frosty staff room. 'It's only *Glenn*. You said yourself you didn't have anything in common.'

'I know,' she warbled. 'We *don't* have anything in common. He's *insane*. Why did I ever go out with him?' She looked aghast at Mildred. 'Oh my God, people are going to know I've slept with *another* loser. Why do I keep doing this to myself? Why do I keep lowering myself?' She stiffened. 'Oh no,' she said, staring into her thoughts.

'What?' said Mildred.

Gertrude looked at her. 'People are going to think I'm a beard!'

'No, they're not!' said Mildred, dabbing her eyes and wiping her nose with a tissue. 'Remember, there's no actual evidence you went out with him, is there?'

'I don't think so,' Gertrude sniffed.

'Well, there you go then! This doesn't have to hurt your reputation. You've got to treat these situations like a police interview and deny everything. Do you hear me? Deny *everything.*'

'Yeah, that's a good idea,' the style advisor burbled. 'I'll just deny everything.'

'Well, come on, say it like you mean it, you daft bitch. I deny *everything!*'

'I deny *everything,*' Gertrude exclaimed, rather unconvincingly.

'Oh, I don't believe you!' Mildred barked. 'That sounds like someone who'd go out with a gimp like Glenn Harding!' She gave her a shake. 'Deny everything!'

'Mildred, I deny *everything!*' cried Gertrude.

'That's more like it!' said Mildred. 'Now come on, louder!'

'I deny *everything!*' shouted Gertrude.

'*Louder!*' Mildred demanded.

'I DENY EVERYTHING!' Gertrude shrieked, banging her fist on the desk.

Shukeena and Norman stared at her.

'We haven't asked you anything yet,' said Shukeena.

'Sorry,' said Gertrude. She discreetly wiggled herself back into alignment with her strapless black stretch-velvet mini dress by Nirah Frazar.

Shukeena studied her notes thoughtfully and looked up from her clipboard. 'How do you feel about Glenn being gay?' she enquired casually.

'Yeah, it's cool,' Gertrude nodded. 'Everyone always knew it. It's no big deal.'

'It's no big deal that your boyfriend is *gay*?' queried Shukeena.

'Glenn was *never* my boyfriend,' Gertrude snapped. 'I deny *everything*!'

'Stop banging your fist on the table,' Shukeena warned.

'Sorry.'

Shukeena looked to the store manager. 'Well, Norman; it seems Gertrude denies everything. What do you think about this?'

'Yeah, I think it's great!' said Norman, nodding approvingly. He smiled at Gertrude. 'I think you've performed well, you obviously know what you're doing, so just keep at it, and we'll see you in another six months.'

Pause.

'This is an investigation, Norman; not a performance review,' said Shukeena.

'Oh,' said Norman, squirming slightly in his chair. 'Right.'

'And, incidentally, performance reviews are every *three* months, not six,' she added.

Norman sheepishly looked to the floor and mimed zipping his lips.

Shukeena took a deep breath, turning her face to the style advisor. 'Look, Gertrude,' she said, 'it's Glenn we want, not you. So I'm willing to cut a deal with you. If you admit you had a relationship with him, I'll make sure the worst head office gives you is a written warning. I'm of course sensitive to your recent. . . . problems, and, as far as I'm concerned you've been manipulated by a nasty piece of work who needs to be finally brought to account.' She leaned forward, smiling. 'What do you say?'

'I deny *everything*!'

'Oh, come on, Gertrude!' Shukeena shouted. 'I *know* you went out with him.'

'No, I didn't!'

'*Yes*, you did!'

'*No*! I didn't!'

'Gertrude!' Shukeena yelled. 'You went out with Glenn Harding for three months! And you'll come clean *now* if you know what's good for you!'

'I deny *everything*!'

IV.VII

Odysseus had at last departed the abode of the witch Circe, and having gathered his personal effects (from the foot of the Dolorous Tower), he returned to Camelot, where he fell back to his fortified residence (the menswear fitting rooms).

Now was his realm wholly mischieved, and outside his cubicle door he could hear his name on everyone's lips, in tones so violent it chilled his heart. *Kill, kill, kill, kill, kill him* they were saying, and he heard on the wind there were even management meetings to which he, the menswear manager, was not invited.

The breach between Glenn and the manager's office was complete.

Still, as he hid there, incommunicado in his cubicle, without a single ally in the shop, he couldn't help but look in the lofty mirror and laugh. For one not made to court an amorous looking-glass, he had certainly caused a lot of pretty elfins a lot of pain. He was almost proud of the trail of destruction he had left behind!

We are all men in our own natures frail, and capable of frailty; few are angels.

Or, as Machiavelli would say, 'It is necessary for a prince, if he wants to preserve himself, to learn how *not* to be good.'

That Gertrude was in a tempest of tears didn't move him, for the fog of mezcal had now lifted, and he remembered that strange man showing up at her door unannounced that time (III.XVII). He was obviously surprised to see another bloke in her apartment, and Glenn sensed there was a lot more to that story than met the eye. Certainly that damned poisonous strumpet was known to the common multitude, judging by her antics with Wilfred.

No, he felt nothing for her, nor any of them—Peggy, Amor, Betty, Chardonnay, Gertrude, the lot. In fact, he felt a sense of relief they were all gone. They had served their purpose, giving him the raw material for his writing. Never mind all the pain, heartbreak, and disappointment they caused Glenn, ultimately they had been beneficial to him; they would even be beneficial to the wider public if, God willing, his artistic show was broadcast to them, the artless masses.

All he needed now was to possess his Guenever, Miss Payne.

And Brigantia, he felt, was guiding him towards that conclusion.

He knew from reading Homer that the gods do not converse directly with men; they mingle and converse with them obliquely, through the words and actions of others. Everything that was happening around him seemed to be telling him that he had no future in Leeds, that the clock was ticking, and that a new life in London, with his beloved Master, his sweet guide, Henrietta Payne, was the panacea to all his problems. That would complete his quest for the elusive *Eudaimonia*. That would be the end.

And what an end. Working for the BBC and coming home to Henrietta. Working her loom and visiting his bed. *Forever.* The thought of such a fantasy becoming his reality brought tears to his eyes. And what if the two of them combined their talents? The possibilities would be endless! After all, his show was set in the world of fashion. Was it really so far-fetched to imagine her label providing a tie-in clothing line? *Did you like the characters' outfits?* the continuity announcer would ask over the credits. *Why not buy them?* And then he really would have brought Beauty back to the high street—while revolutionising the medium of TV forever. For all shows from then on would have their own labels, and channel heads would wonder why they hadn't thought of it before—why it had taken Glenn Harding, of all people, to uncover this economic boomlet.

Then both the worlds of fashion and media would bow down before him.

'And all the people cried, "Arthur is come again: he cannot die",' he hymned.

In a fit of delirium, Glenn became dizzy and had to sit down on the antique piano stool. It's embarrassing to say, but he actually wept. However, a sudden realisation cast a shadow over his countenance. He could not afford to wait until Christmas and New Year to see her again. Meeting her was the only way the action of his great epic could resume—and be resolved. And that's when he realised that all his hopes and future happiness hung on one girl. A girl who despised him, and whose whereabouts were a mystery, and with whom he needed a chance, one-in-a-million encounter, followed by the performance of a lifetime, if he was to have any hope of winning her over again.

In other words, what he needed to happen next was a completely improbable event.

IV.VIII

I have in my hand a sock, and I speak now of those flying moments when the mockery and persecution abates and the gods, out of remorse most probably, rearrange the diorama and place the figures precisely where you want them.

The Victorian novelists are often scoffed at by the cognoscenti, sneered at even, for their use of coincidence—that timely twist of fate that propels us closer to the middle or end. And yet, coincidence happens daily on the wonkbox, in every drama you can name, including the acclaimed ones that clean up at the awards ceremonies. Evidently, TV hacks are not held to the same standard as a pile of bones in Poets' Corner. One has praise lavished on them by the same people who hold the other to an impossibly high standard.

'Life doesn't work that way!' they complain of one. 'It's not real!' they cry.

And they are right. Life doesn't work that way. It's not real.
For them.

But, as I take a long sniff of this sock, I assert to you, gentle hearer, that what is *real* is relative to the life you lead. Some of us are starring players. Others are employed by, attendant on, servants to. What separates one from the other is that starring players understand that drama—*real* drama—exists outside of daily routine, and only those whose spirit drives them continuously to stride beyond it can appreciate the cosmic probability of the completely improbable.

So, I raise my glass to that pile of bones in Poets' Corner, who in life knew better than most how friendly the Fates are to the adventurer.

The catalyst for Glenn was his brother's birthday card. He had been so consumed with fear, waiting for his hour to come, the blow to fall, that he kept forgetting to post it. But nothing happened, his capers having sowed so much discord that Shukeena had too many distractions to concentrate on him. Her favourite, Gertrude, was no longer her favourite; Gertrude despised Ali, and because of that Betty despised Gertrude; but Betty also despised Ali for going to Manchester without her, although obviously she still loved him too; and Mildred, being best friends with Gertrude, despised everybody, and thus everybody despised her. It was so bad on ladieswear that for the first time ever menswear was outselling it!

The skilful warrior stirs and is not stirred.

All of a sudden, a fortnight had passed, his brother's birthday was the next day, and he was desperate to catch the last post as his card contained an urgent plea for money.

The afternoon was dark and chilly. Having posted the card at the Post Office on Albion Street, he breathed the crisp air, felt cosy in his fur coat. His imperial crown was erected impressively. He was glad that he had feigned illness and told Dick to close up for him. Now the evening stretched out enticingly before him, as a Proustian ramble, a Joycean deviation, a Dickensian excursion, beckoned.

He slinked down Saint Anne's Street, past the building work on the dilapidated cathedral, but paused at the junction of Cookridge and Great George Street. The thought that Jimmy might be in the Victoria with his workmates was enough to send him back on himself, towards the Light. There, he ascended the stairs, entering the vast, quiet arcade. As he cast an avid, thirsting look at a nearby bar, he saw something that brought him to an abrupt halt. In fact the sight shook him to his loafers.

Henrietta Payne.

Sitting with an acquaintance and having a pint in the outside seating area.

Glenn's eyes practically flew out from his face on stalks, and he at once turned and ran, the skirt of his fur coat flapping madly behind him as he went. He cleared the steps in a single leap, legged it down the passageway and went headlong into the wan and wintry chill—where he had to lean against the wall, gasping as he clutched his chest.

His nerves were jangling, ears ringing, entrails knotted—he would have vomited had there been anything in his stomach.

Kicking his legs into action, he staggered around the building, trying his hardest to think but finding he couldn't, his brain having short-circuited with the shock of it all.

But stumbling along, spluttering and gurgling, his outstretched hand steadying him against the wall, his thoughts began gradually to assume what could be considered a form. Since the abortive trip to Manchester, his quest for Henrietta had become a quixotic search, a sort of literary exercise. Never for a moment had he seriously expected to find her. And now that he had, he didn't know what to do. Back on Albion Street, he produced his hipflask and took a long, quivering gulp of Jimmy's rum.

He exhaled and took another. And another just for good measure. And another.

Having repaired his nerves, he decided to do another lap outside the Light, and if she was still there afterwards then yes, all right, he would approach her. He wanted to give the gods a chance to move her along, this feeling to him like some sort of divine lapse in concentration that had caught them all by surprise, mortal and immortal.

But no, after completing his lap, empyreal amity was confirmed by Henrietta and her friend *still* drinking outside the bar. Thus, our travelled gallant descended the long, steep escalator, fearing and trembling in his fur coat, brain giddy as he watched them growing slowly larger. Arm me, audacity, from head to foot. Boldness, friend me now. He drew himself up to his full height, assumed his most relaxed, easy smile. Things done well and with a care exempt themselves from fear—and he knew he had given himself enough time to steel his heart. The eagle England was now in prey.

Attack where he is unprepared; appear where you are unexpected.

The day is yours.

'Look who it is!' she said with a note of surprise.

'Look who it is!' he smiled.

His fur coat hung open, and he wore with his black suit a lurid, red and white floral silk shirt by Harvey Pandit that had gobbled up most of that month's earnings.

'You're looking very nice again, Mr Harding,' she said, gaping the prismatic shirt.

'*You're* looking very nice again, Miss Payne,' he smiled.

A pause.

He realised he couldn't just echo what she said all night, and thought he better start rifling his own mental bag for some better, if not original, material.

'Didn't take long for you to drop out then, did it?' he remarked drolly, in his best Jimmy impression. 'What's it been, five weeks? That must be a record for you.'

Shit the bed, she actually laughed.

'I'm back for a few days for some family stuff,' she explained.

His eyes then noted her hands were shaking and he stood stupefied with astonishment, peering disbelievingly at his Master. . . . He had seen things in his frenzies that he knew could not be real, and he hoped now this wasn't one of them. But no, he could *taste* the cognac in the gilt cherubin's mouth; *feel* her firm, sumptuous flesh in his talons. And as he stole sly glances down that body, such view of earthly glory made his brain giddy again. Had he the thousand eyes of Argus, he could never have gazed his fill.

O beauty, till now I never knew thee!

The girl Henrietta was with decided she had to shoot off, and Glenn having never looked at her once could have passed her the following day and not recognised her.

He followed his little Virgil-Beatrice hybrid inside, where they descended some steps and were at once engulfed in the smoky darkness of the immense bar. She got the round in, mercifully, and together they searched the jammed, noisy room and discovered a dimly lit corner to cosy up in. As always her makeup looked as if it had been applied on foot, and she was clad in a huge black scarf over a leather biker jacket on which little imps had been painted, with cropped navy slim-leg trousers and scruffy white trainers. With her hair yanked back behind the blood-red bandana, she looked as if she was about to rock out on the main stage of Leeds Festival. It was perhaps the most ridiculous outfit Glenn had ever seen, and it excited in him infinite admiration. He felt a bit like he was drinking with a celebrity!

'I really do like your shirt,' she exclaimed, staring fixedly at it.

'Have it if you want,' he sighed, looking at her adoringly.

Her thick eyebrows knitted. 'I can *have* your shirt?'

(Softly, gentle patience; she's a wild bird. Don't scare her off.)

'After you peel it from my dead body,' he added.

She laughed, and for once he was glad to be back at Hyde Hill, as it kept Jimmy's act fresh in his memory, making it a lot easier to plagiarise.

Henrietta was good company. Regardless of her looks, she was genuinely fun to be around, and there were none of the awkward silences that punctuated conversation with the likes of Betty, Ali, and even Gertrude. In her presence hours became minutes, rounds were downed and replaced. Yet every time it was his turn to go to the bar, he did so with dread—but somehow, his card kept working, and a strange sense of Predestination began to creep in, as if the night was following its own script. And as the pints poured down their throats all the maddening questions were answered, one by one in dizzying succession: who her mum and dad were; how old they were; what they did for a living; how many siblings she had; what they did; how she knew Jimmy's friend Joe Schofield; every little detail enumerated at long last. How she was doing at university, what she did with her nights, the places she drank, the labels she liked. Who made her fancy jacket. He even learned she was reading a book! Admittedly one written by a living author, and, worse yet, a famous one, but nonetheless; it was impressive that she read. Finally, he was learning it all.

And then, the more they drank, he unlearned it all.

His hands he cast upon her like a snare, as if she might fly off to Manchester at any moment. Priapus had possession of his body, Bacchus his brain, and he was devouring his Chapeltown dish like Pantagruel devouring the cow. And now, servant of Jesu Christ, ye shall be fed afore this table with sweet meats that never knights tasted!

Such nectar from the paragon he would suck. . . .

'Fabric is the medium I use to say what I want to say,' he could hear her saying. 'I use symbolism, I use mysticism—I use *a lot* of mysticism. I use astrology. And I do it all through textiles.'

Glenn grunted.

'At the moment,' she continued, 'everything I make is offensive colours. Blood-red, snot-green, piss-yellow. You say you want to bring Beauty back to the high street? I want to bring *ugly* back to the high street.'

A clanging bell jolted him awake.

'Are you all right?' she asked.

He was stunned to discover her holding his hand.

'I'm *fine!*' he exclaimed.

He shook his head, cast a blurry gaze at the swaying counter. It was last orders.

'Well, this is fun, isn't it,' she sighed, rolling her lovely eyes.

'Henrietta, I'm *fine*,' he slurred. 'Honestly.'

But the table looked inviting to his heavy head, and he nodded forward, lids sagging, only to jerk back suddenly to life. Quietly, he cursed his crapulence. How had he got into such a state? How many pints had they had? He glanced at the dainty one. She looked as if she had been drinking non-alcoholic beer all night, and he remembered now how well the girl could hold her drink. Although in fairness she hadn't been on the street slugging back rum like he had.

He blinked and she was drinking another pint, staring at him thoughtfully.

'Do you know what those women said to me when you went to the toilet?'

'Huh?' he said, drinking his tapwater. 'What women?'

'Those two women over there. They've been watching us all night.'

He cast a glance at the two older women at the table next to them, sipping wine and chattering away. He then looked with mild dread to Henrietta. She was grinning, which traditionally meant she was about to speak heart-wounding words.

'No idea,' he sighed. 'Something cruel that will hurt my feelings, I expect?'

'No,' she said, shaking her head. 'They said they wished their husbands looked at them the way *you* look at me.'

Thou should feel my sword i' the life-blood of thee.

Quoth Venus, in night desire sees best of all; and desire having caught the yielding prey, and Glenn glutton-like having fed, yet never filleth, his lips drawing his rich treasure dry, he wiped the celestial liquor from his mouth and fell on her in delirious longing.

She seized his hips, fixing her gaze on him, her eyes wide and gleaming. In the moonbeam filtering through a gap in the grotty curtains, she assumed an ethereal quality, akin to an angel. 'Twas the sweetest face he ever gazed upon.

'What's wrong?' he whispered breathlessly.

'Come with me to Dinan,' she whispered.

'Is that a club?'

She rolled her eyes. 'It's in *France*, you moron.'

'A club in France?'

'It's a town in France!' she snapped. She then kissed him. 'By the sea,' she said, kissing him again. 'My friend has an empty house there,' she explained, mingling her words with kisses. 'I'm going on the first of January.'

Glenn looked dazed. He was on the threshold of bliss, actually touching it, as her hands held him tightly. 'And you want *me* to go with you?' he said incredulously.

'Yeah. Do you want to come?'

He swallowed.

'Yes.'

'*Good.*' She squeezed his hips. 'January the first, then. Not long now.'
Swilling his tapwater he looked up, and behold, he was in a
reenactment of canto III.VIII, watching with awestruck eyes as she
lunged at him, folded him in her arms and, once again, assailed him
with a riot of kisses. His eyes rolled back in his head.

*Now at last, after failing in Balbec, I am going to discover
the taste of the unknown rose in Albertine's cheeks.*

He began to black out again.
Impossible! Not now. *Please!* With a convulsive effort he was on his
feet. Then shadows. A short walk, but to where? Dialogue under water,
kissing in an alleyway. Now in a taxi, then the harsh lights of an off
licence. A bottle of coke, another of cognac. It was black and he was
floating, floating in the dead of darkness, his arms milling the air. His
recall was that of a newborn baby, until suddenly the dim outline of his
books steadied him. He could vaguely perceive through the murk the
disarray they were in. Had Jimmy knocked them over? In fact, everything
was in disarray. . . . He stiffened. He realised this wasn't Hyde Hill. He
cast his bewildered eyes around the room. Where was he? Round and
round the chamber he reeled, till he bumped into the foot of some single
bed and there she was—all naked to his sight displayed, and whence his
astonish'd eyes more pleasure took than Dis, on heaps of gold fixing his
look.
Mute and amazed he stood, mouth agape. Was he hallucinating? He
tottered over and poked her in the head. She gurgled! He fell back in
terror on the floor.
It was like a shot of paraldehyde, and all of a sudden he felt completely
sober, as the scenes of the night flashed by his inner eye with stunning
clarity. He looked in wonder at her, lying sublime upon her bed like some
descended goddess. He realised she must have brought him here, and
with horror he wondered how many sweet hours he had squandered in
stupor. He leaped to his feet, tottered to the bed. The sight of her body
left him breathless, and he all but fell on her. She awoke with a start but

then her arms infolded him like a band. He tried to kiss her lips, but she turned her head.

'My breath stinks,' she croaked into the pillow.

'I don't care,' he exclaimed.

The right place, with her friend leaving at the right time, before they found the right table, by the right women, who had made the right remark.

By God, fair fellows and lords, saith Launcelot, we have seen this day marvels.

And flying on the airs of Heaven, to Dinan and beyond, what he thought was his heart beating turned out to be footsteps beating the pavement outside. 'What's wrong now?' he said breathlessly. She didn't answer, lying rigidly in his arms. Suddenly, a key rattled in the front door, downstairs. He felt her limbs brace. 'Who's coming home at this hour?' he whispered. Her eyes were wide. 'My *boyfriend*,' she panicked. 'Your *what*!' She leaped out of bed and began hurriedly gathering up his clothes. 'Get out!' she whispered, thrusting the mad bundle into his arms. He heard the front door slam shut and the terrible, heavy footsteps in the hall. 'You have a *boyfriend*!' he whispered, aghast. 'Henrietta!' It sounded like Nimrod himself, loosed from Dante's thirty-first canto and advancing up the stairs. She yanked up her window, and in terror he found himself being shoved into the biting night air.

'*Go*,' she snarled.

But his bare skin shrunk back from the icy cold wind, and the height of the drop, and the slippery looking roof of the bay window. He couldn't do it. But then Nimrod reached the landing, and his footsteps shook not just the floor, but the house itself.

Glenn leaped into the darkness.

IV.IX

Every minute now should be the father of some stratagem.

He must be a wise prince, a skilful warrior—a master of the crooked and straight.

On reflection his sending her uncountable written ambassages, and voice mails, keen to take her up on that invite to Dinan, had probably not been the best move. He had really occupied the yin and not the yang with that one.

Move if there is gain; *halt* if there is no gain.

Wearily, he mounted the wooden high stool, placed his roasted chestnut latte on the high table. He reached inside his fur coat, produced his hipflask and discreetly topped his drink up with a double shot of Hydra's venom. He sipped it while gazing absently into the mammoth silver Christmas tree whose top brushed the stained glass ceiling. The lashing of the fountains softened the raucous din of the rabble.

Behind his humongous sunglasses his eyes were full of sad thoughts and troubles.

His head was as chaotic as his cashdesk drawer. He still was in shock, not quite believing what had happened. He had learned everything then lost it; seen everything then forgot it. He couldn't for the life of him understand how a man of his constitution could be drunk under the table by a small woman. It was impossible even by the standards of a night riddled with impossibilities. It was almost suspicious.

And then there was the matter of her boyfriend.

The thought of another man touching her pained him in his heart's heart. Why had she never brought *him* up before? Was that the reason why she hadn't quizzed him on Gertrude, or that mad, ridiculous incident with Betty? There were plenty of tough questions she could have asked him. Perhaps she didn't want to risk having to answer any herself? He sucked his secret brew, recalling wistfully, longingly, the nectar he had sucked from her. . . . He shook his head. He had been in the same room as immortal fame. He had even shared a bed with it! And the only thing worse than not being able to have Henrietta was having her for one night, briefly; the only thing worse than never being able to hold that body was to hold it once, fleetingly. To know what could be.

He felt like Actaeon, the boy who glimpsed Diana without her veils. Actaeon being the hunter who became the hunted, the goddess transforming him into a stag as punishment for his trespass—whereupon he was torn apart by his own hounds.

Actaeon, of course, was lucky. At least they sprang straight for his throat and it was over in an instant. Poor Glenn was being torn apart from the inside, slowly.

No way could there be a pinch in death more sharp than this.

Another concern was that boyfriend of hers, Nimrod. Glenn dearly hoped that to rescue Henrietta's love, he didn't have to first go through him. He could not shake his sense of lurking peril, that feeling that somewhere in the city catastrophe was looking for him. In his mind, he aways pictured a huge dark shape emerging from the shadows. Ominously, the said shape seemed to comport exactly with the awful sound of that abomination advancing up the stairs.

But then what Glenn in his brain beheld, reviv'd his courage, and his fear expell'd. His inner eye conjured up in order the images of heroes through history who slew the giant: Odysseus and Polyphemos; David and Goliath; Beowulf and Grendel.

Glenn and Wilfred.

He sucked up the remnants of his chestnut-poison concoction. All of a sudden, some wicked day of destiny didn't seem so wicked after all. If that's what you want, Nimrod, then come on, come on straight. You'll be swift to meet your end, child. Your doom comes close on the heels of Wilfred's own, for, by the faith of my body, it is a wise prince, a skilful warrior—a master of the crooked and straight—ye be jousting with. Do not scorn my warning.

Glenn gazed upon Henrietta's gilded sprite, forever imprinted in his eye.

'However hard you try, you won't escape me, you wayward one,' he vowed.

But there was no conviction in his voice. Anon he rose to his feet and lurched unsteadily back to Camelot—his mind not what it usually was.

And so our scene must fly to the other side of the city centre, where another team member was on her lunch. Mildred was sitting on a low-slung sofa in the corner of a compact but lofty undercover courtyard, in one of several deserted seating areas outside the various cafes and winebars. Christmas music was reverberating around the heights of the red brick walls, sleigh bells jingling merrily, as a thick gloom descended through the glass roof. She wore her long, fur trimmed leather coat open over her tight leather mini dress by Nirah Frazar, sipping her gin and tonic as she peered sideways at his huge hands foraging around inside his navy parka's many pockets.

What he produced from one made her jaw drop.

'How the chuff have you got *that?*' she said with stupefaction.

'So you know what it is?' said Derek quickly, fastening on her the single eyeball that peeped out from under the tilted black beanie visor.

'Obviously I know what it is. It's that *vile* red and white polkadot pocket square we sold last year that went straight to sale. Proper minging!'

'Who does it belong to?'

'Well, possession is nine-tenths of the law, so I guess it belongs to *you.*'

'I found it on the floor in my bird's bedroom,' he said gravely.

'That doesn't surprise me. I've seen the way she dresses.'

'Henrietta never bought anything from your shop until she worked there, and that was just uniform, so this pocket square *can't* be hers. You said yourself it's from last year.'

'Mate, have you seen the floor of our stock room? There's shit that's been there since the '90s.'

'Look, Mildred; I know it's all innocent. Henrietta probably packed it in her bag by accident when she was rushing at the end of her shift. But the thing is, she's back in Manchester now, and I just want to return this thing to its rightful owner. That's all. So don't feel like you have to protect your mate.'

'He is not my "mate",' she scowled. 'He's a chuffing *gimp.*'

The cyclops looked fixedly at the sales assistant.

'Oh, so you *do* know who he is?'

Her countenance abruptly fell.

'Ah, bollocks,' she said. 'No, what I meant was—see, the thing is right—look! This is nothing to do with me,' she babbled. 'I deny everything!'

Derek shoved the pocket square back in his parka. 'Mildred, Mildred, Mildred,' he sighed. 'I *really* expected more from my main client.'

'Derek!' she snapped. 'What do you expect? I'm not a snitch. I can't give you his name—even if he is an arrogant little twat who needs a good slap.'

'Are you *sure* you can't give me his name? Because I would hate for my, er, *street pharmaceutical business*—which has, by the way, been so supportive of you throughout your various problems—to have to start withholding your medicine.'

Mildred sloshed back her drink and banged the glass angrily on the table.

'Oh, so you think I'm an *addict*!?' she shouted. 'Mate, I can quit any time I want—in fact, you know what? I'm up to date, I don't owe you owt. I'm going to quit right now.' She grabbed her ruched black leather pouch bag, threw the bicycle chain strap over her shoulder and stood up. 'So you can take your drugs and *shove 'em up your arse!*'

She turned and strutted off defiantly, the heels of her leather kneeboots clip clopping against the tiles. She then lurched to a stop and whirled back around.

'And I mean shove them up your arse as an insult; not like when you have to shove them up your arse to conceal them from the—oh just piss off!'

She threw open the glass double doors and then dissolved into the thick gloom.

Derek's eye was wide, his face slack. He then shook his head, retrieved one of his many Kumquats from one of his many pockets. He clacked away at the keys.

IV.X

Glenn threw open the dungeon door and trudged into the dank and chilly atmosphere. There was a grim look etched on his phizog and his steps clacked sharply upon the stone floor. A shrill and unfriendly voice pierced the air, uttering a curt, '*Hello Glenn.*'

'My job was stacking bricks,' he replied. 'I was twenty-one years old and hard work didn't frighten me one bit, but this job was a killer.'

A pause.

'What?' said the voice.

The effluvia of the manager's office filled his nostrils, and as he peered ahead, two mysterious black orbs seemed to float before his chest. Gradually, Shukeena's striking visage materialised around them. Casting his gaze over her head, he observed that Norman had taken Gertrude's shape, or Gertrude was sitting in Norman's chair, one or the other. Shukeena, his eyes noted, seemed to be looking at him expectantly.

'Yes?' he said.

'What did you just say?' Shukeena enquired with a furrowed brow.

He shook his head to clear the fog. 'O, sorry,' he said, cunningly rearranging his blank expression into a look of alert professionalism. 'I said, "Dive, thoughts, down to my soul; here comes Hell's black intelligencer—let's be calm,"' he stated pleasantly.

Shukeena continued to scrutinise him suspiciously. Her gaze dropped to his fur coat, revealing conspicuous stains—one resembling liquor and another resembling vomit.

She could not repress her shiver.

'Never mind,' the Queen of Furies hissed, turning and clip clopping to Gertrude, at the cluttered desk. 'Just get back on the floor so that one of us is out there, Glenn. We'll be in here for a while, planning the Christmas do.'

Her eyes peered at him sideways.

Glenn said nothing. He removed his ginormous sunglasses, slipped them into his fur coat and hung the huge, shaggy piece on the antique Victorian coat stand.

'I *said*, "We'll be in here for a while, planning the *Christmas do*. . . ."'

The menswear manager stared at her with a vacant expression.

'I thought you'd be upset,' said the hero of villains with a note of disappointment. 'You *love* planning the Christmas do; it's the only job in here you get excited about.'

Glenn sighed. 'Miss Mohammed,' he said, 'a generous ardour boils within my breast, eager of action, enemy to rest; and it urges me to *fight*, and fires my mind—to leave a memorable name-badge behind. Now, I'm hardly going to accomplish that by wasting my time planning some pointless Christmas do, am I?'

'Do you know where we're having it this year?' Shukeena enquired.

'In R'lyeh, where dead Cthulu waits dreaming?' he guessed.

'No,' she said, grinning. 'We're having it at *LS1*. You're finally going to get in!'

Glenn stared at her with a vacant expression.

'What's got into you lately?' she demanded angrily. 'You're not yourself anymore. Are you feeling all right?'

'I'm *fine*,' he sighed. (All days are night to see till I see thee, and nights bright days when dreams do show me thee.) 'Well, maybe not fine,' he said. 'I feel. . . . so so.'

'Soso?' blurted a voice. Shukeena stepped aside and looked at Norman, who was sitting on the office safe, reading a copy of *Medal News*. Glenn hadn't even noticed he was in the room. 'There was nothing "all right" about Soso, I can assure you. It was his generals who did all the work for him. Many times they wanted to make better decisions, but were overruled by his orders. Whole Russian units were decimated because they were forbidden from making tactical withdrawals to better fighting positions, just because this Georgian cobbler whose only experience of combat was knocking over post offices thought *he* knew better. *Soso*,' said the store manager with contempt. 'The man was a liability!'

A pause.

'Great, thanks for that, Norman,' said Shukeena, turning back to Glenn. 'Well, it's a shame you don't care about the Christmas do, Glenn, because, quite honestly, we're lucky to be having one at all, given that head office hasn't allocated us any budget due to our poor figures, and our branch being bottom of the leader board.' She turned to the style advisor, who was quietly typing out invites on the computer, refusing to look in Glenn's direction. 'But fortunately, *Gertrude* has used her contacts to reserve us a couple of tables on the top floor and saved the day!'

She rested a hand on Gertrude's bony shoulder and gazed at her adoringly.

'What with the recent problems in here a lot of people would have done nothing; but not Getrude. And I couldn't be prouder of her. It just goes to show, we're not a team on ladieswear; we're a *family*—and *we* look out for each other.'

Glenn stared at his ex.

'You'll be looking *through* each other if Gertrude gets any paler,' he heard himself say. 'Holy cow—she looks like Jane Grey's ghost!'

'Excuse me?' Shukeena gasped. 'What did you just say!?'

Glenn stared at her in blank wonder. 'Huh?'

The clacking had stopped and Gertrude was grinding her teeth furiously in the glow of the screen. 'What did you just say about Gertrude!' Shukeena shouted.

Glenn couldn't respond because he had noticed that the patch of mushrooms growing on the ceiling had spread into a horrifying mass of blue fungi that was fast enveloping the wall. Hundreds of them gleamed silently in the murk, silhouetting the oblivious Norman, utterly dwarfing his large composition. They looked almost like they were about to swallow him. Glenn choked.

'Well, that's it now!' Shukeena continued. 'Abusive language is gross misconduct! I'm reporting you to head office!'

The avenging deity whirled around and snatched a report from Norman's desk organiser, reaching over Norman in the process, who was lost in his *Medal News*. But on snatching a pen from Norman's pocket she remembered the hundred or so reports she had made to head office about the gross misconduct of Glenn Harding, and suddenly a look of profound fatigue appeared on her face. 'Ah, what's the point?' she groaned, shoving the report log back in its tray. 'Come on, Gertrude, let's get this Christmas do sorted,' she sighed, resting her arms on the back of the executive chair. 'They don't deserve us, this lot. They really don't.'

Gertrude resumed typing out the invites. . . . but she was still grinding her teeth.

Glenn prized his eyes from the horrid mushrooms, shook his head violently.

'I—I better get back to my floor,' he gibbered faintly.

As the door slammed shut behind him, Norman tossed his magazine on the desk.

'Yep,' he said, rising to his feet, 'and I better get back to my office.'

'You're already in your office, Norman!' Shukeena yelled.

'Oh.'

Now turn we unto Kirkgate, down which Gertrude was clip clopping, swathed in a belted black mink fur coat and black silk satin scarf by Nirah Frazar, both items flapping madly in the violent gale. She was still grinding her teeth.

'Gerty!' called a familiar voice.

She looked back and observed Derek lurking in a goods entrance in his navy parka and tilted beanie visor, his chunky gold earrings glinting in the shadows.

His ample figure seemed almost to have walled up the wide doorway.

'What is it then?' she said, drawing near him. 'What's this about?'

'Oh? Are we not doing small talk first?' he said, elevating his eyebrow in surprise. 'Fair enough,' he shrugged, as he reached inside one of his multitudinous pockets. 'I just wanted to tell you that I've got. . . . *this*.'

At the sight of the gaudy red and white polkadot pocket square, Gertrude felt her stomach lurch. Her eyes widened behind her humongous sunglasses.

'And?' she replied, her face betraying no emotion.

'And what do you think about it?'

'I think you can't pull it off.'

The cyclops glowered at her. 'Who does it belong to?' he demanded.

'No idea,' she shrugged. She paused a moment. 'But how come *you* have it?'

She could feel her heart beating faster in her chest.

'It was on Henrietta's bedroom floor.'

Abruptly the style advisor sagged.

'It never was,' she choked. 'Was it?'

He looked at her searchingly. 'Yep,' he nodded.

'*Really?*' she said.

'Yes.'

'Okay,' she said faintly.

'All I want is his name. And for it, as a show of gratitude, my friendly, er, *moving apothecary* would be happy to offer you some *very* competitive seasonal deals.'

'*No*. I'm not doing drugs anymore; it's affecting my appearance,' she stammered. 'And I don't know who that pocket square belongs to. Sorry, Derek.'

But her lip quaked, and teardrops began to stream out from under her sunglasses.

Derek stepped out from his doorway and watched her hurrying away, blown along by the boisterous winds. Thoughts were flurrying through his noodle. . . .

IV.XI

'I don't get it,' blurted an all-too-familiar voice.

The frenetic rat-tat-tat-tat of the keyboard abruptly stopped. 'You don't *get* it?' Glenn said, panting. He stared quizzically at the script in the Leviathan's vasty paws. 'What's not to *get?*'

Jimmy, sprawled athwart the adjacent sofa, in his rags, with his mountainous belly employed as a proxy book stand on which Glenn's script was open, was frowning at the menswear manager, over his reading glasses. 'I thought there was going to be this big, mental house party, but it never happened,' he said.

'And?' Glenn panted.

'And it's a bit of an anticlimax, isn't it?'

'*Exactly*. It's true to life. That's what makes it so clever.'

'You can't build up to something that never happens, Glenn. It doesn't work.'

'Sorry Jimmy, I didn't catch you there—were you talking about my script or *Waiting for Godot?* But go on; tell me about how the idea "doesn't work". Idiot.'

Glenn resumed pounding away at the grubby keys of Jimmy's crappy instrument.

'But this is TV, Glenn. You need, er. . . . plots and resolutions.'

'Do you know what you can watch if you need plots and resolutions?'

'What?'

'*Everything*! Everything ever broadcast, ever! Can there not be one show—*just one*—that dares to explore that dark terra incognita that lies beyond conventional storytelling? That flouts these artificial formulas that were dated in the days of John Logie Baird? And yes, you can pull all the faces you want, Mr Sandaal; scoff all you like; but the fact of the matter is I am attempting to write something no one has ever written before.'

'There might be a reason why no one's ever written it before.'

The din of rattling keys abruptly stopped. Glenn was giving him a feral glower.

'And your characters aren't very likeable,' Jimmy added.

'Joyce's characters aren't very likeable,' Glenn replied tersely. 'Joyce is the greatest writer of the twentieth century.'

'Never heard of her.'

This place is too cold for hell.

'Anyway, I don't really get it,' said Jimmy, removing his reading glasses. He placed them on top of the script, on the pinewood. 'But I wish you luck, obviously.'

He then picked up the remote control and unmuted the wonkbox.

'You're not going to stop reading *now*, are you?' Glenn gasped. He was staring at the behemoth with disbelief. 'Keep going, for I am about a roaring piece of work!'

'Keep *going*?' said Jimmy with incredulity. 'Does it pick up at any point?'

'Of course it picks up! Wait till you read episode four.'

'Episode *four*? Shit the bed. Why does it happen so late?'

'Well, he has to experience *some* bad fortune before he enjoys the good. But by the midway point in episode four things really begin to turn around for Len Farthing—that's when he starts to close in on his big win!'

'But I don't want him to win. I want him to lose.'

'Then you'll be disappointed.'

'I think you're better off letting the BBC judge it, mate. Have you thought much about January?'

'What, you mean with Dinan and Henrietta? Only every second of every day. But what can I do, if that mute cherubin won't pick up the—'

Jimmy threw his paws up defensively. 'No, no; you've told me all about that, Glenn. In great detail. I mean the *move*. You know? Where you're going to *live*.'

Glenn stared at him through his long dangling locks of wet ragged hair. 'The move?' he said cluelessly. 'What move?'

'My tenancy expires in January, remember?' said Jimmy. 'We've got to leave.'

Glenn threw Jimmy's instrument aside and gaped at him. 'What?' he said in falsetto. '*Leave?*'

'*Yes.*'

'So where are we going?'

'Where are *we* going? I don't know where *we're* going, Glenn, but *I'm* moving back in with my family,' Jimmy stated. 'I'm getting married, remember?'

Glenn jerked himself to his feet with his mouth open.

'*Married*!?' he exclaimed. 'Since when are you getting *married*? What the fu—Where the *hell* is all this coming from!?'

'Mate, it was arranged months ago. I've told you numerous times. I didn't think you were taking it in to be honest. You've been all over the place lately.'

Glenn's face had turned a ghastly pale. 'So where am *I* going to go?' he warbled. 'What's going to happen to *me*?'

'Oh, you'll be fine,' Jimmy said soothingly. 'Not everywhere's as pricey as Hyde Hill. You can manage a modest rent, can't you?'

Glenn tilted his head, stared incredulously at the man.

'A "modest rent"?' he said. Glenn reminded him how much he got paid, before tax, and about his uncountable minimum payments on his innumerable debts that were forever growing. 'So, no, Jimmy. No I can't manage a modest rent. Because I have nothing. Do you understand me? Nothing! In fact, no: I have *less* than nothing. And now, to make matters worse, I have nowhere to fizzing live!'

Jimmy cleared his throat. 'Would you consider a hostel?' he ventured delicately.

'THE FLOPHOUSE!' Glenn shrieked. 'You can shog right off with that one, Jimmy! I'll never survive a hostel. The people in those dumps make *you* seem civilized!'

'Well, you know, you can always go home.'

Glenn made a strangled sound.

'Oh come on, mate!' the Leviathan laughed. 'Seacroft's not *that* bad.'

'Would you *really* send me back to the streets of Seacroft?' Glenn said in a tremulous voice. 'Jimmy, I'd be safer in bloody *prison*. At least in there the inmates are supervised! I barely escaped with my life last time.' There was a haunted look in his eyes, and he began pacing the room anxiously. 'You can't expect me to go home, Jimmy. My dad will try "straightening me out" again. Last time he tried to enlist me in the *army*. And that was while my mum was on about sectioning me! I won't be able to pay them any board, I won't be able to do any writing because they don't have a computer. It'll be just me, with no money and nothing to do, surrounded by my dad's shotguns. And how do you think *that* plot will resolve itself!?'

Suddenly he stopped pacing and stood staring at Jimmy. 'Let me come live with you and your new wife,' he begged. 'It'll just be for a few weeks, until I sort myself out, I swear.'

Jimmy drew back in his seat as if a leper had reached out to touch him.

'No way, Glenn; that's what you told me when you moved in here!'

'Please, Jimmy!'

'I said no!'

'Jimmy!'

Suddenly, Glenn froze. His eyes drifted from the underwriter to the tiny window, rattling furiously in its frame. Outside, a tempest howled, black clouds churning across the night sky as rain hammered the glass like his fingers hammered a keyboard. And then, through a jagged tear in the clouds, he saw it: his oldest enemy, the mocking moon, casting its pale, silvery light like an accusatory finger at his oldest friend.

Glenn lowered his gaze from the window and looked agog at Jimmy. 'O my God,' he gasped faintly. 'It's *you*, isn't it? *You're* the catastrophe that's been lying in wait for me. *You're* the lurking peril—the great shape in the shadows, stalking my footsteps.' His expression darkened as he pointed a trembling finger at his flatmate. 'Therefore,' he bellowed, 'when ye see the Abomination of Desolation, standing in the holy place, let them flee to the mountains—for there shall be *great tribulation*, such as was not from the beginning of the world till now!'

Pause.

'Glenn, you really do have some serious problems.'

'I know I do! *You*! You're my problem! You always were my problem!'

'I'M YOUR PROBLEM!?' Jimmy suddenly erupted. 'Mate, *I'm* the one who took you in so you didn't have to go back home! *I'm* the one who keeps lending you money! And who takes you out for drinks, and who lets you get away with murder in here—' Abruptly his face fell. 'Actually, wait. Maybe I *am* your problem?'

'Bullshit!'

'Mildred, I'm looking right now, I swear. It isn't there. It isn't anywhere. Honestly. I've searched the flat high and low!'

'Oh my God. How could you lose the emergency stash?'

'I don't know! Maybe we had it?'

'Are you mad? We'd know if we had that shit.'

'Would we?'

'Are you *sure* you didn't take it yourself?'

'Yes!'

'Gerty, I know what you're like.'

'Mate, I'm not lying to you.'

'Well, you better replace it. I'm broke.'

'So am I. Glenn drank all my money.'

'What! So the gimp is ruining *my* life now? How does he do it?'

'I know, I know. He's like a contagious disease.'

'So what are we going to do?'

IV.XII

But wait, let me say "amen" betimes, lest the devil cross my prayer, for here he comes in the likeness of a formalwear supervisor, emerging from the men's toilets.

'Whatever you want to do downstairs, do it,' Glenn barked, without looking up from his magazine. '*Seriously*,' he said. 'I don't give a shit anymore.'

The chair next to Glenn scraped sharply across the concrete, creaked as his porcine subject planted his vasty buttocks on it. 'Geez, geez, it's nothing to do with work, don't worry,' said Dick quietly, with a reassuring look.

'Nothing to do with work?' Glenn frowned. Through a straw, he sucked his roasted chestnut latte with extra Hydra's venom and fresh blood. 'But we have nothing to discuss that's not work-related?'

'Oh yes we do.'

'Like what?'

'*Drugs.*'

A pause.

'What dost thou mean by this?'

Dick leaned in closer. 'Are you on them?'

Glenn glowered fiercely at the formalwear supervisor.

'Be thou familiar, but by no means vulgar,' he snarled. 'No, I am not on drugs, Dick! And how *dare* thy harsh rude tongue sound this unpleasing—'

'I don't care if you are!' Dick interposed, waving his little hands. 'I'm not going to tell on you. It's just everyone's noticed you've been acting weird lately—well, *weirder*—and what with the Christmas do coming up, and people being skinter than normal cos they're paying off their Thank You cards—thank you very much for that, by the way—it's looking like it's going to be a complete disaster. Unless someone steps forward and saves it, by bringing us all a bit of, er, "good cheer". . . .'

Glenn shook his head with disbelief.

'Authority melts from me, it really does,' he sighed. 'Dick; you do realise that I am the menswear *manager*, and we are at *work*? God's arms and skin! What you are doing here is the equivalent of going to Shukeena and asking *her* for drugs!'

Dick pulled a face. 'It's not *really* though, is it, geez?'

A pause.

'All right, no,' Glenn conceded. 'But it's still bad.'

'You know it's not a free bar this year, don't you? Head office hasn't allocated us any budget. I had to practically *beg* Shukeena just to set out a couple of punch bowls for us! It's going to be the worst Christmas do ever, if someone doesn't do something about it. So if you can find it in your heart to, er, "Let It Snow", it will *really* brighten things up! Come on, geez! Don't you think after a year like this we're owed a great night?'

'Why do I care if anyone has a "great night"? I never have a great night and none of you lot give a toss about me.' He turned his attention back to the copy of *Advert* laid out before him on the table. 'Bah, humbug,' he exclaimed. 'Good afternoon!'

'Well, this is a surprise,' Dick sighed despondently.

'Good afternoon!'

'I thought you'd want to pull out all the stops to make it a great Christmas do, given that Henrietta's coming.'

Glenn spat his coffee across the editorial page of *Advert*.

'*Whattttt?*'

'You heard me.'

'She's definitely coming?'

'She's responded. Said she's coming.'

'I—I can't believe they invited her?'

'They weren't going to—I had to kick off with Shukeena and Gerty over it! I told them it wasn't right, that they *had* to invite her. We invite *everyone* who's worked in the store that year to the Christmas do; it's *tradition*. I mean, obviously we don't invite people like Wilfred who left under a cloud—wink wink—but Henrietta did her four weeks and left on good terms. She wasn't my cup of tea, but she was a good seller. So you see, geez? This Christmas do has the *potential* to be an amazing night. I mean, it's a masquerade ball! How cool is that? But the problem is that LS1 is very pricey, the punch bowls are going to empty fast and, well, you know. . . . Shukeena'll be there.'

'Well I can't help you, Dick. I wouldn't even know how to get any dru—' He stopped.

His eyes were wide, his jaw hanging slack from his head. He had fallen into a trance and was watching himself, way back in III.XI, turning Gertrude's apartment over for money, heaving her mattress up and discovering, what? *A small envelope filled with colourful pills with funny little faces on them.* Down the old grey windowpane wool blazer the envelope went—where it dropped through the disintegrated stitching and settled within the garment and was completely forgotten about. . . . Until this propitious moment.

It is necessary for a prince, if he wants to preserve himself, to learn how *not* to be good.

And so our scene must to Chinatown fly, where a very similar one was playing out.

The spindly body was clad in a provocative red felt cut-off skirt and boob tube with fluffy white Santa trim and knee-high leather boots. Her bare midriff and legs were exposed, and with the garish ringlets dangling from her twisted peroxide knot, and her leopard print silk scarf and long black leather coat flapping in the wind, she looked like a Christmas cracker that had already been pulled.

'Mildred Scragg!' he exclaimed in mock surprise, removing his earphones.

'All right,' Mildred grunted.

There was a sheepish look on her face.

'To what do I owe this pleasure? You can't be here for your medicine because, as we know, you're all better now,' the cyclops said, his eyeball looking at her obliquely. 'How are you finding reality, by the way?' he grinned. 'Very *real*, isn't it?'

'All right, Derek! Stop rubbing it in!' she barked. 'You know exactly why I'm here—the Christmas do's coming up and I need something to get me through it.'

'Hmmm,' said Derek thoughtfully, stroking his wiry beard. 'Let me see what I have shoved up my arse.' He felt about his hulking body and produced from one of his illimitable pockets a small bag teeming with funny green debris.

Mildred rolled her eyes.

'Mate, I'm gonna need something stronger than a bifter. It's *Christmas!*'

'This *is* something stronger than a bifter, genius,' he said. 'It's super strong Lebanese blonde hash mixed with Derek's secret ingredients. Take a puff of this and you'll be blown sky high; finish it and you'll be watching your work party from the *Moon*.

'I call it, "The Gunpowder Pot",' he added proudly.

She lunged for the bag with startling suddenness. 'Give it to me!' she snarled.

He had to hold the bag over his head while his free hand held her off. Her arms were flailing in the air, her mouth foaming. 'Hey, calm down, grabby!' he chuckled. 'You know what I want first.'

'We can't do it out here! It's too cold.'

'Not *that*,' snapped Derek. 'The other thing.' He retrieved the gaudy red and white polkadot pocket square from his parka. 'This *ugly* business.'

The sight of the cursed accessory wrung from Mildred a long, dismal groan.

'Are you *still* on about that stupid hanky?' She closed her eyes and sighed. 'All right, fine. It belongs to Glenn Harding.'

'Who?'

'*Glenn Harding*. He's this psycho menswear manager,' she explained. 'Everybody hates him. He's a total schizo.'

'Really?' he frowned. 'He doesn't sound like someone Henrietta would get with?'

'Oh! You'd be surprised. He's been with Ali, Betty, and Gerty. And those are just the ones I know about! He gets around, all right.'

'Gerty too?' This intelligence flummoxed him, and he gaped the pocket square with incredulity. He glared at Mildred. 'Have *you* been with him?'

'Have I bollocks! I'm the only one in there with any self-respect. Now give me that hash!' She leaped up, snatched the bag and bolted, looking most unladylike as she ran slowly and unsteadily on the icy pavement in her six-inch heels.

'Merry Christmas, you big fat twat!' she shouted back over her shoulder.

Derek put the pocket square back in his parka and pulled out a numbered invitation, addressed to Henrietta Payne. Printed on black glossy card was the gold legend:

THE 20■ NIRAH FRAZAR MASQUERADE BALL.
ALL STAFF INVITED. LS1.
RSVP.

Plus one, it said overleaf. Guests of Gertrude Ogden. His vision hovered forbodingly over the words "plus one".

IV.XIII

'I've got a bad feeling about this night,' cried one over the howling winds.

'I've got a *great* feeling about this night!' cried the other.

'Seriously Glenn; if you've got drugs on you then I'm off home. I'm not getting banged up tonight.'

'Fine! If you don't want to be in LS1, surrounded by the Nirah Frazar girls, then *go*. You are getting married, after all. Adieu!'

Pause.

'Well, I better come with you. Just to make sure things don't get out of hand.'

Glenn strode grimly forward in his fur coat, its skirt flapping relentlessly in the snowstorm. He clung to his trilby, pressed tightly against his head to stop it from escaping, while his free hand gripped the upturned collar of his coat, protecting his mullet. His blue hands longed for the warmth of his long lost leather shooting gloves.

Beside him, Jimmy lumbered along in a bright yellow kagool, stretched over his mountainous rolls of fat, the hood toggled tightly round his vast head. Snow covered his face and trousers, and Glenn was so dwarfed by him that, in the blizzard, he looked like a man out walking his yeti.

Marching through a narrow passageway, they emerged onto a sprawling square, where a magnificent three-storey townhouse stood grandly at the centre, the name LS1 illuminated in lights over the doors. The beat from the building pulsed in the air, and shapes and colours swirled from the eye-like windows. Through the snowstorm, the vague shape of two dread bouncers could be perceived, ogreish and terrible, wielding the petrifying clipboard with the impenetrable LS1 guestlist.

As Glenn beheld the picture, a strong sensation of imminent, inescapable Fate possessed him. After all the years of doodling in his sketch book, and the cackhanded attempts to become a designer, a businessman and model, and now his ongoing struggle to become a TV writer, he had ended up here, at LS1—wherein a genuine talent was waiting for him. With whom he really could *make something of himself.*

And then all his enemies would be ashamed and sore vexed.

At last, the moment of truth had arrived, the night of Destiny was upon him. And Brigantia's burying the city in snow he knew was a plot device—her clever metaphor for the trackless path one must take to make it from the other end of nowhere to *Greatness.* He released his collar, reached inside his pocket, and squeezed Henrietta's sock tightly; he attempted to speak but instead made a gurgling sound.

'Eh?' said Jimmy.

'I said, this is it, Jimmy! LS1! We're here now—so just relax!'

'I am relaxed, me,' Jimmy shrugged. 'It's *you* who needs to relax.'

'Look! Just calm down or you'll blow the whole thing, all right? Let not the bouncers see fear govern our eyes!'

Standing outside the huge Georgian door, under the portico, the bouncers watched the two strange-looking and acting men lurching towards them through the snow.

'Here we go,' Glenn whispered, clutching his trilby. 'Let *me* do the talking.'

'Can I help you?' grunted First Bouncer.

Glenn screamed.

The bouncers exchanged a look.

'We just want to come in,' said Jimmy, smiling amiably. 'Please.'

'Not tonight lads,' grunted Second Bouncer.

Glenn felt his heart contract. '*Whattttt!*' he gasped. 'But—but for what reason?'

'We don't give *reasons*,' grunted First Bouncer. 'Now run along.'

Glenn's jaw flapped in the blizzard. He turned his back on the club and gawped stupidly at the heavens. Was this the obstacle the mocking gods knew all along would thwart him, at the very door of Destiny? Did the Comedy never end?

'Fortune!' he shrieked. 'At last you have wholly defeated me!'

'Er, we should be on the list,' Jimmy remarked. 'We're here for a party.'

The bouncers exchanged another look.

'Names?' grunted Second Bouncer, glaring dubiously at them.

Glenn whirled around and threw himself back into the pother.

'Glenn Harding plus one,' he said quickly, with a quaver in his voice.

'*I'm* plus one,' said Jimmy with great pride.

'We're guests of Gertrude Ogden—my quondam paramour. . . .' Glenn added.

That one got him a long, hard glower from First Bouncer. And from Jimmy. But nevertheless, he found his name on the list and glanced at Second Bouncer.

With incredible reluctance, they stepped aside and let them in.

'I'm glad they had a cloakroom,' said Glenn, thinking out loud as they scaled the U-shaped oak staircase.

Jimmy looked askance at the flamboyant, bright gold silk shirt Glenn was wearing, patterned by little black tigers prowling up and down it. 'I'm not,' he replied.

As they advanced up the levels the drums and strings of the middle floor contested the electronic thud of the top floor, and the wet squelch of Glenn's footsteps. The menswear manager's hands were shaking as he donned his garish, jewel-encrusted Day of the Dead-style skull masquerade mask. It was more chilling than enchanting.

At the top of the stairs, they passed through a large doorway, where the sight that met their eyes stopped them in their tracks.

The vaunted topfloor was like a high hall, grand and gold-adorned, with massive columns rising into the vaulted ceiling. On the dance floor, stylish boys and girls gyrated under polychromatic lights, while great volumes of chatter, laughter and fag smoke rose up from the silhouettes thronging the luminous bar. A riot of pretty phizogs whizzed past the eye pell-mell, all looking to Glenn as if they had leaped straight out of the pages of *Advert*.

He stood glorying in the promised place. He breathed its Greatness.

The music, however, was a vulgar recycling of an old disco hit, the verses replaced by some deep-voiced imbecile gabbling about his new "sneakers" and how much they cost him. In fairness though, this was a *club*; you could hardly expect the common body, no matter how gorgeous they were, to request the DJ spin Rubinstein's rendition of the *Nocturnes*. (Although it would be nice if they did.)

'So this is it—the top floor of LS1,' yelled Jimmy. 'Do you like it then?'

'Like it?' Glenn laughed. 'This locality is so crowded with the presence of divinities that it's easier to find a *god* here than a man!' he exulted dreamily. 'Here is *everything* advantageous to life!'

'Good music, too,' yelled Jimmy.

Glenn chose to ignore one. He scuttled up to the lattice windows, where he gazed in awe at the snowy panorama, making it look as if LS1 was standing atop the fluffy clouds, high in the sky—as if they had ascended to the very roof of heaven.

'Your party's over there,' the Leviathan yelled abruptly. 'Shall we join them?'

Glenn kept his back to the room. 'Not yet, Jimmy; and *stop* pointing at them!' he snarled over his shoulder, swatting his massive arm. 'You'll make us look keen.'

'But we *are* keen.'

He glared at the behemoth. 'We'll go over in our own time, all right?'

Glenn took a deep breath. With trembling hands, he smoothed down the enormous gold shirt he had tucked into his tight trousers. He looked askance at the underwriter, in that dripping wet kagool he insisted on wearing because he was too tight to pay for the cloakroom. And the Mexican wrestler's mask he recycled from Halloween because he was too tight to buy a masquerade one. He could feel his entrails squirming as he wondered what a cruel judge like Henrietta Payne would think of him bringing a plus one like this to the party.

He then wondered what his snobby, hypercritical colleagues would think of him.

700,000 Leodiensians to choose from—and this freak was the best Glenn could do?

And if that wasn't proof once again that Jimmy was the embodiment of that nimbus hanging over him, the catastrophe in his stars, he didn't know what was. He was genuinely too embarrassed to join his own party. He half wanted to go downstairs and give the bouncers another chance to throw them out.

Then suddenly, someone threw themselves at him.

'Hi Glenn,' yelled a familiar voice in its docile timbre. A lad's arms wrapped around him, as two grey eyes peeped at him through a gold, crystal-embellished masquerade mask adorned with a huge black feather.

'How doth, Mr Hussain,' Glenn replied with a quizzical look.

'We were wondering where you were. I'm so glad you came!' Ali gushed.

'*Huh?*'

Given that communication between Glenn and Ali had since IV.V been limited to a stiff, awkward exchange of nods when passing each other in the shop, he couldn't help but search the makeup artist's eyes for evidence of intemperence. He found none.

'Nice shirt, by the way,' Ali grinned. 'Great minds, eh!'

To his horror, Glenn saw they were wearing the exact same golden garment—which meant that his lengthy quest to Manchester, via the Megabus, right to the sale rack at the back of Harvey Pandit, in search of an utterly original outfit for the Christmas do, had after all that been a failure. And momentarily his strength feebled and he waxed passing faint, as he repenteth bitterly that he blew the last of his money on it.

But he was then buoyed by the sight of Ali warmly greeting Jimmy, and introducing them both to his plus one, some stunning cousin in a tight dress, and Betty was there too, as was her plus one, a facsimile of her, as was one of the nameless Christmas temps, with her nameless plus one, and there was much hugging and kissing of cheeks. Glenn's heart was racing, and he and Jimmy exchanged a sly glance in which the behemoth's eyes said, for the first time ever, how glad he was to know Glenn Harding.

'Come on,' yelled Ali, 'come say hello to everyone.' And he grabbed Glenn's hand and dragooned him through the clangorous crowd, followed by the train of nymphs, and Jimmy, unto a roped off corner where the party was.

'Glenn's here, everyone!' announced the makeup artist.

The great roar of approval that rang out from the two jampacked booths sounded like the one London greeted Henry the Fifth with on his return from Agincourt. Glenn's eyes abruptly welled, and as he beheld that bounty of masked divinities thronging the tables, the sparkly whites of their smiles dazzled him and he sensed that Brigantia had interceded on his behalf and permitted him a direct vision of God— whose awesome, supernal face transmitted to him speechless messages that tonight, yes, high fantasy would indeed converge with reality. That tonight he would be *popular*.

Glenn stood with his mouth agape as the rapture flowed through him.

'Shaping up to be a good night, this,' Jimmy yelled. He was clearly impressed.

Glenn's eyes eagerly scanned the sea of masks for Henrietta, but she wasn't there.

IV.XIV

The staircase contorted and wove with every step, and Mildred thought she had never seen a staircase like it. As she looked down and saw her own feet, she thought she had never seen a pair of feet like them. And when she held out her hand, the one that wasn't clutching the wriggling, crazy handrail, and stared at it closely, she thought she had never seen a hand like it, either. Somehow through the fog rolling through her brain she could dimly recall doing this to herself. But where she was going now, or why, was less clear. Her legs were moving, but to those observing her from the landing above, she looked more like she was trying to ride a unicycle than climb the stairs. That she had made it to the club at all in this state was testament to the patience of the taxi driver.

Upon stumbling though the doorway, she cut a striking figure. Platinum blonde hair scraped back and wrapped in a short black bejeweled dress from the Barebones line, with six-inch black heels. The physique was so impressive the masquerade mask being upside down and inside out didn't matter. However, she couldn't lap up the attention she was getting because she was busy gawping at the green lights above, which were spinning so fast that, suddenly, they detached from the vaulted ceiling and began to fly around the room like baby dragons. 'Oh, shit,' she murmured.

Abruptly a jester emerged from the crowd, carrying a pint and grinning insanely.

'Hehnycrdrsprclah!' came his voice through the distortion, as his blood-red visage burst into flames. 'Wabotoo pakofyercrstms bnserrly, he-he-he. . . .'

Startled, Mildred tottered backwards and collided with someone, or something, else. Turning around, she saw a ridiculous mullet draped over a ridiculous golden shirt. She watched an ambush of tigers running up and down it with awe, until suddenly a giant tiger's head leaped out from the shirt and unleashed a terrifying roar in her face.

Screaming, she fled.

'I told you I had a great feeling about this night!' Glenn yelled. 'Gone are the days of Glenn Harding being a social indigent, an outcast from life's feast—and gentlemen in England now a-bed shall think themselves accurst they were not here to see it!'

'I'll drink to that,' yelled Jimmy, clinking his Paint the Town Pink with Glenn's. He had gone to the bar and bestowed the fruity cocktail on the whole Harding herd. 'You do seem to be a lot better in yourself now,' he observed.

'O! I am, Mr Sandaal. It's *amazing* how the writing of five episodes can trepan the old brainwork. I feel as if I have exorcised myself of a ghoul that was haunting me!' He sipped his cocktail. 'What strange arts necessity finds out,' he sighed dreamily.

The menswear manager was in an exalted state, revelling in his newfound popularity, not even bothered by Ali wearing the same shirt as him. The fact someone as stylish as Ali had also bought the shirt validated his fashion instincts. He was a trend setter!

Though you survived alone, bereft of all companions, lost for years, under strange sail you have come home. . . . Suddenly, Betty squeaked something in his ginormous ear.

'What's that, Betty?' he yelled with a dreamy expression on his face.

She slipped her arm around his waist. 'Are you going to sort me out?'

Glenn raised his eyebrows involuntarily. 'What?'

'The toilets are that way. Let's go into a cubicle. I want sorting out.'

'Betty!'

He stared at the lovely green eyes leering at him through the jewel-embellished white swan mask, a mix of shock and titillation crossing his face. Unable to entertain Betty's proposition due to his quest for Henrietta, he at least appreciated the ego stroke.

'*Behave*,' he said playfully, slipping his arm around Betty, who at once cosied up to him, stirring memories of that immortal lunch hour in the Conservatory. . . .

'Don't even *think* about it,' a voice yelled in his face.

'I wasn't thinking of anything!' Glenn yelled, instantly releasing Betty.

'You're not sneaking off into the toilets with *her*,' Ali yelled. He had inveigled himself under Glenn's other arm. 'You need to sort *me* out first.'

'Ali!' Glenn cried.

'The three of us should go together,' Betty suggested to Ali, across Glenn's chest. 'Then he can sort us both out at the same time.'

'All right,' Ali nodded, 'sounds like a plan.'

'What kind of party *is* this!?' Glenn exclaimed.

'Oh, shut up and enjoy it. You're in the gang now,' Ali said in his ear.

Glenn raised his eyebrows, smiling nervously.

Abruptly Lyndsey appeared, his eyes leering through a frightening bird mask. 'Don't forget about *me*, Glenn,' he yelled. 'I need sorting out, *too*.'

Glenn drew back with a look of utter horror on his face.

'Now wait a minute!' he cried, choking on his own outrage. 'It's one thing what you two are on about, but I draw the line at—'

Jimmy leaned into his ear. 'Mate,' he said, 'they want sorting out with the *goods*. That's why they're being friendly to you.'

'Ohhhhh,' said Glenn.

He sighed but felt only a small twinge of anguish really. So what if the goods were responsible for this strange alteration? High fantasy and cold reality could hardly commingle without there inevitably being some real world elements to undermine the experience! At least his being mobbed this way was making him look to the denizens of LS1 like a man about town, a person of prime quality, a true partaker in life's feast—and he hoped everyone was witnessing his adulation.

Especially Henrietta, wherever she was hiding.

'It must be some good stuff,' yelled Jimmy, eyeing him through his wrestler's mask. He looked mischievously at Glenn. 'Give me some.'

'*You* want some? Jimmy, remember—I don't even know what it is!' Glenn cautioned.

'Come on, I'm getting married next year. This might be my only chance.'

Glenn glanced nervously at the synod; their jaws hung slack, and their eyes leered. 'The thing is, there's only so much to go around,' he pleaded.

'Are you *really* not going to sort me out, after *everything* I've done for you?'

A pause.

'All right!' Glenn yelled bitterly. He reached inside his trousers. 'Now look, I took the contents of the pills and mixed them all together in this little bag, so—'

'Hold it, knob head!' Jimmy blurted. 'You're in full view of Shukeena.'

HUNTER

IV.

With a spasmodic jerk, Glenn looked over his shoulder and glimpsed Shukeena and Gertrude together at the bar. Fear gripped him, as he wondered what toil and trouble those midnight hags might be stirring up.

'Come on,' yelled Jimmy, snapping him out of it. The behemoth dragged Glenn to a far corner, by one of the reserved booths. His entourage followed, screening his antics. 'Right, slip me the bag,' yelled Jimmy. 'Just pretend to shake my hand.'

Glenn complied, slipping his hand down his tight trousers and ferreting deep inside his skimpy hipbriefs. He retrieved from some crevice the tiny bag full of powder.

'Well?' Glenn yelled. 'Take it!'

'No, you're all right,' Jimmy grimaced. 'I suddenly don't want it anymore.'

However, as the behemoth waved his paw dismissively, he accidentally knocked the bag out of Glenn's hand. They both watched in horror as it then sailed through the air, over the punch bowl, and for a second time stopped.

But Glenn, in a rare instance of dexterity, managed to catch it between his fingers.

'You *fool*, Jimmy!' he screamed, turning furiously on the underwriter. 'You bloody idiot! You nearly made me drop the goods in the punch!'

'Sorry!' Jimmy cried apologetically. He looked utterly mortified.

'*That* was a close one,' said Glenn with relief. In his peripheral vision, he noticed his entourage parting as a vast dark shadow swept through them. Before he knew what was happening, a massive pair of arms enveloped him and lifted him clean off the floor.

Shrieking with fright, Glenn threw the bag into the punch.

He was then tossed into the air, where he spun 180 degrees and landed in a pair of big meaty hands that hooked him by the armpits.

IV.XV

'DID YOU WRITE ABOUT ME TO HEAD OFFICE?!' Norman yelled in his face.

'What? *No!*' Glenn cried, his loafers dangling in the air. 'I've never written *anything* to head office!' he quavered. 'Ever!'

Norman glared at him suspiciously. '*Really?*' he yelled. His phizog—God only knows why—was a shocking patchwork of contusions and crusted blood, and his breath smelt like an old beer cellar. He wore a fur-trimmed red Santa coat over his rumpled work clothes, and around his neck, leering hideously at Glenn, was a shaggy white Krampus mask.

'Yes, really!' Glenn insisted. 'I'm on my stage 2 written warning, remember? For all my gross misconduct? It would be much too dangerous for me to make contact with head office. The issue teeters on a razor's edge—whether I keep my badge or not!'

Norman, after a long, hard, searching look, plonked Glenn back on the floor.

'Fair enough,' he grunted. 'But *someone's* written a letter about me to head office.' As he put on his terrifying Krampus mask, he vowed, 'And when I find out who the traitor is, they will be on Santa's naughty list, to say the least.

'What did the letter say?' Glenn enquired, as he smoothed down his clothes and looked despondently to his now-empty bag floating in the punch bowl.

'It falsely accused me of being a raging alcoholic, with a short attention span and a—ooh, look. Punch!'

'Er, I wouldn't drink that if I were you, Norman,' Glenn warned.

'Why not?' yelled Norman, snatching up the bowl.

Glenn and Jimmy exchanged anxious looks. 'You don't know what's in it,' yelled the menswear manager.

Norman stared at the punch bowl and then at Glenn. 'Punch, I'm guessing?'

'Norman, *don't*,' Glenn yelled, pulling the bowl away from his lips. 'Please.'

'WHO'S THE STORE MANAGER HERE, YOU OR ME!?' Norman flared suddenly.

Pause.

'That's—that's a serious question, isn't it?' Glenn yelled.

'Yes.'

'*You're* the store manager, Norman.'

'Am I? Great! Well that means you can't tell me what to do, you cheeky bastard.' He grabbed the bowl back. 'And anyway, whatever's in it, I doubt it will have much effect on me. Don't tell anyone, but I'm a raging alcoholic.'

He downed the poison'd bowl in one gulp.

Glenn and Jimmy exchanged an even more anxious look.

'What's wrong with you, boy?' demanded Norman, wiping his mouth with the fluffy sleeve of his Santa coat, dislodging the empty goods bag from his chin. 'Why are you looking at me like that? Never seen a *real* man drink?—whoa!' Suddenly he stiffened, as a thin trickle of spit ran down his chin. His eyes bulged, and his pupils looked like they were riding the tilt-a-whirl. 'Now *that* hits the spot!' he yelled with approval.

'I'm not telling you what to do, Norman,' Glenn yelled. 'It's just that Shukeena has imposed a two-drink limit on us, because we all have work tomorrow—'

'Two drinks, ay?' Norman yelled, swaying slightly. 'All right—if you insist.'

He snatched up the second punch bowl and slugged it back with manic zeal.

Glenn watched in horror as the last of it disappeared down the store manager's throat. A familiar voice then came over his shoulder: 'Shit the bed!'

Norman banged the empty bowl down on the table, next to the other one. 'Right then, you shower of shit,' he belched, turning to his team. 'Who wants a shot?'

'Norman, are you sure you're feeling all right?' said Glenn fearfully. 'That was a lot of drink you just downed.'

A sort of film descended over Norman's eyes as he stared at Glenn with unparalleled scorn—with a look that seemed almost to question his manhood. 'You really are a lightweight, aren't you?' he growled. 'Don't you worry about *me*, lad. Believe it or not, some of us can hold our liquor.'

Pause.

The next thing Glenn knew, Krampus was dancing atop the bar, bare-chested in his unbuttoned shirt and Santa coat. Somehow he had procured the DJ's mike, and was belting out a rocking old Christmas number to the delight of the top floor crowd.

'Oh a turkey and some trimmings,
Today would sho' be nice!
And a little Christmas givin',
From a girl who ain't my wife!
YEAH!'

He lolloped heavily down the long counter, kicking his feet and shaking his hips, as the denizens of LS1 roared their approval. It was as if they had never heard rock 'n' roll before, and there was a feeling that Christmas had come early in the stout shape of this foaming, sweaty Santa Claus.

'Leave out a carrot and a mincepie,
When Santy comes-a-rockin'!
But you know it won't be Christmas,
If he don't get in your stocking!
WOOO!'

Dick was watching the spectacle from the sidelines, from behind his full-face blood-red jester's mask, which had a little hat attached, complete with little gold bells.

'So Norman got all the goods, then?' he yelled at Glenn, standing beside him.

'Is it that obvious?' yelled Glenn, looking into Dick's spooky mask.

The store manager was performing a perilous one-legged hop down the counter, hammering at his imaginary guitar, as the crowd went into ecstasies.

'Geez, your ability to organise a party is on par with your ability to manage a shopfloor,' Dick yelled with disgust.

'What are you doing, babe?' yelled Ali. 'Are you going to sort us out or what?'

Glenn found himself again engirted by his dazzling coterie of masked divinities, all of them leering hungrily at him. 'Sadly not,' Glenn sighed. 'I am afraid that Encolpius alone drank all the aphrodisiac.'

'Eh?'

'The goods are gone, Ali,' Dick yelled. 'Kiss arse here gave them all to the boss.'

The makeup artist stared at Glenn for a moment with his mouth open. He then rolled his eyes, shook his head bitterly and skulked off into the crowd.

The Nirah Frazar circle and its extended family enfiladed Glenn with their eyes.

He lost his entourage as quickly as he lost the goods, and in an instant he was back to being the most hated man in the shop. A bitter groan burst from his lips.

'Ah, don't get upset, geez; shit happens,' yelled Dick philosophically. He sipped his pint. 'Have you spoken to Gerty at all?' he enquired innocently.

Glenn reflexively glanced over to the booths in the far corner, catching Gertrude peeping back at him through her extravagant mask. When they made eye contact, she looked away, shielded her phizog and pretended to be absorbed in conversation with a Christmas temp.

'No,' he sighed.

'Good,' yelled Dick. 'Keep it that way. She's still angry at you, remember? And the last thing we need tonight is an embarrassing scene.'

'And so I will be waiting,
Under mistletoe, miss!
It's only once a year,
When Santy needs his—'

Norman shrieked an obscenity as he slipped in a puddle of beer and flew into the air, plummeting parabola to the floor. There was a great gasp from the crowd as they felt the horrific thud. Glenn and Jimmy exchanged a look of terror, but when they waded through the throngs and looked where Norman fell—they found him body popping on the oak flooring as the denizens went into ecstasies.

Unto the snow-wrapped street do we now shift our scene, where a little Skoda was parked down a deserted alleyway, its engine humming loudly in the silent night. The shadowy forms of two mountainous looking goons filled the frosty windscreen.

'And LS1's just down here, is it?' said Derek, sitting in the passenger seat.

'Go through that passageway there,' said Wilfred Woods, sitting in the driver's seat, 'and you'll come out into a big square. It's there. You can't miss it.'

Derek sat mute, pondering the passageway.

'I wouldn't wait too long, fella,' Wilfred advised. 'The way the snow's coming down, I won't be able to get the car out of here soon.'

'So what's the deal with this Glenn Harding bloke?' Derek enquired casually. 'Is he really a schizo?'

'He's definitely a shampoo bottle short of a gift set, aye.'

'Yeah?' Derek stared at the passageway. 'Do you think he's dangerous?'

'Only to himself.'

Derek nodded. He then donned a black masquerade mask that looked more like a robber's mask, zipped up his parka and stepped out of the car.

IV.XVI

The night felt like it was escaping Glenn, who hadn't managed to corner Henrietta yet, in spite of his constantly pacing the busy room, searching for her in the moil.

He missed his entourage, but if he played his cards right there would be even greater entourages later, in London. He would once again partake in life's feast.

O, immortal one! Thou hast beat me several times, and I have nightly since dreamt of encounters 'twixt thyself and me. . . . The DJ was back to his recycled disco hits with garrulous rhymers babbling over them, and as Glenn threaded his way through the gyrating knots of bodies he observed the columns of the club actually vibrating.

What he didn't see was Shukeena step out from behind one.

'Hello *Glenn*,' she shrilled, as he walked into her and bounced off her bosom.

'O, veni veni, Mephistophile,' he yelled, reluctantly pulling his eyes from the crowd and looking down at her. 'Is this the face that launch'd a thousand stomachs?'

'Huh?'

But his heart wasn't in it, and with a brusque flick of his hand said it was nothing.

'So,' she shrilled, holding him with her eye. 'Who would've thought someone would make a fool out of themselves at the Christmas do, and it not be *you*?'

'The night is still young.'

He heard a strange noise and thought she had been sick. But when he looked down, he saw that she was smiling under her stunning black cat mask—complete with cute little ears, fur, a diamond nose, long whiskers and slanted eye holes—and he realised to his amazement the barbarian queen had *laughed*.

She wore a short black silk dress from the Egomania collection, and when he saw the outrageous plunging neckline descending all the way past her naval, his eyes nearly shot out of his masquerade mask. And with the exquisite legs on display, and the studded anklestrap heels and the cocktail in her hand, it seemed as if some new, even more breathtaking creature had stolen Shukeena's shrill nasal whine. She looked glorious.

'Well,' she shrilled, 'just remember you have work tomorrow. I need you to unbox your gift vouchers, set out the pre-sale, the pre-spring, update the—'

Glenn goggled the woman.

To be on your Christmas do, in a masquerade mask, half-naked and drinking a cocktail, and *still* be thinking about unboxing gift vouchers, required a deranged level of professionalism. Holy cow. You would think she was *married* to Nirah Frazar!

What art thou, Shukeena Mohammed, I bid love ask. And now that it assume thy body, some lovely glorious nothing I do see.

'Right!' he yelled, interrupting her. 'If you insist on breaking the rules of the Christmas do by talking about *work*, then I'm afraid I am going to have break your rule about the two-drink limit.' He threw the straw out of his glass, sank the pink remnants and slammed it on the counter. 'Hell and night, Miss Mohammed! It's no marvel you're standing here on your own.'

She looked flustered as she stared up at him, her dark maroon glossed lips pursed. But then her face broke into a rare smile—one that was without the malevolence normally observed in a Shukeena smile. She put her glass aside and began reaching inside her bodybag-shaped leather clutch by Nirah Frazar.

'Is that a hint?' she asked.

Perhaps something other than goods was the celestial ambrosia that infused reality with fantasy, for they were all gone and yet still an air of improbabilty hung over events, as the two warring managers were propped against the bar, sipping cocktails and, unbelievably, having a *friendly* natter with each other.

It was like Beowulf having a drink with Grendel's mother.

'Obviously *I* don't know who wrote that letter,' said the quaffer of Styx' corroding water, 'it could've been anyone. But I do think head office overreacted a bit. It's *Norman* who needs investigating, not the whole shop.' She laughed awkwardly. 'They should have just let me run the shop, while they assessed him!'

Glenn sighed. He quietly sucked his cocktail, felt it tingle in his empty tummy. Even when she tried, the poor girl had nothing but shop talk. 'Come bad chance, and we join to it our strength, and teach it art and length, itself o'er us to advance!' he yelled rhapsodically. He threw an amiable arm around her. 'Now please, my ne'er-touched vestal—cudgel thy brains no more about it.'

'What does that mean?' She peered up at him suspiciously. 'Are you being rude?'

'It means. . . . To Shukeena! The *finest* ladieswear manager Leeds has ever laid eyes upon,' he exclaimed merrily, clinking her glass. She must have been starved of compliments, because at that moment he felt her sag against him, as if melting.

'All right. And to you, Glenn. The most. . . . *interesting* menswear manager I have ever worked with.' She slipped her arm round his waist and clinked his glass too.

And she looked up at him. . . .

And he looked down at her. . . .

And then he looked away for some reason—and beheld Henrietta Payne, who had halted in front of them and was stood open-mouthed, her glare flitting back and forth between the two cosily entwined middle managers.

With the roll of all eye rolls the airy spirit was on her way.

White-faced terror seized Glenn, and he slammed down his drink, flung the Gorgon aside and went bounding after his Beatrice, with a swiftness of foot that would have impressed Achilles. 'Oh, what do you want?' she snapped as he grabbed her arm.

'For you to stop bombarding me with messages!' he yelled, smiling.

It was a prepared ad lib, a wry reference to the numberless cringeworthy written ambassages he had sent her (see IV.I), all without reply. 'Okay,' she replied, her eyes registering the joke but her face refusing to simulate any amusement. She gave his daring shirt a dubious look, turned her back and sauntered off.

With burning eyes, he pursued her, and in one spasmodic leap obstructed her path. Her eyes widened. 'Henrietta!' he cried. 'Are you not going to speak to me at all?'

'You looked busy with Shukeena.' She smiled knowingly. 'You've nearly got the full set now, haven't you? Bless those poor shopgirls.'

That one threw him. He watched as the awesome one with ponytail sauntered off again, in her bizarre costume—some weird frowsy cream golf jumper over a salmon buttoned-up blouse, with high waisted, buttock-twitching vintage stonewash jeans and a pair of mad, painted shoes. She hadn't even bothered to invest in a mask.

The outfit was completely inappropriate for a formal party in a select club. It was pure insolence on her part, an insult to her former employer. It was genuinely offensive.

He loved her more than ever.

'I was just *talking* to her,' he yelled imploringly, emerging from behind a column and obstructing her path. 'And anyway, you have a boyfriend, and you did a lot more than just talk to me. How do you explain *that*?'

'I don't have to explain anything, mate.'

Glenn stared into her cold eyes and radiant visage with intolerable longing; he felt like Pygmalion, in love with a statue. Come on Mr Ovid, come on Mr Donne, shew me the words. Why standest thou afar off, Sweet Swan? A young lover needs your help!

'But *Henrietta*,' he squalled. 'You admitted you missed me when I wasn't at work. You invited me to France! And you kissed me as if—as if you felt something for me.'

'I'm not being one of your shop conquests.'

Glenn wobbled. He watched helplessly as she turned and legged it, dissolving into the crowd like goods into a punch bowl. . . .

Well that was anti-climatic.

The coda of his great canticle had at last arrived and he had failed, and not even spectacularly. He had simply flopped.

It was like that scene in *The Canterbury Tales*, when the fictive Chaucer's turn comes to tell a story, and instead of stealing the show, he nervously blunders through some tedious tale until told to shut up in his own book.

Glenn bitterly regretted everything he had just done and said.

He hadn't weighted the situation carefully before making his move and had thrown himself into the fray and failed. In fact, he had pretty much violated every axiom of *The Art of War*. He had advanced uphill; attacked keen troops; he was fairly certain he had pursued an enemy who was feigning flight.

He could sense Master Sun looking down on him, shaking his head despairingly.

Well, anyway. That was that then. Farewell, Miss Payne; thou art too dear for my possessing. The dream of Dinan was over, and with it his new life and the infinite possibilities therein. January was fast approaching, and he *still* had nowhere to go.

He turned his back on the club, stood forlornly by the lattice window. He half wished Henrietta's colossus of a boyfriend would come and put him out of his misery. For the magic of fantasy was gone, dull reality had triumphed again, and this truly was the day of doom. Suddenly he felt a hand reach out and grasp his arm.

'All right, the punch has gone so you can buy me a drink,' Henrietta yelled.

Glenn gave the heavens a look. Thank you, Mr Donne! Thank you, Sweet Swan! '*Fine*,' he yelled, grabbing her hand. He galloped to the bar with such speed he yanked her clean off the floor. In a moment they were there. 'O!—I just remembered,' he yelled, remembering his crushing penury. 'I left my bank card with my plus one. Will you wait here while I go get it?'

'Just bring my drink up to the VIP room.'

'The *what* room?' he asked with amazement.

'The VIP room. It's upstairs. It's reserved for us.'

He followed her eyes to a mysterious door in the corner, guarded by a bouncer.

'You mean there's a yet higher floor in LS1, just for VIPs—and it's reserved for *us*?' he asked, his voice trembling.

'It's reserved for the Nirah Frazar party, you moron.'

'O. O, well that's still good. Right!' He pinched her hips. 'I'll see you there.'

The fleeting yet impassioned kiss she gave Glenn dazed him.

Cocktails? He was already thinking ahead to the transcendent nectar he would suck from the gilt cherubin. He wheeled around and galloped headlong into what he thought for a moment must have been a column. Stunned, he felt the humongous hands of a monster reach out and clasp his spindly arms.

He looked up, and lo, he beheld an unfriendly face staring back at him.

'Jimmy!' he yelled. 'Quick. Give me thy card. There's no time for questions!'

But the behemoth looked unusually perturbed. 'No. You need to come with me.'

'Jimmy, whatever the problem is, I don't care; I've got Henrietta waiting for me in the VIP room—*yes*, there's a VIP room—and I need to buy her a drink *fast!*'

'You don't understand, Glenn—this is *serious*. You need to come with me *now*.'

'What the devil for, man? What could possibly be wrong now?'

'Norman's dead.'

IV.XVII

A bored looking Ali was sitting with Betty and their plus ones, and some nameless Christmas temps, in one of the reserved booths. 'Where is everyone?' Ali yelled, casting his eyes around the heaving club. 'I can't believe even Mildred's gone. We usually have to drag her out. I wonder where she went?'

Lyndsey glanced back over the backrest of the next booth. 'Look under the table,' he yelled. Ali and Betty traded a look of puzzlement. They dipped their heads under the table and found Mildred squatting there, holding herself tightly, quivering in her sparkly dress. Her face was a mess of sweat, makeup, and sputum, and her mask was still inside out and upside down.

'Mildred, you're here!' yelled Ali. 'What are you doing under the table?'

She looked back at him uncomprehendingly. There was panic in her eyes.

Ali and Betty laughed. 'She's off her tits!' yelled the makeup artist. 'Here, Mildred,' he said, 'do you know it's your round?'

'Yeah, Mildred,' squeaked Betty, 'do you know it's your round?'

It sounded to Mildred as if they were speaking under water. She saw Ali waving his hand, and watched in wonder as his shirtsleeve left a glistering trail of golden vapour in the air. As she squinted her eyes at his magical shirt, she saw the pack of tigers scuttling up and down it. Her mouth was slack, her eyes spellbound.

With a mighty roar one tiger leaped out, lashing its gigantic claws at her cheek.

She jumped up with a shriek and banged her head on the table. Tumbling out of the booth, she scrambled to her heels and fled screaming.

'*Wow,*' squeaked Betty, watching her run off. 'What a tight bitch.'

Mildred clattered her way down the steps in her six-inch heels, only to fall straight into the hulking arms of the street pharmacist.

'Mildred!' yelled Derek. 'This Glenn Harding dude. What's he wearing?'

'TIGERS!' she shrieked in his face. 'TIGERS! TIGERS! TIGERS!'

'*Tigers?*'

She wriggled herself out of his bearhug and ran yelling down the stairs.

On the top floor of the club, Derek's eyes raked the room, staring fixedly into the tangle of bodies gyrating in the smoky, green-lit miasma. He squinted at each male but there were simply too many of them, their monochrome apparel merging into one dull blot—until suddenly a bright light flared in his periphery.

For a moment he thought someone's camera had flashed in his eyes, but then he realised it was a shiny gold shirt floating by in the foreground. Derek marveled the gaudy piece. It looked baggy enough to fit him. But when he espied the tiger print the music suddenly was stripped of everything but its core beat and everyone but the man in the shirt seemed to stand still. . . .

Rage bubbled in his brain as the steam shot out of his ears.

He lifted his glower and stared into the eyes of the masked boy, gliding by him.

That's when Ali saw the big handsome man looking at him. He flashed the stranger a smile and gave him a cheeky come-hither wink.

'O my God!' said a hoarse voice in stage whisper. 'What did you do to him!?'

'*Me?*' said Jimmy in a hoarse voice, also in stage whisper. 'I didn't do *anything* to him! *You* gave him enough drugs to give Pablo Escobar a hard-on!'

Glenn looked again at the store manager, slumped on the toilet in the semi-darkness, dead as a door-nail. It was no easier the second time, and he felt the same ghastly shiver of revulsion. The case of Norman's huge spirit was cold, his knot of life untied, and as the menswear manager beheld the grotesque expression on his blue dead face the horror almost overcame him. This couldn't be happening to Glenn Harding.

'But he wasn't meant to take all of it! He's dead through being too debosht!'

'He didn't know he was taking class A drugs, Glenn; you should have stopped him!'

Glenn stifled a cry. His hair with terror stood; fear shrunk his sinews, congealed his blood. Erethism was attacking his nerve endings. He was positively willing the scene to reveal itself to be another phantasmic event, but he knew that it was real, unbearably real. O God, was he in trouble this time. He watched as his dream world of Dinan and Henrietta, of London and the BBC—not to mention his delusions of Predestination—was crushed under an avalanche of images that were as vivid as they were terrifying: the sight of him in the dock at Leeds Crown Court; the shame on his mum and dad's faces; the public revulsion, the prison sentence; the unavoidable suicide required to escape his crimes— all of it played out in the press with a series of humiliating revelations about his creepy private life.

This couldn't be happening to him.

He was a nice boy who just wanted to be back in his bedroom in Seacroft, reading a book and waiting for mum to put out dinner.

'What are you doing!' Jimmy whispered.

'Going home,' Glenn replied, his hand on the lock. 'This is nothing to do with me.'

The Leviathan tossed him back into the tiny cubicle and barricaded the door with his girth. 'Oh no you don't! You can't run away from this one, Glenn! It's *serious!*'

'Then neither can you, Jimmy. You're part of this too.'

Jimmy's eyes bulged. '*What*!?' he choked. '*How?*'

'You've been complicit from the beginning.'

And as they went back and forth, Glenn's eyes welled, and he began to hyperventilate. In a flash he saw everything with awesome clarity: the dark premonition that had plagued his thoughts had at last come true. The sinister shape that was his brain's outline of the mysterious calamity had *not* been that patch of mushrooms in the office, but rather the man who had been sitting under it, Norman Mountain—and it was *Glenn himself* who was responsible for it.

Like Oedipus, he realised he had been destined all along to bring about his own misfortune—his discovery of drugs in River Tower being the day he sealed his fate.

He had carried doom in his underpants and waltzed gaily into his own annihilation.

And with nothing left to lose, his big Nosferatu hands sprang out and seized Jimmy by his stupid fat neck while he was mid-sentence.

'This is *your* fault!' Glenn screamed. 'You've put me under so much stress lately, I haven't been able to think straight! *You* made me do this!'

Jimmy made a strangled sound as he reached out and tried to grab Glenn by his throat, but with thumbs pressed into his windpipe, and Glenn's skin being too lubricious with Starstuff, he couldn't get any purchase. Instead, he grabbed his mullet, only to feel Glenn's power increase, presumably from the raging adrenalin produced by having his hair messed up.

'You could have stopped Norman drinking that punch,' Glenn gasped, the tears rolling down his cheeks. 'Murderer!'

Jimmy's tongue was protruding, his eyeballs ready to pop out of his skull. He rammed Glenn against the wall but couldn't hold him there as his feet kept slipping on the piss-drenched tiles. They wrestled, wriggled and fell, slipped and squirmed, banging back and forth in the narrow cubicle. It looked like a dancing bear fighting its trainer. Jimmy was grossly unfit, and Glenn could feel the behemoth's awesome power beginning to ebb with each passing second, as his own wiry strength asserted itself. He took the opportunity to ring Jimmy's neck some more, making his massive head flop back and forth as the behemoth's knees gave out, and he began sinking before him.

'Ha-ha! Now art thou better of a size to deal with than thou wert!' Glenn shrieked. 'Thou most gross and heathenish son of Simon!'

The behemoth raised his arm in desperation, and the next thing Glenn knew a fist the size and weight of a bowling ball was hurtling towards his unguarded chin. Jimmy smote him athwart the visage and there was a terrible crack, as the two of them went tumbling onto Norman's corpse, bouncing off his humongous beer belly and landing with a splash on opposite sides of the toilet bowl.

Norman emitted a low, grisly moan.

Glenn and Jimmy stared wide eyed at each other over his lap.

Gertrude was staring wide eyed as she paced the busy room, searching desperately for Glenn, wearing the black jumpsuit she knew was his favourite. As she threaded her way through the crowd, she didn't notice the columns of the club vibrating—or the grinning formalwear supervisor emerging from behind one.

'You look lost,' Dick yelled, as she walked into him and bounced off his bosom.

'Dick!' yelled Gertrude, grabbing him by his hideous electric blue Hawaii shirt. 'Do you know where Glenn is?' Her eyes raked the room. 'I saw him at the bar with that slut, Henrietta, but now he's disappeared.'

'Oh, are you *still* chasing Glenn?' Dick groaned. 'Gerty, I've told you; he hates you! So just stay away. The last thing we need tonight is an embarrassing scene.'

'He. . . . *hates* me?' she trilled. The eyes in her black mask adorned with giant, technicolour butterflies welled almost instantly. 'But I didn't do anything to him!' She remembered throwing his possessions out of her apartment window. 'Much,' she added.

Her bottom lip began quavering uncontrollably.

'Oh, Gerty. Rejection is never easy. Your self-esteem must be rock bottom right now.' Dick slipped a consoling arm round her tender waist. 'Let's get you a drink, and we can talk all about it.'

In a daze, Gertrude allowed Dick to lead her to the bar.

IV.XVIII

The door to the men's toilets swung open and Derek, in his robber's mask, filled the doorframe. His baleful eyes swept the gloomy, foul-smelling room.

The urinal troughs were unpeopled and two of the three cubicle doors closed.

When the door nearest opened he stiffened. But on seeing an obese Asian man emerge in a weird gimpy mask, and with another man's arm draped over him, a man who looked like he was dressed as Santa, he turned and moved toward the urinal trough. He lingered there with his back to the deviants, hiding his phizog.

It sounded like several people were vacating the cubicle, whispering nervously to each other, apparently out of breath.

Derek, pretending to use the facilities, could not repress his shudder.

But as the reprobates exited the toilets he immediately whirled around and strode down the cubicles, slowly and heavily, to the last one. He rapped on the closed door.

The toilet flushed and the cubicle door was unbolted. Ali opened it curiously as he zipped up his fly. When he saw the hulk from outside staring at him, he smiled.

'Hello,' he crooned.

'Glenn Harding?' said Derek tonelessly.

Ali lifted his mask. 'What about Glenn Harding?' he said quizzically.

'I want to speak to him.' Now Derek was smiling.

'You want to speak to *Glenn Harding*?' he replied incredulously. 'Why?'

'Oh, I think he knows.'

A pause.

'I hate to break it to you,' said Ali, 'but you're not really Glenn Harding's type—'

'I don't mean it like that!' Derek snapped irritably. 'And knock it off with the third person, mate. I heard you were weird.'

'"*Third* person"?' said Ali. His eyes searched the room. 'What are you on about?'

'Do you know Henrietta Payne?' Derek growled.

'Yes. Although, to be honest, I'd forgotten she existed until I saw her tonight!' he laughed. 'Why?'

Derek's face clouded over, and he clenched his massive fists.

He threw Ali back and followed him inside the cubicle. He slammed the door shut behind them, at which point the makeup artist up-sent a shriek that nearly shattered the mirrors. The panels of the cubicle began to rock and shake, as the doors of the LS1 fire exit banged open, and Norman's limp body was tossed out into the dazzling drift.

He hit the crystallin snow with a soft wet crunch.

'All right, go steady with him!' came Jimmy's voice.

'Go steady with *him*?' Glenn panted. 'I nearly broke my back frogmarching that lump down those steps.' He staggered out in his trilby and fur coat and was smote by the night. 'God's bones!' he cried. 'Did we upset Juno? It's colder than the Ninth Circle!'

'Oh, it can't be that bad you big puff,' said Jimmy, pulling his hood up. He stepped out into the subzero temperature. 'Shit the bed!' he cried.

Horrid confusion heaped upon confusion rose, as they were attacked on all sides by sounding showers, rapid rains, and rowling torrents. The surrounding buildings of the lamp-lit square had been reduced to faint white hills.

'This cold night will turn us all to fools and madmen,' said Glenn with terror in his voice. He turned to Jimmy. 'Let's just leave him here and go back inside!'

'What! We can't leave him like this. He really will die!'

'Yes, but this time the culprit will be *winter*.'

'Not when they review the CCTV, you moron. We'll just bung him in a taxi and send him home where he can sleep it off. Then we can go back in and enjoy the party.'

'All right.' Glenn was still clinging to his hat, his mullet and fur coat flapping in the violent cross wind. His eyes searched the wide square. 'One thing, Jimmy.'

'What?'

'Where are we going to get a taxi? This area is completely pedestrianised.'

Jimmy stroked his multitude of chins contemplatively.

'But *how* can he hate *me*?' she burbled. 'I loved him! I did *everything* for him! And all he ever did was treat me like an inconvenience.'

'It's not you, Gerty; it's *him*. That's the problem with young men today. They don't want to settle down. That's why if you want someone who's serious, you need an *older* man.'

Gertrude sipped her cocktail, wiped her eyes. 'Yeah,' she yelled thoughtfully, 'I think you're right. I'm sick of boys who just use me. I want an older man!'

Dick swallowed hard. He shuffled closer to her.

'Yes,' he yelled. 'Yes, you do.'

'An older man who's loaded.'

'*Shit.*'

'Every tedious stride I make will but remember me what deal of world I wander from the jewels that I love,' Glenn murmured bitterly under his breath. 'How much further, Jimmy?' he called out with annoyance. Norman's legs felt like a pair of heavy trunkcases, and all he could see in front of him through the blustering snow was his slack dribbling face outlined by Jimmy's enormous yellow back.

'I'm not sure,' Jimmy called back, panting. 'We might be here. . . . Or it might be another mile.'

Glenn released Norman's legs and wailed at the wrathful skies in anguish.

'O, we're never going to make it to the main road, Jimmy!' he protested, panting. 'Let's to the club and book a taxi from there. Weakness possessth me, and I am faint!'

With a sigh, Jimmy let go of Norman's arms, who slapped down heavily against the snow. He laid there spread-eagled, as if to make a snow angel. 'What, with that 45-minute waiting time? I don't think so. Let's just flag down a passing taxi and be done with it.'

'A passing taxi?' Glenn howled. 'Mate, there's not even a bloody *road* anymore. Come on; retire! We have engaged ourselves too far!'

'There's a car coming now.'

Glenn jerked in his freezing loafers. 'What!' He leaped over Norman and huddled up next to the behemoth, peering around his bosom. 'In that case we must be on the main road.' He gave Jimmy an excited jiggle. 'I told you we'd make it!'

They squinted into the tempest. A pair of yellow lights were growing slowly larger, and there was a faint gleam of blue between them.

'Thinkst thou that's a taxi?' asked Glenn dubiously.

'No. I think it's a police car.'

'*Run.*'

Jimmy grabbed him by the fur and yanked him back. 'Don't run, you prick! A police car is *better* than a taxi. They'll see our friend has *slightly* overdone it at his Christmas do, and they'll take him home for us—for *free.*'

'And then we can return to LS1?'

'And then we can return to LS1.'

'Then for England, cousin, go!'

The Leviathan was all smiles as he waved his massive arm in the air. He then remembered to pull off his sinister wrestling mask.

The police car pulled to a stop as the window rolled down.

'Hello!' said Glenn and Jimmy, in unison.

The two officers said nothing. Their eyes were drawn to the unconscious figure sprawled in the snow, his exposed gut protruding from his Santa coat. The officer in the passenger seat lifted his gaze to Glenn and Jimmy.

'He's twatted, isn't he?' said the officer.

'Just a bit,' said Jimmy, laughing nervously.

The officers nodded.

Glenn and Jimmy's jaws flapped in the wind, as they stood watching the police car shoot off into the night.

IV.XIX

He stood in the brunt of the stormy gust, trying to thumb a ride from the sporadic cars that came, at very long intervals, skidding crazily down the dual carriageway. Unfortunately, the sight of two masked figures and a prostrate, and possibly dead, Santa Claus, lurking around in a deserted part of town in the middle of the night, only seemed to encourage motorists to speed up. Glenn watched another one zoom by.

'O, this is never going to work,' he protested. 'We look like killers!'

Jimmy was crouched down beside Norman. 'Calm down, it's not that bad. Look: I've buttoned his coat up now; you can hardly tell that

his stomach's blue.'

At length another car came careering madly out of the snow. The driver slowed down, took one look at Glenn grinning desperately at him in his spooky mask, and rammed the accelerator—gunning it down the wet, icy road.

'Pluto and *Hell!*' Glenn cried. 'Are we doomed to roll this restless orb all night? How long a time lies in one little world? My grief doth make one hour ten!'

Retrieving his precious love trophy—Henrietta's sock, inadvertently shoved into his hands in IV.VIII as she bundled him out of her bedroom—he began kissing it, nosing it, and rubbing it all over his face.

'What the hell is that?' the behemoth demanded.

Glenn told him.

Jimmy responded with his favourite catchphrase. Then:

'I don't get you, Glenn Harding. I really don't.'

'What mean'st thou?'

'I mean'st thou could have *Gertrude Ogden* but instead you chase Henrietta Payne.'

'So?'

'So, from what you've told me about her, she doesn't sound like a very nice person. And looks-wise. . . . Come on, mate. Gertrude was getting chatted up by guys all night! But Henrietta? I only saw one bloke speak to her—and that was to say, "Excuse me, can I get past?"'

'Yes, well. Love reasons without reason, Jimmy Sandaal.'

'And what does that mean?'

'It means what it means.'

'Is this unhealthy obessesion with Henrietta the reason why you didn't pull Shukeena when you had the chance?'

'*What?*' Glenn said. 'I never had the chance to pull Shukeena!'

'Yes you did. It was the last thing I saw before I went to the pisser and found this dickhead.'

'No,' said Glenn faintly, shaking his head. 'We—we were just talking about work.'

'She wanted more than work talk, Glenn. Just think, if you weren't so clueless with women, you could've left with her. And it'd be me out here in this shitstorm with Norman—while you were snuggled up in bed with Shukeena!'

Glenn's face turned deathly pale.

He tried to reply, but no words came. His eyes glazed over as he tottered to and fro, then staggered back and collapsed beside Norman. With a ghastly convulsion, he was rendered spread-eagled and still.

'Taxi's coming!' Jimmy exclaimed.

The window rolled down and bhangra music thumped and jangled into the night. The little greybearded driver peeped nervously at the two limp bodies lying in the snow. He stared at Jimmy.

'Don't worry, it's just Santa who needs a ride; the other one's my problem,' the behemoth explained, beaming. 'We need him to get home safely, brother.'

'No, sorry.'

'I'll pay you double?'

'No, sorry.'

'Triple?'

'Put him in.'

Jimmy yanked open the rear door and then bounded over to Norman.

The taxi driver watched Norman's head flop to and fro as Jimmy hauled him up by his limp arms. 'He won't be sick, will he?' asked the driver nervously.

'Absolutely not,' said Glenn, suddenly revived and scrabbling to his feet. He grabbed Norman by one floppy arm. 'This man has an iron stomach—he can keep anything down, believe me. Just you watch!'

The driver watched as Norman responded to being sat upright by spraying the snow with a torrent of projectile vomit, which even speckled the passenger door.

The man slammed his foot on the accelerator and whizzed off into the night, his rear door still hanging open.

'Well, that's it,' sighed Jimmy. 'This night officially could not get any worse.'

Glenn sniffed the air and frowned.

'What's that smell?'

Gertrude stood under the portico outside LS1, smoking a cigarette and shivering uncontrollably, her short leather jacket being less wind resistant than her rock-solid beehive. Dick, in a battered, tan leather coat, stood to the side of her, trying to shield her from the worst of the weather.

'Fancy,' exclaimed Dick in merry tones. 'Gerty Ogden smoking a cigarette! I never thought I'd see this girl again. What's happened?'

'I don't know,' she said glumly, teeth chattering as she gazed absently into space. 'I've been craving a fag all night.'

'Yeah, I noticed,' said Dick under his breath. 'Did you see them all talking about us as we went out?'

'No?'

'Well, they were. I bet they thought we were leaving together!'

She forced a half-hearted laugh. She continued to gaze into space.

'Can you imagine how much it would hurt Glenn? One of his own team members pulling his *ex*? He'd go mad!' Dick chuckled.

Now she was looking at the formalwear supervisor.

'Hurt him?' she said.

'Oh yeah. A lad with his fragile ego? It'd be devasting for him.' He looked at her. 'Then he'd know how you feel.'

'Do you want to come back to mine?' she asked.

Dick's face fell abruptly. 'Gertrude! Didn't anyone teach you that it's wrong to toy with someone's emotions—'

'Do you want to come back to mine or what?'

Dick stood with his mouth agape.

The bouncers watched with amazement as the unbelievable girl disappeared into the snowstorm with the little fat man.

'He must be loaded,' grunted First Bouncer.

'Yep,' nodded Second Bouncer.

Glenn and Jimmy were taking cover down a street off the main road, with Norman sitting between them, slumped drooling and comatose against a garage door.

'It's not coming!' Glenn wailed despairingly.

343

'It *is* coming,' the behemoth insisted. 'It'll be here any second.'

'You can't even read the street signs!'

'They know their way round town.'

Pause.

'Do you think they'll give us a lift back to LS1?' said Glenn hopefully.

'I wouldn't think so, mate; it's an ambulance.'

Glenn cried out with an exceedingly great and bitter cry. 'Jimmy!' he yelped 'Thy future is set; give me leave to go back to LS1 and secure mine. *Please*!'

'You're going nowhere, sonny-jim. I'm not taking responsibility for this mess.'

'Well then let's both go back! Just leave him here. The ambulance will find him. Then he can sleep it off in hospital—'

'NO, GLENN!' Jimmy erupted. 'What did I tell you on your birthday? It's time to *grow up*. Adults don't run away from their problems, and I'll be damned if I let you run away from this one. Okay!? Now come on; I think I hear them coming. Let's get out where they can see us.'

Jimmy squatted down and threw Norman's arm around his neck. Glenn tried to help him hoist the weighty store manager up, but his legs shuddered then gave out.

He lay supine in the snow again, spread-eagled.

'Jimmy, I can't lift this idiot any longer,' he gasped. 'I can't even feel my limbs!'

'Get up, Glenn!' Jimmy threatened, as he struggled to keep Norman upright. The behemoth hauled the store manager out of the alley and along the side of the building, where the siren was sounding, the rotating shafts of blue light piercing the snowfall.

'You do the talking,' said Glenn nervously, bolting upright.

'No! *You* did this to Norman, *you* do the chuffing talking!' Jimmy yelled. 'I told you, I'm not letting you run away from your problems anymore. Be a man!'

With one mighty grunt Jimmy swung Norman round the corner and into the main road—where the ambulance drove straight into him.

BANG!

Jimmy found himself stood with his belly pressed against the side of the vehicle, and Norman ten yards down the road, strewn facedown in the snow.

He looked back at Glenn in horror.

And then turned and legged it.

Glenn and two medics waded through the snow to where Norman was lying, rolling him over and checking his face. His eyes had opened.

'Oh, Christ,' he groaned, 'my head is killing me!' He looked up impatiently at Glenn and the medics. 'Whose round is it?'

IV.XX

Now with a general peace the world was blest. The blizzard had past and LS1 was shining, gloriously bright, like the Mount of God, that sacred hill, the seat supreme, that John Milton described in his great canticle, aside from which I turn for envy.

'Can I help you?' grunted First Bouncer.

'We just want to return from whence we came,' Glenn smiled, nervously.

'Not tonight lads,' grunted Second Bouncer.

'Why?' said Norman, with puke streaking his Santa coat, and a shocking lump jutting out amid his other ghastly facial injuries. 'What's wrong with us?'

The bouncers stared at him.

'Yeah, that's fair enough,' Glenn sighed, nodding.

Fortune, at last you have wholly defeated me.

The pair of them hobbled off through the horrid stillness of the void-like square.

'I don't get it,' Norman remarked, rubbing his head, 'why did you make such a fuss? I always sleep if off in the end. You should have just left me where I was!'

'Great, *now* you tell me,' Glenn moaned. He gazed back at the golden rays shooting forth out of the club's eye-like windows. 'And while we're down here, they're up there—in that amazing VIP room, having the time of their lives. . . .'

He burst into tears.

'*And I'll never know what it's like!*'

In the VIP room, Shukeena was still holding Glenn's cocktail for him.

'Shall we go downstairs?' she said, squished up between Lyndsey and some nameless Christmas temps, the room not being much bigger than a utility cupboard.

'But then we won't be in the VIP room,' said Lyndsey disapprovingly.

'Would that be such a bad thing?' she said.

'Yes,' said Lyndsey. 'It doesn't matter that it's a shit room; it's the *VIP* room.'

He took a sip of his cocktail and smiled smugly.

She sighed. She then glowered again at the huge man who seemed to be taking up half the room with his girth.

'I think it's all right, me,' said Jimmy.

He sipped his cocktail and smiled contentedly.

SALE

V.I

■-DECEMBER-20■

Dear Glenn

*Thank you for sending us your script **That's All We Have Left in That Size, Sir ep 1**, which we have now read and return, enclosed. I hope my below comments may be of some use to you:*

That's All We Have Left in That Size, Sir is an ensemble comedy with a topical premise and an interesting milieu. The array of twenty-something characters all aspire to lifestyles beyond their means, epitomising contemporary British consumer culture. The writing demonstrates a sound sense of visual grammar. The storytelling is economic yet detailed and includes effective use of montage and fantasy sequences. The dialogue also works well – convincingly naturalistic with an engaging energy.

The characterisations, however, are superficial and insufficiently differentiated. They are essentially an array of schematic types who never quite manage to convince. Arguably too many are introduced at once and it is hard to sympathise/root for any of them. Critically, the central protagonist does not possess any likeable qualities. The key story elements also seem familiar and the narrative is without any genuine sense of drive. The tone falls between two stools, never really managing to be either funny or dramatic enough. There is insufficient insight into a very pertinent problem.

We are sorry we are not able to discuss your script in any more detail. Good luck with your writing.

Yours sincerely,
Bunsari Patel
Script Reader writersroom

The letter slipped from Glenn's hands and fluttered to the pinewood, settling between his fluffy slippers.

He stood speechless in his satin pyjamas, gaping vacantly at the bare green wall.

At length he reached behind the sofa-bed and retrieved his dictionary. Schematic. *adj.* Of or like a scheme or diagram.

Placing the book back on its pile, he turned and clambered up onto the adjacent sofa, where he opened the little window. It was a black morning, and he could feel the bitter chill against his face. He poked his head out and contemplated the precipitous drop down to the inner courtyard. The bottom was shrouded in a swirling, eerie murk.

He walked in a daze down the corridor, opened Jimmy's door without knocking.

'Jimmy,' he said, 'I'm going to—'

There was an unmade bed but no Jimmy. He must have gone to work.

To Glenn's right, between the foot of the bed and the wardrobe, was the bulk of the underwriter's possessions, boxed up and ready to move. He walked up the side of the bed to the window, where he fingered apart the blinds and peeked out at the madhouse. What he beheld there, in the ward, froze the very current of his blood.

Mr Hyde from Hyde Hill, waving back at him.

In the kitchen, he dizzily drew the stainless steel chef's knife from the block and held it to his throat. Thoughts, whither have ye led me?

His hand trembling, he let out a scream.

An awesome white light flashed before his eyes.

His mullet was wet and when he lifted his head he discovered himself sprawled on his back in boggy grass. It was light but the sun was nowhere to be seen, and on sitting up and looking around he recognised the vast, desolate surroundings of Hyde Park.

His furry slippers were caked in muck and he was still wearing his satin pyjamas. And yet, despite the fact his clothing was sodden and clinging to his skin, the cold didn't bother him at all. Here, in the very slough of despond, he felt nothing.

In his hand he discovered the letter from the BBC. He brought the sheet to his face and read it again carefully, twice. It was still a rejection.

And still, strangely enough, he felt nothing.

It was a curious reaction. Like that of Oscar Wilde in *The Portrait of Mr W.H.*, who, having poured everything into a theory that the *Sonnets* were penned for a boy-actor the Bard was secretly in love with, found that he had exhausted all passion for the subject and was now completely indifferent to it. Had Glenn, too, done his subject to death?

Proust said, "If we are to make reality endurable, we must all nourish a fancy or two", but Glenn's fancy had not made reality endurable. His fancy had made only for an enjoyable *unreality*, and he realised now that there would be no fee for his pilot script, or a fee for each script in the series, or a request to extend the series from six episodes to eight or ten (which was a relief because he hadn't been able to think of a plot for a sixth episode, let alone an eighth or tenth). There would be no producer credit for him, no starring role in the show, no executive producing the soundtrack, no writing a tie-in book for the Christmas market, no clothing line by the house of Henrietta Payne who didn't speak to him anymore anyway; there would be no swank penthouses, no new life of London and largesse, no entourage and no ascension to Fame's immortal house. He would *not* be the lowly menswear manager who made himself into a celebrated writer, like a new Martin Eden. In short, he would not be escaping his irons and bondage. For he was no more a writer than he was a fashion designer, or a model, and the question of where a lifetime's reading and writing would lead him had finally been answered.

It led to four short paragraphs, on a single side of A4 paper, in which all of his hopes and dreams were destroyed forever.

Still though, he couldn't help but admire its structure. Whether by accident or design he knew not, but the letter seemed almost to possess a story of its own. From the opening lines that gripped you immediately with their cryptic nature, to the second paragraph where expectations were masterfully built up as a series of virtues were delineated with great brio. The suspense was so skillfully executed you could barely wait to read the next paragraph!

And then it happened. The unexpected twist, where a series of shocking revelations, each one more devastating than the last, exposed the awful truth and brought the story to its tragic climax. And reading it, Glenn had been struck dumb, left gobsmacked. He felt as if the rug had been pulled out from under him.

Now *that* was writing.

It was the sort of effect he had been striving to achieve with his scripts. And the letter even ended on a joke! *Good luck with your writing.* A preposterous remark to make, after such a condemnation of his talents. It was a brilliant punchline, set up sublimely, and he gazed in awe at the letter. Ah, what a shame they were not able to discuss his script in any more detail; he felt that if the BBC would let him collaborate with this Bunsari Patel woman, together they could write something truly incredible!

His musings were interrupted by a quarrelsome crow walking around near his muddy slippers. His gaze drifted beyond the rowdy bird, inexorably to Leeds University, the faint outline of which he could perceive through the thick mist. O! how he envied those students starting out on the right path. Acquiring the right degree that would lead them to the right job (probably in London). Students who were no better than he was, but who were simply better guided—who were simply *lucky*.

He wondered whether a degree was the only thing now that could put him back on track. And yes, all right, it would mean adding to his Barry Lyndon-level debts, but this time the debt would be *strategic*, a loan taken out with a clear objective, that. . . . but no, the idea wasn't worth pursuing. Because his GCSEs were poor, he didn't have A-Levels, and he had quit his GNVQ.

And being unprepar'd, his will had become servant to defect.

Poor Glenn Harding! He had dreamed of being the first great writer to have risen from the gutter. Literally, because the notion had come to him while he was lying flat on his back in the gutter (in the forty-ninth canto of this great canticle). And this is where it had got him. Lying flat on his back, again, but this time in a bog. In winter.

He cringed at the memory of that mawkish night in the sixty-third canto, when he had posted his script and projected the dead in the sky, beheld his own star rising. He had felt in his bones that he would be big, and he was right. He would indeed be big.

A big embarrassment!

He blushed with shame at the awful script he had written, and the vitriolic rants he had made about it to Jimmy. Burying his face in his hands, he groaned in anguish.

He then flung his head back and laughed aloud at the very idea of him ever having his own TV show. What monstrous madness could have blinded his eyes!

To the present day I cannot understand the beginning or the end of this strange passage in my life.

He lowered his gaze, looked at the crow. There was a worm dangling from its beak, and while the putrid sight turned Glenn's stomach, the more he studied it, the more he realised that as puny as the crow looked, outlined by yon mighty university, still it was the picture of contentment, down here in the bog, with its little worm. And it gave him an idea. A new idea! A radical idea! His boldest idea yet. And the idea was this:

To grow up.

To stop looking for some better life and accept the one given him, like everyone else did. With education he was past the point of no return. And without his artistic pretensions, and his constant striving for advancement, what was he left with?

Nirah Frazar.

He worked for one of the finest names in the fashion world. And while Bunsari Patel's masterful letter had proven that he was not and never would be a writer, he *was* a menswear manager. And he was now free to devote all his time and attention to the day job, such was the strange and wonderful power of resignation. What was that line he liked from *A Life*, that the Italo Svevo character said? "A balanced life, a hard working existence with modest aims, was worth more than the pleasures that riches could give."

O, Italo Svevo, you brilliant philosopher you! Another reason to love Joyce: his gifting Svevo to the world. Yes, lack of self-content really *was* the worst of all misfortunes; the middle station of life *was* the place to be. Conformity divine. Upper low life.

That was where Glenn belonged. And, fortunately, that was where he already was.

He had long been possessed by a strong sensation of imminent, ineluctable Fate, and at last he understood it. His fate was to be the best department manager Nirah Frazar had ever seen. Better than Shukeena. Better even than Sylvanus. For the pursuit of what he thought was a dream life had plunged him into a nightmare, and it was time now to turn what he thought would be a nightmare into his *true* dream life.

Glenn looked to the bleak sky and beheld his new dawn.

He shambled to his feet and began trudging through the gloom, back to Hyde Hill. Back to where his life began—and where his life would now begin again.

V.II

ABANDON ALL HOPE, YE WHO DON'T SHOP HERE was written in large gilt letters on the Nirah Frazar shopwindow. Inside it, a group of mannequins stood tall, bedecked in the most luxurious winter ensembles, while beneath them was a darksome ditch of mangled naked ones, piled on top of each other in a mini abyss that was rimmed by sheets of red foil shaped like hellfire.

That abyss was where every fool in Leeds who was embarking on a *creative* project, or attending lectures for a degree they would never use—who was dissatisfied with the station wherein God and Nature had placed them—would find themselves in the end. For every one successful fashion designer there were a thousand failures, and the miry slough had space to swallow them all. And though, on that cold dark morning, the long tragicomedy of their lives was just beginning, Glenn's tragicomedy was over; for the Sunshine Day had arrived, and walking under the green and gold of County Arcade, passing by the window and thinking of their plight, he breathed a sigh of relief that he was no longer one of them.

I will be no companion of such misled, fantastical fellows.

The staff were sitting in silence on antique piano stools, the animosities between them running so high that, like *Tramecksans* and *Slamecksans*, they wouldn't even speak to each other. Yet Glenn Harding, the man responsible for all the schism, was sitting right in the middle of them, on a Scandinavian swivel chair, beaming brightly.

Indeed, he had been the first to arrive on the floor.

When Shukeena broke the silence by clip clopping down the stairs, she was met with a burst of applause. The team all gaped in unison at the menswear manager.

He was on his feet, clapping.

Shukeena stopped mid step. She gripped the banister, as one heel hovered in the air. She didn't know what was more alarming. That Glenn was applauding her, or that he was in at this time at all.

It seemed he intended to prove himself the better manager not by the complots and intrigues that she employed against him, but rather with a big smile and oodles of enthusiasm. He would esteem the yang and avoid the yin at all costs.

The other way was all abyss.

'Thank you, Glenn, for that warm welcome,' said Shukeena dubiously as she marched onto the floor wearing her sleek black mohair-blend suit over a black rollneck and wielding a folder of paperwork. 'You can sit down now.'

He obediently did as instructed as she stood behind her lectern, laid open her folder.

'Good morning, everybody,' she exclaimed shrilly.

The staff murmured a response which was drowned out by Glenn's booming 'Good morning, Shukeena!' She gave him the eyeball. Sitting erectly, smiling enthusiastically at her, something in his black eyes and bright smile provoked in her an involuntary shudder.

'*Right*,' she said, scanning her notes. 'Before I start the meeting, I'd just like to thank you all for coming in on New Year's Eve.' She looked up at the room and smiled. 'And if you're planning on going out tonight, I hope you have a good time.'

The staff looked touched by the ladieswear manager's uncharacteristic amity; suddenly a rare, joyful air of goodwill swept through the shopfloor.

Then her voice hardened.

'When you signed your contract of employment, the terms and conditions stated that, "Nirah Frazar does not recognise *any* public or bank holidays." I can confirm that, in spite of the rumours that have been going around this week, and regardless of what other shops in the arcade are doing, we *will* be opening tomorrow, and you are *all* contractually obliged to work your full shifts.'

That rare, joyful air of goodwill passed in an instant and all the staff seemed to sink with despair into their own piano stools. All except Glenn.

'And it's a 6:30 start everyone,' she continued. 'So again, have a good time tonight—but *don't* forget you need to be up early and in here *on time*. Do *not* be late.'

Glenn held his smile, as some of the temps dotted around him openly wept.

'Any questions?' said Shukeena brightly. 'No? Right then. Let's begin—'

A hand rose into the air.

Shukeena stared at it for a moment as if she couldn't comprehend what it was. She squinted her eyes and followed the arm down to a fair, lambent face.

'Yes, Betty?' she said faintly.

'I can't work tomorrow,' Betty squeaked. 'I promised Ali I'd visit him.'

The room at once fell silent, with eyes fixed on the hardwood.

Shukeena was glaring darkly at the sales assistant—as was Glenn.

'Well of course we *all* wish Ali a speedy recovery,' she said in a low, measured tone, speaking through gritted teeth. 'But I'm already understaffed because of him, and, with all due respect, Betty, I can't afford to lose *two* team members over one head injury.'

355

'Hear, hear,' Glenn murmured.

'But his family's restaurant is open tomorrow!' Betty squeaked pleadingly. 'He'll be all alone on New Year's Day!'

'Betty, if you don't come in tomorrow, then don't bother coming in the next day,' Shukeena warned. 'Because you will *not* have a position here anymore.

'And by the way,' she added. 'January is the hardest time of year to find a job.'

'It's also the month with the highest rate of suicide,' added Norman, tottering through the floor in his camouflage jacket, followed by a waft of night that cut through the perfumed air. He eerily reeled up the stairs and then vanished.

After the meeting, Betty clip clopped over to footwear and returned her piano stool. It was as she turned to face the floor that she was met by a pair of leering black eyes.

'Nice try, Betty!' Dick giggled. 'But if there's one thing I've learned in all my years on shopfloors, it's this—*they've got you by the bollocks.*'

Betty returned a disconsolate hum.

'I see you're demoralised,' he said. 'Don't worry! Everyone goes through it early in their retail career.' He slyly looked her petite figure up and down, barely covered by a strapless black mini dress, with an explosion of black ostrich feathers encircling the high hem. With her black leather ankle boots she looked to him like the love interest from a Bryan Ferry music video. 'But,' he continued, in a slightly breathless voice, 'if you ever need a shoulder to cry on, we can always go for a swift half after work? Maybe in, I dunno, the Conservatory—'

'Dick,' Betty squeaked.

'Yes babe?'

'If I go for a drink with you, will you lie and tell everyone you did it with me?'

Dick turned purple.

'I *DID* DO IT WITH GERTRUDE!' he yelled, waving his little fists in the air. 'IT WAS AFTER THE CHRISTMAS DO! WHY WILL NO ONE BELIEVE ME?!'

The floor's hubbub of chatter and clip clops abruptly fell silent.

Gertrude, marching through ladieswear with a haul of dismembered limbs under her arms, came to a halt. She glared fiercely at Dick. 'You slept on my *sofa*!' she shouted. 'And if you lie about it one more time, I'm going to report you!'

'That's enough, you two!' ordered Shukeena, who was hunched over the cashdesk, writing out the rota. 'Gertrude, go and put those mannequin parts in the window; Dick, stop spreading lies about my staff.'

Dick screamed.

As he went storming off, stamping up the stairs with his body jiggling convulsively, Glenn sprang up in front of the tills. 'Morning Shukeena!' he said cheerily. 'That was a great meeting you put on there; *very* informative. I feel briefed!'

'What do you want, Glenn?' she asked, not lifting her eyes from the rota.

'Nothing!' he laughed. 'I just wanted to compliment you on your talk. You put it all in the plan, and now I just want to run up those stairs and realise it for you.'

'If you're fishing for what time we'll get out tonight, I have no idea.'

He flung his head back and gave a jolting, one syllable guffaw.

'No! It's nothing to do with that. In fact, I'm planning on working late tonight.'

A pause.

'You're *what*?' she said faintly.

'So, if you have plans and want to shoot off early, I'm happy to take on whatever needs doing. *Very* happy.' He leaned in. 'Remember, I am here to support you.'

Shukeena drew herself up and looked Glenn square in the eye. 'All right, what the hell are you doing?' she demanded.

'Nothing, my warlike Amazon!' he cried, laughing. 'I just want to ensure everything gets done, so that New Year's Day runs as smoothly as possible. After all, it is the biggest date in the retail calender.'

Her massive eyes remained fixed on Glenn's. 'All right, Glenn,' she nodded. 'Good luck with that,' she said.

'Thanks mate.'

Shukeena visibly shuddered.

'And you really think you can get men's ready for the sale by the end of the day?' she asked doubtfully.

'I don't see why not.'

V.III

I was on the bridge with the skipper and the bridge officers and we were all peering anxiously at the fog.

The ship was going "dead slow", the captain had made two slight alterations of course and I realised that we were lost. To make matters worse we didn't have any radar, only a magnetic compass, when most ships at this time had gyrocompasses. After a while there was the noise of engines and a voice from a loud hailer came across saying, 'To regain correct station bear 303 for 3,000 yards; I repeat, to regain correct station bear 303 for 3,000 yards, if you understand flash an Aldis Lamp.' I flashed the lamp assuming that the ship's officers had heard the message and understood it.

When I looked around the skipper was staring at me and asking, 'What was that?' I told him what the message was and how I understood it, and he immediately gave the necessary instructions to the helmsman and we changed course.

I want you now to put yourself in my position. I was a youngster, twenty-one years old, and my knowledge of seamanship was very limited. I knew quite a bit about visual communications, but the complexities of compass bearings and the like was beyond my meagre capabilities. Most of the troops were standing on deck and I noticed that many of them were wearing life jackets. The jungle telegraph must have been in operation and I suppose they thought we could be in trouble, as in fact we were.

I began to wonder if I had heard the message correctly, and it occurred to me that if anything went wrong I was going to be to blame. I realised that 4,000 troops could be in mortal danger because I might have heard a message wrongly, and I began to be frightened. We cruised along steadily and after a while I asked one of the bridge officers if we had travelled 3,000 yards. 'More,' he said.

Two minutes later we suddenly broke through the fog, only to find ourselves heading straight for another large ship.

The captain screamed out, 'Hard a-port, full speed astern!' (Of course this was in French but Fernand told me afterwards this is what he said.) This manoeuvre saved us from a fatal collision, but unfortunately we lost the convoy again. The main body of it disappeared into the mist, where frayed reams of tinsel were hanging limply from the pictures and mirrors. Empty rails dotted the department, stuffed robins and boughs of holly had been kicked about the hardwood, and, on the main display, a neglected, possibly dead Christmas tree was encircled by its own shed needles.

Brummell, stood beside it in a dusty blazer, was missing his head.

Glenn stood at the centre of the floor with his hands on his hips, legs spread apart.

'How on earth did I let menswear fall into this state?' he said, shaking his head in astonishment. '*Again*,' he added, after a moment's thought.

The junto of Dick, Lyndsey, and Mildred, gathered by the cashdesk, heard his words and exchanged with each other looks of outrage.

'Us!' gasped Dick. 'Here, you can't blame us, Glenn; *you're* the menswear manager. It's *your* job to—wait, hang on a second. Did he say "I" just then?'

'He did say "I",' nodded Lyndsey with disbelief. 'He's actually taking responsibility for his actions for once,' he said with amazement.

'Who is he? And what has he done with Glenn Harding?' demanded Mildred.

Glenn turned and showed his team a perfectly cheerful face.

'O well!' he said. 'With labour I must earn my bread. The time 'twixt six and now must by us be spent most preciously,' he smiled, rubbing his hands together.

The remark wrung from his underlings a weary groan.

'Dick, Lyndsey, you stay on your sections; Mildred, you cover front and cashdesk,' Glenn instructed. 'Leave the floor to me.'

The team gaped at each other with disbelief. 'Glenn,' said Dick, 'did—did we *hear* you right? You're going to let us just stay on our sections while *you* sort the floor out?'

'Ay, good friend,' Glenn nodded. 'I don't want menswear missing out on any sales, or my yoke-fellows suffering, just because *I* didn't manage to prepare the department in time,' he smiled. 'We are no tyrant, but a Christian king!' he chuckled.

'Whoa, *geez*,' said Dick, staring fixedly at him. 'You don't seriously expect to prepare the whole department, single-handedly, *today*, do you? You'll never do it!'

'Not with your three naps a day in the fitting room you won't,' remarked Lyndsey.

'And the other things he does in the fitting room,' added Mildred knowingly.

The other two nodded in agreement with that remark.

'Pish,' said Glenn. 'The fewer the men, the greater the share of honour. And stop worrying, you lot! You're not going to be working late, irrespective of whatever *I* do. *I* got us into this mess—and *I'll* get us out,' he vowed sombrely.

'My, Glenn,' said Lyndsey. 'That certainly is. . . . *ambitious*.'

'I know it is,' Glenn nodded, smiling. A single tear rolled down his cheek.

The junto watched him turn and march off decisively, if somewhat unsteadily.

'Oh my God, Glenn's gone mad,' Dick gasped. 'Well. . . . madder.'

'He does seem to be behaving very strangely,' said Lyndsey.

'He's gone gimpy in the head,' said Mildred. 'But who gives a chuff? At least he said we're not going to be working late.'

'I know, what a result,' said Dick. 'It's unbelievable!'

Lyndsey frowned at Dick. 'Glenn being weird is hardly "unbelievable", Dick. It's a daily occurance.' He grinned. 'You and Gertrude—now *that's* unbelievable.'

Mildred snorted.

'I *DID* DO IT WITH GERTRUDE!' Dick yelled, waving his fists and stamping his feet. In his rage there was some looseness of speech which it is unnecessary to quote but essentially contained a surfeit of graphic detail in relation to the event. There was a pause, followed by the staff members realising to their horror that the first customers of the day were standing at the top of the stairs gaping Dick, who turned a violent crimson. Set down properly the incident would perhaps wrap up the scene on a satisfying comic note, but that ultimately is a *creative* concern, and that way madness lies.

So let's shun that and instead end things in an abrupt and unsatisfying manner.

V.IV

For the first time in a long time Glenn was wearing his set of manager's keys.

Usually, he would leave them lying around the shop and then scream at Dick or Lyndsey to go find them for him, but this morning they were clipped securely to his belt loop, jangling authoritatively as he traversed Camelot. He found the noise they made quite pleasing, and was surprised by how much he had missed it.

I weep for joy to stand upon my kingdom once again.

He grabbed a binbag from inside the grotty utility cupboard, made a mental note to clean it in January after things quietened down. It was a task he could delegate but preferred not to, knowing he would do a better job than any of those schematics on his team. He jangled happily—if unsteadily—past the stairs, to the far side of the floor, by the rusty suit of armour, where he then shook the binbag open.

He reached up past the velour business trousers to a vast painting of a man in black stood before three nude maidens and pulled down the tinsel draped across its ornate frame. He dropped it in the bag and then had to beat the dust off his face. He laughed. Apparently he would also have to go around his realm with a duster later! But one thing at a time, H. One thing at a time.

'Pssssst,' came a low, demonic whisper from behind him. 'You boy.'

With a sensation of horror so overpowering it defied description, Glenn realised that Mr Hyde from Hyde Hill had tracked him down to his place of work. At once he sagged, and as he glanced back, he braced himself for the ghoul's appalling sight.

He breathed a sigh of relief when he saw the still horrid but mercifully human face peeping out of the office. 'Yes, Norman?' he replied.

'Do me a favour, will you? Go and find Glenn Harding, the menswear manager!'

'All right. Here I am.'

'Marvellous, you work quickly. Come in!'

'It's no one's fault, Norman,' said Glenn reassuringly, squinting to read the figures under the weak light of the bare lightbulb. 'It's just that time of year. Shoppers are holding back you see, waiting for the sale to start.'

Norman was lying on his back on the desk, his huge arms and legs dangling from the sides, staring vacantly at the ceiling. 'Yeah, tell that to head office,' he sulked.

Glenn glanced at his watch, but remembered it had stopped working again, and he no longer had Gertrude to get it fixed for him. (D'ye think Henrietta would ever have got your watch fixed for you?) His eyes searched for the clock on the wall but found that it too had succumbed to the mushrooms. The blue fungi had engulfed the office like a living, breathing wallpaper, and their unholy presence chilled the very marrow in his bones.

'The figures aren't *that* bad,' he assured the store manager, turning his attention back to the sheet. 'All right, our classic lines are down, but I'm working on that now. Or at least I will be, when I'm back out there. But if you look, the figures for some of the new talent boutiques have actually been creeping up.'

'Really? Which ones?'

Water began dripping from the lightbulb. Glenn moved the sheet aside.

'Burn, House! has been growing steadily this week; You Must Eat Men, they've had a sudden surge in the last few days; O, and Kill,

Kill, Kill, Kill, Kill, Kill! looks set to meet, and possibly exceed, target tomorrow—'

It was the oddest thing, but the image of the mounted moose head over the tills flashed in Glenn's eyes. And at the sight of its vast horns, a chill tingled his spine.

There will be blood on the moon tomorrow.

'Well, that's a good sign!' said Norman, sitting up. 'That's a *very* good sign.'

'Things are looking up! I'm taking down the Christmas decorations— or I will be, when I'm back out there—and then I just need to put them in the basement, get the fixtures and fittings in position, update the mid-season favourites, bring the racks of sale out and put up the new signage, and men's will be good to go. *We're on track!*'

He was surprised by how rapidly the floor had filled with customers, but then remembered that it was New Year's Eve, and that most people, normal people, were liberated from their irons and bondage today. He scooped up his binbag and took two slightly painful steps to the wide leg, olive shearling slacks, and the next piece of tinsel, which was draped over a picture of a beautiful young man that always made him think of Dorian Gray. As he reached up, a loud crackling sound pierced the perfumed air.

'Can Glenn Harding report to ladieswear immediately,' came a harsh, shrill voice. 'Glenn Harding to ladieswear immediately.'

He took a deep breath.

'Thou dost love the new PA system most unfeignedly, don't you?' Glenn laughed, wincing slightly as he walked over. 'Would thou lov'd me but half so much!'

Shukeena was standing by the little mike stand on the counter of the ladies' cashdesk. She glowered at him and said in a stern, shrill voice: 'Is it true you told your staff they could leave *early* tonight?'

'Yes,' Glenn smiled.

'Are you *mad?*' the Infernal Serpent asked.

'Nay,' said Glenn, holding his smile. 'I just don't see why the *team* should suffer, because the manager has, by his own errors, work more plentiful than tools to do't.'

He sneezed, saw the dust blow off his unkempt scraggle.

'Glenn,' said Shukeena tersely, 'your floor is a *trainwreck*. You are *weeks* behind. There is *no way* you can get it ready for tomorrow on your own. It's impossible!'

'My firm nerves shall never tremble, Miss Mohammed,' he said, his smile looking slightly strained. 'I am doing it *now*. Or at least I would be doing it now, if you hadn't called me down here. But the truth is, I'm better off working without those wavering commons upstairs, lacking as they do the firey ardour for battle that *I* possess.'

'Oh, give over with the arrogance, Glenn; it's *you* who's on a stage 2 written warning, not anybody else! Now listen to me: you don't have the authority to be making decisions like when to send staff home on New Year's Eve; *I* do. And *I'm* telling you to go upstairs, tell everyone they'll be working late, and start delegating tasks so that *my* team doesn't have to come up and sort out menswear for you after we've finished—*like we did last year.*

'Crack the whip, Glenn! That's how you get things done. And if you're this great manager you think you are, you'll do it. Crack the whip. *Crack it!*'

The witch shall die.

He snatched up his binbag, made great dole under his breath. I'll fizzing crack you, you thirty winter age hag. Beware! Approach Glenn not too nigh, for he hath vanquished more than one queen, and hath made him a coat full of name-badges!

'Excuse me,' said an unfriendly voice.

'My lord?' said Glenn, wheeling around with a forced smile.

'Do you have this in a small?' asked the boy. He was holding up the drop shoulder, open-knit piss-yellow lambswool jumper.

The sight of the garment stirred painful memories in Glenn, reminding him as it did of the sort of designs he expected Henrietta would one day produce. 'Ah yes,' he sighed. '*This* one. . . . I'm afraid that's all we have left in that size, sir.'

'Oh, I always get fobbed off with that line,' the boy huffed.

'Pardon me, sir: little joy have I to breathe this news: yet what I say is true,' Glenn insisted. 'You see, the London store occasionally sends us items from the new talent boutiques they're trialling, and this was one of them. And I do mean *one*; that's the only size they sent us. It's by a St. Martin's graduate named—'

'Can you not have a look in the back for me, just in case?'

'As I say, sir, that *was* the only size they sent us.'

'So you're not going to check for me?'

'Sir, I know for a fact—'

'So you're not going to check for me?'

Glenn held his polite smile, as he felt his eyelid begin to twitch.

'Have you considered trying that one?' he suggested. 'It's not meant to be worn *fitted*; that's why it has drop shoulders. That ribbed trim at the bottom will draw it in at your waist and give the garment its relaxed, boxy shape. Seriously! I'm a small too, and I would buy the medium. If I could afford it.'

The lad looked down and saw the state of Glenn's shoes, and the binbag he was dragging round. 'Yeah, that's great mate, but I *can* afford it, and I want to buy it now, but you don't seem arsed about making a sale.'

Pause.

'All right, sir!' said Glenn brightly. 'I'll go upstairs and check the stock room for you, just in case there's an ancillary jumper that has hitherto evaded our detection.'

'It is your job,' replied the boy derisively.

Glenn's eyelid went into spasm.

He dumped his binbag, zigzagged the gabbling duncery, making great dole under his breath. He looked over the mass of heads, to the chalet cuckoo clock, but remembered smashing its face in months ago. He skulked behind the partition and discovered that the lift doors had vanished behind a phalanx of rails, wedged tightly together and weighted down by masses of sale stock hanging from them.

He smiled.

'Tis good for men to love their present pains; so the spirit is eased!

He trudged up the chilly stairwell, every step stinging his feet. One of his soles began to emit a squeak, and the irksome sound travelled up the heights of the narrow shaft, carried on the thick stench emanating from the bins on ground. And as he stood in the cold stock room, contemplatively stroking his scraggle, his narrowed eyes searching the half-dark for a garment that did not exist, it suddenly occurred to him, to his horror, that it was only a matter of time, a few years at most, until London began sending them lines by. . . . fashion graduate Henrietta Payne.

Abruptly his pulse beat as if he had a fever, as he thought of the indignity of him having to sell her costly creations while he was on barely more than minimum wage. What name would the sylph dream up for her label, he wondered. Not One of Your Shop Conquests? He fell into a trance, beheld the dark dawn that her first batch of wares arrived: Predestination in a delivery box, a manifestation of the gods' cruel mockery—and his job to sell it. O, product knowledge? Features and benefits? *Origins?* Yes, sir, I think that I can fill you in on this designer. Tell me, do you like reading scripts? Let me just run up to my locker!

God's nails and blood.

She'll easily get the cover of the *Yorkshire Evening Post.* Local girl made good. Buzz of fashion world. And that's when it hit him, like a dread bolt from Jupiter:

One day she'll get the cover of *Advert.*

'Gape wide, O earth, and draw me down alive!' he shrieked.

Suddenly, right on cue, the pit of hell opened her mouth just whereabout he stood, and from whence came smoke and coals of fire, with hideous noises. And as he looked, and beheld the gulf of Tartarus ready, opening wide its firey chaos to receive his fall, the heat singed his scraggle and with a scream of terror he drew back from the brink.

With an almighty groan the aperture closed back up.

Glenn stood to one side panting, a hand pressed to his fluttering heart. He shook his head forlornly. God, he envied Wilde and his ability to exhaust his passion for a subject. When was *he* going to exhaust his passion for Henrietta? And how was he going to devote himself to the day job, embrace the middle station—*how was he going to survive in the straight world*—knowing she was out there doing the exact opposite, in bustling London, in the pursuit of Greatness? With some dullard boyfriend who doesn't even know he is the luckiest man on earth; who certainly doesn't know that Glenn Harding would *sell his soul to the fizzing devil* just to swap places with him—for an eternity in Dis was a more than acceptable price for a life on earth spent with an angel.

He sighed.

It was going to be hard bondage, living through the next 70, 80 years without her. He cast his eyes upward, into the crushing darkness of the rafters. . . . *How gladly would I meet mortality, my sentence, and be earth insensible.*

But then he thought of those mannequins in the abyss, and himself passing them by. *For every one successful fashion designer there were a thousand failures—and the miry slough had space to swallow them all.* Remember the letter, Glenn Harding; remember your name-badge. Learn thou of manly fortitude, and scorn those joys thou shalt never possess.

Let the sylph go and live her enjoyable unreality.

Watch from afar as she is authoring her own tragicomedy.

Bide thy time while she ventures gaily, O so gaily, unto the wrath to come—for on the Day of the Schematics we shall stand back and watch as the abyss swallows her whole. . . . *And enjoy every minute of it.*

He jumped as he remembered his customer.

'I'm afraid we don't have any more upstairs, sir,' he panted to the customer, 'but this cotton blend white sweater from our classic range is similar. Except for the studs.'

The boy glared at the garment. 'I didn't ask for that.'

Glenn glanced over his head, at the tinsel still drooping over Dorian Gray.

'I *know* you didn't ask for it, sir, but we don't have any other sizes in the jumper you asked for, therefore I am humbly offering you this alternative.'

'Don't get snappy with me; it's not my fault you're unhappy in your job.' The lad grinned. 'Maybe you should have paid more attention in school?'

Glenn stood with his mouth open as he watched him walk off down the stairs.

A loud crackling sound pierced the perfumed air.

'Can Glenn Harding report to the manager's office immediately,' ordered a harsh, shrill voice. 'Glenn Harding to the manager's office immediately.'

V.V

'I am worried, Norman! We are the lowest performing branch of Nirah Frazar! Head office are investigating us! We don't just need to exceed target tomorrow—we need to *smash* it. Our careers depend on it!' Shukeena jabbered anxiously.

Norman was rolling along the walls, twirling and flailing. 'How's menswear coming along?' he asked dreamily.

'It's *not*,' Shukeena said. 'Glenn hasn't made any progress on his floor at all.'

Norman abruptly stopped spinning.

'*What*!' he boomed, teetering unsteadily over his desk. 'No progress *at all*?' He gaped at Glenn. 'What have you been doing?' he demanded.

Glenn was sitting next to Shukeena with his face pitched in his hands.

'I have been *trying* to make progress, Norman,' he growled through gritted teeth, 'but people keep dragging me away from my work.' His eyelid was twitching again.

'You've been *trying*?' the store manager gasped. 'Well, you better try harder, laddy.' He looked to his wrist—no watch. 'You're running out of time!'

'I've got all *day*,' Glenn replied roughly.

'It took ladieswear all *week* to get ready,' said Shukeena gravely.

'Then maybe you should work on your time management?' Glenn grunted.

Shukeena jerked in her mill worker's chair.

'*My* time management!?' she screeched. 'Don't you dare talk to me about time management, Glenn Harding! That garland has been hanging on your back wall since *last* Christmas!'

Glenn groaned something that sounded like mezcal.

'Glenn?' said a voice.

He dropped his binbag, threw back his head and emitted a long, moaning cry.

'What now?' he replied eventually.

'You know you're on the twelve lunch, don't you?' Dick queried.

Glenn shrugged his shoulders. 'So?'

'Well, it's one now. I should be going! But I can't until you've had yours.'

A pause.

'Just go, Dick.'

'Why? When are you planning on going—'

'Just *go*!'

Dick grabbed him. 'Geez!' he chuckled, 'what's wrong? Why are you getting yourself all worked up?' He jiggled him affectionately. 'Do you need a little. . . . *symposium?*'

Glenn tipped his head back and took a long, sweet slake of blonde ale.

He smiled, sat glowing in his dirty fur coat, at a small table down the end of the long, narrow room. He was resting against the dark wood-panel wall, sideways on to Dick, who was sipping his lager thoughtfully. Glenn closed his eyes and breathed the boozy air, revelled in the fun, relaxed atmosphere. What a relief it was, to be off his aching feet! His unkempt crown of monstrous size actually felt lighter on his head.

'Wow,' said Dick. 'Well, thank you for sharing all that, geez. You certainly got a load off your chest.' He sipped his lager.

'Told thee I could a tale unfold, whose lightest word would harrow up thy soul.'

'Well, yeah, I knew you fancied Henrietta; I just didn't think you had such. . . . *intense* feelings for her. I didn't think *anyone* could have intense feelings for her.'

'Love reasons without reason,' Glenn shrugged. He took another slake of his ale. He cocked a curious eye at the formalwear supervisor.

'Hast thou never beheld a woman and been swallowed up in an abyss of love in an instant?'

'Yep. Debbie Harry performing "Heart of Glass" on *Top of the Pops*, 1979.' He sipped his lager. 'And then Gertrude.'

Glenn glared at his underling. 'I'st time to jest and dally now?' he said darkly.

'It *happened*, geez,' said Dick, grinning from ear to ear. 'Sorry.'

'How, you fat fool! I scorn you.'

'Do you want to test me on any distinguishing features her body has?'

'As though I had not pain enough to bear, Mr Zabledore!' Glenn cried. He sighed, swigged his ale. 'Her earthly vehicle hast not a blot or a mark; 'tis flawless.'

'I *know*,' said Dick with a lusty growl.

'False knight, get thee gone, or this will grow to a brawl anon.' Glenn slammed his tankard on the table. 'Before God, I am exceeding weary!'

'Let's talk about something else, shall we?' Dick said in an emollient voice.

'Let's. What have you got?'

Dick turned his attention back to his tattered newspaper. 'Four across: your face. Six letters, ends with an E.'

'Visage,' Glenn said, after a moment's thought.

'*Visage*? What's that?'

Glenn stared at him. 'Your *face*.'

Dick's visage contorted. '*Really*? Is that what it means? I just thought it was a band.' He looked at his crossword. 'Ooh! Chuffing hell, it does fit though. Thanks.'

Glenn watched him scribbling cheerily, his black gelled side-parting glinting in the sun streaming in pleasantly through the frosted windows. Over his head a gallimaufry of older patrons lined the counter, aglow in the smoke-whorled glare of the dangling lightbulbs. He looked again to the windows. The duncery was scurrying to and fro through the alleyway, their breath blowing in the bitter chill. The rush led his thoughts to New Year's Day, and targets to exceed, and all the work still to do, and his eyelid began to twitch again. He quaffed his tankard, when, all of a sudden, he beheld the denizens behind Dick turn his way and begin to advance on him—garments in hands and questions on their lips—and he jerked in his seat.

'Did you say something?' Glenn asked, discombobulated.

'Yes, geez,' said Dick. 'Ghost that haunts Macbeth. Six letters, starts with a B.'

'Banquo.'

'*Really?*' He looked down. 'Yeah, it does fit!' He scribbled it in. 'You're quite smart, aren't you, geez?' he chuckled. 'Do you ever think you're wasted in retail?'

Glenn blinked.

I want to do more with my life than work in a clothes shop in—He shook his head violently.

Chains in hell, not realms expect.

'Right, we better get moving,' said Dick, checking his watch. 'I still need to get me sarnie. Fancy a walk up to Thornton's?'

Glenn looked dismally at the slither of ale in his glass. But then he glanced at Dick's and saw that it was still half-full. 'You get off,' he said, wiping his mouth. 'I'm going to stay here a while and think of a plan of action for tomorrow.'

'Hairy muff,' Dick nodded.

The moment the formalwear supervisor left, Glenn snatched his pint and threw it down his throat. And with the room's attentions fixated on the bar, he was able to stand up, squeak over to the next table and pour the remnants of a couple of discarded glasses into his. He returned to his table with a half.

He smiled as he sipped his warm, flat lager, glowed dimly in the gloom.

Do you ever think you're wasted in retail?

Glenn retrieved the rejection letter from his fur coat and unfolded it on the table.

[*Reads.*]

The characterisations are superficial and insufficiently differentiated. They are essentially an array of schematic types who never quite manage to convince.

He looked, and beheld himself sitting in the staff room. He had a shaven head, wore a hideous, off-brand, pink-striped shirt, and was bathed in a nervous first day sweat. A grief of shopgirls was clip clopping to and fro, completely ignoring him, when suddenly Mildred trudged in looking worse for wear, and reported to the room that she had woken up that morning face down, fully clothed.

The remark shocked Glenn as much as it amused him, and it served to introduce him to the world of Nirah Frazar. It was a sentence that seemed to contain a story all of its own. It worked on two levels, conjuring up an amusing image of Mildred while also summing up her character in one line. He liked it so much he had included it in his script. But what struck him now was that the remark could have been made by any of them. Swap Mildred with Gertrude and it still sounded right; swap Gertrude with Ali and it fit like a glove; the words come out of Wilfred's mouth and no one thinks, *Well, that's out of character*—such was their strong influence on each other, and the parochial nature of the north, their narrow life experience being acquired at the same time, in the same place, growing up surrounded by the same people.

Mildred had never even read a book, a fact she took great pride in. Ali told him that he had read only one book in his life, at school, but he couldn't remember its title or any details of its plot. Gertrude had at least applied a theory to her incuriousity. She didn't read fiction "because it never happened". Was it any wonder they were facsimiles of each other? With their frame of reference so minute, their worldview so myopic?

It was one of the main themes of his story.

Writing demonstrates sound sense of visual grammar. Storytelling economic yet detailed, effective use of montage and fantasy, dialogue works well – convincingly naturalistic, engaging energy. The characterisations are superficial and insufficiently differentiated. Schematic types who never quite manage to convince.

Good. So he had succeeded with the effect he was going for.

There is insufficient insight into a very pertinent problem.

And he had failed to achieve what he had not attempted.

Because to provide the sort of insight Bunsari Patel thought was required, the staff would have to explain that which they could not explain themselves. That which they were not even conscious of. They would need their life experience to be rewritten, their horizons broadened. They would need to acquire a capacity for reflection. Essentially, they would need to stop being themselves—in which case the script would no longer be true to life. And all because by sitting down to write he had somehow inherited an obligation to adhere to the established principles of formulaic TV storytelling—to write in a schematic style, essentially—in order to appeal to the inferior parts of the public.

Glenn's view? Laymen should be encouraged to think.

And James Joyce agrees with me. Who have you got?

Tone falls between two stools, never managing to be funny or dramatic enough.

Subjective! What about Jimmy, who thought parts of it were, and I quote, "chuffing funny"? And no one watches more TV than Jimmy. Or what about Polyphemos, that literary cyclops whose writing was courted by the Playhouse, and who laughed all the way through his script, comparing it favourably to *A Midsummer Night's Dream*? Who was this desk-dweller, this Bunsari Patel, who so casually issued her rejections? Her critique reeked of checklist. It was as if she read scripts while referring to someone else's set of rules. Clearly she didn't know her Aristotle, or her Joyce. What qualified her to dismiss Glenn Harding's personal experience? And how could someone who gets paid to sit inside the BBC and preside over artists *possibly* relate to the world he was writing about? And to recognise those rare writing traits such as the sound sense of visual grammar, and the dialogue that was naturalistic with engaging energy, but *still* return the script with a letter of rejection, was to stop and admire the work of a skilful street artist and then swipe the change out of his cap.

He wondered whether she had ever written anything, this Bunsari Patel. O! He would love to read that. A script that described her great struggle, the long and uphill battle that led her to Television Centre and the life of a script reader, being paid to destroy people's dreams one after another, Monday to Friday nine while five. He knew she had never written an original piece in her life. He *knew*. She had failed, and now she ensured that every poor bastard who crossed her desk would fail too.

It was Jack London who said, through his alter ego Martin Eden, that "every portal to success in writing is guarded by such watch-dogs, the failures in writing." And yet it was they, *of all creatures under the sun the most unfit*, that were the very ones who decided what shall and shall not find its way into the wide world.

You saw the hacks Bunsari Patel approved of on the morning news sofa from time to time, promoting their latest show. Overfed Home Counties greyhairs waffling on about how touched they were by the stories they heard from the poor suffering shop assistants, in the brief research chats they conducted before first classing it back down south. Sat in the study of their sprawling penthouse, writing their scripts, they lamented the tragedy of our youth at ten grand per episode. Manufactured drama. Improbable exposition. Characters that were at heart "good" rather than difficult.

Real insight into the lives of people that never existed.

And you can watch Bernard Brakespeare's moving new northern drama *Shopworn* tonight at nine o'clock on BBC1. Don't worry—it has a redemptive ending so that you don't all kill yourselves!

They were so accustomed to artificial depictions that they could not recognise the real thing when they saw it. Sorry you aren't able to discuss my script any further, Bunsari Patel; but are you able to discuss a vocation to which a failed scriptwriter *is* better suited? How about script reader?

Glenn wiped the tears from his eyes, slipped the letter back inside his fur coat.

He finished his warm lager while inwardly lamenting his unpaginated existence.

He felt a burning desire to run home and write his frustrations away; to channel all of his ressentiment and *really* give voice to it. . . . But he couldn't, because he had to go back to work. He cursed his irons and bondage, bitterly regretted his script's failure to win him a new life. God, how he wished that reader had been somebody with a bit more *gamble* in them! And then, as he looked, he beheld in his eye-beams a hazy vignette from III.XVIII: It was Henrietta telling him how everyone in the shop spoke ill of him, and when he asked her whether it had put her off him, she replied:

No, quite the opposite, actually. I like *the fact you don't fit in.*

Now *that* was the kind of reader his script required.

Glenn twirled his scraggle. . . . Would Henrietta give up if somebody said no to her? Would she even *care*? No. She would saunter back to her sewing machine and continue anyway, until some better audience inevitably recognised the strange originality of her vision. He thought of his revised scripts, the idea *That's All We Have Left in That Size, Sir* had transmogrified into—titled either *Leeds Libretto* or *A Shopworn Symphony*, (or *Leeds Libretto: A Shopworn Symphony*)—and how superior they were in every way to that rough work he had rashly submitted. His new scripts had better storytelling, grander scenes inspired by bigger events that occurred after he wrote the pilot. And they had characters that were even *more* superficial—that were even *harder* to sympathise/root for. The new episodes were so much more mature and refined than that silly thing Bunsari Patel had read. If anything, he had submitted a crude pencil sketch—and still it had impressed on some level!

Could he really give up now, just because one decision went against him, rendered by some embittered watch-dog of failure? Insane. Utterly insane. And as he thought of the common drudgery of the shopfloor, and its infinite labour, he knew then that the middle station of life was *not* for him. He wasn't that Italo Svevo character, whose name he couldn't even remember. He was Robinson Crusoe, Lemuel Gulliver. He was an adventurer—and just imagine how well you could write that sixth and final episode, on an adventure in Dinan. Wouldn't that give you all the raw material you need? Stanley Aristophanes, the erstwhile Len Farthing, gets the girl and runs away to France.

It's *perfect.*

It dawned on him then that this rejection letter was just another obstacle in his epic odyssey, issued by the gods as the final challenge to his faith. And having fought this fight at the expense of his mental wellbeing, liver function, and credit report, he would not give up now. He lifted his tankard, threw his head back and shook every last warm drop from it. He wiped his mouth with his hairy sleeve.

'I have followed this quest this twelvemonth, and either I shall achieve it or *bleed of the best blood of my body*,' he vowed solemnly. He then belched.

Victory goes to he who can hold out fifteen minutes longer.

V.VI

Engaging his duties, the common drudgery, his infinite labour, had never felt more arduous. He looked at his department with disdain. "Interesting milieu"? Yeah right.

His thinking was that if he could get the work done today, men's would be set for the biggest day in the retail calender tomorrow, and he could at least go out on a high note.

That tonight he would run into Henrietta was a given; it was ordained from above. Brigantia would take his mental compass and direct him straight to her, as she had done once, twice, and now thrice. Dinan was his destiny.

Eudaimonia on earth.

He had made progress. Tearing down decorations and stuffing them in binbags, he slung most of them in the basement. Others he dumped in the bin passage in the back of the shop, so difficult was it to navigate the mounting detritus while carrying lots of binbags down the narrow stairwell leading to the basement. Particularly with his throbbing, possibly bleeding feet. He laughed impishly. What did those lost bags matter, really? One thing was for certain, he wouldn't be here next Christmas when they were looking for them!

He plodded limping and squeaking onto the shopfloor, where Dick and Lyndsey were preparing their sections and Mildred was who knows where. He compared the floor he was looking at with the layout on the floorplan in his hands, perceived no correspondence between the two and felt his strength flag.

But then the thought of Henrietta's mouth, the touch of her body, the taste of her nectar, produced in him a spasm of energy and he was off, threading through the dwindling dunciad and hauling antique furniture aside to make room for new displays. All the time he was planning lines of conversation to use with her, such as: How have you been? And:

Would you like your sock back?

He would think of better lines tonight when he was out with Jimmy.

He was up on the main display, trying to inveigle the rigid limbs of Brummell into a blood-red chunky rollneck. Straining with the stiff joints and thick fabric, he began to feel dizzy. He could feel Shukeena checking the time and watching him. He could sense the mounted moose head over the cashdesk eyeballing him. Even Brummell's faceless face was staring at him impatiently. He was paying for that round Dick had bought with interest, and desperate thoughts began swarming his skull. Of leaving work sometime before midnight; of meeting Jimmy; of getting in somewhere good before the queues and the dreaded clipboards came out.

He had to look his *best* tonight for Henrietta—look as good as he did in III.XVIII, when he was primped to perfection in his Vincent van Gogh shirt, and her eyes lit up; or that night in IV.VIII, when he was decked out in his red and white floral silk shirt and she was gaping at him. *They wished their husbands looked at them the way you look at me.* He felt his heart grow lighter, as she enfolded him in her arms and began devouring his lips. He closed his eyes, and when he opened them again, behold! He saw her, all naked to his sight displayed, and whence his astonish'd gaze more pleasure took than Dis, on heaps of gold fixing his look. . . . O fruit divine! Fair to the eye, inviting to the taste! To the bar Glenn is destined tonight, make with all due haste!

He could *taste* the cognac in the gilt cherubin's mouth; *feel* her firm, sumptuous flesh in his talons. He was lapping up every last drop of elixir from her lips.

'The shop's closed,' said Dick's voice.

Glenn found himself stood on the display, passionately tonguing Brummell.

'*What!*' he yelped, opening his eyes and looking down at Dick.

'It's six o'clock geez, Shukeena's closed the doors.' He stared up at Glenn, grinning. 'Are you practicing for midnight?'

Glenn unhanded Brummell, jumped from the platform and hit the floor, his shoes emitting a ridiculous squeak. 'Closed?' he gasped.

'Already?' He cast a nervous glance around his department, beheld the multitude of empty sidebars and forward facers. 'How ready do you think we look for New Year's Day?'

'We could be ready for *next* New Year's Day,' opined Mildred, wiggling over.

Then Lyndsey appeared, rubbing his hands.

'Speak for yourselves,' he said cheerily, 'footwear's done!' He then looked very seriously at his colleagues. 'And by done, I mean I've left sale out and locked up the full price, away from the scum.'

The team looked as one to footwear. There was barely a shoe on it.

'Lynn,' said Dick in a curious voice, 'why are you always so weird about your shoes? We are here to sell, you know?'

Lyndsey let out a short, loud laugh.

'I'm not *weird* about my shoes! There's just no point having the best stuff out when the worst customers are in, that's all. It's hardly *weird*.'

Lyndsey looked weirdly at his colleagues.

'Shukeena will want to review the floor soon,' said Mildred ominously. 'You better go find her, Glenn; she's gonna be proper mad when she sees this.'

Glenn felt a knot in his stomach. His right eyelid was actually convulsing.

He knew Shukeena was crazy enough to keep him working past midnight to get the floor ready. Which admittedly would get the floor ready—but would also mean that he would miss New Year's Eve, and Henrietta, and his only chance to escape the straight world. The thought chilled the very marrow in his bones, and abruptly he announced that they were leaving—via the backdoor, secretly, by the dumpsters in the passage.

The junto gasped.

'Leave *now*!?' Dick cried. 'But what about the floor, geez? We're not ready!'

'Vex not yourself, Dick, nor strive with your breath; for all in vain comes counsel to mine ears!' Glenn thundered. 'Look, I'll just get in early tomorrow and finish it off.'

'Get in early on New Year's Day!' Mildred laughed. 'You really have gone mad.'

'It'll be *fineeeee*,' said Glenn assuringly. 'I'm not even going to drink tonight.'

V.VII

CHUG! CHUG! CHUG! CHUG! CHUG!

The duncery cheered as Glenn reached the bottom of the beeryard and staggered to and fro before stumbling backwards into the Leviathan. His belly tried to shoot the liquid back up, but he covered his mouth with his hand and forced it back down.

'Say something funny!' called one face in the crowd as a beefy hand reached out, grabbed his shoulder and jostled him. 'Yeah,' said another, 'tell us a joke, funnyman!'

The great comedy writer grinned sheepishly but said nothing.

'Jimmy,' he belched, turning to him. 'Why do they keep asking me to tell them a joke?' His phizog darkened. 'You didn't tell them about my script, did you?'

Jimmy looked genuinely baffled. 'No.'

'Did you?' Glenn yelled, holding a bony fist to his myriad chins.

'I swear, I didn't!'

The wretches gradually rescinded and returned to their shadowy circles, silhouetted by the stark green wall. The pink-lit ceiling was spangled by fairy lights and behind the long counter was a pandemonium of strange bottles from every corner of the globe. Glenn took a long, sweet slake of the Cannibal Coast Jimmy bought him and exhaled. He peered down the length of the counter, through the writhing cluster of bodies, to the glass entrance. Outside there was a frightful fog, immense and still, cloaking the street, while inside there was an equally frightful fog of fag smoke, and it looked as if darkness itself had come to visit. He could feel his anxiety growing, a sort of queasy terror rising up within him, and he took a long manic slake to wash it back down.

'You might want to go steady with that stuff, mate, it's eight percent,' Jimmy yelled. 'Remember, you've got work tomorrow.'

'O, I'm not thinking about *work* tonight,' Glenn slobbered with a flick of his hand, the execution of which knocked him off balance, obliging him to grip the counter.

'The curse of Cromwell on Nirah Frazar! And all its staff!' he screamed.

But he was thinking about work. And the notice he had scribbled in a fever at home, dictated to him by Mr Hyde from Hyde Hill. What if he didn't run into Henrietta tonight? Without that escape route he would *have* to go into work tomorrow. But what if they sacked him for abandoning his floor? The plan, if you could call it that, was to hand in his notice before they could sack him. But then what?

He lifted a shaky hand and slurped the zesty ale.

His scripts would save him. After work he had sat down with the instrument, popped open Jimmy's bottle of glimigrim and, in one concentrated assault, reworked episode five, lifting whole chunks of dialogue and action directly from recent events in order to speed up the process. Now all he needed to finish the thing was an episode six, but he couldn't write it because he had reached that huge, horrifying creative void last sighted by Joyce in the final throes of writing *Stephen Hero*, prompting his departure from Dublin to seek in Trieste the conclusion his novel needed.

For Glenn to bring his story to a close he first had to know how this saga with the estranged sylph, the mute cherubin, his lost Virgil, Henrietta Payne, would conclude. The events of his real life had so preoccupied him during his writing they had gone from informing his story to invading it. Stanley Aristophanes was now hopelessly in love with a young fashion student named Zelda Vayn, his obsession for the girl so consuming him that he had begun writing his own dramatic work about her within the script, called *The Conquest of Gall*, which he hoped would one day be staged in the West End. His fictive self had literally caught up with the flesh and bone one—and now they were both lost!

He yanked out his Kumquat and tried again to call her.

Still switched off.

'Are we going to talk to some birds or what?' yelled Jimmy impatiently.

'I'm trying to talk to a bird *now*,' Glenn moaned.

'I meant some birds in *here*.'

Glenn reluctantly put away his Kumquat. 'Aren't you married?' he frowned.

'Not yet I'm not,' the behemoth answered with a wink and a nudge.

'These are not women for me, Jimmy,' Glenn yelled, his eyes lingering hopefully on the door. He lifted his glass to his lips but found it empty. 'Although perhaps another round would get me in the mood?' he added with a wink and a nudge.

'*Another* round! I already bought us beeryards! It's expensive in here, you know?'

'It'll be even more expensive if we start talking to women.'

Jimmy's face turned serious. 'Good point.'

Glenn took a long slake of the Old Savage the behemoth handed him and wiped his mouth. The din of the crowd drowned out the jangling guitars and the shadowy huddles were full of grinning yellow teeth. Everyone seemed to be having a great time and Glenn, as always, was standing to the side watching, waiting for something to happen.

Just like his story was watching him, waiting for him to do something.

He smoothed down his garment, the stunning eighteenth century frock coat he had bought at the West Yorkshire Playhouse costume department summer clearout. The coat was green with a gold floral print and massive ruffled white collar and cuffs. It was a provocative piece to wear out on a night; the kind of courageous fashion gamble that normally only a famous person would make. He had resolved to finally debut it as a reply to the growing number of vintage shops popping up in Leeds, and the new wave of students who increasingly seemed to be assimilating the look he had been working for years with pieces annexed from his late grandad's wardrobe. Well, it would take them many years to catch up with him this time. Try a couple of hundred!

'I keep telling you, Glenn, she's never going to reply,' yelled Jimmy's voice.

'You don't know that,' Glenn yelled, again staring at his Kumquat.

'I *do* know that. Mate, just accept it—the best moment of your life was a forgettable night in hers. It's *over*.'

'When we need your use and counsel we shall send for you!' Glenn flared.

He was staring holes in his Kumquat. Still nothing. He moaned.

'Glenn, I know you're in pain, but it's not the end of the world. You've been through this before, remember? With Peggy? It's not nice, but you get over it, find someone better.' He thought for a moment. 'And, hopefully, she's interested this time."

Glenn stared at Jimmy with a look of utter hatred. He slammed down his ale and in one movement was halfway down the bar, standing by a blonde in a silver dress.

'Hello!' he yelled in her face. 'Are you having a good night?'

She looked somewhat startled. 'Yes thanks,' she smiled, her eyes giving his virtuosic ensemble the once over. 'Are you?'

Glenn leaned coolly against the counter, assumed his most charming smile.

'I'm having a *great* night; although I was arguing with my *tenant* over there about you and whether you work in Victoria Quarter. He thinks he's seen you, but I'm in there every day—I'm the manager of Nirah Frazar, you see—and I'm sure that if *you* worked in the arcade I would remember a face as pretty as yours.'

'Well, it looks like you win the argument. I don't work in Victoria Quarter.'

'I *knew* it! What do you do? If you don't mind me asking?'

'I work at ITV.'

Glenn's charming smile abruptly dropped. 'ITV?' he gasped.

'Yes.'

'As in the TV channel?'

'That's the one.'

He stared at her in wonder. 'So you work in *television*?'

'Yes!' she laughed.

'Wow,' he replied. 'That's—that's amazing.'

'It's a job.'

Pause.

'Do you work in the studio where they filmed *Rising Damp*?' he queried excitedly.

'*Rising* what?'

'No, never mind,' he blurted quickly. His eyes were fastened on her, his face hanging slack. He could not quite believe his luck. If Henrietta wasn't going to show, what better woman was there in all of Leeds for him to run into? It was a coincidence worthy of a Victorian novelist, and it corroborated for the umpteenth time the cosmic probability of the completely improbable. 'It's funny I should meet you actually,' he smiled. 'You know how I said I was the manager of Nirah Frazar? Well, that's true, but I'm also a *writer*.'

'Oh right?'

'Yes! And I've written this show, a really good show actually, that's set in a shop, in Victoria Quarter—a fictional shop—and it's, er, it's like one of those classic, um, northern dramas, but it's also a *comedy*—a comedy drama, really—and it's all about, er, fashion—it's a high fashion shop—and real life—'

She grabbed his wildly gesticulating hands. She was laughing. 'What's your name again?'

'Glenn,' he answered nervously.

'Tell you what, Glenn—why don't you get us a drink, and then we can discuss your script?'

'*Deal*.'

It turned out he was buying the woman and her little circle of dressy, phosphoric friends a bottle of wine. His heart was beating hard enough to break a rib but, thanks to his mum and dad's Christmas money, the transaction went through without issue, and once again he could feel Predestination tingling in the air. He heaved the fat bucket up by the handles and passed it excitedly to the blonde's friends, as the vapour whirled from the ice, mingling with the dark, rowling fag smoke.

Glenn turned beaming to the blonde.

'I realise I didn't explain my script quite as succinctly as I should have just then,' he chuckled. 'Let me try again. *Leeds Libretto* is an inversion of *Doctor Faustus*—'

'Mate, I don't care. I work in accounts.' She turned away and followed her friends, disappearing into the crowd.

Glenn stood in his frock coat with his mouth agape.

He had blushed to the very tips of his ears. The back of his neck felt so hot it was as if fire-belching Moloch was stood behind him, his molton breath scorching his mullet. A gaggle of nearby rogues, a dunciad of bearded thirtysomethings with beer bellies, were grinning at him. 'Ere he is!' called one malefactor. 'Mr Chuckles!'

'Ay up, make room, ee looks like ee's about to perform a funny song!'

Glenn looked anxiously to the door and beheld the eerie fog. A dark mist of death was lapping over Leeds, a gloom at the world's end. He sensed the powers of darkness, carrying in it a bloody doom for him, beckoning him out.

O immortal madness, why do you have this craving to seduce me?

He checked his Kumquat. Nothing.

He sniffed, turned his mullet on the door and wiped the tears from his eyes. He steadied himself on the counter, produced his Kumquat and, infused with the spirit of John Donne, composed the following romantic couplet: *Hey sexy! U out tonight??? X.*

Betty Work, check; Gertrude Work, check; Mildred Work, check; and then, since he had gone this far and nothing mattered anymore: The Gorgon Work, check. He even hovered over Ali Work. Ah, why not? Check. He dispatched the ambassage.

He then sent a long, maudlin missive to Henrietta, but I shall not trouble the reader with the particulars.

'Look who's back,' yelled Jimmy with mock surprise at the figure limping wretchedly towards him. 'The loaded bankrupt! What was that bottle I saw you buying? Flunec?' He poked Glenn in the chest. 'Well *you're* getting the next round in, I can tell you.'

Glenn looked up at the Leviathan with a grave expression on his face.

'Prithee, friend, be advised and hark what I counsel thee: that girl you're marrying; I've seen her in Bar Phono, doing Jägerbombs and taking men to the toilets.'

Jimmy sipped his tankard. 'Well that's quite an achievement, Glenn,' he nodded. 'Because Sukhjinder is in India, and has never set foot in the UK.'

'That's what you think.'

Glenn stumbled down a steep staircase on rubbery legs, steadying himself against the narrow walls that were shaking with the thump of the music. Fie, fie upon her! There's language in her eye, her cheek, her lip, nay, her foot speaks! His piss tinkled in the toilet. Her wanton spirit looks out at every joint and motive of her body, and she will sing at any man at first sight—just so long as he isn't Glenn Harding.

I'm not being one of your shop conquests.

And what *are* you going to be? A fashion designer? Ah, cease, rash youth! Desist ere't is too late, for thou seek'st the greatness that will overwhelm thee! For every one successful fashion designer there are a thousand failures, and the abyss has space to swallow them all. And while you may have won the battle with Glenn, you must ultimately lose the war, for never yet did I hear tell of anyone succeeding in all their undertakings, who did not meet with calamity at last, and come to *utter ruin.*

And all I have to do is *wait.*

And I can wait. O believe me, my little gilded pillar of infamy, I can wait as long as it takes! I have all the time in the world. And I am more than happy to spend it praying for you to *fail.* And if you fail—sorry, *when* you fail—what do you have? A useless degree and a debt you can never repay. And then can you afford London rent? Can you even afford Manchester rent? Nay, child. You'll be back living with your mum and dad—*working in a clothes shop in Leeds.* And with the way you carouse and swill, your frail beauty must decay, the glow of youth go the way of all flesh, the way of all buttons, all shall fade, and she who scorns a man will die a maid—*and all I need is for God to hear my prayers and answer them.* O! You don't think He'll do it for me? Well, He gave you to me, didn't he? Twice! Just you wait for my next prayer to be answered. You denied me my *Eudaimonia;* but *I* will deny you your *dreams.* . . . Go now, deluded woman! Go and seek again new toils, new dangers, on the dusty plain! For that happy shore, that seems so nigh, will far from your deluded wishes fly.

385

Go, you bitch unparalleled! The gods are calling deathward! And upon thy stone, sadly, it shall be written:

SHE TRIED AND FAILED.

With trembling hands, he typed a number into his Kumquat and held it to his ear. Unbelievably, it was ringing.

'Hello,' came a faint, nasal voice.

Pause.

'Hellooooo,' came the voice again, singing the O, convoking all at once a psychic tapestry of floors, bars, and bedrooms lost. 'Is anyone there?' the voice asked.

He burst into tears. He tried to regain his composure but instead cried harder, the teardrops rolling down his cheeks. He cried almost to roaring into the speaker.

'*Glenn?*' said the voice.

He held out the Kumquat and stared at it in wide-eyed horror.

'What's wrong now?' asked Jimmy with genuine concern. 'You're doing that weird shaking thing you do, when you've tallied up how much you've spent shopping.'

'I just cried down the phone to Peggy.'

Jimmy responded with his familiar catchphrase.

'I know you deleted her number from my Kumquat, Jimmy, but it doesn't matter. I remember it. I could type it with my eyes closed.' The bar was now packed to capacity, the bodies pressing them into the counter. 'This New Year's Eve is a disaster, isn't it?'

'So far, yes,' Jimmy acknowledged.

Glenn once again checked his Kumquat. There was no return call from Peggy. Or from Henrietta. Or anyone. 'Ah, shall we just go home?' he asked despairingly.

'No way!' cried the behemoth. 'The night's not a lost cause *yet*. There's still time for us to drink, get ourselves merry and, at the stroke of midnight, dive into that crowd and find two birds even more desperate than we are—'

Abruptly the furious guitar music cut out and, to everyone's surprise, the countdown to New Year's playing over the PA was already at five. Half the room clocked on at four and by three they were all counting, two they called with rising suspense, and then, with a great peal of cheers, they welcomed in the New Year—as outside a bevy of fireworks thundered overhead and made the ground tremble.

Pinioned to the bar, Glenn and Jimmy watched as the many-coloured confetti showered the smoky maelstrom. Everyone in the room was sharing a kiss, and there was laughter and cheers as people locked arms and began to sing "Auld Lang Syne".

'Is the night a lost cause now?' Glenn yelled over the clamour.

'Yep,' Jimmy nodded. 'Let's go.'

As they left the bar the fog swallowed them whole.

V.VIII

It was about 1:30 in the morning, bitterly cold and very clear and moonlit. There was a slight breeze and one could see small waves breaking on the beach. In the trenches I was in was Don Hill and a Cockney youth named Shorty Nolan. We conversed for a while about various topics, had a quick drag on a cigarette (strictly forbidden) and stood in the damp cold dugout shivering and cursing our unhappy lot. After about an hour, when we were expecting a stand down and a return to our warm bunks there were two large explosions at the south end of the camp, then several smaller bangs and a crackling sound of small arms firing. I've got to say that I was absolutely terrified and paralyzed with fright, convinced that within a very short time I would be dead. Don Hill was all for moving out of the camp and making his way home. Shorty Nolan had a round up the spout and was threatening to kill the first "bastard" that came anywhere near our trench. All three of us had live ammunition ready to fire but in my case I was shivering with fear and I think my two companions were in the same state. Don kept saying, 'Let's beat it, we've no chance against these Germans! What do they expect us to do with ten bullets?' I was inclined to agree with him but I was too scared even to run. All this time explosions and gunfire were coming nearer. We were facing the chalet rows because the sea behind us was empty and we assumed the invaders had landed further down the coast. At this point we hadn't actually seen anybody but a few minutes later as the sky seemed to be getting lighter, men could be seen moving quickly at the top of the chalet rows about two- or three-hundred yards away from where we stood in our slit trench. We had all got a round up the spout of our rifles and as they started to come down the chalet rows we all fixed one of the figures in the sights of the riles. Shorty said, 'Well, here goes,' and he was about to pull the trigger when to our amazement a naval officer with a large armband said, 'You lot are eliminated; consider yourselves dead.' Apparently the OCTU (Officer Cadet Training Unit) who were stationed south of Skegness were having a night training exercise and the plan was to take over Royal Arthur in a simulated attack! I should imagine those army lads would not have come running down the chalet rows so quickly had they known we hadn't been told it was an exercise and had live ammunition. How someone was not killed or gravely injured I'll never know. We mentioned it the next day to our signal instructor but nothing was ever said about it and it is my opinion that either the throbbing of his skull or the work of some internal clock roused Glenn from his unconscious state.

He found himself lying face down, fully clothed on the sofa-bed, and when he raised his head from the pillow and saw the empty vodka bottle strewn sideways on the sheets, he groaned. His head felt like Jimmy had been jumping on it.

He tightened, as his eyes quickly darted around the room. The green walls were enveloped in darkness and the storm rattling the little window seemed of the type that occured only in the deep of night. He checked his watch. It made no sense and he remembered for the millionth time the watch had stopped working.

In a growing panic he groped around his bed. He looked over the side and saw his Kumquat lying face down on the floor. He snatched it up, but the battery was dead.

He screamed.

Leaping from the bed he looked frantically for something, anything, that could tell him the time. All he could think through his pounding skull was Shukeena and the 6:30 start. *And don't be late.* . . .

He turned on the wonkbox and glared impatiently at the black screen, bracing himself. As always, the voices came before the picture.

'Come on, come on,' he croaked.

The BBC news presenters appeared on their sofa, and by them was the time:

8 a.m.

'O, *pluck!*' he screamed, hurtling out the door and down the winding staircase. The door slammed so hard it knocked his framed "no further action" letter off its hook.

He ran out of the old building, where he was met by a ferocious monsoon. 'PLUCK!' he screamed, hurtling down Hyde Hill, headlong through the tempest, remembering now with mortal terror the state he left his floor in.

You are eliminated; consider yourself dead.

V.IX

The wind howling furiously outside the window and the rain lashing against the glass at least drowned out the awkward silence gripping the staff room.

Shukeena had worked ladieswear so late last night there wasn't anything to do that morning, so the whole staff had no option but to sit together at the table.

Betty hadn't turned up, choosing Ali Hussain over Nirah Frazar, thus effectively handing in her notice, much to Shukeena's chagrin. And with that one decision the shop's chief flower clip clops off the stage of history. So long, fair one!

Gertrude and Mildred were too hungover to speak, and were sat waiting quietly for the painkillers to kick in. Dick was reclining back at the top of the table, peeping at Gertrude over the *Yorkshire Evening Post* he was pretending to read. Down the other end Lyndsey was sitting with his feet on the table, gazing admiringly at his own bright-red clown shoes by Kill, Kill, Kill, Kill, Kill, Kill!

'I wonder if Glenn's in yet?' said one of the nameless Christmas temps.

Gertrude's eyes narrowed. 'Why do *you* care if Glenn's in?' she said hoarsely.

'I was just asking.'

'Yeah?' said Gertrude. 'Well *don't*.'

Dick dropped his paper and glared at Gertrude. 'Why do *you* care whether she cares if Glenn's in or not?' he said suspiciously.

'No one cares whether anyone cares if that gimp's in or not,' Mildred croaked, slumped on the table in a heap of bony limbs. 'So *shut up*.'

'He must be in,' Dick remarked, 'his locker's open.' He got up and waddled over to it, where he opened the door fully. 'Oh, but there's no coat; I guess he's not in.'

But he couldn't resist a nosy peep at the menswear manager's odd possessions. The gold-topped formal day cane that he could only recall Glenn using once was in there, as was an umbrella that said AIG Insurance on it that he must have nicked from somewhere. His old suit was hanging there, as was that weird, smelly World War II-era suitcase. In the top compartment, under some screwed up old bus tickets, a couple of pocketsize paperbacks, one called *The Yorkshire Ripper*, the other *Panzer Commander*, and the latest *Advert*, he spied something.

'Hey up,' Dick said, 'what's this?' He pulled a wad of paper out of the locker, held together by a bulldog clip. '"*Leeds Libretto*",' he read out loud in a puzzled tone. '"A commedia, by me, Glenn Harding."'

Mildred looked up from her arms. 'You *what*?' she said hoarsely.

'What is it, Dick?' asked one of the nameless temps, screwing her face up.

Dick lowered the paper and grinned at the room. 'A *script*,' he exclaimed gleefully.

'Oh my God,' Mildred groaned. 'Just when I thought he couldn't get any sadder, he writes a *script*.' She stared at Dick. 'What's it about?'

Joy sparkled in the formalwear supervisor's eyes. 'Us!' he squealed.

'*What!*' Gertrude ejaculated, jumping to her feet. She was wearing her strapless black jumpsuit with her back and arms exposed to the chilly air, and yet could feel herself growing hotter by the second. 'No, it isn't, it's all made up!' she said. 'Isn't it?'

'Not from what I'm reading it's not,' said Dick, leafing through the pages. 'This is all stuff that actually happened!'

'*Really. . . .*' said Gertrude. She gazed into vacancy as a thousand-and-one questions about Glenn Harding and Henrietta Payne, and Len Farthing and Helena Layne, were answered all at once.

She had to sit back down.

'God, our Glenn loves writing about himself, doesn't he,' Dick remarked, flicking through the pages. 'And look! It says "episode four"; there's more of them!'

'Oh, *Glenn*,' Lyndsey groaned, 'that's *so* tragic.' He grinned. 'Let's read it!'

The great roars of laughter that came from the staff room echoed along the corridor and travelled all the way down the depths of the stairwell. The bulldog clip had been tossed aside and Glenn's sheets scattered around the table, the best of them, or worst, going from person to person. Dick was in ecstasies over the material.

'Oh, here we go!' he cried. He held the sheet closer to his eyes. '"Stanley, brackets, brusquely, holding his script: *I do not seek official approval in any aspect of my life or art.*"' Dick looked up. 'Well, that's a relief—cos your art's a load of shit!'

The table exploded with laughter, as Dick wiped the tears from his eyes.

'What does brusquely mean?' asked one nameless temp, amid the din.

'Oh God, hang on,' said Mildred, waving her hand. She leaned over to Gertrude and pointed at the scene. '"Stanley, brackets, con. . . . tum. . . . eliously: *Let's make this a more literary quarrel, Shakina. Name me one book you've read?*'

Gertrude, grimacing, followed Mildred's finger. '"Shakina, brackets, shouting: *The employee handbook, Stanley—and may I suggest you read yours!*"'

Dick screamed with laughter, as Lyndsey slapped his thigh and flung his head back howling.

'I can't take it,' Mildred moaned, covering her face. 'It's just too embarrassing.'

'Wait,' said a temp who no one had heard speak before, 'I think I've found the worst one yet: "Stanley, brackets, profoundly: *I am one that converses more with*"'—she snorted—"'*the buttock of the night than with the forehead of the morning.*"'

The table exploded again.

'I don't know about "conversing with buttocks",' cried Mildred over the clamour, 'but if he thinks that's good writing, he's talking out of his arse!'

They all yelled with laughter, reeled in their seats, and in the excitement Dick fell out of his. Suddenly he shot up and looked serious.

'Hey,' he said, checking his watch. 'It's ten past.'

'We better head down,' nodded Lyndsey solemnly.

The staff rose to their feet with a contented sigh.

As they filed out of the room, Gertrude remained. She stood, hands on hips, staring at the strange and deeply uncool project her ex had poured himself into. And as she remembered how obsessed he had been with it, and how it had excited him more than she ever did—and how that pocket square of his had been found in the bedroom of that absolute minger, Henrietta—her countenance darkened, and her heart grew hard in her chest cave.

She turned her back on his pages and hurriedly clip clopped after the group.

Together, they sauntered down the stairwell, still sniggering and reciting lines from the script. They were once again the best of friends.

V.X

Glenn ran through Leeds like Paris through Troy, swift-footed and with long strides, as from the wrathful skies proceeded lightnings, thunderings, and noises as had not occurred since men were on the earth. And as he skidded off the Headrow and arrived at the top of Briggate, he stopped to catch his breath.

Sheets of rain were lashing the high street on all sides, and the pavement looked to be under several *glumgluffs* of water. He beheld the many-coloured waterproofs huddling under umbrellas in the pale cones of streetlights outside the darkened shopfronts. It was the one day in the year when the customers had to get up early and stand around waiting for *them*, but he was in no condition to drink in the sweet change. In fact, the thought of drinking anything was enough to make his belly contract. He lurched along under the tempest, halted outside the arcade. There he looked, and behold, a pale horde was gathering outside the Nirah Frazar shutter. Puke at once swelled in his cheeks, and he ran into the little alleyway between Gieves & Hawkes and Envy, where with one violent convulsion he painted the walls and pavement.

'Happy New Year, Norman!' said Mildred. 'Shukeena says she needs you to come down for the health and safety talk, the expectations and goals discussion, the current events and promotions reminder, and "to briefly share any relevant news you might have with the team."'

She lifted her eyes from the mysterious box Norman had quickly closed as she popped her head in, noticed that his burly frame was visibly trembling against the mushrooms.

'Any relevant news?' he replied at length, in a sort of strangled, quavering voice. 'Yes,' he said, 'I think I have some *relevant news* I'd like to share with you all. . . .'

'I look forward to it!' she exclaimed. She then slammed the door shut.

With trembling fingers, he combed back his sodden crown over his throbbing sconce as he stumbled down the arcade, still drunk, squelching and squeaking against the marble. The shops were blacked out, while lightning flared across the fulminous skies beyond the glass ceiling. Rain cascaded on the glass, its sound resonating fiercely through the arcade as the raw wind blasted the dawn shoppers therein. He nervously checked his watch and remembered *again* it was dead.

Fumbling for his Kumquat he realised he had left it at home.

He began to be troubled and deeply distressed, fearing that he had gone down to the night of the underworld, was approaching the house of Death before his time. A shadowy presentiment that the Abomination

of Desolation was lying in wait for him, somewhere inside the shop, pervaded his nervous imagination—and it dawned on him that the last day, the day of trouble, was finally upon him.

'Excuse me, please, I need to get in,' he said hoarsely, breathing heavy as he threaded his way through the heathens. He banged on the shutter, the effort of which sent his equilibrium swirling. He had to lean against a pillar to stay upright.

A particularly rough looking yahoo in jogging bottoms stepped forward. 'What time do you open, pal?' he grunted. *What time do you open? What time did he say they open? What time do you open?*

'I don't know, soon?' Glenn croaked. 'Prithee, people; it's too early for questions. What's thy passion? Ho!'

A she-yahoo with dimensions beyond the Nirah Frazar size guide limped forward. 'Are the No Label-Label cashmere ponchos in the sale?' she growled, leering.

That was when three teenage hardfaces draped in chunky gold chains piped up. 'What about the Egomania pantaloons, bruv? Are they in the sale?'

'A plague upon this howling!' Glenn cried. 'I told you, I don't know!'

He knows! He knows! He's the manager, he knows! They began to advance up the steps as one with their arms outstretched, their outspread hands reaching for him, their looks harbouring naught but death.

Glenn sprang off the pillar and staggered backwards. 'Will you be gone?' he begged. 'I pray you stand outside the portico until we open!' His back then hit the shutter. 'Go! Get you home, you fragments! Hence to your homes; be gone!' he yelled.

But the eerie flock closed in on him, their deathly tentacles reaching for his body, and he stood paralyzed with fright.

He gave vent to his horror with a loud, prolonged, and terrible shriek. . . .

V.XI

Some lazy ages, lost in sleep and ease no action leave to busy chronicles. Not so this age. Not on this day.

Glenn found himself spread-eagled on the Iranian silk kashan carpet, staring up at the painted blue sky. He heard the grinding screech of old hinges as the shutter came down, lifted his head to espy Dick bolting shut the double-doors.

'Ah-ha, the Distant One has arrived!' exclaimed the formalwear supervisor cheerily. 'I take it your New Year's resolution wasn't to improve your timekeeping, then? Ha, ha!' His face fell abruptly. 'Oh, geez; what are you wearing?'

Stretched out on his back, the Distant One sighed.

'Well demanded, knave; my wardrobe provokes that question,' he croaked, rising to his grotty loafers and smoothing himself down. Rain was dripping off him. 'It's a frock coat,' he stated proudly, 'and it's from the eighteenth century.'

'Do you think maybe you should have left it there?'

All armed prophets have been victorious and unarmed ones have come to ruin.

'We are less afraid to be mocked than thou art, Mr Zabledore!' said Glenn crossly. 'And I don't care what *you*, or anyone else in this shop, thinks about my so potent art; nothing more than dogs thou art, easily won to fawn on any fashion designer!'

Turning on his heel, Glenn squelched off with his nose in the air.

'Christ these people up north really are a bit thick!' he shouted.

'Ooh, he's changed his tune,' laughed Mildred at the makeup stand, applying some volcanic-red lipglòss. 'So we're "thick" now, are we? Last night we were "sexy".'

Suddenly remembering last night's drunken ambassages, Glenn's eyes bulged as the hot shame erupted on his cheeks. He quickened his pace to the staircase, desperate to escape the cruel stares of his colleagues when abruptly his path was blocked by a massive pair of blood-red clown shoes by Kill, Kill, Kill, Kill, Kill, Kill!

He glanced up at Lyndsey's leering face.

'Gone for the slicked back hair today, Glenn?' Lyndsey smiled 'My, that certainly is "the forehead of the morning".'

'What?' Glenn rasped.

'Why are you talking to him, Lyndsey?' said a voice. Glenn looked to the fitting rooms, where some schematic type he'd never even seen before was grinning at him malevolently. 'You know he prefers conversing with "the buttock of the night".'

With those words the shop fell a-laughing, as Glenn felt his blood congeal with horror, and his heart die within him. His whole head turned a violent scarlet.

He shoved past Lyndsey and literally ran for the stairs, only to find his escape route obstructed once again—this time by a pair of rock stud black pumps by Nirah Frazar.

'How doth, Miss Mohammed,' he murmured, wincing. 'Sorry I'm a bit late.'

Hell's dread empress wore a black long-sleeve, stretch-jersey midi dress with a neckline right up to the chin, and an alluring split all the way up one leg, by Nirah Frazar. The skeleton earrings flashed him some feral, evil grins.

'A *bit late*?' she repeated with incredulity. 'Oh, you're more than a *bit late*, Glenn,' she said, beginning to scream. 'You're *two hours late*!'

He glanced back at the antique Dutch grandfather clock behind the till.

'An hour and a *half* late,' he asserted.

'I said we all had to be in at half-*six*,' she shrieked. 'It's half-*eight* now!'

'Sixteen minutes past eight.'

'And your breath reeks of alcohol! And you've got sick down your front! And you've left muddy footprints all over my floor! And you snuck out last night, after *promising* me you were going to work late—'

'A POX O' YOUR THROAT, THOU BAWLING, INCHARITABLE NOISEMAKER!' Glenn screamed, so loud she jumped from her skin. He climbed a step, so they came face to face. 'Now be collected; no more amazement,' he snarled. 'Tell thy piteous heart there's no harm done, O thou rib crooked by nature, or taste thy folly, and learn by reproof not to contend with a man when he hath caroused potations pottle-deep!'

Shukeena looked gobsmacked, her jaw dangling in the air.

'Out of our way, I say!' Glenn grunted, shoving past her. He stopped a few steps up and looked back. 'O, and sorry about the text last night,' he said sheepishly.

He then squelched and squeaked his way upstairs, disappearing onto his floor.

Shukeena's mouth was still wide open.

Pause.

'What the hell are you lot looking at?' flared the snaky sorceress, abruptly snapping out of her trance. 'We'll be open in half an hour; get back to work, all of you! *And somebody mop that bloody floor up!*'

She cast a dark gaze up the staircase and seethed with blind fury.

V.XII

He slung his sodden frock coat on the floor behind the tills, slumped over the bed of jackets and buried his face in his arms. Under the mounted moose head and the smashed in face of the German cuckoo clock, he could still hear the mocking laughter, echoing in his ears. And that eerie premonition. It was still niggling him. . . .

You must be mad. Or you wouldn't have come here.

He knew he was a much better writer than that script suggested. It was a first draft, that's all. It's not like he would send that version to a channel, would he? No! He would revise it, work it up. And anyway, what did that lot know about scriptwriting? He could transcribe one of those acclaimed US dramas and *still* those dunces would disparage it. But how different would their verdict be of his writing if they had instead experienced it via the useful mind-warp of the wonkbox? If Glenn Harding was just a name on the credits, a man they had never met? The cast full of familiar faces, people they saw all the time on their telescreens. There's no way they would have laughed at it then. They would have accepted it on its own terms and laughed *with* it, like the sheep they are. Also, how the hell could they distinguish good writing from bad? They knew as much about letters as they did history, philosophy, politics. The world. More than one of them couldn't name the Prime Minister. One of them genuinely didn't know whether she lived in the United Kingdom or not. The truth was, to get any story at all out of those schematics took an artist of enviable skill and imagination!

He was a much, much better writer than that script suggested.

His moan was muffled by the golden jackets. He was too crapulent for such intense thinking. His head was pounding, entrails convulsing. The stillness of the floor was being repeatedly disturbed by the sharp footsteps of Dick and Lyndsey, going back and forth as they gave the department a last polish, and the constant locomotion was making him nauseous, let alone the hushed discussions they seemed to be having. . . .

A mad conception was fomenting in his brain.

He was beginning to think that he should abandon whatever self-respect he had left and just go by himself to Dinan. *Today*. Actually, it wasn't even mad, for twice his expeditions had led him directly, impossibly, to Henrietta, and he knew he could do it again. Like Victor Frankenstein venturing blindly into the Alps and happening upon his Creature, it would be just another Victorian coincidence—the likely impossibility that only life's adventurers could understand. If Glenn was incautious, audacious, *crazy* enough to go there, he would find her eventually—even if it meant having to spend a few nights in the woods first. Henrietta? he said, wiping the muck from his face, peeling dead leaves off his dirty frock coat. Fancy meeting you here!

The phone you are ringing is switched off. Please leave a message—he slammed down the cashdesk phone, sank bitterly into the bed of jackets.

He gave vent to his frustration with a long, low, and desolate moan.

His great epic, this busy chronicle, *had* to end with him winning her back. *It had to.* He had to pass the final stage, from bad fortune to good, and begin his new life. . . .

And he would do it. The end is not yet, the last chapter is not written.

The event is yet to name the winner.

Suddenly he sensed a dark shadow pass over him. He shivered involuntarily.

'Geez!' ejaculated a familiar voice.

'What now?' Glenn murmured into his golden pillow.

'Is there a reason why the sale wallets aren't out?' Dick enquired.

Glenn's corpselike colour as he lifted his head froze the current of Dick's blood.

'Pluck knows,' croaked the menswear manager with immense effort. His head then declined back down behind his spindly arms. He moaned again.

'Okay! I'll run up and get the box. Best I do it, in case Shukeena wants a one-on-one with you. I know she wants to talk to you about health and safety, expectations and goals, current events and promotions, as well as the other news we heard today—'

Glenn drew himself up. 'A one-on-one?' he said feebly. Bile shot up into his mouth, and he swallowed it with some difficulty. 'You stay here, Dick,' he gurgled, 'I'll go up and get the wallets—and probably a glass of water while I'm at it.'

[*Exeunt* King Glenn. *A dead march sounded.*]

V.XIII

Gertrude had changed into a long sleeve black mini dress with a low neckline and white laughing skull print, with black leather ankle boots, by Nirah Frazar, and she had accessorised the look with a pair of rubber gloves, a bottle of disinfectant and an all-purpose cleaning cloth. Jangling down the staircase, she found her path obstructed by the store manager, who was sitting halfway down them with his broad back to her, brooding over the floor. He was wearing an oversized white T-shirt with a big red target print on the back, by Nirah Frazar.

'Happy New Year, Norman,' she said. 'Shukeena sent me to clean the mushrooms in the office, but they seem to have vanished. Where did they go?'

Norman looked back over his beefy shoulder at her, masticating feverishly.

'No idea,' he snarled, wiping his mouth.

'Okay then,' she nodded. 'And how are you doing, anyway? Are you all right?'

'Me? I'm fine, love. I've done more January sales than I can remember. It's just another day at the office as far as I'm concerned.'

'No, I meant, you know. . . . your news. From London.'

'Dumdum?'

'*London.*'

'Dumdums are expanding bullets, love. Extremely deadly and *not* Geneva compliant. Shoot a man with one and you'll make a hole so big you can put your fist through. He won't be getting up anymore after that.' He belched and wiped his mouth. 'But the scariest thing? How easy they are to make. Just imagine if they fell into the wrong hands. Oh! Doesn't bear thinking about.'

Norman turned back to the shopfloor. He appeared to be thinking very deeply.

'Eh?' said Gertrude.

Glenn, meanwhile, was still reeling from the scene he beheld in the staff room.

He had ventured in there for a glass of water, only to discover his script, episode four—easily the weakest one—discarded like litter on the floor. He had sobbed as he gathered them up, reddened as he read them over in the day's detested glare. The key story elements *did* seem familiar, the narrative *was* lacking any genuine sense of drive. And as for the tone? Well, it never managed to be either funny or dramatic enough.

After re-reading the episode, Glenn had no choice but to admit the BBC was right—he wasn't good enough. He wasn't a writer.

And for that reason, he was doom'd for a certain term to remain in Nirah Frazar.

Yes, he would stick to the day job, his Epsilon Semi-Moron work, for another year, saving up to move to London where he could pursue his dream of being a TV writer. And he would re-read the classics, watch the wonkbox in a less derisive, more analytical way, and practice his writing until it reached the level required to bring his vision to life. He couldn't do it right now. He didn't have the correct distance from the events he was describing. As Joyce said, "A poet's job is to *write* tragedies, not be an actor in one".

He wasn't going to worry about where he would live, either. The truth was Jimmy would never let him be homeless. He would just have to move in with the Leviathan and his new wife, and his mum and his dad and sister, if only for a few weeks.

After which, Jimmy would lend him the rent and deposit just to get rid of him.

One day Glenn would live and thrive, indebted to no prince or peer alive, Alexander Pope-style, through his writing—but this morning had shown he was a long way off.

Cudgel thy brains no more about it.

His head was drooping, as were his eyelids. From head to toe he hurt, in particular his head and toes, and as he spied by the delivery box the faulty returns dumped on the floor, he thought how soft and inviting the garments looked. The rain was beating the blackened windows, the monsoon assailing the roof, and the rhythmic sound of nature in all its fury was almost soothing, under the sheltering Nirah Frazar.

He couldn't stop himself. He wanted to slither onto that strange bed, lie down and, just for a second, rest his eyes. He wanted a rest from the world, and from himself.

Just for a second. . . .

In a second, he had slipped into the heavy honey-dew of slumber.

The office phone was ringing loudly. Head office didn't work on New Year's Day, so it couldn't have been them calling. The store manager was opening and slamming drawers, pulling out filing cabinets, lifting bags from the bin, looking in all his secret hiding places he thought no one knew about but evidently someone did.

He swallowed hard.

Sweating and panting, he dropped to his knees before the safe. The door opened easily as he never locked it because his shaky hands couldn't negotiate the dial. He was feverishly yanking out fat bags of float and slinging them over his shoulder. He found the bottles at the back, hiding behind the fake internal wall he had made for it, and cried out in excitement. But as he lifted them out, he felt how light they were.

He screamed as he rose up and smashed them across the floor.

'PLEASE!' he yelled. 'Just one,' he whimpered feebly.

The gleaming of the freshly polished Trench Broom caught his eye.

He turned to look upon it, resting gently in its padded velvet bed.

He began staring at the evil-looking weapon with zealous intensity, and as the phone continued to ring in his ears, he began to hyperventilate.

V.XIV

I finished my watch at 4 o'clock one morning, it was very dark and the ship was rolling heavily. I went straight to my bunk and slept like a log. At around 11.30 I was given a call to prepare for my watch. I could tell the weather was bad as the ship was pitching and tossing and rolling heavily at the same time. It was most disconcerting. I said, 'It appears to be a bit grim out there.' He replied, 'You ain't seen nothing yet.' He wasn't kidding. Our bunks were situated in a small cabin in the very rear of the ship's deck proper and I couldn't believe the evidence of my own eyes.

The ship must have been on the crest of an enormous wave and it appeared as though I was looking down a great hill of water at a small ship at the bottom. Within a couple of seconds the position had reversed and we were surrounded by the great hill of water, far above the ship's mast. The waves were like rows of mountains rolling by and I've got to say I was scared witless. The crew had slung long ropes from the rear of the ship to the bridge structure across the cargo hatches and one had to time one's run across the decks because waves were breaking across it. It would have been very easy to have been washed over the side and that would have been certain death, because it would have been impossible to have lowered a small boat and in any case it wouldn't have stayed afloat five seconds. Another aspect was the inflexible rule that no cargo ship was allowed to stop once the convoy set sail. It didn't matter what the circumstances were, the rule was keep going. There may have been men in the water or survivors in small boats or life rafts but the vessels were forbidden from stopping and saving them, because a stationary ship is a sitting duck and quite easy for a sub to torpedo.

HUNTER.

Well I negotiated the dangerous deck and scrambled up the ladders to my station on the bridge. It was a terrifying sight to look out over the sea. The waves were ginormous and the wind screamed and howled, what the wind speeds were I have no idea but to say they were strong would be an understatement. I could only see about three ships out of the 30 or so we had commenced with and they kept disappearing in the huge troughs. The senior officer of the escort was a mere spot on the horizon and the only reason we knew he was there was because he was attempting to make contact with us with a signal lamp. Our ship was not in first class condition and he was trying to warn us that the lift doors had parted and through them was passing a formidable shape that had espied Glenn, alone in the dark, lying face down on the faulty returns, snoring.

He was so still the pigeons were pecking at his warped soles.

Slowly the presence advanced on the prostrate and gurgling menswear manager, whose head was resting in the thick folds of a luxurious fur coat, with a blissful smile on his face. O whence and what art thou, execrable shape, that dar'st, though grim and terrible, advance thy miscreated front athwart my way to yonder boy?

The acoustics of the lofty roof amplified the rain pouring upon it, and it was hard to believe that anyone could sleep so peacefully in such a terrific racket.

The presence blocked out the light, engulfing him in a shadow of great darkness, and in his sleep he choked restlessly. Black it stood as night, fierce as ten Furies, terrible as hell, and shook a dreadful dart, as a monstruous thunderclap exploded overhead.

Glenn's eyes opened with a spooked look.

He glanced upwards, and as he beheld the complete realisation of the Abomination of Desolation, he knew that his last hour had come, and his doom was fixed.

He gave vent to his terror with a long and violent shriek.

But now prepare thee for another scene.

The staff were keeping the shutter down and the doors locked to try and silence the inhuman chorus of moans, gnashings, and exhalations that were building in intensity outside. Throughout the department the hoards of goblins, owls, and elvish sprites ornamenting the displays glared fiercely at the staff; even the figures in the paintings had taken on an indignant look.

One nameless Christmas temp clip clopped up to the shopgirls gathered by the main display. 'It's past nine now,' she said anxiously. 'Do we open or not?'

Another faceless temp looked fearful. 'We need a grown up to tell us!' she cried.

Mildred lay sprawled on a bed of silk scarves with her hands tucked behind her head, a picture in her grey leopard print mini dress and black boots. 'Oh, just calm down and enjoy the skive,' she groaned. 'The only other break you'll get today is your spirit.'

'I hear they're forecasting the busiest sale in years,' Dick intoned. 'Get ready, guys; this one's going to be *mental*.'

The shutter rattled ominously.

'*Really?*' said another faceless temp, looking perturbed by his words.

Mildred laughed. 'Yeah, because if Dick says so it *must* be true.'

Dick spun around furiously. 'I AM *NOT* LYING!' he yelled.

When the floor responded with a chorus of titters, he turned on his heel and stomped jiggling to the cashdesk. 'Are you happy now?' he growled in a low voice. 'You've turned me into a laughing stock with your constant denials!'

'I deny everything,' said Gertrude, who was putting out the float.

'*Fine.* You're only lying to yourself. We both know what happened after the Christmas do. And what happened again, in the morning, in those 30 seconds the taxi was outside waiting for me—'

'*Dick!*' Gertrude snapped, 'I might have slept with you *once* in a moment of madness—well, all right, twice in a long moment of madness—but I will never, *ever*—' She realised her voice sounded weirdly amplified. She looked to the mike stand and realised Dick was pressing a sly finger on it and grinning deviously.

As she looked to the floor and took in the sea of stunned faces, her stomach lurched.

'Ah-ha!' cried Dick, pointing at Gertrude's face.

The room once again fell a-laughing, as Gertrude quickly turned her back on them to hide her mortified face, which had turned a violent purple.

Suddenly, a heavy thumping sound shook the floor. It was Lyndsey coming down the stairs in his clown shoes. 'Pipe down, all of you!' he shouted. He cast a grave look at the trembling shutter. 'I want to see what it's like out there.'

The room watched as the nameless temp nearest to the entrance put her finger to the shutter's control pad. She looked back over her shoulder. 'Ready?'

Lyndsey swallowed hard. He nodded.

Nothing could have prepared them for the sight that met their eyes when the shutter went up: a horrid mass of dreadful depth, in guise of seasons old, was crushed up against the double-doors and violently trying the door handles.

The Nirah Frazar staff collectively shrieked.

The mob shrieked in response, and as they eyed the luxurious world within, broke into conniption fits. One woman was seen to be running side to side dementedly, like a caged animal. A short, beefy hardface with a shaven skull began to headbutt the lock. An old man, slapped up against the glass, pissed himself.

And Mildred, observing the scene from her bed of silk scarves, said: 'Not as bad as I thought.'

V.XV

All right, so it wasn't the actual Abomination of Desolation, but it was still pretty bad: Shukeena Mohammed standing over him, pointing a Kumquat in his face.

'What are you doing?' he spluttered nervously.

'Oh, nothing much, Glenn,' she smiled. 'I was just filming the menswear manager, asleep on the job, on the biggest day in the retail calender.'

'You think I was *sleeping*? Shukeena, I was inspecting the faulty returns.'

Suddenly the sound of bestial snoring filled the air. She was playing the footage.

Glenn closed his eyes and grimaced.

'That's it, Glenn!' she said triumphantly, locking the gizmo. 'Sleeping on the job is gross misconduct, and this time I've got proof.'

'Shukeena, please—I can't afford to get a third warning,' he begged.

She returned him an incredulous stare. 'No, you don't get a "third warning", Glenn; there is no "third warning". Don't you understand? The policy is three strikes and you're *out.*' She chuckled. 'This is it now. You're *finished.*'

Glenn sat up so abruptly the pigeons flapped.

'But Shukeena!' he cried. 'You can't do this today. Do you not think Norman has enough on his plate without you showing him that video?'

'I'm aware of Norman's problems!' she barked. 'Any normal store manager would have sacked you years ago. But fortunately, not even Norman can save you this time.'

Glenn rose unsteadily to his feet, wiped the drool from his scraggle.

'He's always found a way to preserve me so far,' he intoned gravely. 'He likes me, Shukeena. And he won't want to lose me now—*on the biggest day in the retail calender.*'

The submerger of souls smiled.

'You're right, Glenn, he *does* like you,' she said, nodding. 'And he won't want to lose you now, on the biggest day in the retail calender.'

'I sense there's a *but* coming.'

'*But*, had you bothered to show up for the morning meeting, you would have heard *his* news, and know that he's got bigger problems than the sale.'

'What's happened?' Glenn warbled.

'Head office concluded their investigation into the store. They rang him last night and told him they were unhappy with his management and think that he's responsible for our poor sales—which I suppose is half right. He's been served his notice.'

Glenn's knees gave out. He fell against the racking.

'*What!*' he yelped. 'But—but they can't terminate Norman! He's the longest serving staff member in the whole company!' His mouth was agape, his mind whirling. 'Who's going to be store manager if not him?' he demanded.

The gaper's torment grinned a terrible grin.

'Oh my God,' said Glenn faintly.

'That's right, Glenn! There's a new sheriff in town, and things are going to change around here!' She glowered demonically. 'Starting with the menswear manager.'

Locking eyes, the pair began slowly to circle each other.

'Soft, I pray you, Miss Mohammed—for my name-badge I hold dear as my breast,' he snarled. 'Who dost thou intend to make menswear manager? Or, *ladieswear* manager, for that matter, O thou holder of the sharp two-edged sword? Give me particulars!'

'That's not your conern,' Shukeena grinned.

'It is *your* concern, though,' he warned. 'The only realistic contenders are Dick and Gertrude. Thinkst thou those enemies to peace will be pliant subjects to thee? Nay! Ranker routs of rebels never was than those upstarts. And if you do crown them, let me prophesy: thine tears shall manure the ground of the manager's office, and future shifts groan for this foul act! All these curses will come upon you and overtake you, and you shall surely perish—and Dick Zabledore inherit the throne of glory!

'I see this all *fulfilled*. . . .' he darkly concluded.

'Oh really?'

'*Yes*, really. You are being manipulated, Shukeena! By perhaps the most consummate villain that has ever existed—a latter-day Uriah Heep! And while I'm used to dealing with Dick—you're *not*. You're going to need me around, if only to police his perfidy.'

'Thank you for your concern, Glenn; but I *always* keep my staff in check.'

'When you're not accustomed to history, most facts about the past do sound incredible,' he said with an upraised finger. 'So *please*, I beg thee, in the name of all the gods at once: delete that recording.'

'You really don't get it, do you? I've told you: this is *it*. I'm going to be store manager, and I don't want *you* in my shop!'

Glenn looked genuinely injured. 'But *why?*' he asked.

'Why? Seriously? All right, Glenn, I'll tell you why: you're late every day, you swear at staff, bully them, sleep with half of them, steal from the till, insult mystery shoppers, and use interviews to chat up girls! You got your top seller fired, tried to get your cover manager fired, stole thousands of pounds worth of stock, and you hired that stupid fashion student knowing *full well* she was going to Manchester! And you've been given *two* warnings! And both times you got *worse*! And, to top it all off, you've reeked of booze for *months*! You're insane, Glenn! Completely insane! And we've all had enough of your *shit*!'

A pause.

'No offence is so heinous as unorthodoxy of behaviour,' Glenn said philosophically, after a moment's thought. 'Good Ford, Shukeena, that is quite the memory you have there!' he chuckled as they continued to circle each other, pumps clip clopping, loafers squeaking and squelching. 'There's just one misdemeanour you left out.'

'Oh yeah?' she said, panting slightly after her lengthy rant. 'What's that?'

'Me snatching your Kumquat and smashing it on the floor.'

She laughed aloud. 'You wouldn't dare!'

He halted. 'Wouldn't I?'

Her countenance darkened. 'You're stupid, but you're not *that* stupid.'

'O, you think so? Interesting. Very inter—'

He lunged at her, but she stepped aside with ease, sending him crashing into the phalanx of customer reserves. Smiling ruefully, he turned to face her.

'You'll have to do better than that to catch *me*, Glenn!' she laughed derisively.

'Shukeena; I *am* going to smash that Kumquat, and I *will* tell everyone you dropped it. It's going to be my word against yours. And while you may not think much of me on the shopfloor, you should see how well I perform in a formal grievance procedure. I can bombard head office with letters of complaint; appeal against every decision taken; contest

every letter of *every* word of *every* note written during hearings. You think you're going to turn this store around? Ha! You'll spend so much time in the office defending yourself, you'll forget what the store looks like.'

Now it was Glenn's turn to grin at her, his beady eyes glinting darkly. His face fell as she held her gizmo out to him.

'There you go, Glenn.'

'Huh?'

'Take it,' she said. 'Smash it if you want.'

He stared at her face: inscrutable. He snatched the Kumquat anyway. Her expression didn't change.

'Shukeena!' he cried, 'I don't *want* to smash this, you know? Just unlock it and delete the video and we'll say no more about it. It's a new year. Let's start afresh.'

'No.'

'*What*! You don't want me to break your Kumquat over this, you demented witch. These things are expensive!'

'It's all right, Glenn, I'm insured. And anyway, I'm due an upgrade.' A pause.

'O, I get it,' he groaned. 'You've already Forkbearded it to everyone, haven't you?'

She smiled, shook her head. 'Nope.'

'Then what is it then!' Glenn demanded. 'What are you up to? What do you *know*? Fiend!' he yelled hoarsely. 'Thou torment'st me ere I come to hell!'

'I haven't Forkbearded anyone the footage of you asleep on the job, Glenn,' she said reassuringly. 'However, I *have* Forkbearded everyone the footage I filmed last night of the Christmas decorations you dumped in the bins, because you couldn't be bothered transferring them to the basement.'

Glenn tightened. On intractable terrain do not encamp.

'Decorations which include numerous antiques that Nirah Frazar himself collected,' she continued. 'So while you *could* destroy the evidence of your being asleep on the job, it's too late for you to destroy the evidence of you destroying company property—which is also a third and final strike.'

The colour drained from his face. On dire terrain do not linger.

'I suppose you *could* get the skeleton key—assuming you can find where I've hidden it—and go into each locker and smash *everyone's* Kumquats, but then it wouldn't just be Nirah Frazar prosecuting you for his losses.'

Glenn watched as his whole world began tumbling down before him.

All of his plans, his fusing his two goals by working hard for a year, while he honed his craft and repaired his finances, were going up in smoke—and there was no magic of fancy that could lengthen his song now. He watched her mouth pronouncing his black sentence to a soundtrack of white noise, grew furious as he gazed upon his conquering foe. Why these insulting words, this waste of breath, to souls undaunted, and secure of death? 'Tis no dishonour for the brave to die; nor came I here with hope of victory!

On death terrain do battle.

With a loud yell he closed his eyes and with a full swing the fatal weapon flew.

A pause.

Glenn, although never known for athletic prowess, was still stunned to see the gizmo lying so close to his feet. He thought he'd hurled it against the wall in a fit of rage. But as he looked up, he saw Shukeena staring at him over her hands clamped to her mouth, her eyes wide with shock. For a split second, time stopped.

And then the black Gorgonean blood began to seep through her fingers, a trickle that in the blink of an eye became a deluge, and Glenn with a thrill of terror perceived that this wasn't just the end of his Nirah Frazar career—it was the end of *any* career.

'Sorry,' he whimpered.

If thou ask me, the real sound is the devilment brewing downstairs; for there our bloody sister is bestowed on ladieswear, not confessing the cruel parricide she is plotting.

He breathed the salt-sea breeze, goggled the bloody sun on the grey horizon.

Men's is below target, it's not meeting standard, and head office are asking questions.

413

Norman's mouth was gaping, as he watched in wonder his spectral staff.

Nothing's changed since our emergency meeting last month, Norman. The new collaboration still isn't out; his faulties are still piling up in the stock room. Oh and all those Homme boxes are still cluttering up the basement. Quite honestly, I've seen mannequins more active than Glenn.

Norman's head was tilted back, the red fluid flying down his throat.

And thus we penetrated deeper and deeper into the heart of darkness.

V.XVI

A nameless temp put down the cashdesk phone. The staff stared expectantly at her. 'That was the arcade manager asking why we're not open yet,' she said anxiously. 'Has anyone seen any managers?'

The dunciad was butting repeatedly against the double-doors, a hideous gabble rising loud among them. The bolt was starting to give.

'No,' answered Gertrude. 'But we should probably stay closed until a manager tells us otherwise.'

Mildred, lounging on her silk bed, smirked. 'Well, given how shit your judgment's been lately, that probably means we should open.'

Gertrude choked as the room broke into laughter.

'Let's just open now,' said Dick. 'If we miss out on business we're gonna be screwed.' He grinned. 'And Gertrude knows how *that* feels!'

'That's *it*!' cried Gertrude. 'I'm telling Norman!' She stamped up the staircase, gave Dick an almighty slap, then disappeared into menswear.

Dick rubbed his sore cheek, giggling impishly.

'Look!' said Lyndsey, 'if we don't open now, those animals will break the door down. And then we'll all have to stay late while Shukeena finds a locksmith. And remember—people with trades don't *need* to work on New Year's Day.'

The team exchanged fearful glances. Even Mildred sat up and began to look nervy.

The nameless temp who mocked Glenn was stood trembling by the doors, holding the keys. She looked back to Lyndsey for final confirmation.

'All right, everybody!' exclaimed the footwear supervisor, polishing his pince-nez. 'This is the New Year's Sale; I expect a tough, clean shift; protect your till at all times; any questions from ladieswear? Any questions from menswear?'

Pause.

'Underling,' he called. 'ADMIT THE VULGUS!' he screeched.

As the temp opened the doors, the trampling rout swallowed her whole.

O miserable mankind! To what fall degraded, to what wretched state reserved! Wave after wave they came, a darksome cloud of locusts swarming every corner of the shop, screaming and shouting, snatching up garments in search of a deal, ripping off swing tickets, tossing them to the ground and stamping on them, as the hallowed shop filled with inhuman sounds the likes of which few staff members had ever heard before.

Highly they raged against the highest, and fierce with grasped arms clashed on their sounding shields the din of war, as they sacked fixtures and fittings, turned over display tables and ripped mannequins limb from limb. In the imbroglio, the antique medicine cabinet toppled, spilling its bottles of Finite, which shattered across the hardwood.

'The medicine cabinet is down!' Lyndsey cried. 'Someone replenish the parfum!'

Mildred had her back to the wall, fending off the rascals with a mannequin's arm she swung like a chain-whip. 'Do you do half sizes!' 'Are there anymore bags in the back!' 'The stitching's coming out—can I get a further discount?'

'No!' she yelled. 'That's it! Piss off!'

She screamed.

The room was rocking, and as Dick and Lyndsey cowered on the stairs they saw a pack of ape-men, with foreheads villainous low, storm the central aisle, vault the displays and trample the mannequins.

'They're coming this way!' yelled Lyndsey, his face turning pale.

'RUN!' Dick yelled.

LEEDS—Stock room, Nirah Frazar, Victoria Quarter

In the morning's feature affair, smoking hot Shukeena 'The Gorgon' Mohammed, 105lbs, Chapel Allerton, was matched with 'Gentleman' Glenn Harding, 135lbs, Hyde Hill, a loquacious character who had talked rings around his opponent through a long and protracted buildup to this much anticipated grudge match.

The self-styled 'Gentleman' Glenn, the flamboyant champion of menswear, certainly looked the part as he towered over his diminutive opponent, although some sceptics question his listed height of 5'11½". Whatever his exact dimensions, Harding did sport every conceivable physical advantage over Mohammed, the long-reigning ladieswear champ, including an always welcome 30lbs of added musculature. However, size matters little to the pocket pistol from north Leeds, who likes to swarm her opponents, slip their punches, and return her own heavy fire.

There is no more attractive pairing in boxiana than a dueller and a brawler, and with Harding promising a battle so epic its only parallel in history would be the time Alexander the Great fought Darius on the field hand to hand, the air of excitement in the stock room was palpable.

No one could have predicted that Harding would prove to be such a disappointment.

In spite of his 'Gentleman' moniker, the man from Hyde Hill proved to be no respecter of the rules as set down by Queensbury. Commencing hostilities not by throwing fists but by throwing an actual Kumquat at Mohammed, he rocked her back on her heels and drew blood from her mouth, although she seemed more surprised than hurt. Alas, with that opening gambit the Ungentlemanly One appeared to have shot his bolt, for when 'The Gorgon' responded by bounding forward and burying a knee between his legs, all the fighting spirit seemed to depart him.

With Harding bent double, Mohammed went to work, treating his exposed head and body to a vicious barrage of lefts and rights that sent him reeling to the customer reserves rail where, still cupping himself, he begged for a reprieve. Mohammed does her best work on stationary targets, and when she saw her opponent lying against the rail, she licked her bloody lips. Moving in for the kill, she slipped his pawing left and sprang up with an uppercut to the jaw that sent the hair product flying from his head.

With Harding in peril, he lifted Mohammed clean off the floor and flung her into the faulty returns, whereupon he proceeded to run screaming for the stock room door, pulling out his set of manager's keys and trying desperately to find one that would fit the lock.

If the menswear champ really is the bibliophile he claims to be, it's too bad he never got around to reading the boxing rulebook, of which the first instruction is PROTECT YOURSELF AT ALL TIMES. *With his back turned to his opponent, Mohammed saw the opportunity to get even for the earlier cheap shot and ran after him, leaping into the air and landing a flying elbow on the back of his undefended occiput, dropping him to his knees as the pigeons cooed and flapped their approval.*

As he shook his head and tried to clear the cobwebs, Mohammed went into finishing mode. She reached out and grabbed a metal wire coathanger, wrapped it around his throat and started to garrotte him.

Gertrude burst into the office and froze. Shards of glass glittered across the floor, drawers hung open and moneybags were strewn about as if they'd been robbed. Also on the floor was a strange black box with a red interior, empty and dumped on its side.

As she turned to leave she saw it—smeared across the wall in massive letters, in what looked like blood, was the word:

BLUTBAD

She staggered back and screamed at the top of her lungs.

And as the shop was pitching and tossing and rolling heavily all at the same time, the mannequins in the abyss began screaming too.

V.XVII

WHAT! I'VE GOT TO TELL HEAD OFFICE WE'VE LOST HOW MUCH!? FORGET PROSECUTING THE BASTARD—I'M GOING TO KILL HIM! He could feel every fibre in his body shaking. *This is an investigation, Norman; not a performance review. Right.* He shook his head violently, found himself back on the white beach. He looked with wonder at the label on the bottle but couldn't read the ingredients because the words kept moving. He went to swig it again but found it empty. Fortunately, there was plenty more where that came from, and he threw the bottle on the sand and grabbed another one from the box at his feet. Within moments his mind had again unlocked those amazing phantoms, projecting them over the thrashing green waves. *I better get back to my office. You're already in your office, Norman!* He closed his eyes, tilted his head, and took a long swig from the bottle. *DID YOU WRITE ABOUT ME TO HEAD OFFICE?!*

He gave vent to his fury with a prolonged and hellish scream.

Kill think we do if the of are yourself only body the all a you and families atoms! favour could the Norman you! and have head you the run another will have atmosphere! away drink die children you're laddy, then of just you your making don't could own them want actually you into to think! *wouldn't atmosphere be want early! here them to come to harm! You're already in your office, Norman! You're already in your office, Norman! You're already in your office*—'Norman!'

Norman wheeled round on the sound. 'What!' he barked.

A nameless temp stood by the lift doors, the light from inside the lift shining on the store manager, who was standing alone in the dark catacombs under the shop, his eyes red and wild. 'I, er, just need to replenish the perfume,' she stammered.

That's when she noticed the torn delivery box at his feet, and all the empty bottles of Finite. She stared at him, aghast, as he wiped his mouth with his beefy forearm and belched. 'All right!' she said. 'I guess I'll go back up—'

When he pulled the Trench Broom from his trousers, she let out a piercing shriek. Her eyes rolled back, and she collapsed in a heap by the lift doors.

Norman looked surprised. Marching determinedly towards her, he stepped over her prone body, entered the lift and mashed a button with his fist.

The doors closed on him.

As the coat hanger cut into Harding's throat, his eyes rolled back in his head and, being the cultured lover of literature that he is, was no doubt thinking at that moment how reminiscent the scene was of Menelaus choking Paris with the oxhide chin strap.

Mohammed saw his hand reach feebly for the keys in the door and countered by squeezing the metal wire tighter. The move brought down Harding's outstretched arm, cutting off both his escape route and the oxygen to his brain. The ladieswear larruper is nothing if not a great finisher.

But what was this? Like the gored bull that finds within itself the will to launch one last charge, Harding suddenly heaved up one knee, planted a mangled loafer on the concrete and thrust himself up. He ran backwards and rammed Mohammed into the customer reserve rail, as her weapon went spinning under the stock, coming to a stop somewhere in the tenth row.

Harding had been expected to dance and move, and when he teetered away on unsteady feet some in the crowd thought he was indulging in a display of flashy footwork. In fact, his funny dance was the result of fatigue and disorientation, and as he fell against the door, slid down it and slumped on the floor in a sweaty heap, it was clear he'd had enough for one morning.

Perhaps the beeryard, ten pints, and bottle of vodka he was rumoured to have trained on did rob him of his strength and fitness. John L. Sullivan he is not.

Mohammed stood over him with her legs apart, hands on her hips, the image of a conqueror, standing victoriously on the field after another bloody campaign. Certainly the question of supremacy between the departments had been settled. Get me an application for ladieswear. 1-1-■

Shukeena stared disbelievingly at the blood on her hands. 'Well that really is it now, Glenn,' she said, panting. 'You are fired! Get out of my shop!'

'No.'

'*No!* What do you mean no? I'll have arcade security drag you out if I have to!'

'You're not the store manager, Shukeena! You don't have the authority to fire me! Only Norman does!'

Bloody death, a black nightmare of death, is close upon you.

'What did I just tell you, Glenn? Norman has been served his notice! I'm the store manager now!'

'Not yet, you're not! What's Norman's notice? A month? That gives us plenty of time to figure out a way to stop you!'

'Oh please! If you think Norman can save you this time, you're even more deluded than I thought! I saw him in the morning meeting, and I can assure you he is a broken man, a has-been! He's finished, Glenn! Do you understand me?

'*Finished!*' she roared, shaking her fist.

They were so busy arguing they didn't hear the subtle hum of the lift in motion.

As the doors parted, a thunderous explosion outside blew the windows wide open, causing the thousands of garments to flap convulsively in the fearsome gale. Stunned, it took them a moment to register the light emanating from the lift.

As they turned towards the parted doors, a silhouette emerged that made the hair of their flesh stand up. What the lift had transported up was not from men's, or from ladies, or even the basement. It looked like something that had come from the infernal regions.

[*Enter* THE ABOMINATION OF DESOLATION *in warlike manner.*]

It possessed the body of a man, the head of a moose, and the horns of Lucifer—and as the lightning flashed, momentarily illuminating the monster, they perceived the gore that drenched its massive hands and bare chest and were seized by terror.

Your last hour has come, you die in blood.

Glenn and Shukeena clung to each other and screamed.

Behold the great doom's image! The Chimera drew the Trench Broom from its trousers, waving it wildly as it joined their screams, its inhuman cry echoing along the passageways and through every level of the old building. Meanwhile, on the ground floor, the mannequins had clawed their way out of the abyss and pressed themselves up against the shop window—as if desperate to escape the store itself.

BLAM!

Had Glenn's crown been up the bullet would have shot straight through it. He screamed again, grabbed Shukeena by the hand and ran, as the monster gave chase.

BLAM! BLAM!

Loud peals of thunder! Flashing lightning the transient light renew! And from the skies proceeded brimstone and fire, voices and the trumpet, as Glenn and Shukeena ran screaming down the aisle, with the Chimera on their tail, squealing, shrieking, and shooting.

BLAM! BLAM! BLAM!

Glenn bolted left down one of the narrow walkways, dragging Shukeena with him, where they disappeared behind a mass of garments flailing in the wind. BLAM! Stood with his back to the wall, unseen in shadows, he peeped over her head, his hand slapped over her mouth, watching with terror as the Chimera went rampaging by. BLAM!

Shukeena made a muffled sound.

'Huh?' Glenn whispered. He uncovered her mouth.

'I said I think that's Norman!' she whispered. 'You've finally driven him mad!'

'*Me*! I didn't drive him mad! *You* drove him mad with your incessant nattering!'

She leaned to one side, looked up at him. 'Don't even try it, Glenn!' she whispered. '*You* drove him mad with your constant shenanigans!'

'It was *your* nattering!'

'No, it was *your* shenanigans!'

'Nattering!'

'Shenanig—' BLAM!

Glenn felt the air blast by his face. They looked, and behold, the giant moose head was leering at them from the central aisle. They screamed again.

'Quick!' said Glenn. They dropped to the floor, scrambling under rows of garments toward the door. Reaching it, they sprang up, and Glenn threw it open. He hoisted Shukeena through, darted out after her, then locked the door behind him. BLAM!

It was lucky he had crouched to lock the door, because the bullet tore through the wood exactly where his head had been, leaving a gaping hole.

Shukeena was already halfway down the stairwell.

'You're still fired!' he heard her call up them.

V.XVIII

He watched them devastating Rome, the khaki mob upturning his palace, storming the senate, climbing his main display. When he saw that Brummell had been stripped of his clothes and ghoulishly hung naked by his heels from the woodbeams, he felt the current of his blood freeze.

And so, having failed—but at least attempted—to scale the Helicon with his High Verses, and having failed—but at least attempted—to win

Eudaimonia with the sylph, Glenn found himself unable to look upon such people, indulging in such wanton depravity, without feeling like Lemuel Gulliver, for whom the sight of man, after living so long among the noble Houyhnhnms, filled him only with hatred.

Whatever goes upon two legs is an enemy.

Dick stood atop a clothing island on formalwear, using his measuring tape to fend off the swelling babel around him, who were waving clothes and asking him questions. 'Now look,' he cried, 'if you can just form an orderly queue I will be happy to help all of you! Please, form a queue!'

The horror! The horror! (How loathsome, how incredibly loathsome, was reality.)

Lyndsey hurled the last of his shoes into the shoe stockroom as the enemy closed in. 'No, you don't have the look to pull off metallic leather ankle boots!' he yelled. He swung a try-on sock loaded with a bottle of Finite like a cosh to fend off a rough group of young hardfaces. 'And I am not having your stinking feet in my galoshes, even if they are on sale! We have an image to uphold! Piss off!'

The horror! The horror! (The portion's equal whether a man hangs back or fights his best.)

This was not the coda Glenn had envisioned for his great wonder-work, his canticle. A tear ran down his cheek, while far below him the abyss yawned, waiting.

Suddenly a hellfire print silk shirt was thrust in his face.

The brute holding it paid Glenn's disfigured head no heed, such injuries being no uncommon sight on this morning. He himself was sporting a fresh blackeye.

'You got this in an extra large, pal?' the brute grunted.

The horror! The horror! (And he would forget the books he had opened and the world that had proved an illusion.)

'That's all we have left in that size, sir,' answered Glenn with infinite bitterness.

Shukeena burst into the manager's office but froze at the bloody shards of glass littering the floor. Carefully stepping around them, she propped a hand on the desk, picked up the phone and dialed 999.

'Hello?' she said breathlessly. 'Hello!'

Silence.

She stared at the receiver, noticing the severed wire dangling from it, and tossed it aside. Frantically, she checked her coat on the coat-stand for her Kumquat, then stiffened as she remembered—it was still upstairs, on the stock room floor. . . . Where Norman was now tying empty delivery boxes into a crude cudgel. With a lighter, he set the tip ablaze. As the flame roared to life, he ran through the walkways, torching clothes.

In a moment the stock room was ablaze, the garments burning in an unquenchable fire, as vapours of smoke and fumes began filling the cavernous heights, while far below, the heathens ripped garments from each other, trading bone-cracking blows.

The carnage staggered Shukeena, and her bloody mouth hung open. She tottered to the cashdesk.

'Where've you been? It's mental down here!' cried Gertrude, ringing a cropped silk organza top through the till. 'That's 165, please, madam.'

Shukeena was bent over the counter, breathless.

'Upstairs. . . . Norman gone mad. . . . again. . . . have to call the police!' Trembling, she picked up the cashdesk phone and dialed 999.

'What's Norman mad at now?' asked Gertrude as she handed the customer the bag. 'He'd be happy if he saw the takings. We're on five grand already!'

'999, what's your emergency?' asked the operator.

'Hello,' gasped Shukeena, 'I—wait, *five grand*? Let me see that!' She printed out the itemized takings from the till and checked over it. The receipt was longer than her arm. 'Oh my God, you're right—and it's only twenty-five past!'

'That'll be 220 please, madam,' said Gertrude.

'Hello?' called the operator. 'Are you in need of assistance?'

'*No*,' Shukeena answered, slamming the phone down. At once she opened the second till, next to Gertrude's. 'Keep going, Gerty; next customer please!'

Outside the shop, in the arcade, a woman pointed upwards and screamed.

V.XIX

Has the ship arrived from Delos, at the arrival of which I must die?

Orgy porgy, Ford and fun, kiss the shopgirls and make them One.

The hour has come to cook your Lordship's mutton.

There, at the highest point of the arcade, through the rowling smoke flying out of the broken stock room window, the Chimera stood, gripping onto one of the iron mullions supporting the great glass dome, its toes perched on a stone pilaster. The monster hung perilously in the air, drenched in blood and sweat, swatting the smoke with the Trench Broom. The black cloud was rapidly filling the dome and beginning to seep out and spread along the length of the glass roof in every direction, darkening the arcade and blotting out the tempest raging above. It was difficult to hear exactly what it was saying over the roaring flames, but it was babbling something like, *Where once was people the beast is loosed; don't feed it, you must destroy it, it is your only hope—I am* not *crazy*!

'Dick, I'm going now,' said Glenn over the hubbub.

Dick, serving on the cashdesk, looked startled. 'It's a bit early for lunch, isn't it, geez? That'll be £180 please, sir.'

'No, I'm *going* going. I quit.'

'You quit? Geez, don't quit—this will have quietened down in a week! If you'd just like to put your credit card in the machine, please, sir—thank you very much.'

'I'm going not because of the sale. I'm going because I am too courtly, and thou art too cunning.'

'You what?'

'Cursed is the one who attacks his neighbour secretly,' he intoned. 'And now thou hast deliver'd me to my sour cross, thou art bound for the devil's maw—*you Brutus*.'

'Oh, geez, what are you on about now!'

Americano? This bad place for you. Deese hombres, malos, cacos. Bad people here. Brutos. No buenos for anyone. Comprendo? Glenn was wading through the warring apes, squeaking and squelching his way to footwear. The displays were ravaged and there wasn't a shoe to be seen, or a section supervisor. The door to the shoe stock room was

HUNTER

V · XV 11

locked. He took out his keys, unlocked the door and threw it open.

'Lyndsey, I'm—'

What he saw Lyndsey doing to a two-tone dance shoe is too horrifying to relate. He slammed the door shut and hastily locked it—and left his keys dangling there.

Wherever you turned the abyss was waiting for you round the corner. He limped dizzily behind the cashdesk, picked up his trampled frock coat and slipped it on. It was still sodden. 'Farewell, Mr Zabledore,' he crooned, kissing his fat cheek. 'If I live till next New Year's Day, I'll visit you; if not, Faustus is gone to hell.'

O would I had never seen Seacroft Library, never read a book.

'Glenn!' Dick called after him. 'You're not *seriously* leaving, are you?' he said, aghast. 'Who am I going to *talk* to?'

'Shukeena Mohammed,' Glenn smiled. He stopped, looked back over his shoulder. 'Don't miss me too much,' he winked.

The fire was blazing, the Chimera perspiring heavily in the brutal heat. It was trying to waft the smoke away with its gun, its every swipe showering the crowd with droplets of sweat and blood. Again, it was difficult to decipher its ravings, but it was something like, *It feeds on wallets, purses, and fear! If we're to slay the beast we must refuse to be cowed by it—you must take me* very *seriously!*

Descending the stairs, Glenn beheld with wondering eyes the tumult mix'd with shrieks, laments, and cries: bodies falling, foreheads striking hardwood, garments sullied by muddy footprints like 'twere the pages of some bad sitcom script. A din of troglodytic hoardes through perfumed air rose to the painted sky all brazen, brawled with the shrill, jangling shriek of the unheeded fire alarm.

'Morning Gertrude,' he said nervously.

'Oh, what do *you* want?' she groaned, not looking at him. 'That's 545, please—ooh, that's a good bargain.'

'I know you don't want to speak to me right now,' he said, 'or ever, for that matter. But. . . . well, I haven't really planned this, but—' He observed to his utter amazement a silver hair in her beehive. (Harding, thou art damned to hell for this. This deed is chronicled in hell.) 'I just wanted to apologise to you for my, er, *sensual faults* foiling—'

She looked him square in the eye. 'Glenn, I really don't give a shit.'

Glenn tottered.

'No,' he replied, faintly. 'Why would you?'

Ugly hell, gape not! I'll burn my books!

'Glenn, are you *still* bothering my staff?' Shukeena said from behind the second till. 'Get out! You don't work here anymore!'

'I know I don't work here anymore, Shukeena!' he snapped back, 'I just quit!'

'Quit! You can't quit—I already fired you! That'll be 300 please, madam.'

'I told you, Shukeena! You don't have the authority to fire me! And head office don't work today, and Norman has lost his mind, so there's no one who *can* fire me!'

'Oh yeah? Watch me. You're *fired*!'

When there is no way out, you are on Death Terrain.

The crowd outside the shop had grown so large it had gridlocked County Arcade and was rapidly filling up Cross Arcade, right back to the fountains. Arcade security couldn't push through the phalanx of glazed, gawping faces pointing their Kumquats at the lunatic flailing his gun in the surging black smoke.

'Chuffing jump then, you daft bastard!' yelled a voice in the crowd. 'Yeah, just do it! Jump!' yelled another. 'Jump!' And then the chant rose up from the mob:

JUMP!

JUMP!

JUMP!

JUMP!

JUMP!

And with the crowd baying, and its mouth still muffled by the moose head, it became almost impossible to understand what the monster was saying, but it was something like, *I'm not up here to jump—stop pointing your pissing Kumquats at me, you imbeciles*—listen *to me, I'm trying to help you!*

But the intensity of the heat was getting to it, and lowering the

Trench Broom it sagged in the surging fumes. It said something like, *Christ, can somebody chuck me a bottle of water?*

'You know what, Miss Mohammed?' Glenn sighed. '*Fine.* Let's just say you fired me. I hope that makes you happy.'

'Byeeeee,' said Shukeena, with a mocking smile.

Eyes, look your last!

Gertrude's avoided his.

Now go not backward; no, Faustus, be resolute. He turned away and limped towards the doors, through which the savages were pouring in from the arcade. He halted as his eyes scanned the sea of uniform faces hopefully. He had almost fallen into the *barranca*—now would she not come in, wheeling her suitcase behind her, and save him? It seemed as if everyone in the city was coming into the shop except her.

Orgy-porgy, Ford and fun, kiss the girls and make them run.

Don Juan he was not.

O Brigantia! Of all the gods and goddesses, none is more cruel to the hopeful than thou art! Why make Glenn fall for a wandering rogue who ravages boys' hearts? Why let him taste the cup of elixir then snatch it away?

Woe to the innocent who view her body divine.

JUMP!

Now in Glenn the evocation of that image stirred new longing and an ache of grief. *O that you had perished, and mine eye had not seen thee.*

JUMP!

Does the soul grasp truth? For whenever it attempts to examine anything with the body, it is clearly deceived by it. Approach the object with thought alone: *The best moment of your life was a forgettable night in hers.*

JUMP!

The body confuses the soul and does not allow it to acquire truth and wisdom whenever it is associated with it. The body keeps us busy in a thousand ways because of its need for nurture. Approach the object with thought alone: *You already saw everything; what more can you gape after?*

I glory in the glory I have seen! The fame of that event will never die!

You must stop imagining that posterity will vindicate you, Winston.

JUMP!

The body fills us with wants, desires, fears, all sorts of illusions and much nonsense, so that no good thought of any kind ever comes to us from the body. Approach the object with thought alone: *All things that are, are with more spirit chased than enjoy'd.*

What did Greatness get you in the end, anyway?

A bronze statue, smothered in birdshit.

JUMP!

The cold morning enwrapped him, and emerging from the portico the first thing that caught his eye was the smoke cloaking the arcade in darkness. It looked like the Styx itself was exhaling its fog and mists.

Scanning the faces in the crowd, Glenn suddenly realised they were all looking up. With a start he remembered the madman running amok upstairs, but rather than leg it he chose to turn back and look up himself.

All he could see through the smoke rushing out of the broken window was a vast pair of horns protruding from it.

Then suddenly, in a transitory gap in the effusions, he glimpsed the moose's head and locked eyes with its dead black gaze. It seemed to come alive at the sight of him, before being engulfed once again by smoke.

It was then that a single eye emerged from the fumes and fastened itself on him. It looked like the monster was almost winking at him.

It was only when he heard a hideous shriek that he realised it wasn't an eye at all, but a muzzle.

Wretched queen, adieu—

BLAM!

[*Dies.*]

V.XX

The gazing crowd around them stood, the Trench Broom on one side, the moose head the other, both in blood. Glenn's twig-like limbs were poking out from under Norman, whose broad, sweat drenched back was breathing fitfully. It was as he rolled his bulk off the erstwhile menswear manager and spread-eagled himself beside the recumbent boy that the onlookers screamed.

Glenn was lying dead on the ground, his cracked crown staining the marble with his foul life-fluid. It was pumping from his skull at such a rate that the red disk encircling the remnants of his head had soon encompassed his whole body.

The crowd had to keep edging back to protect their footwear.

Here was a boy who had read the pre-eminent poets, who could recite the mightiest shade, who had filled his brain till it was brimming with knowledge—and now that knowledge was decanting like wine drops over the arcade floor.

And if you looked close enough, yes, you could actually *see* the discontent draining out of his decimated mazzard.

All the grunt and sweat, the ignoble stooping, was squirting out in rivers of crimson, as chunks of brain went bobbing along in the dark spillage.

Did that grey morsel there contain his great dreams of becoming a writer? Did it hold everything he had wished to share with the world?

If so, he had shared it now.

And lo, at that nugget glinting between someone's shit-covered Converse; is that where his happier times with Peggy resided? Or did it contain his burning love for Henrietta, and the golden future his deluded fancy had conceived for them?

Might it contain the hazy image of her tender thighs?

And that slimy little hunk you see wedged in the massive, ruffled collar of his stupid frock coat—did that minute crumb hold the entirety of his life's learning? Was that small particle responsible for his feeling superior to Seacroft and its many thousands of inhabitants?

Could that tiny fragment be the source of all his antics?

Strange thing, the brain. It only weighs three pounds, yet it feels as if it carries in it the weight of the world.

Poor Glenn Harding! That head that throbbed with big ideas was empty now. His great quest, his epic odyssey, had taken him five steps from the shop. His search to find somebody had left him without a body. Had he been alive to see himself lying reversed on the marble, he might have thought of *The Satyricon*, the world's first novel, written by Petronius in 1 AD, where two travelers find a corpse washed ashore and lament its fate—wondering who awaited the dead man, unaware of his end; who had kissed him goodbye before his final journey. For all his hopes and dreams, the man was now prostrate upon the sand, food for fishes and wild animals. *This is what mortal plans come to; this is the result of all our great dreams and ambitions. A man in this world is simply at sea!* Glenn's eyes were rolled upward into their sockets, protruding hideously, and his jaw hung slack at a frightful angle.

Look at this, mortals, and then dare to fill your hearts with great ambitions.

That was the truth Glenn Harding ultimately shared with the world. That was the message of his epic saga.

Fool.

Petronius already did it—2,000 years ago!

ADDENDUM

Yet not for a moment did I suppose myself actually dead.

His head hurt, his limbs were weak, and his feet in tatters, but it was not the bottom even now, he realised. It was not the end quite yet.

His eyes scanned the departure board. There were trains to London, but how one got to France he knew not. He *did* know that the Channel Tunnel was in Dover; but there were no trains to Dover that he could see. Did you change at London to get to Dover? God, he felt naïve and almost childishly unworldly at that moment.

You never leave Leeds, do you? Do you not think that's a bit sad?

He didn't know where Dinan was and he didn't speak French. In fact his knowledge of the country was limited to its wars with English monarchs and a handful of authors. It did feel like a long way to go for a man with nothing in his pockets but some spent plastic and an old sock. Wearing a frock coat.

If the good Lord willed it, she would waltz through the station shortly and take him with her. She would show him the way.

She would make him human.

The hall resounded with clamour, and as he sat down on a bench he beheld a great multitude which no one could number, pouring through the ticket booths and filling the air with hubbub strange, a jangling noise of words unknown.

[*The clock strikes eleven.*]

He sat there waiting; waiting with the faith and the patience of the saints; waiting for his prayers to be answered; waiting for the *miracle*. For he knew it was written that come the infernal hour, in the last minute, at the last second, at the very last moment, when all hope seemed lost—one last windfall from the gods would come.

[*The clock strikes twelve.*]

With a sigh he rose to his feet. He didn't have his passport on him anyway.

He limped out to the taxi rank, where the driver wound down his window and looked up at him. Glenn smiled.

'How much to Seacroft?'

Neil Hunter is a TV and digital
producer from Leeds. He presently
lives in North Yorkshire.

Paul Hunter is an
advertising illustrator and former games
developer from Leeds. He lives in London.